LOOK TWICE

AN INGRID SKYBERG THRILLER

EVA HUDSON

VENATRIX

First published 2021 by Venatrix.

978-1-9160195-9-1

LOOK TWICE

1

INGRID STARED at the defendant as he took the stand, searching his face and demeanor for signs of remorse. She hadn't seen a new photo of James Jones since his arrest two years ago, and the man on the screen didn't look much like his mug shot. Or the man she had seen on a dark night twenty years beforehand.

She had always imagined she would be in the courthouse when Megan's killer was brought to justice. At first, she had assumed she would be giving evidence as a witness to her best friend's abduction. And then, as she graduated high school without Megan, as she went to college and started work aware that Megan had been denied those milestones, Ingrid resolved to join the FBI and become the agent who arrested her friend's murderer. But Ingrid had played no part in Jones's arrest, and now she was watching his trial over the internet four thousand miles away at her office in London.

Ingrid had envisaged this exact scene countless times in the intervening decades, but nothing felt the way she had anticipated. Bile was not coiling in her stomach.

Hatred was not raising her temperature. Disgust was not pooling under her tongue. Her overriding emotion was impatience. More than anything, she wanted the trial to be over. She knew she wouldn't be good for much until James Jones was convicted and handed a life sentence.

Due to exceptional interest in the case, and the infirmity of Megan's mom, Judge Isaacs had allowed three cameras into the courtroom. One was focused on the witness box, one was positioned above the jury's heads allowing a wide shot of the court while keeping their identities private, and the final camera targeted the spot in front of the bench where the defense and state's attorneys conducted their cross-examination. This meant the moment Jones took the stand was the first time anyone outside the court had seen what he looked like for two years. Like most monsters, he was disappointingly ordinary.

Jones was 42 but appeared a decade older. A combination of bourbon, meth and guilt. Despite the haggard face, the tabloids had dubbed him a Bruce Willis lookalike. He had a firm jaw, electric blue eyes and close-cropped hair that had turned a little grayer since his arrest. Ingrid thought he looked more like a guy who would make you a gyro than a Hollywood actor. The 'House of Horrors' case was always going to get a lot of attention. Twelve victims buried in the basement and the yard, another three chained and starved in outhouses. Add in a killer with 'movie star looks' and the trial was guaranteed a regular slot on the nightly news. Newspapers from both coasts had sent their crime reporters to Minnesota for the duration.

The cameras were not allowed to zoom or pan, but what the trial coverage lacked in production values, it had more than made up for with content. Some of the testimony from his three surviving victims had been so harrowing the cameras had gone black. Court TV was getting its highest ever viewing figures, and everyone from the BBC to Al-Jazeera had billed it the 'Trial of the Century'. Lurid headlines all over the world gorged on the crimes of a depraved man who abducted young women and forced them to make brutal and sadistic pornography in the basement of his house. The videos that made him the most money had been the ones in which he killed them.

Jones raised his right hand, held the Bible in his left, and took the oath. 'I swear by almighty God..." His voice retained a trace of his Texas childhood, but it was lighter and softer than Ingrid had expected. A tattoo poked out from under the cuff of a white shirt that the clerks would have given him from the Goodwill. Judge Isaacs never allowed defendants to appear in jailhouse jumpsuits. Ingrid knew exactly where the Goodwill cupboard was in the Jackson County Courthouse. A memory surfaced of two hookers she'd arrested when she was a deputy. They'd changed into shapeless smocks for their arraignment, but still tottered into the court room in six-inch stilettos.

Jones's shirt was a little too tight, bulging over his torso and giving the impression that his time in the county jail had been spent working out. The jury was made up of eight women and four men: it looked like Jones intended to flirt his way to a not guilty verdict. Notorious killers always got fan mail, and it sickened Ingrid to think Jones probably got a sack of the stuff every month. He sat down, smoothed a hand over his chin, and smiled at his attorney. The movie star was ready for his close-up.

Ingrid threw the brown cardboard bowl that had contained her lunch in the trash, then picked it out. Not only had the embassy's commissary started serving food in recyclable packaging, but there were now recycling points throughout the building. The nearest one was just outside her office door, but she didn't want to step away from her monitor for even a second. She pushed the bowl away and saw that yesterday's was still on her desk. Dried lettuce encrusted around its rim, an oily stain blooming at its base.

The Criminal Division office was a dump. In the previous six months, Ingrid had torn through a string of temporary assistants, none of whom had come to grips with the filing or the computerized systems. House plants that had been lovingly tended by Jen, Ingrid's assistant for the previous four years, were now wilted and parched on the window sill. The calendar on the wall hadn't had any appointments filled in since a bright young woman from Delaware had enthusiastically sat at the opposite desk for a couple of weeks in February. Ingrid had no idea why she'd burned through assistants so rapidly: she didn't think it was anything she'd said or done.

She had stopped seeing how rundown the place had become. She'd stopped noticing the light that had been flickering above her desk for the past two weeks, and she no longer thought anything of having to restart the printer every time she needed a paper copy of something. It had been a very long time since she marveled at how the best crime fighting agency from the richest nation on earth could operate out of something that hadn't had a lick of paint in her lifetime. There was no point calling maintenance as the answer was always the same: we will be moving to our new building shortly and a budget for these issues has not been allocated. 'Shortly' had lasted for at least two years, and the move to the new embassy had just been delayed again. Ingrid was grateful that the air conditioning worked: it hadn't dropped below seventy degrees Fahrenheit—even overnight—in London for the past six days.

Footsteps and whispers from the courtroom dribbled out of the feeble speakers, and Ingrid remained glued to the screen as Jones's attorney got to his feet.

"Mr. Jones, over the past three weeks, the State of Minnesota has laid out its case against you. We have heard from witnesses that you—"

The door flew open, and Ingrid gasped audibly. She turned quickly, guilt flooding her brain for being found watching TV. It was Jacob DeWalt, the newly promoted Supervisory Special Agent. "Boss, hi."

"You don't need to call me that." DeWalt's shirt stuck to a belly that was just overspilling his belt, and sweat patches stretched from under his armpits. "Geez, it's cool in here."

Ingrid sat up straighter and stacked the cardboard bowls in a vain attempt to make the place look tidier. "The AC is just about the only thing that does work in here."

DeWalt—forties, balding, and affable like a dad in a teen melodrama—nodded at her screen and winked. "Hey, we're all allowed to watch a little TV on our lunch break. Any news?"

"Jones has taken the stand."

"I meant about the Tilbury bust."

"Ah." Ingrid squirmed. Heat flamed her cheeks. "Final planning meeting in a couple of days. Can I update you then?"

"Sure." DeWalt raised his eyebrows. "And just to make

sure that update actually gets scheduled, let me introduce you to… Zeke, your new assistant."

Ingrid stood up as a neatly dressed man in his early thirties walked in behind DeWalt. He extended his hand. "Zeke McDaniels, pleased to meet you." Zeke had deep brown eyes, soft hands, a smooth accent that Ingrid guessed was from somewhere in Georgia, and a shy smile.

Ingrid shook his hand. "Ingrid Skyberg."

"Oh, I know that. You're the one who saved the First Lady, aren't you?"

Ingrid looked at her shoes.

"She sure is," DeWalt said. "Our very own hero with an entire cabinet of medals and commendations. But be warned Zeke, you think she's this big hero, but you're her seventeenth assistant this year."

"It's only June," Zeke said.

"We haven't figured out what she does to them yet. Maybe she buries them under the floorboards."

Ingrid's eyes widened, and DeWalt knew his gag had landed a heavy blow. He looked at her screen, then back at her. "I'm sorry. That was thoughtless of me." He bit his lip. Embarrassed, he took a step backward. "Okay," he said, keen to exit. "I'm going to let you two get acquainted. Go easy on him."

DeWalt left the door open and the sounds of the bullpen where most of the civilian staff worked—ring tones, keyboard strokes, printers, chatter—filled the awkward silence that had suddenly solidified between Ingrid and Zeke. His demeanor had changed. The bright, smiling man she'd met thirty seconds ago seemed nervous, anxious even. He could no longer make eye contact and instead looked at the floor. What had happened to him? Perhaps her eighteenth assistant wasn't very far away.

"Okay," Ingrid said. "So, first things first, I'm real sorry about the mess. If I'd known you were coming, I'd have tidied up. I wouldn't want you to think I was a total slob, I just have a lot on at the moment." She glanced over at her monitor. "Apart from watching TV, that is."

Zeke kept looking at the floor. The carpet was worn and stained from too many late-night pizzas and dropped cigarettes from the days when agents could smoke at their desks. It didn't warrant a close inspection. "Mr. DeWalt mentioned the Jones case was happening in your home town. You must know the house where it happened."

Actually, Ingrid didn't. The House of Horrors was a farm about thirty miles west of Jackson, but when she'd been a deputy, she would have driven past it a hundred times. "It'll be a long time before the town talks about anything else," she said, clearing some of her paperwork off Zeke's desk and stacking it on the third desk in the room that was occasionally used by an intern. "Once we get you onto the system, I can show you where the leads from the field offices are. Your main task will be assessing their priority and making sure—"

"I, um." Zeke tried to say something. He raised his hand and looked up. His eyes rolled backward. His head jerked suddenly. His torso twisted round, and Ingrid stepped toward him. She broke his fall as he tumbled, cradling his head as he hit the floor.

2

INGRID LAID Zeke down on the carpet in the recovery position as his body continued to jerk and twist. His tongue lolled out of his open mouth. Ingrid closed her eyes and took a deep breath. At some point in the past ten years, she'd done a first aid course that covered epileptic fits. *Come on, think!*

She checked the time. 14:31. If he was still fitting in five minutes, she'd call for help. She shoved the trash can out of the way so he wouldn't hit his head, got up and closed the door. Then she killed the lights to stop the flickering. She was about to call maintenance to come and fix the light, but she knew they wouldn't arrive in time for Zeke.

Ingrid cleared a stack of newspapers off one of the visitor chairs and placed it on her desk, carefully wedging the legs between abandoned files, stray external drives and piles of business cards from people she could no longer remember. She checked on Zeke: his seizures seemed to be less jerky, but maybe that was just because she was less afraid. Action was always the best antidote to fear.

Ingrid climbed onto her desk, then stood on the chair to inspect the reprobate light fitting. It was one of those old-fashioned fluorescent tube lights inside an aluminum rectangular box. The bulbs were notoriously fragile. In the new building, the lighting would no doubt be LED and so high-tech they'd have to employ electrical engineers rather than maintenance operatives, but until the much-anticipated move, they were stuck with technology from the 1980s. Ingrid unclipped the aluminum casing and gently lowered it onto her desk. She checked on Zeke. He had stopped jerking. His chest moved visibly. She checked the time again. 14:35. If he was still unconscious in another five minutes, she'd phone down to the embassy doctor on the second floor.

The bulb wouldn't budge. It was welded in place with eons of grime and there was no shifting it without shattering it. The only alternative she could think of was to disconnect it. She pushed a stained ceiling tile up out of its aluminum framework, moved it to one side, then stretched a hand into the void. She patted around in search of the cable and tugged on it.

The circuitry was so old it was the same vintage as the wiring in her childhood home. When you grow up on a farm thirty minutes from your nearest neighbor, the skills you acquire by the age of ten include basic wiring, small-bore rifle shooting, tractor driving and simple dentistry. She could do this.

Zeke let out a moan.

"Hey," she said, clambering down from her perch. "How you doing?"

Zeke moved an arm, then stopped. It was too soon. Ingrid crouched in front of him and resisted the urge to stroke his face. Instead, she placed what she hoped was a reassuring hand on his shoulder. "Take your time."

He nodded and squeezed his eyes shut.

"Can I get you anything? A glass of water?"

He didn't respond. Ingrid stayed still: she would take this at his pace. A minute or so later, he opened his eyes and gave her a look filled with terror.

"It's okay." She smiled at him.

He blinked several times, then pushed himself slowly up to a seated position. He scanned the room. "Is it just you?"

"Yup."

He stretched out his arms. "Really?"

"You want me to call for help?"

"No, God no. Normally..." he swallowed hard to lubricate his throat. "Actually, a glass of water would be good."

"I'm on it."

Ingrid fetched a glass from the watercooler in the bullpen. When she returned to the Criminal Division office, Zeke was sitting with his head in his hands. Ingrid closed the door. "Here," she said. "You want some Tylenol?"

He took a sip. "You're way nicer than they said."

Ingrid screwed up her face. "Who's they?"

He nodded in the direction of the bullpen.

"And what did they say?" She paused. "Do I want to know?"

"Nothing that bad. I was just expecting someone, I don't know... Whatever it was, you're not it."

Ingrid was used to colleagues thinking she was aloof. She was just slow to open up. She rummaged round in her desk drawer for a pair of scissors and some tape and spotted a pack of Tylenol. "Would these help?"

"Sometimes they help. Thanks. And thanks for not, well, for not making a scene. Most folks dial 9-1-1 and panic. I guess you must know someone who's epileptic?"

Ingrid stepped up onto her desk. "I don't, actually, but we get first aid training fairly regularly. I suppose some of it came back. 'Make sure the patient doesn't hit his head or swallow his tongue.' That's mostly what I remembered. I also figured it was highly unlikely to be your first seizure, but if it had gone on much longer, I might have yelled for backup." She stepped onto the chair. "Did I do the right thing?"

"Yes, you did. And I didn't pee my pants, so that's a bonus."

"That would not be a good move on your first day! But… I do have some track pants in my locker, so we'd have had you covered."

"You got a solution for everything?"

"Try to." She smiled and tugged on the cable. "You going to be okay? You need to lie down?"

He didn't say anything for a while. "What are you doing?"

"Disconnecting the light. It was the flickering, right? That set you off?"

Zeke got unsteadily to his feet. "You know how to do that?"

"Fairly sure I know enough not to get myself killed."

"Fairly?"

Ingrid was at full stretch, up on her toes.

"Here, let me help." Zeke grabbed the legs of the chair, and Ingrid froze.

"It's better if you don't," she said.

"Just trying to help."

"Please let go."

It was an order, not a request. Zeke took a step back and raised his hands. "You're the boss."

Ingrid looked at the wire, then looked over at the light switch and mentally mapped the likely route of the cables. If she was right, the switch had cut the current to the entire circuit and cutting the wire between her fingers shouldn't be a problem. She studied the other lights and figured the distance between them meant they weren't daisy chained. She rested the metal blades against the cable, exhaled hard, and squeezed the scissor handles together.

No boom. No puff of smoke. No dead hero. She craned to see where the plastic tape was and saw that Zeke was already holding it up for her. She gave him a smile. "Thanks. Seems you're not clueless about wiring yourself."

"Seven years with USAF."

"Cool."

"Medical discharge."

"The epilepsy?" Ingrid wrapped the tape around the ends of the wire as the phone on her desk rang. Zeke didn't miss a beat before swiping up the receiver. "Special Agent Skyberg's phone… I'm sorry… No, I said Sky*berg*. If you mean Special Agent Skyberg, she'll just be a minute... Be like that then." He shrugged. "Whoever it was put the phone down."

Ingrid slipped the scissors into her pants pocket and gripped the roll of tape between her teeth.

"He insisted he wanted to speak to Sky*lark*. No 'Agent' no 'Miss'—you aren't a 'Mrs.' are you?—just Skylark."

Ingrid mumbled that she was a 'Ms.' and the tape fell out of her mouth and bounced onto the floor. "I've been getting about one call a month for Skylark. Must be a sales call." She fumbled around in the void to retrieve the ceiling tile and her hand hit something. She pulled it back sharply. "*Govno*!" Ingrid always swore in Russian.

"What?"

"I touched something. I don't think it was a rat."

Zeke's eyes widened. "You got rats up there?"

"I'd bet on it. This place is falling apart."

Ingrid swallowed. Her heart pounded. Her physiological responses were in overdrive. *Deep breath. Whatever it is, it's not going to kill you.* She reached up again and blindly padded around for the tile. She touched the object again and let out a squeal.

"If you tell anyone I squealed…"

"Scout's honor."

This time she grasped deliberately for the object. It was light and moved without much force. She gripped it with the tips of her fingers and pulled it toward her, flicking it into the void with a puff of dust. She reached out to catch it and tumbled. The chair went flying in one direction while she vaulted in the other. Ingrid tucked and rolled, clattering into the trash can she had moved to protect Zeke. She righted herself to a seated position and held the object aloft.

"Huzzah!"

"You okay?" Zeke asked, his voice a mix of alarm and amazement.

Ingrid almost laughed. "I do parkour. Usually when I fall, it's off a roof."

"So, you're okay?"

"I'm fine."

"No 9-1-1?"

"Not necessary. And by the way, it's 9-9-9 in the UK."

"Noted. So, what is it?"

The two of them stared at the rectangular orange box covered in what looked like a decade of dust.

"I haven't seen one of those for years," he said.

"Not since everyone got a smartphone."

Ingrid was holding a disposable camera, the sort that was briefly fashionable to leave on tables at weddings, or that kids were trusted to take to their first summer camp.

"What do you think is on it?" Zeke asked.

Ingrid looked up at the square hole in the ceiling. "Something someone didn't want anyone to see. It didn't accidentally end up there, did it?"

"Good point."

They fell silent for a few moments. "My bet, judging by the dust," Ingrid said, "is the 2007 Christmas party."

"An elicit office romance, eh?" They locked eyes for slightly longer than was necessary.

"Something like that." Ingrid got to her feet and brushed off more dust. "Guess there's only one way to find out."

"The embassy has a processing lab?" Zeke asked.

"Oh, you need to downgrade your expectations of this embassy's facilities. But there's a branch of Snappy Snaps on most main streets. Heaven knows how they're staying in business in the iPhone era, but I'll drop it off later."

Zeke's brow furrowed. "You really think you should?"

"You telling me you're not curious?"

"I am *deeply* curious. But aren't there, like, privacy issues? Isn't that someone's private property?"

"What course have you just taken?" Ingrid scrunched up her face. "I'm fairly sure I don't need a warrant for this one." She picked up the chair and placed it back on the desk.

"What are you doing?"

"The ceiling tile isn't going to replace itself."

This time, Ingrid let Zeke hold the legs.

3

"WHY ARE WE HERE?" They were standing on a busy highway at the entrance to a mid-century apartment building.

"River views," McKittrick said. "Trust me, it's amazing inside."

When Ingrid had told Natasha McKittrick that she was house hunting, her closest friend in London had immediately decided to help. Since her dismissal from the Metropolitan Police two years beforehand, the former Detective Inspector had forged a new career as a presenter on a BBC show called *Crimewatch*. It evidently earned her a decent paycheck for a part-time job, and the rest of the time McKittrick bought, developed and sold property. She called it 'flipping', and every time she flipped, she banked six figures. Ingrid wasn't quite sure, but she was beginning to suspect that her once matronly friend was spending some of her profits on Botox, filler and personal training sessions.

It hadn't been Ingrid's plan to stay in London, but the notoriety Ingrid had gained in the US for saving the life of the former First Lady meant she wasn't able to return home and remain a case agent. Even in the UK, her higher profile had encouraged her to spend the first five months of the year as a Supervisory Special Agent. Ostensibly, the temporary promotion had been to fill the position made vacant by the death of Marshall, her former fiancé and boss, but the reality was that desk duties had kept her out of public view long enough for people to forget what she looked like.

In February, Ingrid had learned to her astonishment that she was the main beneficiary of Marshall's will. She had broken off their engagement two years before his murder, but he had never updated it, and so she had inherited his apartment in DC and his 401k and investments. Quite how he had saved so much by the age of 35 having reached the rank of Supervisory Special Agent, she couldn't comprehend; he had certainly never flipped a property. Even after death taxes and conversion to sterling had taken their cuts, Ingrid was left with enough for a deposit to buy a property for the first time in her life.

While her feelings about Marshall would forever be filed under 'complicated', Ingrid had always considered Marshall's younger sister Carolyn to be her own flesh and blood. Ingrid had known her since she was a tot, and as a consequence the girl brought out Ingrid's protective side. When Carolyn announced she was returning to London to complete her studies, Ingrid insisted that they move in together. It felt appropriate to use Marshall's money to buy a home for his baby sister.

Not only did the property have to be in a safe neighborhood and be the sort of place that Marshall would have wanted his sister to live in, it also needed a third bedroom so Marshall's parents could visit and check up on their only surviving child. Ingrid was more than a little flabbergasted she was contemplating having Meredith and Preston Claybourne as houseguests, but they hadn't challenged Marshall's will, so she figured that maybe, perhaps, they felt a little more warmly toward her than they had ever let on.

"Natasha, hi!" The realtor waved as he marched down the pavement, a zipped leather document file under one arm. A trim, eager twenty-something, he wore a pale blue suit that screamed the kind of confidence that only came from attending a school like Eton, Harrow or Winchester. They shook hands vigorously.

"Hi, Harry. This is my friend, Ingrid."

"Lovely to meet you. Shall we?" He produced a bunch of keys and gestured to the door.

The building smelled stale and the vinyl tiles on the hallway floor were warped and split. Harry pushed a switch. The lights did not come on.

"What's the service charge?" McKittrick asked.

"Very reasonable. For the area. About two thousand pounds a year."

"And how much would it be if they actually replaced the light bulbs?" Ingrid inquired.

The elevator doors slid open, releasing a sour aroma that probably emanated from the discarded McDonald's bag in the corner. "I thought you said this was an upmarket neighborhood."

"It is," Harry said. "Someone told me there are more blue plaques in Pimlico than anywhere else in London."

"Blue plaques," McKittrick explained, "are put on houses where famous and brilliant people lived. Something to do with English Heritage."

"I know," Ingrid said, as the car lurched upwards. "I've lived in London for over five years."

"Of course you do. Sorry." McKittrick made a zipper gesture in front of her lips.

The doors opened onto a long corridor. A skylight that hadn't been cleaned in decades let in enough light for the temperature to have reached triple figures.

"It's like Kew Gardens," McKittrick said. "You know, where the hothouses are."

"I do know."

McKittrick grimaced apologetically, revealing lipstick on her teeth. "Shall I stop telling you how to suck your London eggs?"

"That'd be great."

Harry tried several keys before one opened a door that would once have been white but was now the color of neglected teeth. It was even hotter than the hallway. "Let's open a window, shall we?"

A short corridor opened out into a large, empty room with windows on two sides. The décor was dated and the carpet was even worse than those at the embassy, but the apartment wasn't as awful as Ingrid had feared.

"Well, you haven't completely turned your nose up, so that's better than last week."

"Last week was Kilburn. At least we're in Central London here."

"Exactly," McKittrick said. "That's what I learned. No further out than Zone 2, Zone 1 if at all poss." Ingrid had noted how often realtors' particulars mentioned these zones, which referred to the Tube map. Ingrid very rarely got public transport—her motorbike was way more convenient—but by the time Carolyn finished her studies, Ingrid would have spent the best part of a decade in a city she didn't much care for. She didn't want to look back and think she had spent her days in somewhere called Brent. Or Erith. Or Penge. When people back home asked where she was living, she wanted to say Kensington, or Chelsea or Covent Garden, not somewhere that sounded like a fungal infection. She was aware that getting a three bedroomed home in such pricey locations was going to involve compromise, but this place was stretching her imagination.

Ingrid stuck her nose into the other rooms. A bathroom with a rose-pink suite and a kitchen with the sort of melamine cabinets that could generously be called 'vintage'. The sale was a probate instruction, code for 'an old person died here and the kids want their inheritance as quickly as possible'.

"Am I missing something?" Ingrid said. "Like a third bedroom?"

"Ah! You could be a detective."

"Funny."

"Well, see, what you can do is turn the kitchen into a box room, which is fine for guests, and then have an open plan living-kitchen arrangement. The living room is huge, so that's not a problem. You haven't even seen the view yet. Come on. It's better from the living room."

Harry had opened all the windows and was pacing around, happy for McKittrick to do the sales job for him.

"See. Look at that," McKittrick pointed. "You're on the sixth floor so you don't really hear the road and—ta-dah—you have a river view."

Ingrid stood next to her friend and looked out. Natasha was right. The building was opposite a handkerchief-sized garden square, and beyond it was the Thames.

"So, the compromise is that you're buying an ex-council flat, but you're getting great square footage for the price and the opportunity to add value. What's not to like?" McKittrick asked.

Ingrid pointed. "That."

"That? Really? I thought that was the pièce de résistance, the deal-sealer. You can walk to work."

"I usually run to the office. I'm not going to get many miles under my belt from here, am I?" The two friends looked out at the new US embassy, a modernist cube nearing completion on the south side of the Thames. "I'm not sure I want to come home and look at work."

McKittrick wilted, either with disappointment or the heat. "I was sure this was the one. Harry, have you got the details?"

He handed her the particulars. "All in there. I should say that we're going to get a heap of interest in this place. The river view is going to attract a lot of people, so if you do want to put an offer in before it officially goes on the market, you'll have to let me know tomorrow."

McKittrick let out a sigh. "Really? You're not going to bite?"

"I'm thinking about it," Ingrid protested. "I'm allowed to think, aren't I?"

"If my money wasn't tied up in my current development, *I'd* be buying this place. The chance to turn a semi-derelict two bed flat into a three-bed riverside penthouse in one of the best neighborhoods in Central London? You're not going to turn that down, are you?"

She had a point. "Okay, let's grab a coffee," Ingrid said.

"Or a nice cold glass of Sauvignon Blanc. You weren't going back to work, were you?"

Half an hour later, they were outside a recently renovated pub. It hadn't been where McKittrick had intended to take Ingrid, but a branch of Snappy Snaps had altered their plan. Ingrid could get the photos back in an hour, so they counted down the minutes in the Queen's Arms opposite.

A cold glass of wine—small for Ingrid, large for Natasha—in the sunshine before everyone else clocked off for the day made London feel momentarily glorious. Ingrid really didn't want to go back to the office, but she had a call scheduled with an agent in the Pittsburgh FO at 19:00.

The chat about property didn't last long, primarily because Ingrid just couldn't get over the fact that, for the price of two bedroomed apartment in London, she could buy a ranch in Minnesota. What London offered in square feet, she could have in acres back home. *Home*. An image of Jones on the stand reared up, making her shudder.

"So," McKittrick said, "I hear you're working with wee Ralphie Mills at the moment." She raised her eyebrows. "How's that going?" The lipstick was still on Natasha's teeth, but it felt weird to say something after so long.

Ingrid took a sip of her wine. "Not nearly as strange as you'd think. It's not like we dated for very long. And it was eons ago."

"But he was very, very sweet on you for a long, long time."

Ingrid demurred. "You do know he's got married since, right? I am no longer on a pedestal."

"I was at his wedding, remember? I honestly half expected him to say your name rather than Shelley's."

"Shelbie," Ingrid corrected.

McKittrick nodded. "That's a dog's name, isn't it?"

Ingrid didn't answer.

"Well, it should be."

Ingrid watched a young couple walk past, both fanning their faces with their phones. "Did you know that Shelbie is going to have a puppy?"

McKittrick put down her glass. "I had not heard that, but I bet Ralph is delighted."

"Every meeting we have he's either got paint on his forehead or in his hair. I think he's decorating every surface in their apartment before the baby arrives."

The bartender came out of the pub and placed two bowls of fries on their table. "Do you want any sauces?"

"Ketchup and mayo, please," McKittrick said.

"And some salt and pepper?" Ingrid popped one in her mouth and licked her fingers. "Ralph will be a good dad. He'll love all the early morning cartoons and the late-night feeds."

"Boy or a girl?"

"Boy."

"Just as well. He'd absolutely smother a girl. He wouldn't mean to, but he'd end up with a right princess."

It felt to Ingrid that they had veered into bitching, so she buried her discomfort in a fistful of fries.

"And how is Operation Pinball?" McKittrick asked. "All going to plan?"

"You know I can't talk to you about that. You shouldn't even know the operation name."

"But it's big? I've gathered that much."

"Several agencies. The Met, NCA, Border Force, us, the coastguard, the Gendarmerie."

"Ooh, nice pronunciation. So, it's drugs then?"

"Yes, I don't think it's too much of confidentiality breach to say it's drugs." Ingrid took a sip.

"Must be the Tilbury bust then?"

Ingrid avoided eye contact by repeatedly dipping a fry

into the ketchup. "I can neither confirm nor deny. Do you miss it?" she added. "The job?"

McKittrick stared into the middle distance. "Some days. I mean, I don't miss getting spat at and being called a bitch, but, you know, I wasn't ready for it to end." She pressed her lips tightly together.

"But." Ingrid formed her words tentatively. "It wasn't good for your health, was it? You seem much healthier now."

McKittrick made eye contact. "You mean because I'm no longer a junkie?"

Ingrid was a little taken aback by Natasha's bluntness. "Well, yes, that. But, actually, I've been thinking you look happier these days. Flipping property and Botox clearly suit you."

McKittrick prodded her forehead. "Is it that obvious?"

Ingrid didn't reply.

"I only had it done two weeks ago. I thought she was sticking a bit too much in. It'll calm down in a week or two." She drained her glass and gestured at Ingrid. "Those of us who weren't born with blonde hair, blue eyes and the physique of a superhero have to work a little harder."

Ingrid looked at McKittrick's empty glass and knew she should offer to buy a round. "Talking of work."

"You really are going back to work?"

Ingrid checked her watch: the photos would be ready. "The bad guys aren't going to arrest themselves, are they?"

"Fair point. So, I'll keep looking then?"

Ingrid wiped a drop of ketchup off the realtor's details. "I'll think about this place. I hear everything you're saying about it, but—"

"You're just not feeling it?"

"I think it's more that I don't want a view of the office."

"So, leave the FBI and take the flat!"

Ingrid smiled at her. "Maybe I just need to imagine it after you've renovated it for me."

The two friends kissed on the cheek, and Ingrid crossed the street. Snappy Snaps wasn't air conditioned, and the aroma of the young men who had worked there all day invaded her nostrils.

"You're back!" The youth in the Lou Reed tee seemed genuinely surprised that a customer would return to collect their photos. He put the packet of images on the counter. "I should have said, but I didn't notice when you dropped it off, that camera still had unused photos on it."

"Oh." Ingrid hadn't noticed either.

"So, there are only sixteen photos, but I have to charge you for the entire roll of twenty-four, anyway. I hope that's okay."

"Sure." Ingrid fished her card out of her pocket.

"So, that'll be ten ninety-nine." He held out the card reader for Ingrid. "Do you need a receipt?"

"That'd be great, thank you."

Ingrid picked up the pack of photos and took a peek.

"Oh." She flicked through them. They were not what she was expecting. Not at all.

4

Ingrid walked back to the embassy, and unusually for her, she strolled rather than marched. It was partly down to the heat, but she also found herself looking in windows and glancing up at balconies and wondering how much every property would cost to buy. Maybe the place McKittrick had shown her wasn't such a bad option.

Every pub she passed had a large throng of office workers having 'a cheeky half' on the sidewalk and chatting noisily before descending into the fetid underground for the long slog to the suburbs. Sidewalk swilling was a feature of London life she'd not seen anywhere else in the world. A combination of good weather being a novelty, air-conditioning being a rarity and outside space being expensive, she presumed.

By the time Ingrid walked into her office, many of her own colleagues had departed for the summer ritual of a cold beer on a city street. Zeke was still there. "Hi. I'd have thought you'd be off home by now," she said, depositing the realtor's details on her desk.

"I didn't want to disappear without saying anything."

"You can always send me a message, or leave me a note. I thought maybe the seizure would have wiped you out?"

"No, but your filing system is exhausting." Zeke leaned against his desk, notebook and pen in hand.

"Hey, don't knock it. It works for me."

Ingrid woke her computer to find she was still livestreaming KEIS, which was now showing a property renovation show. She checked her cell for messages to see if Svetlana had sent an update on the trial. She hadn't spoken to her mother this much since she'd left home. It was like they were in a book group, constantly making sure that the other hadn't missed a key revelation or plot twist.

"What have you got for me?"

They ran through the most pressing requests that had come in from field offices across the States. Mostly, they were appeals from case agents needing to access UK records, or requiring a witness or expert to be interviewed to support the bureau's investigations back home.

"You seem to have the hang of this already," Ingrid said. "Must seem very dull after the air force."

"Says the woman who rescued the First Lady from the roof of the ambassador's residence."

Jesus, you have a cute smile.

"Are they what I think they are?" Excitement inflected Zeke's voice as he nodded at the Snappy Snaps wallet on her desk. "Is it like the morning after the wrap party on *Love Island*? Strewn underwear and scattered champagne bottles? Naked bodies with only strategically placed Santa hats to protect everyone's modesty?"

She wrinkled her nose. "You need to seriously downgrade your expectations of the Christmas party. No, it's more like one of those art house European movies from the 1970s where nothing makes sense."

He raised an eyebrow. "Now I'm really intrigued. Show me."

Ingrid got up and closed the door. Zeke watched her as she brought the photos to his desk where the lack of clutter and a working overhead light gave it advantages over her own. "Do I need to remind you about your duty to keep everything you learn in this office private? Secret, even?"

He lifted his eyebrows. "No, no, you do not. But you do realize I am now burning up with curiosity?"

"I think these will dowse your flames pretty swiftly."

The first image she placed on his desk was the one she'd seen in the store. It was a map of Scotland. To be precise, it was a photo of a map of Scotland on a computer screen. The next photo was of a pocket-sized diary showing two facing pages displaying a week in March; it wasn't clear from which year. There were only two entries. On Monday the fifth, the word 'dentist' was circled, and on the Friday the entry read 'submit expenses'. The only other entry was a scribble on the Wednesday that looked like someone was testing out their pen.

Ingrid poked her tongue against the inside of her cheek, glanced at Zeke, then carried on. "I told you they were… art house."

The next image featured the word 'sois' written on a notebook. The one after that was another photo showing something on a computer monitor, a bird that Ingrid was fairly sure was a starling. The next image was of a bird she didn't recognize. Possibly a female blackbird? Brown and nondescript.

Zeke looked at her and ran a palm over his close-cropped hair. "Is this some kind of prank for the new boy?"

Ingrid gave him a half smile.

"Cause if it is, I think I'd prefer the trash can balanced on the top of the door."

"They get weirder." Ingrid continued laying out the photos, all of which were of images on a computer screen. An Amazon.com listing for a book called *National Affront* by a writer named David Steiner. The physicist Stephen Hawking. A Google Street View image of the kind of mock-Tudor 1930s family home that made up most of the outer London boroughs.

Zeke looked at her. "Why would someone take photos of these things on their computer?"

"And then hide the camera in the ceiling?"

They stared at the images, utterly disbelieving someone would bother to do either thing.

"Where's the embarrassing Christmas party kompromat?" Zeke asked. "I thought this was going to be fun."

Ingrid sensed they were standing a little too close together, and took a side step as she peeled the next photo out of the packet. This one showed three Post-it notes. One bore the number 36, another the words 'west park', and the third just had the letter E and the number 16 on it.

Zeke's lip curled and he tilted his head. "Is this, like, some real-life game of Clue?"

"If it is, maybe the color of the Post-its is significant."

Zeke stroked an imaginary mustache. "Why yes, Inspector, I see it now. One yellow, one blue, one green." He faked a French accent. "It is so… *signifique*."

The next three photos were what she had expected from a camera hidden in an office ceiling: images of a party.

"Is that outside?" Zeke asked, nodding in the direction of the bullpen. "Do you recognize any of them?"

Ingrid peered at the photos. Three white women in their twenties held a birthday cake between them and smiled for the camera. The three images were nearly identical, presumably because whoever was taking the photos was struggling to center the women in the frame: they were so far to the left of the image, one of the cake holders was nearly cropped out of it.

Ingrid's mouth fell open.

"What is it?" Zeke asked.

One of the women was Jen, her former assistant, looking much younger than the woman who had left London the previous Christmas. The photo must have been taken shortly after Jen started work at the embassy. She barely looked old enough to have graduated high school, let alone Vassar. "Don't get your panties bunched up, but I do know who that is." Ingrid pointed to Jen. "You may occasionally hear me refer to her as 'Saint Jen'."

Zeke's eyes twinkled. "My predecessor?"

Ingrid was surprised. "You've heard of her?"

"Or perhaps you mean my nemesis?" There was something gleeful and theatrical about Zeke. Ingrid sensed he was going to be fun to have around. "DeWalt may have mentioned I'd have a hard time living up to her."

Ingrid scrutinized him, narrowing her eyes. "You know when you start dating someone?"

He looked wistfully upward. "Vaguely."

"It's never a good idea to bad mouth the ex until you're sure of your ground."

"Ex?"

"You are so hungry for office gossip Zeke McDaniel that you are in danger of making it up."

Ingrid looked again at the photo of the very youthful Jen. Then she scanned the table for the photo of the diary. "What year would the fifth of March have fallen on a Monday?"

Zeke snapped his fingers. "Good thinking." He blitzed the keyboard, and a few seconds later a search result popped up on his screen. "Twenty twelve."

"Five years ago." Jen had done so much growing up in that time. She held the photo closer and looked at the people in the background. As far as she could make out, none of them still worked for the Legal Attaché Program.

Zeke picked up one of the other birthday cake photos. "It hardly looks like the sort of office party you need to hide in the ceiling."

There were four photos left in the packet. One showed a spiral bound reporter's notebook turned on its side with four arrows drawn perpendicular to the faint printed lines. Three small arrows were bunched together near the spiral, and a heavier, taller arrow was towards the bottom of the page.

Ingrid ran her fingers through her hair. It was just so bizarre.

She laid out the final three images: two more photos of a computer screen, one showing a Google image search displaying a grid of thumbnail photos for the search term 'yard', and a close up of a code made from letters, hyphens and mostly numbers. The final photo was of a page from the *Evening News* reporting on a gala at a nightclub called Mojito Joe's. Actors, socialites and millionaires in tight-fitting evening wear posed for the camera.

"Would you like me to get you a copy of that newspaper?" Zeke asked.

Ingrid pursed her lips. "Yes, yes I suppose I would.

And that book."

They stared at the matrix of images on his desk. Scotland, a starling, Post-its, handwritten notes, a low-key birthday celebration, Stephen Hawking, a book. "Taking one of these photos would be weird—"

"But taking *all* of them," Zeke interjected, "is just borderline psychotic." He planted a hand on his hip. "But it sure makes you want to know why though, doesn't it?"

It did. Ingrid started to pace the room. Not only had someone taken these photos, they had then hidden the camera with eight unused frames behind a ceiling tile. It's not like it had been placed on top of a locker, or behind a book on a shelf. To hide it in the ceiling required balancing on a chair on top of a desk, or using ladders. Why would anyone want to take such images and then go to such lengths to hide them? Why didn't they finish the film? Why didn't they get the film developed?

"Oooh."

"What?" Zeke asked.

Ingrid swiped up one of the photos and dashed to her own computer. She'd recognized what the string of letters, hyphens and numbers was. "See this," she said. "Two letters, hyphen, five numbers, hyphen, six numbers, hyphen three letters? It's a code for an FBI intelligence report."

A wide smile lit up Zeke's face. "Now it's like one of those Le Carré movies."

"Yeah," Ingrid said, waiting for her ancient monitor to flicker back into life, "one with Alec Guinness rather than, oh, what's his name?"

"Gary Oldman?"

"That's the one." The database finally loaded, and she typed in the code and waited. And waited. An egg-timer rotated slowly in the center of her screen and then, finally, the documented loaded.

Ingrid peered at it, her lips pursed, her brow furrowed, her heart thudded. Zeke leaned over her shoulder. He had a pleasant earthy smell. "Threat Assessment of Far-Right Groups in the UK." It was dated October 19, 2011.

"So," Zeke said, cautiously, "it's linked to the photo of the book in the Amazon listing. That was also neo-Nazi related, wasn't it?" Ingrid scrolled through the report, hoping for a cross heading or an image to pop out at her, something that would explain why the file was so important someone had photographed its database number.

Her cell illuminated. It was Svetlana. Ingrid inhaled deeply. "I need to take this." She swiped to answer. "Mom, hi."

"*Malyshka*."

Svetlana hadn't called her that for years. "What is it, Mom?"

"You have not seen?" She sounded more anxious than normal.

Ingrid leaned back in her chair and stared at the ceiling. She hadn't replaced the tile correctly; it was slightly slanted within its aluminum holder. "No, Mom. I've had to work. What is it? What's happened?"

"I can't believe you have not seen it." Svetlana's accent was a thick as the day she defected from the USSR. "I thought you watch news all the time."

"There's a time zone difference. Mom, please, what is it?"

Svetlana paused to take a deep drag on her cigarette. "He says he didn't do it."

"Jones?"

"He says he didn't kill Megan and he will prove it."

5

INGRID BECAME aware of a buzzing sound and then, moments later, that the sound was her phone. After Svetlana's bombshell the night before, she'd done a hundred lengths of the Hilton pool in an attempt to exhaust her body—but mostly her brain—into sleeping. It had worked. She reached out a stiff arm to the nightstand and grabbed her phone before it buzzed its way onto the floor. "Mom, what is it?"

"Did I wake you?"

"It's six a.m."

"So, I woke you?"

"Yes, you woke me." Ingrid stretched the muscles in her face, a cat-like silent yawn. She blinked at the sunlight framing the edges of the hotel drapes. "What is it, mama?"

"You haven't heard?"

"Mama, what is it?" When had she started calling her 'mama'? Was it because they were talking so often? Ingrid didn't like it. 'Mom' was intimate enough. 'Svetlana' was preferable.

"It is Kathleen."

Megan's mom. Ingrid's unofficial aunt. "How is she holding up?"

"She collapsed last night." Svetlana inhaled on a cigarette as Ingrid found the remote control under the sheets and flicked on the TV. The BBC's Breakfast show was interviewing the UK's Secretary of State for Justice about the government's refusal to impose new gender equality legislation. She switched over to CNN. "I know what you think, *Kroshka*. How can someone collapse when they are in bed already?" Kathleen's obesity had meant she'd not left her bed for the past five months.

"I wasn't thinking that. Did something happen to her?" Ingrid still hadn't processed the news that Jones claimed he hadn't killed Megan. She slung her legs out of the bed and slowly opened the drapes. The sky was hazy and yellow. There was no indication that the weather was about to break.

"Yes, something happened to her. The EMTs came. They're still there. I think he broke her heart, that's what happened."

"Mom, wait. It's on the news."

Ingrid unmuted the TV. A reporter stood outside the house on State Highway 49 and spoke in serious tones. It had been recorded before the EMTs showed up. "Speculation is mounting," she said, clutching a huge furry microphone, "about the identity of the man James Jones claims carried out at least some of the killings that happened in the property behind me."

Speculation. Ingrid had come to hate that word. It was the only excuse a journalist needed to prod and probe outlandish accusations and persist with hurtful intrusions. Ingrid changed channels, well aware that her own appetite for trial news was fueling the blanket coverage. But it was different for her. It was personal.

"You rather listen to yesterday's news than what I have to say?"

Ingrid rolled her eyes. "No, mom. I just thought—"

"I'm here, aren't I? Don't you think I would know more than some reporter?"

Ingrid deflected the accusation. "How is Kathleen?"

"She's dying."

"Mom!" Even for Svetlana that was alarmist.

"They're not even taking her to hospital, *that's* how sick she is."

"Mom, they can't take Kathleen to a hospital because she can't fit through the door. We've discussed this before. They'd actually need a builder to take out the wall." Ingrid cracked open a bottle of water from the minibar and took a sip. "And a hoist."

Ingrid waited for her mother to say something, but Svetlana always chose silence rather than uttering the words 'I suppose you're right, honey'.

"And can you imagine doing that with all those cameras outside her house?" Ingrid's pity for Kathleen surged. "Will you give her my love when you see her?"

Svetlana didn't respond directly. "If Kathleen dies, she will be his tenth victim, you know that? He won't be able to say he's not guilty of that. Causing her all this stress."

Ingrid worked out the time difference. "Shouldn't you be in bed, Mom?"

"You think I can sleep? With Kathleen like that?"

Ingrid's alarm sounded, and she turned it off. Six fifteen a.m. "Mom, I have to get ready for work now. You should try to rest. Turn off the TV and go to bed."

Telling Svetlana what to do was a mistake. "What you work today, *Kroshka*? Big case?"

Ingrid stretched her legs, rising onto her toes. "Still putting together that sting at the docks. The one I told you about."

"I remember. The one where nobody does anything right."

"I didn't say that, Mom. It's just that different agencies have different ways of doing things."

"And your way is the right way."

"I never said that either. There are just lots of gaps, a few misunderstandings. It doesn't take much for something like this to collapse, or for us not to get the evidence in a way that lets us bring a prosecution."

Svetlana said nothing for a while. "The problem with you, *Kroshka,* is that you don't trust people."

Ingrid considered hanging up.

"And that is something else that man is responsible for. Ever since Megan vanished, you have never been the same."

Ingrid inhaled deeply and exhaled slowly. She held her phone away from her face and silently screamed at it. "I have to go, Mom. I need to fit in a run before it gets too hot."

"That is also his fault. All this running."

"Mom. I have to go. Give my love to Kathleen. And get some sleep."

On her five-mile run around Hyde Park, Ingrid relived her mother's words. She was right of course, that's why Svetlana's words always stung so much. Ingrid had taken up running because of Megan. They had been the two heaviest girls in their grade at school, and if Megan had been a little faster, he would have grabbed Ingrid instead of her. 'Do you think you run because you are still afraid?' How many therapists had asked her that over the years? Svetlana was right about trust, too. When your dad dies when you're ten, and your best friend disappears when you're fourteen, you go out of your way to protect your heart from pain. Ingrid accelerated, trying to outrun Svetlana's judgment while knowing that she never would.

Just before eight a.m., Ingrid took the five flights of stairs to the Legat's suite of offices in the US embassy on Grosvenor Square, one of Mayfair's best addresses. She pushed through the door from the stairwell just as several people noisily exited one of the elevators.

"I thought we were never going to get out of there." A woman theatrically fanned her face.

"I'm not getting back in," her friend said. "Come on, let's take the stairs."

"They still haven't fixed it?" Ingrid asked them. The elevator had been acting up for weeks.

"When do they ever fix anything round here?"

The other elevator dinged and its doors slid open. "Sam!" Ingrid said. "Just the man I need to speak to. *U tebya yest' pyat' minut*?"

"*Da*. For you I might even be able to spare six minutes."

If it was possible to lay a bet on who would be the first Black director of the FBI, Ingrid would happily wager a hundred bucks on Samuel Sherbourne. He was serious and hard-working while being friendly and cooperative, the perfect characteristics for someone to rise through the ranks without making enemies. Although he was in his thirties, he gave the impression of not quite being fully grown. His features were still a little too large for his face, and his shoulders were permanently slouched.

Ingrid followed him into the office used by the counter-terrorism squad. Five agents made up the CT unit, three of whom monitored the threat from Islamist cells, one China, and Sam who managed the Russian threat. Ingrid and Sam had worked closely on several cases. In another office, in another part of the world, Ingrid would be the Russia expert, but her time undercover monitoring Putin's allies in the UK precluded her from that role in London. Instead, she fed intel to Sherbourne, and he sought her out for advice and guidance.

He slung his messenger bag under his desk. "What do you need?"

He looked tired. His boyish features were starting to sink behind dark circles and crow's feet. "You okay?"

He inhaled deeply. "I'm fine. Baby was awake the whole night. Nothing three triple espressos won't fix. What do you need?" he repeated.

"Who's our far-right specialist?" Ingrid asked.

His mouth crumpled. "In London?"

She nodded.

"We don't have one. We should have, though, don't you think?"

"After what happened in Oslo, it does seem a little near-sighted."

"Why are you asking?"

Ingrid paused, unsure what to say. "I've got this weird case. It may be nothing, maybe big. I need to find a copy of a book called *National Affront*, which seems to be out of print. I certainly haven't found it for sale anywhere. Anyway, I've got a couple of loops a far-right expert might be able to close."

"I'll keep my ear out," Sherbourne said.

"*Spasibo.*"

"You're welcome."

The clock on the wall said 07:55 when Ingrid switched on the lights in the Criminal Division office. Maintenance hadn't been to repair the fluorescent tube above her desk. She didn't expect it to ever get fixed. A permanent reminder of the fact that someone once saw fit to hide a disposable camera behind the stained and chipped ceiling tiles.

Out of an abundance of what she was calling caution, but what was really paranoia, Ingrid had locked her desk drawer overnight. She grabbed the pens out of her black mesh penholder, tipped it upside down, and the small silver key tinkled onto her cluttered desk. For some reason, she had half expected that the green and yellow wallet from Snappy Snaps would have disappeared from her locked drawer, but it was just where she had left it.

She flicked through the wallet and selected the photo of the small brown bird, before putting the rest away and closing the drawer. The photocopier grumbled into life and she placed the photo on the scanner bed.

"Good morning!"

Ingrid turned. "Hey there. How are you feeling this morning?"

"Much better," Zeke said. "This still my desk?"

"Most certainly is."

He dropped his satchel on to his desk and unbuckled it. He pulled out a gift wrapped in vivid geometric paper. "This is to say thank you. For yesterday." He handed it to her.

Ingrid's head tilted. "For what?"

His hand was still outstretched. "For not making a scene. And being so nice."

Ingrid moved away from the photocopier. She was always wary when people called her nice.

"It's nothing, really. To be honest, it's more a joke." He waggled the gift until she took it from his grasp. Ingrid tore off the paper and smiled: it was a first aid kit.

"I thought after yesterday, with me having a fit and you falling, we might need it."

Ingrid's eyes brightened and she handed it back to him. "Good thinking. You better keep it in your locker because I will forget where I put it. If you stick around, it's something you'll learn about me. I am terrible at filing." Ingrid glanced at the photocopier, then at the clock. She had time to brief Zeke before her meeting with the Met. "You drink coffee?"

"You want me to get you a coffee?"

Ingrid's mouth widened. "No, God no. I'm not the 'go fetch' kind of boss. At least I don't think I am. I certainly don't mean to be. But I need a long black and you need a notebook and pen. I'm going to show you the commissary in the basement."

Ingrid briefed Zeke on her caseload and brought him up to speed with Operation Pinball at Tilbury. Three coffees later, he put down his pen. "So, what are my priorities for today?"

Ingrid didn't have to think. "I need you to get me a copy of *National Affront* by David Steiner. Obviously, I've tried all the online shops and databases. Maybe the British Library has a copy—"

"You don't need to tell me where to get a book. I'll get one for you."

Ingrid smiled an apology.

"Anything else?"

Her phone rang. A forwarded call. They were never good news.

"Hello?"

"Mrs. Andrews?"

Ingrid took a beat to remember who that was. "Ah, yes. Speaking."

"This is ATX Security. The alarm has been set off at your property in Tilbury."

6

"COULD you come back in an hour and collect me?"

The black cab driver glanced round at the industrial park. "Where am I going to get another fare round here?" He had a point. The only people within a mile radius were truck drivers and warehouse workers. "I'll keep the meter running if you like and wait for you."

Ingrid weighed up the risks of him sticking around. "I'll pay now, thanks. I'll call when I need picking up."

"Fair enough. Seventy-three sixty, then."

Ingrid was a little taken aback by the cost. She normally rode her new Ducati in London, but the bike wasn't on brand while she was posing as the director of a medical supplies company. As soon as Ingrid stepped onto the cobbled yard, she realized the cab's air conditioning had been far better than she'd given it credit for. The blanket of humidity reminded her of getting off the plane in Charleston when she used to visit Marshall's family in July. It was like a furnace.

Ingrid watched the cab driver leave, then delved into her shoulder bag for the key to the padlock. Several of the buildings in the Napier Yard complex had, one way or another, been leased by Operation Pinball over the past year. A collection of Victorian and early twentieth-century architecture, they were no longer big enough for the major importers who now used the new hangar-like metal sheds on the neighboring land. Most of the Napier warehouses surrounded a central yard, but behind them, down narrow alleys, were a haphazard cluster of buildings that predated the invention of forklift trucks.

The 'yellow' warehouse—so called because it had originally been built of yellow London bricks, although they looked brown to Ingrid—had only recently become vacant. The Pinball team decided to rent it, thereby extending their control of the yard and reducing the risk of anyone finding out about their operation. The best way to do so without alerting anyone about Pinball, was for a legitimate company to rent the warehouse and make use of the landlord's existing security arrangements. Ingrid—under the guise of Jayne Andrews—had been made the keyholder and security director of Shoreham Medical, a cover company that exported used medical equipment for recycling. If anyone ever told her that working for the FBI must be glamorous, Ingrid made a mental note to tell them about her knowledge of used bed pans and specimen bottles. She wended her way through a network of thoroughfares just wide enough for a horse and cart, crouched down and inserted the key into the padlock. With effort, she pushed up the metal roller shutter, rattling it skywards, to reveal the building's original Victorian facade.

The ATX patrol had inspected the property and found no sign of forced entry, but they needed Mrs. Andrews to reset the alarm as it required a key and a code. A constant beep beep beep pulsed in her ears as she fiddled with the lock on the sliding gate, followed by the final lock on the door. If someone had broken in, they definitely hadn't done so via the main entrance.

With Pinball just days away from completion when the MSC *Laussat* was due to dock and unload its cargo of cocaine, they decided not to send the Met to investigate the alarm. It was unlikely, but just possible, that whichever officer they sent would be recognized by a docker they had previously arrested or pulled over, and months of planning would have been for naught. And just in case the smugglers had Napier Yard under surveillance, it was felt a woman arriving alone to reset the alarm wouldn't frighten anyone off.

Ralph and his team had checked the security cameras remotely, and they hadn't seen any nefarious activity. It was probably just the heat. Several alarm systems had malfunctioned in the past week, and the Pinball team was relatively sure the heatwave was to blame. Nevertheless, Ingrid kept her phone in her hand, ready to call for backup.

She closed the door behind her, locked it and slipped the keys into her bag. After a couple of steps, she changed her mind. She scooped out the keys and put them in her pants pocket. That way, if anyone separated her from her bag, she could still escape. Her nostrils stung: the heat-wave clearly hadn't agreed with something that Shoreham Medical was storing.

The interior of the old Victorian warehouse was filled with aisles of brand-new cobalt blue metal shelving. Her footsteps echoed on the concrete floor as she marched quickly between the shelves. A rivulet of sweat tadpoled its way from her collar to her waist. The further she got from the front of the building, the darker it got and the more the odor intensified. Ammonia. She fought the impulse to gag. A buzzing sound joined the pulse of the alarm, making her wince. A single bee flew past her head.

"How did you get in?" she asked out loud.

The office was up a flight of metal stairs. She pulled hard on the handrail and took the steps two at a time to arrive on a metal walkway that ran along the entire back wall of the warehouse. Between her clanging footsteps on the stairs and the rattle of the shutter, there was no way she hadn't announced her arrival to any trespasser. She unlocked her phone, ready to make a call.

At the end of the walkway was a door. It was open. Was it meant to be shut? The constant pulse of the siren chased away her ability to know the answer. The bee accompanied her as she walked through the open door into a short corridor that was lined on one side with half-glazed doors. The alarm was even louder now, making her screw up her face. Nervous, she fumbled with the keys, looking for the one that unlocked the office door. She couldn't do it one-handed. After checking left and right, Ingrid pushed her phone into her pocket and selected the right key.

Take a deep breath, kiddo. There's no one here.

Ingrid pushed open the door. There was no evidence that the office had been violated. Her sweaty palm slipped on the handle as she opened the alarm's cover panel. She stared at the control, wincing as the alarm repeatedly assaulted her ears.

Something made her turn sharply.

Another bee? No, it was something else. Footsteps? She crept toward the open office door and stood behind it. She strained to hear over the siren. A loud clatter.

Ingrid poked the keys between her fingers and formed her hand into a fist. Definitely footsteps. Someone was on the metal walkway. She reached into her pocket for her phone. It slipped from her sweaty hand onto the floor.

Govno.

The floor moved with the heavy stride of whoever was approaching. She glanced down at her phone. She didn't dare bend down to pick it up. She tightened her hand around the keys as a figure stepped into the open doorway, obscured by the frosted glass. Ingrid held on to her breath. She didn't even blink. He strode out from behind the door and into the office.

"Oh, for fuck's sake!" She hyperventilated. "Ralph! You fucking moron!"

"Hi." He smiled at her and stuck a finger in both ears. "Sorry I'm late."

Ingrid raised her fist and showed him her impromptu knuckle-duster.

His eyes widened. "What?"

Ingrid pushed him to one side and punched in the code to the alarm panel. She fell against the wall with relief when the pulsing stopped. She hauled air into her heaving chest. "What the hell are you doing here?"

"I sent you a message."

Ingrid scooped up her phone from the floor and showed him the screen. "Well, I haven't got it." She had a sudden flash of one of the training courses at Quantico and her instructor telling the class 'What's received is what's communicated.' A fundamental maxim that prevented fuck-ups.

Ingrid's chest hurt. She started shaking her head, and then a smile started to stretch its way across her lips. The idea that anyone would find Ralph Mills scary was hilarious.

"Are you laughing at me?" Ralph asked.

"Maybe."

He checked his fly. "Have I got paint in my hair? What? What is it?"

Ingrid had never understood why laughter was a response to discomfort, but she couldn't stop herself.

"What have I done?"

Dear sweet wonderful Ralph Mills. The nicest, kindest, dumbest fool she'd ever dated. Her shoulders hurt with the movement. She couldn't stop, and he couldn't stop from joining in.

"I have no idea what I'm laughing at," Ralph said, a minute or so later.

"I know." Ingrid just about managed to get her words out. "That's what's so funny."

Ralph shook his head suddenly. He slapped his cheek. "Jesus. What's a bee doing in here?"

Ingrid's hearing was recovering well enough for her to realize the sound she could hear wasn't just one bee. She stepped out into the corridor. Now the alarm had stopped, there was a persistent buzzing, simultaneously high and low pitched.

"What is it?" Ralph asked, stepping out behind her.

"You hear that?"

"What is it?"

Ingrid had a pretty good idea. "I think it's what set off the alarm."

They walked down the corridor, and the hum got louder as they reached the final door. Ingrid looked down at the floor, her eyes distracted by the sight of two honeybees crawling through the gap. She placed a hand on the doorknob.

The second she opened the door, dozens of bees escaped. Ralph waved his hands in front of his face. "What the—"

"Don't flap. You'll make them angry," Ingrid said.

In the far corner, under a broken skylight, a seething, surging mass vibrated. Thousands of bees. Maybe tens of thousands. The swarm was massive enough to have triggered the motion sensors.

"What's that?" Ralph said.

"A swarm. Looks like the queen has found a very inconvenient new hive."

"Ow!"

"You been stung?" Ingrid asked.

"Yeah, the little—" He looked up at her with his puppy dog eyes. "You can't really call a bee a fucker, can you? Even if it does bloody hurt."

Ingrid thought of Zeke's seizure and wondered if she was about to see a second medical incident in two days. "You're not allergic, are you?"

Ralph turned to her. "Wha?" He couldn't make the T sound because his tongue was swelling up. His eyes enlarged even further.

"Ralph?" Ingrid took a step toward him. "There'll be a first aid kit in the office somewhere." She pushed past him but he grabbed her wrist and pulled her back. She turned and saw that he was smiling.

"Fooled you."

Ingrid looked down at their hands, then back up at him. They both pulled away at the same time.

"Now we've both laughed at each other," he said, slightly pleased with himself. "It's only fair. What are we going to do about those?" He pointed a thumb in the direction of the bees.

"Well, back home, I'd call a local beekeeper. Maybe animal protective services. Don't you have some sort of Royal Society for Animals, or something? Or, like, the Department of Agriculture?"

"The RSPCA?" He shrugged. "I'll call the office, see what they suggest."

Three hours later, Ingrid was in the back of another cab riding back into Central London. As the bees didn't pose an operational threat, Director Aziz of the National Crime Agency made the call to leave them where they were. Ultimately Pinball was his rodeo, and he determined the greater threat was a beekeeper turning up in the body suit and mesh hat only for one of the dockworkers to film them. A light-hearted report on the local news was just what they didn't need.

Ingrid's taxi stopped at traffic lights near London City Airport. Sitting at the intersection of four roads, she saw that each of the four road signs all had the code 'E16' on them. She was still thinking about the colored Post-its—west park, 36, E 16—when the driver pulled away from the lights.

She knocked on the dividing glass.

"Yes love?" He made eye contact via the rearview mirror.

"Is there a street near here called West Park?"

"Yes," he said slowly as the cogs in his brain clunked and whirred. "You want to take a detour?"

Four minutes later, he pulled up outside number thirty-six.

7

INGRID HAD to remind herself of several things on the drive back into Central London. One, she had no idea if the three Post-it notes containing three separate pieces of information referred to an address, let alone the one she had spent twenty minutes staring at while the cab driver kept the meter running. Two, she couldn't come up with a good reason why someone wouldn't have just put '36 West Park E16' on a single Post-it if they wanted to write down an address. And three, she really was utterly clueless about why any of those photos had been taken. Even though, or possibly precisely because, she would never know, her thoughts kept returning to the packet of photos locked in her top drawer.

Thirty-six West Park was a newly built row house, part of what a realtor would call 'a boutique development' of twenty small houses, all clad in charcoal timber to resemble the wharf buildings that would have once lined the Royal Albert Dock. They overlooked a small rectangle of grass that was barely bigger than a decent-sized back yard—she certainly wouldn't have called it a park—but if the good weather held, Ingrid planned to return with a beach towel and some sun tan lotion. It wasn't often that such an easy surveillance opportunity presented itself.

The downstairs window of number thirty-six offered a glimpse of the room beyond, but in the bright sunshine all she had seen was the cactus on the window sill and backs of several photo frames. The window above was filled with stickers and lined with a row of soft toys. Ingrid had called Zeke and asked him to find out everything he could about who lived at the address. It would be a good test of his competency and skills.

As she didn't yet have proof of Zeke's abilities, Ingrid asked the driver to drop her off outside Foyles bookstore. Foyles was one of the oldest and biggest book stores in the world: if anywhere in London had a copy of David Steiner's book, it would be Foyles.

The air inside was cool, but not cool enough. The good thing about living at the Hilton in such heat was the prospect of a swim when she finished work. Maybe today she'd even go straight to the plunge pool. Ingrid navigated her way through aisles of books to a map of the store, and from there she plotted a course to the information desk on the second floor. The assistant behind the counter looked exactly like every other bookstore clerk: studenty, hipsterish, one of those metal holes in one earlobe, unsmiling.

"Hi."

The clerk didn't even say anything. The heat was clearly getting to him.

Ingrid loosened her shirt from her damp skin. "Can you tell me which section has a copy of *National Affront* by David Steiner? Please?"

His eyes bulged slightly before he wordlessly turned to

his computer screen and typed in her request. "It's out of print."

"Does that mean you don't have a copy?"

He tilted his head. "That means we don't have copy." He could use a little customer service training.

"You know where I might get a copy?"

"There's this really big website these days that sells books. You may have heard of it?"

Such wit. "Amazon doesn't have it."

"Have you tried the secondhand shops? Atticus on Charing Cross Road has quite a lot of Nazi stuff." His lip curled as he uttered the word 'Nazi'. Ingrid was suddenly very aware of being blonde, blue eyed and, well, Aryan. She thanked him, then walked the short distance south to Atticus.

Charing Cross Road was one of those London thoroughfares that always disappointed American tourists. If they had read Helene Hanff's book, or watched the Anne Bancroft movie, they had an impression of a studious street where every shop sold books, and where the knowledge and beauty that wasn't on the page was lurking in the minds of the charming people behind the counters. The remnants of its bookish past were still visible in small shops like Atticus, but most of Charing Cross Road was now taken up by clothing chain stores, pizza-by-the-slice joints and Chinese supermarkets.

A small and neat store on ground level, Atticus became a meandering warren of small, airless rooms in the basement that ran beneath the neighboring stores. Every two minutes, the hot sticky caverns vibrated as the Northern Line rumbled just a few inches beneath her feet. Ingrid searched the British History section, the World War II section, the Social Affairs shelves and the Politics department. She didn't spot *National Affront*, but she did learn that its title was a play on a defunct, or dormant, far-right political party called the National Front.

She emerged back at ground level with sweat running between her shoulder blades.

"Did you find what you were looking for?" The assistant was more like a university lecturer than a student. The kind her students had crushes on. Her curly hair was buffeted cinematically by a desk fan.

Ingrid told her about the Steiner book, and the helpful woman gave her a list of other titles about British far-right groups. "I really am just after this particular book." And then for no particular reason, perhaps because she was worried that this nice woman would think she was a far-right sympathizer, Ingrid felt the need to add: "It was written by a friend. More a friend of a friend."

The woman's eyes brightened. "Does that mean you know Daisy Steiner?"

"Um."

"The crime writer? She's his daughter."

"I can't say I do."

The woman shifted on her stool, and leaned in, conspiratorially. "Don't tell anyone, but I *love* her books. They're a bit infra dig, especially if you work somewhere like this, but I could read one every day if she wrote more quickly. Here." She got to her feet with more energy than Ingrid had seen anyone display since the thermometer topped eighty degrees. She zipped to the rear of the store and Ingrid followed. "Yup. I knew we'd have some. I'm going to give you this one because it's the first in the series."

Ingrid held a slim volume. A slim, *pink* volume. This really wasn't Ingrid's sort of thing.

"I love a bit of crime fiction," the assistant said. "Especially the cozy stuff. So much more of an escape than romance. Plus, you always get a resolution, unlike half the stuff that wins the awards."

Ingrid flicked through the pages. "It's not much of an escape when you're an actual detective."

The woman's eyes popped. "Really?"

"Kind of," Ingrid said, keen not to have to reveal who she worked for. The Brits tended to overreact to any mention of the FBI. "Any idea where I can get hold of her father's book?"

"You tried Amazon?"

8

INGRID KILLED the engine and hauled the Ducati onto its stand. She eased off her helmet, draped her jacket over the warm seat, and took a deep breath. She stretched her bare arms toward the sun. For the first time in she didn't know how long, she was smiling so much her cheeks hurt. God, it was gorgeous out here.

The valley sprawled below her toward a hazy horizon where the lion-colored fields bled white into the palest of pale blue skies. Behind her, a cluster of stone-built farm buildings basked in the heat like seals on a rock. She hooked her helmet on the handlebar and stepped away from the sting of gasoline and toward the rich summer scents of warm grass and wild flowers.

"Can I help you?"

Ingrid turned back to see a teenage girl carrying a saddle at the threshold of a barn. "I'm looking for Daisy Steiner." Her throat was dry, but her hair was drenched in sweat.

The girl looked Ingrid up and down and suppressed a smirk. "She's down with the pigs."

"And, where are they?"

"Down thataway." She nodded at the valley. "See the trees at the bottom of that field?"

Ingrid shielded her eyes. "Yes, yes I do."

"Well, if you get that far, you'll not be far away." The girl slipped back inside the barn.

Ingrid fetched a bottle of water from her top box and quenched her thirst. It was warm and musty after two hours inside a plastic bottle, inside an aluminum box, inside a heatwave, but it felt like the elixir of life. She exchanged the half-finished bottle for a tube of suntan lotion. Arms and face duly smothered, Ingrid climbed over the gate and walked through the field. She followed a hedgerow that bounced with the nodding bells of bindweed and waving hands of cow parsley. It hummed with bees and on the short walk through the sunshine she spotted three different types of butterflies. She needed to get out of London more often.

Ingrid reached the small stand of trees and was instantly grateful for the shade they offered. A hand painted sign on a wobbly wooden gate said 'Pigs—Keep Closed'. She unbolted the gate and closed it behind her. Birds sang in the canopy above her head, and in the distance, she heard more singing: Daisy Steiner was belting out a dire rendition of Springsteen's *Blinded By The Light*.

"Hello!" Ingrid raised her voice and shouted through the trees. "Hello!"

Daisy stopped singing and turned toward Ingrid. "Hello?"

Ingrid picked up speed, glad of the biker boots to stride through the undergrowth. Up ahead, Daisy Steiner held a bucket of feed as a gaggle of brown pigs truffled at her feet. "Daisy, hi, it's Ingrid Skyberg. We spoke on the phone?" Ingrid waved as she approached the clearing. "Hi."

Daisy didn't move. "You're an FBI agent?"

Ingrid looked down at herself. Boots, jeans, sweat-stained tee shirt. "To be fair, you don't look much like a crime writer either."

"Touché." She put down the bucket and extended a welcoming hand. "You're early."

"It only took an hour and a half."

"I've never made the journey from London that quickly." She pushed her collar length hair behind an ear. "Did you have flashing blue lights?"

"No, just two wheels."

"Ah." Her eyes widened. "That explains it. I had planned to be back at the house for your arrival. Just wanted to get these fellas fed."

"Tamworths?"

Daisy took a step back. An eyebrow lifted with disbelief. "You know your pigs."

Ingrid smiled as she crouched down to get closer to the animals. "I grew up on a hog farm. I had four thousand of these as my childhood pets. Is she pregnant?"

"Yup. Scan says a litter of twelve."

"Oh, wow. That's a lot for a Tamworth. She'll be glad of the shade."

Ingrid stood up and Daisy moved toward her. She reached out a hand and touched Ingrid's face. Her fingers smelled of the Kalmbach feed her father used to swear by.

"Gosh, sorry," Daisy said, embarrassed. "I don't know what I was thinking. You've got some sun tan lotion on your cheek. I, um. I'm sorry. I was going to rub it in for you. Sorry. That was totally inappropriate."

Ingrid raised her own hand and wiped her face. “Thanks.”

“I wouldn’t want you to look in the mirror later and think I hadn’t said anything. Don’t you hate it when that happens? You have a really nice lunch with a friend and you go to the ladies and you’ve got a bit of lettuce tucked between your incisors.”

“Yes, I do hate that.” Ingrid pictured the lipstick on Natasha McKittrick’s teeth. She should have said something.

Twenty minutes later, they sat under an umbrella on the terrace behind the farmhouse, a pitcher of iced water and a plate of bite-sized Greek spinach pies on the table.

“These are delicious,” Ingrid said, grateful for being fed.

“Special offer at Waitrose.” Why did the Brits always find it so hard to take a compliment? “I have a farmhouse kitchen, but alas no farmhouse cook.”

“I take it today isn’t a writing day?” She reached into her messenger bag for her notebook and pen.

Daisy lowered her head. “I write in the evenings. Four hours after dinner.”

“You work late.”

“That’s what seems to work for me.”

Ingrid placed her notebook on the table. “Writing and farming is an unusual combination, isn’t it?”

Daisy’s lips stretched slightly into a half smile. “The farm was my partner’s idea. Her dream, really. And now her ashes are scattered on the top field, I can’t ever leave.”

“I’m so sorry,” Ingrid said.

“It’s fine.” Daisy waved her hand in front of her face. “It’s been a few years.” The tears moistening her eyes meant it clearly wasn’t fine. She swallowed and continued.

"The farm isn't much of a business. More of a small holding, really. Luxury sausages at local markets, that sort of thing. A felt maker from the nearest village takes the wool. The honey is excellent, though. You must take some when you go. It's all organic. If it was just me… If it *had* just been me, I'd be in a penthouse in New York. But," she gestured to the far horizon, "it ain't bad."

Ingrid took a beat before answering. She was wistfully taking it all in. "It's wonderful." She thought of the shabby apartment on the river McKittrick had showed her. "I'd much rather be somewhere like this than the center of a city. But, then, this is what I grew up with." She needed to pull the conversation back to the reason for her visit. She had to focus. "Thank you so much for agreeing to see me. It's very nice of you to be so generous with your time."

"Don't be daft. I write crime fiction. I never pass up the chance to speak to a cop. You get double points for a Fed."

"Ah. So that's why we've got pies!" Ingrid paused. "Do you mind if we talk a little about your father?"

"Of course not. That's why you're here, isn't it? You mentioned one of his books on the phone. Which one was it?"

" *National Affront*. You don't happen to have a copy, do you?"

Daisy shook her head. "Nope, I don't think many copies were printed of that one. It wasn't well reviewed."

"Why?"

Daisy flared her nostrils. "Makes me a little angry now, but when it came out, he was the first person to say that Russia was funding the resurgence of the far-right in the UK. Now, of course, after Brexit, we know damn well that Russia is meddling in our politics. What better way for Putin to create havoc than by breaking up the EU?" She paused. "Sorry. Didn't mean to rant. Still can't believe we actually voted to leave. Anyway, so Dad said that Russia was behind groups like EFE—"

"EFE?"

"England for the English. Thugs. Absolute thugs. But with a few rubles they sort of became the paramilitary wing of the UK Independence Party. Sorry," she stopped abruptly. "Is this what you wanted? Is this even relevant?"

The girl from the barn appeared at the open back door. "I'll be off then, Daisy. See you in the morning." She turned to Ingrid. "I suppose I'll see you in the morning, too."

Daisy spat her water out. "No, Amy. Ingrid's here to talk about… It's not like that."

The girl's cheeks bloomed with embarrassment before darting back into the house. "Sorry about that. It's probably the motorcycle. She's only fifteen. She thinks in clichés. Though, to be fair, she has seen quite a few women come and go this year. Who knew pigs and sheep would be such lesbian catnip?"

Ingrid suddenly thought of her mother, still looking after the pigs twenty-five years after her husband's death. It had been a long time since Svetlana had even hinted at an overnight visitor at the farm, male or female.

"You're not gay, are you?" Daisy asked, raising one eyebrow provocatively.

"Um, no." Admitting to her one night of Sapphic exploration would be highly inappropriate.

"It's just the bike. In the Venn diagram of women who ride motorcycles and lesbians, there is quite a large shaded area."

Ingrid didn't know how to respond.

"So, I didn't realize," Daisy put down her glass

purposefully to change the subject, "that the FBI operated outside America."

"I'm part of what's known as the Legal Attaché Program," Ingrid explained. "There are, currently, ten agents in London. No, twelve."

"And what sort of cases—should I call them cases—do you work on over here?"

Ingrid picked up another pie. "We have a mandate to investigate federal crimes anywhere in the world, so long as we do so with the approval of local law enforcement."

Daisy took a sip, the ice cubes tinkling in her glass. "You'll have to forgive me, but I don't know what constitutes a 'federal crime'. It's not really a distinction we have here."

Ingrid had expected to be the one conducting the interview, but she obliged. "A federal crime is a crime against the US government, or a crime that has been committed in multiple states, or a crime against a federal employee." It wasn't an exhaustive list, but a cozy British crime writer didn't need to know the intricacies of the American legal statute.

Daisy pushed her unruly hair behind her ear. Ingrid hadn't yet worked out Daisy's age, but she'd wager she was early forties, about five or six years older than she was. "And I thought it was all serial killers and profiling."

"We do that too. Just not every day."

"So why is the FBI interested in my dead father?"

"As I mentioned when we spoke, I can't go into details, but I'm re-investigating a case that, if your father was alive, I believe he may have had information that would have been useful."

"To do with the far right?" Daisy pressed her lips together. "Not what I was expecting."

Ingrid furrowed her brow. "Why did you think I was coming?"

"I thought you were going to tell me who killed him."

"Your father was murdered?"

"Ever since you called, I've been thinking that he might have been."

"Because the FBI investigates serial killers?"

Daisy shook her head. "Well, maybe. But." She pushed her chair back and stood up. "I'll be right back."

Ingrid sat back and listened to the breeze in the distant trees and the low moan from a far-off tractor. Insects buzzed closer by and birds serenaded each other from unseen perches. Daisy's footsteps clattered onto the stone slabs behind her. Ingrid turned to see that Daisy was holding a business card. She held it out for Ingrid.

At first Ingrid thought Daisy was handing her back her own card. US Department of Justice. Federal Bureau of Investigation. It had the embassy's Grosvenor Square address. But the name on the card was Dennis Mulroony.

"Do you know him?"

Ingrid was so shocked she couldn't speak. She hadn't heard Mulroony's name for years. "Um. No. He was my predecessor," she managed. Ingrid looked up at Daisy's concerned face. "Where did you get this?"

"The coroner. When my father's things were returned after the inquest. It was in his jacket pocket the day he died."

9

THE SENSE of foreboding grew the closer Ingrid got back to the city. When her Ducati rounded a bend on the three-lane freeway and the skyscrapers of Docklands came into view, she almost considered turning around and heading back out to the undulating folds of Suffolk. When Jones's trial was over, when Zeke had found his feet, she promised herself a vacation. Hiking in the Dolomites, or renting a Vespa in Agrigento. No phone, no email, just the lure of the horizon and the warmth of adventure in her legs. She had never been very good at taking time off, but her afternoon on the farm had made her realize she was in desperate need of some R and R.

A rider on a Honda CBR pulled alongside her, and nodded. He was asking her for a race. On her old bike, a beautiful retro-styled Triumph, Ingrid got nods of appreciation. Now she got morons thinking they could take her for a ride down Thunder Road. When most of them saw a woman was inside the helmet, they lost their competitive streak and zoomed off into the traffic. Some, like the idiot to her right, actually tried to flirt at seventy miles an hour.

She mouthed the words fuck and off at him, but he took this as an invitation to ride even closer. Ingrid responded by slowing down and moving into the inside lane: the only way to lose an idiot like him was to make it very clear she wasn't playing.

A slower pace was no bad thing. She wasn't concentrating nearly hard enough on the road as her thoughts surged with the revelation that it must have been Mulroony who had taken the photos. It made sense of why she'd found the camera where she did—her desk used to be his—but why would an FBI Special Agent use a disposable camera? The only reason she had been able to come up with was that he didn't want to leave a digital trace.

When Ingrid had first arrived in London in 2012, Mulroony's name was like Macbeth's in a theater, or the one without a nose in Harry Potter: cursed. She'd asked questions at first, but had been told in no uncertain terms by Sol Franklin, her SSA at the time, to park her curiosity and move on. The rumor, or maybe it was just her suspicion, was that Mulroony had been a double agent. For whatever reason, he had become the one who couldn't be named, but whether that was out of fear, or shame, or national security concerns, Ingrid never knew.

It had bugged the hell out of her at the time. She was taking over Mulroony's investigations but not allowed to ask questions about him. She was his replacement as the chief Met liaison, but she hadn't even been given the right security clearance to access his files. She scoured her memory for every detail she knew about him as she rode closer and closer to London. Ingrid yanked up a recollection about a jackass of an arms dealer—Brewster something, or something Brewster, either way it hadn't been his real name—who'd insisted on speaking to Mulroony and refused to deal with her.

Another memory surfaced. This one was muddier. Walking round Grosvenor Square waiting for her cell to ring. Why had she been in the square? Ah, that was it. She had called Marshall—they had still been engaged at the time—who was working in DC. She'd asked him if he could find anything out about the mysterious Mulroony, and Marshall had arranged for someone to call her. Who? Ingrid tried to dislodge the information from a crevice in her brain. She was fairly sure he hadn't given a name. Nor had he revealed anything interesting. Only that virtually all records of Mulroony's service had been scrubbed from the bureau's files. Now that Marshall was dead, she would never know who her anonymous caller had been.

A truck thundered past, spewing sand and grit from its open load straight into Ingrid's mouth. Its backdraft pulled on the Ducati, causing her to wobble. *Concentrate.*

The fact that the photographs had been taken by a double agent meant she was no longer thinking that the images of birds on computer screens, or collections of Post-its, or badly framed birthday celebrations, was random. Ingrid knew it sounded far-fetched, but were the photos some sort of code? Was this the sort of material a double-agent passed on to his handler? And if that was the case, were the photos a matter of national security? She needed to let DeWalt know.

Another motorcycle came alongside her. She turned her head and saw it was the same Honda CBR. He must have turned off at the next junction and looped back. What for? All to get another look at a chick on a bike? What a jerk. She kept her gaze firmly forward. She did not want to encourage him. She did not want to rile him. She definitely didn't want to die in a pile up on the A12.

He tooted his horn.

What hell was his problem?

He honked again. This time Ingrid looked at him and raised her left arm. It was hard to give someone the finger in motorcycle gloves, but she hoped he'd get the message. He waved at her, pointed at the bike. She shook her head —no, she was not going to play with him—and slowed further, only for the car behind to blast its horn as it swerved to avoid going into the back of them.

The Honda was not backing off. She glanced down at the speedometer: they were still doing over fifty. He was playing a reckless game. Ingrid had no power of arrest in the UK. If this was the States, she'd ride him into the verge, show him her badge and scare him with threats to summon her buddies on the local force. The best thing she could do was ignore him and ride as safely as possible.

He started shouting at her, but between the road noise, the muffling effects of his helmet, and the insulating effects of hers, he was wasting his breath.

Don't take the bait. He'll get bored soon.

Out of the corner of her eye, she could see he was still gesticulating at her. Ingrid weighed her options. She could steer closer to him and scare him off, but it was risky move in heavy traffic. She chose the other option. Ingrid checked her mirrors and reluctantly signaled before pulling onto the shoulder and out of the flow of traffic. The moment she did this, he sped off, waving at her as he steered between cars.

Furious, Ingrid came to a stop and put both feet on the ground. Her heart was pounding. Her head felt like it had swollen with rage inside her helmet. She killed the engine and kicked down the side stand.

"You absolute tosser," she shouted, pleased at how satisfying British swear words felt in her mouth. She needed a few moments before setting off again. Riding angry was not a good recipe for maintaining four fully working limbs. Ingrid got off the bike and saw it. The strap of her messenger bag was hanging out the top box, drooping dangerously close to the spokes of her back wheel.

Ingrid pushed off her helmet and ran her hands through her hair. Her skin trembled. *Govno*. He wasn't a tosser, was he? He had probably just saved her life. *If the strap had got caught…* she didn't want to think about it. He had even looped back around to make sure she got the message. She could hear her mother's voice: "When are you going to learn to trust people, *Kroshka*? Eh? Not everyone means harm to you."

Ingrid crouched down and stared at the cars speeding past. She shivered despite the heat. In her profession you accept, while never really acknowledging, that you're putting your life on the line. You always think about the bullet in a shoot-out, or the booby trap on an arms cache, or the pile up at the end of a high-speed chase. Now she needed to add 'not checking a strap isn't flapping out of your top box' to her list of ways not to die.

She took the last ten miles easy, finally getting back to her desk after five. Zeke had already left. No note. She hoped he hadn't had another seizure. It certainly didn't look like he'd left in a rush. His desk was meticulously clean. In fact, there wasn't any sign that he'd actually used it all day. But a copy of the *Evening News* from April 2012 that he'd left on her desk was evidence that he had done a useful day's work.

Ingrid turned on her computer then stared out of the window at Grosvenor Square while it creaked into life. After-work picnickers vied for space with military fitness classes and canoodling couples. She remembered again the mysterious phone call she'd received from a contact of Marshall's about Mulroony and strained to recall anything more. The guy had had an accent of some sort. Boston, maybe. She had a thought: how many agents from Boston would have worked at headquarters in the summer of 2012? She sighed. If it were an official investigation, then the resources would be found. But this wasn't even an investigation at all.

She logged on and immediately pulled up Court TV. Jones was still in the dock, his second day of testimony. She sneered at him. Just be a goddamn man and take responsibility. She pictured Kathleen Avery watching the trial and how much pain his performance was causing her. She'd been ill for a long time and Ingrid feared Svetlana was right. The stress of the trial might be too much for an already broken heart that had to keep an eight-hundred-pound body alive.

Ingrid logged into the system and searched for Mulroony. It wasn't a surprise to find there wasn't any trace of him. Next, she accessed DoJ records: if Mulroony had been arrested in 2012, surely his trial would be on the system? It was five years ago, after all.

Okay, she reasoned. If he was a double agent, if he was a spy, then maybe he was tried in secret. That would explain why the Department of Justice had nothing logged for his trial. She tried a Google search and found a few college basketball team sheets and an obituary for a John Dennis Mulroony. It was a more common name than she would have imagined. She needed a way of whittling down the numbers.

She wrinkled her nose. It might work.

On the inside of her locker door was a ripped and faded sticker for the Cleveland Browns. Maybe the locker used to be his? She added 'Cleveland' to her search and the first return was a news report about Dennis Mulroony Snr who had donated his kidney to a co-worker at the high school where he taught. She clicked on the link and saw the smiling faces of two men with their arms round each other, outside a high school building in bright sunshine, above a caption that read 'Donor and recipient start new semester with smiles'. Mulroony Snr was beaming, his exuberant face almost bisected by a thin, hooked nose. Ingrid did the math and reckoned there was a good chance the all-American man she was looking at was the father of a Russian spy. She could only imagine how much his son's actions had hurt him.

She was about to search for something else, but stopped. She had the sense there was something she had forgotten to do. And then she remembered. The bird! The photo of the bird! She pushed her chair back and practically ran over to the photocopier. She lifted the lid and exhaled hard when she saw the photo of the bird was still there. Her heart pounding, she pressed the copy button and stared at the printout as it was delivered into the paper tray. It really was such a dull looking bird. Like a big sparrow. Brown and lacking any distinctive feature. Why on earth had Mulroony photographed it? She picked a pen out of her holder and wrote a message under the image.

Does anyone know what type of bird this is?

Ingrid stepped out into the bullpen. It was quieter than normal for the time of day, something she attributed to the weather. She pinned her sheet of paper on the bulletin board below a framed photograph of Frank Geest, the legend of an agent who'd been the London Legat in the 1990s, and who was the FBI's director in the early 2000s when Ingrid joined the bureau. Ingrid smiled: Geest's signature was on her certificate from Quantico.

Ingrid returned to her desk where James Jones was gesticulating silently in his muted rectangle. She was about to turn up the volume when she had an idea. Jones was going to prison, no matter what his defense said or did. Prisoners had records. Even if Mulroony's trial had happened in camera, he would now be in a federal prison. He'd have a number. He would have to exist.

Ingrid entered her password and signed into the Federal Bureau of Prisons database.

Hmm. No record there either.

She tried a different spelling.

Still no record.

It was starting to feel like the packet of photos in her top drawer was the only tangible proof that Dennis Mulroony had ever existed. What the hell had happened to him? Did he get a bullet in the back of the head and dumped in the Atlantic? Is that what the United States government really did to traitors?

Ingrid opened the drawer and pulled out the Snappy Snaps wallet. She looked again at the case file number, the suburban house, the map of Scotland. What could these things possibly mean to a man who was betraying his country? Were they evidence of a plot against America? A plot that was thwarted only because Mulroony was arrested? She slid the photo of the bird back into the packet and closed the drawer.

Then she opened it again.

What if this plot was still operational?

10

"Mom, stop. Slow down. You're not making sense."

"That is because you don't listen to me."

Ingrid rolled her eyes to the ceiling. Svetlana was impossible. "Mom, I am listening. I *have* been listening to you. For the past half hour."

"So now you don't have time for me. Now? Now is when you turn your back on me?"

Jesus! "Mom, I'm at work. My assistant hasn't come in. I have over a hundred cases. I can't watch the trial the whole time." In the corner of her screen, muted, a reporter was standing outside the courthouse, trying to find new ways to say the same things, only with more words.

"Kathleen needs you. *I* need you."

Ingrid gripped the phone so hard her knuckles were white. "I know that. And you also know that I haven't been called as a witness. If I had been, I would be there, but the prosecutors decided they didn't need me." *Or want me.*

"But you could say it was him."

"Mom, I *couldn't*. I'm an FBI agent. I can't take the stand and make things up."

"But you did see him, didn't you?"

They had been over this at least four times. "Mom, I was fourteen, I was terrified, it was dark. It was twenty-one years ago." Ingrid inhaled slowly. "Any defender is going to take my testimony about the man who chased Megan and me and persuade a jury they can ignore it. *That's* why they're not calling me."

It sounded like Svetlana was crying. Svetlana never cried. "Hang on, Mom." There was a commotion out in the bullpen, and Ingrid got up from her desk and closed the door. "I'm sorry I'm not there, but you must realize this is hard on me too. I'm the one who has flashbacks. Me and Megan on the path running so damn hard to get away from him. I'm the one that has PTSD every time I hear carnival music. It's not like this doesn't affect me."

Sometimes it felt to Ingrid that Svetlana, and maybe Kathleen too, took Ingrid leaving Minnesota as a sign that she was somehow over what had happened to her. "Another three or four yards and it could have been me."

Svetlana unleashed a howl. "Don't say that *Kroshka*. Never say that."

"But it's true, Mom. Isn't it? The reason I run every day, the reason I do this job for chrissakes, it's because of him. So please, please don't ever say that this doesn't matter to me." Ingrid blinked back tears.

James Jones had told the court he had nothing to do with the first three victims, one of whom was Megan. "They was already in the basement when we put that kid from Alabama down there," he said. The 'we' he was referring to was himself and a man he was calling Bill Starr. Jones's defense was that he was just another of

Starr's victims. "I was just a hick from out of town. I didn't know what I was gettin' into, what I was bein' roped into."

According to Jones, Starr made pornography—Jones kept referring to them as 'dirty pictures' like they were harmless—back before digital cameras and online streaming. Not only did he make the films, he distributed them on VHS cassettes, sending them out mail order. He specialized in abusive and degrading material. Women and girls being told they were worthless as they were raped and tortured.

Ingrid had worked four years in Violent Crimes Against Children, but even she found listening to Jones's testimony unbearable. The thought that Megan—shy, funny, sensitive Megan—could have been a part of what he described was too painful. She had watched most of it on mute. They had beaten the girls, they had mutilated and humiliated them. In Megan's case, they had starved her, tormenting her with food, forcing her to perform degrading acts before letting her eat and then ridiculing her for her size. Jones claimed the first girl died by accident, but when Starr discovered that tape was in high demand, he had a financial incentive to carry on killing.

Jones testified that he'd been hired for his looks. His lack of family connections and low self-esteem—it sounded to Ingrid like he'd had therapy while he was on remand—were additional benefits. He claimed he was just as much a prisoner on the farm as the girls had been. "I'm real sorry to the ladies present," Jones told the court, "but when Billy Boy couldn't get hard no more, he was looking at losing more than his manhood, ya know? This was how he made his money. He needed a stud, and he found me."

Ingrid's desk phone rang. "Mom, I have to go. I'll call you tonight. Okay?"

"Any time, *Kroshka*. You call any time."

Ingrid snatched up the desk phone. "Agent Skyberg."

"Ingrid, hi."

Her shoulders instantly relaxed at the sound of a friendly voice. "Ralph. Thanks for calling back."

"You got news?"

"News?"

"On Pinball?"

"Ah, no." Her brain was still in Minnesota. The noise coming from the bullpen didn't help her concentration either. "I was after a favor… well…"

"Spit it out."

"Do you remember when we first met?" That was the wrong thing to say. She could almost hear him blush. "You probably don't remember—"

"I have a very clear memory, actually."

Now she was blushing. "I asked you for a favor. I was new to the Met liaison role and I wanted to find out who my predecessor had worked with."

"This is sounding vaguely familiar."

"You don't happen to remember who that was?"

"Your predecessor at the embassy?"

"No, the officer in the Met he dealt with."

"Ah." There was a long pause. "Why do you need to know?"

She wasn't going to tell him about the photos. "Tying up some loose ends. I'm sure you told me at the time, I just wish I could remember now."

"What was your predecessor's name?"

"Mulroony. Dennis Mulroony."

"A bell is faintly ringing. Leave it with me." He inhaled audibly. "Will I see you later?"

"You bet."

"See you then."

Ingrid clicked to unmute Court TV when her door opened.

"So, you are still here," he said, beaming. "What do you say? Can I buy my hero agent some lunch?"

11

"Sol!" Ingrid got to her feet. "I didn't know you were coming to London."

"Impromptu visit." He was beaming. He was twenty or thirty pounds lighter than when she'd last seen him, and his beard was significantly grayer. "Madeleine's speaking at a conference. The organizers were offering spouses a free airfare, and I thought, well, why not?"

Ingrid shut down her computer and made sure her top drawer was locked. She grabbed her wallet.

"You're not going to need that," Sol said. "This is on me."

Outside in the dreamy midday heat, he led her deeper into Mayfair where he'd made a reservation at Sabrina's, an understated Italian restaurant that usually had a couple of paparazzi outside hoping to spot a minor royal or a major movie star. "Sabrina's, eh?" Ingrid said as they walked briskly through the hazy streets. "Your bureau 401k is obviously serving its purpose."

"Well, I just thought I haven't seen you since your heroics at the ambassador's ball. I wanted to do something nice for you. Let you know there's a lot of people in the bureau who are very grateful to you. We need all the good publicity we can get."

"We? You're talking like you didn't retire."

"Believe me, this job never leaves you."

Sol Franklin had been Ingrid's Supervising Special Agent when she started work in London. He was part of the reason she took the job. He was friendly, and wise, encouraging and easy going and one of the few agents she had worked with who didn't want to be higher up the ladder, or back working as a case agent. Sol had been a steady, nurturing presence in her career when that was exactly what she needed. Although the bearded, Jewish mensch looked nothing like the blond, Scandinavian father she remembered from her childhood, it didn't take a psychotherapist to tell Ingrid that Sol was one of the many replacement father figures she had sought out in her life.

The maître d' showed them into a courtyard at the rear of the restaurant. Circular tables under calico parasols were dressed with stiff white tablecloths and polished glassware. The white painted walls of the terrace were clad in a trellis burgeoning with sweet-scented jasmine. In the heat, it could almost be Rome. Ingrid was glad to be wearing sandals.

Ingrid recognized one of the diners at a table in the corner. He was an obese, heavily tanned man in his sixties who combed his thinning hair over his greasy head. He wore more jewelry than most women and his shirt was open at the neck to reveal a tangle of chest hair. His name would come back to her, but he had been in the headlines recently. A fraud trial. Some kind of retail magnate. He was talking intently to a younger man in an expensive shirt and aviator shades.

"Anything to drink?" the waiter asked.

"*Acqua frizzante*," Ingrid said. "*Al limone, per favore*."

"I forgot Italian was one of your languages," Sol said. "I hope you just ordered a bottle of Gavi."

Ingrid gave him a half smile. "Some of us aren't on vacation. Sparkling water, but you should definitely have a drink drink."

"In that case, I'll just have a glass of Gavi. A large one," he added before the waiter could ask. "Hopefully you can translate the menu too."

Their conversation meandered easily through DeWalt's promotion and her time as acting SSA, Madeleine's conference and the events of the ambassador's ball, though they stumbled when Sol awkwardly consoled her over Marshall's death. There was only really one topic Ingrid wanted to talk to Sol about, but she was unsure how wise it was to bring up: Mulroony. She hadn't yet mentioned the photos to DeWalt, but if there was a chance they related to an active plot, then she needed to know how to get him to take a discarded disposable camera of dubious prominence seriously.

Behind Sol, a table of four noisy coworkers ordered their third bottle of wine. With each top-up they got a little rowdier. They occasionally pointed at the sweaty retail billionaire in the corner, and then dropped their voices to whispers. If an actual celebrity was in the restaurant, they would probably ask for a selfie.

"Sol?" Ingrid put her fork down, a stuffed sardine fillet on the end of it. "Can I ask you something?"

"Sure." He dabbed some puttanesca sauce from his beard.

"It's kind of weird that you'd show up, because I can't actually think who else I could ask about this."

The lines on his forehead bunched between his eyebrows. "I'm intrigued."

Ingrid took a slow sip of water, taking a last opportunity to weigh up the wisdom of saying anything. "Remember Mulroony?" A tremble rippled over her skin as she crossed the Rubicon.

His eyes narrowed. "I do." He spoke slowly, quietly.

"Do you know what happened to him?"

He looked down at his plate before replying. "Why are you asking, agent?"

Ingrid's pulse pounded under her shirt. "Something came up."

"Something?"

"Are you not answering my question because you don't know?"

"I may have retired," he dropped his voice to whisper, "but I'm still bound by my signature on State Secrets Act."

"So, you do know what happened to Mulroony?"

Sol leaned back in his seat. He glanced at the noisy table before returning his attention to Ingrid. "Why now, Ingrid?"

"I inherited his caseload, didn't I? I think I've stumbled across something that feels significant."

"Significant how?"

They were both willing to call and raise, but neither of them wanted to show their cards.

"Well, see, I don't really know because no one," she raised her eyebrows to emphasize her point, "told me what happened to him. And when I look for his records to find what did happen to him, it turns out there aren't any records." She picked up her fork. "You were his SSA at the time, Amy Louden was the Special Agent in Charge, and you've both left the bureau since then—for very different reasons, obviously—so I don't know if this information I have is significant, or who to pass it on to. Do I give it to DeWalt?" She popped the sardine in her mouth.

Sol's pupils dilated behind his glasses. "No," he said carefully. "No, that would not be a good idea."

Okay, that was at least a straight answer. "Do I get to know why not?"

Sol took a sip of wine. "Because he doesn't know why Mulroony disappeared. This information you have. Does it relate to national security?"

Ingrid shrugged. "I honestly can't make that judgement because," she leaned in, "I don't know what Mulroony did or where he is. But let's just say that what I found out does impact national security, how do I escalate this if I can't share it with DeWalt? Do I tell you?"

"No," he said deliberately. "I am no longer authorized. If you think this is serious, you absolutely cannot tell me."

"Do I take it to the Legat?"

Sol chewed the inside of his lip. "It would really help if you told me what it is you've found."

Ingrid looked down at her plate. She tried to work out how she could talk about the photos without sounding like a crazy person. "I found some notes," she said. "Handwritten notes." It felt like a good lie. "The light was flickering and so I tried to fix it. I found them hidden behind a ceiling tile."

Sol scratched his beard, trying to cover the surprise with his hand. "And what do the notes say?"

Again, she didn't want to sound like someone in need of a psych referral. "They appear to be in some sort of code."

"Hmm." Sol raised an eyebrow. "And you're sure Mulroony wrote them?"

"Not entirely, but he's the most likely candidate."

"And where are these notes now?"

"Locked away."

Sol rapped his fingers lightly on the table. "Okay, I'm going to tell you something, but—"

Behind Sol, a drunken coworker pushed his chair back. Its legs caught in the paving stones and clattered onto the ground. He swayed slightly, grabbed the table to steady himself and pulled on the tablecloth sending two glasses of wine spiraling to the floor. The splintered pieces scattered across the stone slabs. Silence descended like a heavy mist. The entire courtyard froze. Then the drunk man's friends started clapping and the waiters scurried toward them.

Ingrid put down her knife and fork.

The drunk man turned on his heels, shoved a waiter out of his way and staggered toward Ingrid and Sol. Ingrid pushed her chair back, readying herself. Chatter returned, rising slowly from the tables like coils of steam. The man stumbled past them. Ingrid feared he wouldn't make it to the bathroom before he threw up. Then she realized what he was really doing.

"Excuse me," she said to Sol and stood up, just as the drunk man swiped a glass of red wine off a table and lurched toward the retail magnate. He threw the wine at him, catching the side of his face, spraying his open-neck shirt.

"You fucking thief…"

The magnate was too fat to get up, so he shifted his body weight away from his attacker and fell sideways off his chair into the raised flower bed. His dining companion erupted out of his seat and aimed an uppercut to the drunk man's jaw. The drunk arched his back to avoid the blow, then swung an arm at his assailant. Ingrid grabbed his arm, turned him round, and yanked his wrist up behind his back.

"What the fuck?" He sprayed spittle as he spoke.

Ingrid pressed her knee onto his right calf, forcing him down into a kneeling position. She instinctively reached to her waistband for handcuffs—muscle memory—but only found the phone in her back pants pocket.

The entire courtyard was silent apart from the obese man's whimpering. His dining companion stood motionless, fist still raised, jaw hanging loose. Diners poised with forks mid-air, waiters like statues with bulging eyes.

"Give me a hand here, will you?" Ingrid said.

The tension dissolved. Diners took out their phones and started filming. Sol got to his feet and together they lifted the fat man back onto his chair. Waiters dashed toward them. More appeared from inside the restaurant. The table of drunks mumbled half-hearted apologies.

"You okay, sir?" Ingrid asked the fat man. His shirt was stained from collar to elbow. "I think you may be bleeding."

He was too shocked to speak.

"No, signorina, it is you who is bleeding," a waiter said.

Ingrid looked down. Her ankle was covered in blood. A piece of the shattered wine glass was still protruding from her skin. She hadn't felt a thing.

Back at the table, she grabbed a napkin and wiped away the blood as a uniformed police officer barreled into the courtyard, followed by the maître d'. Within five minutes, the drunk had been arrested, his friends had made an embarrassed exit, the glass splinters had been swept up and retail entrepreneur had offered to pay for

Ingrid's lunch. Complimentary limoncello was distributed to every table.

Sol raised a small glass of yellow liqueur. "To our heroine." He took a sip and immediately screwed up his face. "Wowser, this stuff is lethal."

Ingrid figured she could allow herself a small shot of alcohol. To steady her nerves. Besides, limoncello made her so nostalgic for the semester she had spent in Florence as a student. *"Cin cin."*

"Cin cin."

One tiny sip and she was back on an endless evening on Piazza della Signoria talking to Paulo, or was it Mauricio, in the warm night air about nothing and everything.

"How's your ankle?"

"Seems fine," she said. "You had been about to tell me something."

"Had I?"

"You know you had."

"Hmmm."

"Look, it would help a lot if I at least knew what happened to Mulroony. I checked the trial records. There has never been one. I checked the prisoner records. He doesn't exist there either." She leaned in and lowered her voice. "Mulroony's like a goddamn ghost. How does someone disappear like that? Why?"

Sol cradled his chin. "Okay," he said, "but not here. You don't know who's listening. You okay to walk?" He pointed to her ankle.

"Of course."

"Come on then."

They finished their limoncello and stood to leave. As they walked between the tables, a woman grabbed Ingrid's wrist. She turned sharply.

"You shouldn't have done it, you know that?" The woman's hand was trembling. "That bastard," she nodded at the fat man, "deserves whatever is coming to him."

Ingrid shook off her grasp. "I don't know who he is, but he has as much right to eat his lunch in peace as you do."

Shock widened the woman's mouth.

"Have a nice day," Ingrid said, then followed Sol into the restaurant. "Do you know who that guy is?"

"Can't say I do." He opened the door for Ingrid. "But I'm damn sure he didn't buy his Rolex on Canal Street."

There were even more photographers outside Sabrina's than when they had entered, drawn by the police cars and unnecessary ambulance. A few took images of Sol and Ingrid as they hurried away.

"Where are we headed?" Ingrid said.

"Doesn't matter," Sol replied, popping a tab of nicotine gum in his mouth. They wended their way through the streets, heading vaguely east, away from the embassy to reduce the risk of bumping into anyone they knew. "I'm only telling you this because I care about you, you understand that?"

Ingrid glanced over at him. "Sure. Understood."

"My aim is to keep you from doing something stupid, you hear? Mulroony was a traitor, a stain on the bureau and one of the biggest screw-ups in our history." Sol spoke quickly but quietly. "Here, let's go down here." They turned into a narrow alleyway that spilled them into a small cobbled square. "First off, I only know about ten percent of what happened. My clearance only allowed me to know the basics. But I know who leaned on me, and I don't want them leaning on you. Okay?"

He steered her at a pace through a maze of streets too narrow for cars.

"The reason Mulroony wasn't tried, the reason why you can't find a record for him, is we never got a chance to arrest him."

That was not what Ingrid was expecting. She'd been picturing Guantanamo and orange jumpsuits. "Why not?"

"Someone beat us to it."

Ingrid slowed as she absorbed the revelation. "Explain."

They emerged from the warren of streets onto Berkeley Square. Sol hurried across the road and opened the gate for her. Then changed his mind. Too many picnics, too many people. He piloted them south toward Piccadilly, then abruptly pulled up.

"What is it?" Ingrid asked.

"I need to look you in the eye."

"Are you trying to scare me?"

He leaned closer. "Yes. Most definitely. The people who made him disappear could make it happen again. You weren't there, so you don't know what it was like. One day he didn't come into the office. At first, we thought he was ill. Then we thought he might have choked on a pretzel in his man cave. But he had vanished. We reported him as a missing person, we *investigated* him as a missing person, and it was about three weeks later when an asset in the field told us what had happened to him." He started walking.

Ingrid resisted the urge to interrupt as they strode past the galleries of Cork Street.

"He was about to be exposed as a double agent. The Russians yanked him before we could arrest him. I say 'we' loosely, I mean the Agency." Sol pulled a handkerchief out of a pocket and mopped the sweat from his brow. "We'd had intel for a while there was a Russian asset inside the Met. It kind of made sense when we found out. Mulroony worked closely with the Met, just as you do now, and he'd been covering his tracks that way for years."

They crossed over Piccadilly and headed into St. James's. "So, you're saying Mulroony's in Russia?"

"Probably got a nice pension and a balcony overlooking the Black Sea."

Ingrid's attention was drawn to a poster outside a bookstore. A face on it was familiar. She slowed down as Sol marched ahead. It took a couple of beats for her to work out the face belonged to Daisy Steiner. Younger, more serious looking. 'Book signing, Monday, 7pm.' Ingrid skipped a few steps to catch Sol up. "Still doesn't explain why there are no records of his service."

Sol sighed. "We had to scrub him from the record. It's one way of monitoring who knows about him. The moment someone mentions him, a flag is going to be raised."

She remembered the cold shoulders she got when she first arrived in London and asked questions about him. They entered St. James's Square where the tall trees sweetened the city air. "Thank you for telling me this, but I am still unclear what I should do with what I have."

Sol stopped walking. He checked behind him and looked over Ingrid's shoulder. He took a half step toward her. "Nothing. Nothing is what you should do." He was close enough for Ingrid to smell the nicotine gum on his breath. "I will find someone for you to talk to. But we still don't know who his Russian handler was, and we still don't know why he was pulled." He rolled his lips over his teeth. "Honestly, Ingrid, without those two pieces of information you gotta sit tight." He placed a warm hand on her shoulder. "Look, you're going to get your medal from the president for what you did at Christmas. You're going to get a commendation from the Director. Right now, whatever you've got on Mulroony is a grenade, and the more you poke it, the more likely it is it's going to blow your career apart. Unless and until you know why Mulroony was vaporized from the record, you risk the same thing happening to you."

12

INGRID ARRIVED BACK at the embassy with a new appreciation for the air conditioning. A brief fantasy about a swim in the Hilton pool further lowered her temperature.

"Hi."

"Hey, Zeke. How are you settling in?"

"Good, thanks. Something came for you." He signaled to a package on Ingrid's desk. It was heavy and rectangular and wrapped up like a cartoon mummy. Zeke crossed the floor and offered Ingrid a pair of scissors.

"Thanks." Zeke's nostrils twitched ever so slightly. Ingrid feared he had smelled the limoncello on her breath. Ingrid slid the scissors under several layers of sticky tape.

"So," Zeke said, excitement inflecting his voice. "You want to know what I found out?"

Ingrid looked up from her task and couldn't help but smile at Zeke's enthusiasm. "Shoot."

"I spoke to HR. They were mighty pleased I wasn't getting in touch with a request transfer, by the way, and asked them for the names of the people who have worked in this office for the past decade."

She cut through another tangle of tape as he placed a list of names in front of her. "I figured one of them must have taken the photographs."

"I like the way you think." Ingrid scanned the list. Mulroony's name wasn't there, just as it wasn't on any other list in the history of Christendom. Ingrid snipped through the last of the tape and a thick hardback book thudded onto her desk.

National Affront by David Steiner. "You found a copy?"

"I thought that might have been what it was. Definitely not a light read, is it?"

"Good work, Zeke. Really good work." Ingrid flicked through the densely typeset pages and sighed: it would take a week to plow through it.

It didn't matter how dry or how dense it was. There was nothing Ingrid wanted to do more than read it now Sol had told her to leave the Mulroony thing alone. Although she respected Sol, she had taken an oath to serve and protect. If it turned out something in the photos could prevent a plot against the US, Ingrid was very clear her duty was to pursue her investigation.

"Zeke?"

"Yep." His tail was bushy and his eyes were bright.

"Can you see if you can get me five minutes with the Legat?"

"Agent Munsden?"

Ingrid nodded.

"Um, sure. Today?"

"No, I'm out all afternoon. Tomorrow would be great, though."

"Leave it with me."

She was hoping that by the time she got in the room with Peter Munsden, she'd be able to talk about the photos without sounding like a basket case. Ingrid checked the clock on the wall. 14:55. She had ten minutes before she had to leave for her meeting with the Met. She logged into Court TV where a caption stripped across the bottom of the screen told her the judge was meeting in chambers. There was no way of knowing how significant that was, but Svetlana would definitely ask for her take on the significance when they spoke later on. She listened to her messages, replied to the urgent emails, but her concentration never totally left David Steiner's book. She pulled it closer and read the back cover. 'A comprehensive analysis of the past, present and future of the far right in Britain.' It was published by a university press and looked as dry as a cracker without the cheese. She flipped it open and scanned the chapter headings.

Mosley and the Cable Street Riots. Powell and his Rivers of Blood. Punk vs Mods. Moscow on Thames.

Ingrid stopped flipping at the mention of Russia. Daisy had said her father had been pilloried for claiming Russian rubles funded a group called England for the English. She turned to the index. Mulroony wasn't in it, but EFE had seventeen references. She suddenly had an idea.

"Zeke?"

"Hi." Her eager new assistant beamed at her across the office.

"Can you find something else for me?"

"Shoot."

Ingrid picked up the book. "Can you get me the author's death certificate? David Steiner. Maybe also the coroner's report?"

"Sure thing."

Ingrid skimmed the rest of the index, flipping through from the back, looking for anything that suggested why a

Russian double agent had deliberately taken a photograph of the book's Amazon listing.

She stopped at a name she recognized. More than that, it was someone she *knew*. Angela Tate, former chief reporter of the *Evening News,* was someone Ingrid had crossed paths with a few times. Tate got three mentions, so Ingrid thumbed through to the relevant chapter. It was about a former Prime Minister's ties to EFE that Tate had reported on. Angela had always told her she'd brought down the government: seems she hadn't been lying.

Ingrid never relished the prospect of dealing with Angela Tate—the journalist was brash, opinionated and slightly out of control—but there wasn't much she wouldn't do in exchange for a story. Ingrid made a mental note to call her.

Ingrid found the key to her drawer and took out the packet of photos. She flicked through them without removing them from the wallet. Now that Sol had confirmed Mulroony was a Russian asset, she looked for a Kremlin connection to each of the images.

She came to the photo of Jen and the other women holding a birthday cake. She was about to photograph it on her phone and send it to Jen, but then remembered the lengths Mulroony had gone to so as to not leave any digital breadcrumbs. Sol had made her paranoid, and the air conditioning suddenly felt very fierce. The hairs on her forearms perked up. A twitch troubled her jaw. She pulled out the photo with the case file number on it: she had already left a digital trace, hadn't she? Sol's warnings swirled through Ingrid's thoughts. There was one way to find out if he was right. She logged into the system and called up the file.

Ingrid blinked at her screen. E411 error code. No such file.

She checked the number against the photograph. She typed it in again. Same error code. Her jaw dropped. Her mouth dried. Two days ago, there had been a file on the system called the Threat Assessment of Far-Right Groups in the UK. Now it wasn't there. Erased like every other trace of Mulroony.

Ingrid swallowed hard. Fear trembled her top lip. This wasn't a coincidence. She had walked into someone's trap. She'd laid the same trap for others numerous times. You create a file, or a web page, that only people with specific knowledge would know to look for, and when they access the file, or visit the website, an alert is triggered. She was in no doubt. She was being watched.

13

INGRID CHECKED over her shoulder and kept running. The asphalt was sticky in the sun, but she drove her legs into the surface and accelerated. The fire escape was up ahead: if she was quick she'd be gone before Danszak made it to the roof. A loud clattering erupted behind her as the roof hatch opened. She twisted her neck: Danszak wasn't alone. Two men gave chase. The bulges on their thighs were Glock 17s.

This was kind of fun.

She vaulted over the ventilation ducts and access hatches that dotted the roof, noting that they were perfect foxholes to drop into if she wanted to take a shot at them. But she didn't. Her task was to evade capture.

Gunfire at street level. Shouting.

Change of plan: if she took the fire escape, she'd run into the crossfire. She turned sharply right and headed north toward the river. The two cops behind her shouted, but she couldn't make out any actual words. It's not like anything they said would stop her. She powered forward, and her vision lasered in on the edge of the building.

Seven strides, six, five… she filled her lungs, three, two… Ingrid pushed her right foot down and launched herself into the air.

The building opposite was further than she'd calculated. She wasn't going to make the roof. Her outstretched arms reached for the windowsill on the top story. She gripped it, tensing her body so her knees didn't slam into the wall. Her sneakers hit the brickwork a little more heavily than she'd have liked, but she quickly hauled herself up and scrambled through the open window.

It felt like cheating when there wasn't any glass. But, she reasoned, if they glazed every window in this place, they'd have to re-glaze them every damn week.

It was cooler inside. Darker too. Her eyes couldn't adjust quickly enough, but she figured it would be an empty shell, like all the other buildings on the Metropolitan Police's training center. Some of them were just flat fronts, like the ones she'd seen on the Universal Studios tour as a kid. Ingrid craned her neck and saw Danszak and his mate through the window. They stood on the roof of the building opposite, their bodies silhouetted against the bright sky as they looked for her at ground level. When they didn't see her, they turned back. Now she had a real advantage: no one knew where she was.

The fake building smelled of kerosene. In a previous exercise, it must have been the Molotov cocktail factory. Her vision adapted, and she saw the entire building was hollow: on the outside it looked like a row of houses, but the inside was barn-like with exposed struts and trusses. It wouldn't be long before Danszak would figure out where she was. Her footsteps on the bare boards would give her location away to anyone at ground level. She needed an escape.

Ingrid ran through the darkness until she heard voices enter below. She climbed out of the next window she came to and stood on the ledge. A lone officer walked down the fake street, moving his MK5 in an arc. Her chest bellowed as she pressed herself against the sun-warmed bricks. *Please don't look up.* At the far end of the street was a car repair shop and a convenience store, painted with generic signage. If she squinted, they looked real, but the lack of painted lines on the road gave the place a surreal quality, like a dream or a distant memory.

"Get back," he shouted.

Ingrid turned her head slowly and saw two participants playing the part of civilians had entered the street, pushing a buggy with a doll in it. Their arrival meant his job was now to protect them: he wasn't going to be looking two floors up and spot her. The ack-ack-ack of rapid gunfire from the next street split the air, followed by shouting from the other side of the block.

Behind her, through the window opening, someone clattered up a ladder.

"Where are you?" Danszak's voice. "Where the fuck did you go?"

"She's gotta be in there," his mate said.

Ingrid breathed hard. It was too far to jump to ground level, but she didn't want the exercise to end like this. Keeping her back against the wall, she slowly reached out for the drainpipe two feet to her right. She didn't know if it was fake, or if it could take her weight.

"Shit, we've lost her."

"There's nowhere else for her to be."

They would be humiliated at the debriefing if they'd let one of the officers posing as the drug smugglers get away. They'd never live it down. Ingrid heard their footsteps as they moved toward her. She pushed against the drainpipe. It seemed solid. She slid a foot sideways, off the window ledge and onto a metal bracket holding the pipe in place. Her body made an X against the wall.

Ingrid filled her lungs and spun around, clinging on with one arm until she could grab it with both hands.

"Ow." The black metal was baking hot to the touch.

"What was that?" Danszak said.

"Sounded like it came from outside."

Clenching the pipe between her knees, Ingrid shimmied upwards, reaching up for the guttering. She pulled herself onto the sloping roof tiles just as Danszak stuck his head through the opening.

"How the fuck?" He was open mouthed.

Ingrid beamed at him. "Gotta try harder, sucker."

She pushed herself upright and started to run. A tile slipped under her foot, and she stumbled, sliding downward and tumbling over the edge. She stretched for the guttering and held on with both hands.

"Look up there," the man with the buggy said.

Ingrid strained over her shoulder as she dangled from the gutter. The armed officer took up a position. The gutter dug into her hands. She was going to fall.

"Come on!"

Ingrid curled her body and hooked her right leg over the half pipe. She hauled herself back onto the roof just as a rubber bullet bounced off the tiles.

"You bastard," she shouted. This was an exercise. If he'd hit her, she could have fallen. She could have been seriously injured. There was no way they were going to catch her now. Ingrid scrambled up the roof as more rubber bullets flew at her. She reached the apex, then dropped down on the far side of the roof, out of sight from the officer in the road. She lay flat against the tiles, and her chest heaved as she replenished her oxygen.

She was right at the northern edge of the training center. Ahead of her was the center's perimeter fence topped with razor wire, guarded by a regiment of floodlights on thick metal poles. Beyond the fence were the grassy banks of the Thames, which curved its way slowly toward the sea. On the opposite bank of the river was the Napier Yards complex and Tilbury docks where cranes reached up out of the flat landscape. Colored shipping containers stacked like LEGO bricks glinted in the sun. She looked east where a huge cargo ship approached from the North Sea. Next week, one of Tilbury's arrivals would be the MSC *Laussat*.

The shouting from ground level told her the building was now surrounded. She checked the Glock 19 in her holster. New magazine. Seventeen shots. She had another mag in the leg pocket of her fatigues. Ingrid calculated the odds. She had the perfect vantage point. Unless they had ladders, or a helo, or an officer who also did parkour, they couldn't shoot at her. How many officers could come for her? Six? Eight. If she hit her targets, she had the ammo to shoot her way out of it. She rolled over onto her front and crawled up to the apex of the roof. And then she stopped. The moment she popped her head over the roofline, a marksman would take a shot. She had the wrong weapon. An AK would do it, but the Glock couldn't fire rapidly enough. Ingrid felt her heart thunder against her ribcage. She had forgotten how exhilarating these exercises could be.

She looked again at the perimeter fence and had an idea. She was not going to let them capture her, even if it did mean breaking the rules. Her pursuers would find their way to the back of the building soon enough, and that meant she didn't have a second to waste. Ingrid scrambled to her feet and ran. She needed to pick up speed if her plan was to work. Using the slope to her advantage, Ingrid ran toward the apex, then used gravity as she curved back down toward the guttering. As she neared the edge of the roof, she bent her knees and powered herself at the pole holding a floodlight. She used her momentum to swing round the pole and vault over the fence, dropping down onto the grass beyond.

The earth was still soft from the river water, and she rolled on impact. She came to a halt and lay prone in the grass, unseen by the black-clad officers who had finally made their way round the building. MK5s shouldered, they stalked the perimeter, calling to each other as they passed each hiding place.

Ingrid buried her face in the grass and smiled.

Ingrid helped herself to a Pepsi from the fridge and stood in front of the pedestal fan in the corner of the conference room. Her mobile phone vibrated on the table, jiggling until it bumped into the Glock.

"Hi."

"Where are you?" Ralph asked, breathless.

Ingrid smiled. "Where you should be."

Ralph held the phone away from his mouth. "She's okay," he said. "You can stop looking." There was a pause. "Yep. Yep, that means it's over."

Ingrid sat down at the head of the table, put her feet up, and waited for the door to open. Danszak was the first one through. Sweat dripped off his face. "What the fuck? How the fucking hell did you escape?"

One by one, as each officer tumbled into the room, their eyes widened, expletives dripped from their lips and half of them slammed a palm against the wall. The split between admiration and loathing was also fifty-fifty.

"How the hell did you do it?" Ralph asked when he stepped in, his cheeks red with heat and exertion. "Minty on the gate says you walked through half an hour ago. How the hell did you get over the bloody fence?"

Before Ingrid could answer, Deputy Director Tariq Aziz from the National Crime Agency walked in. He smiled at Ingrid. "Right, apart from the fact we need aerial support next week, double the amount of ammunition, and a fleet of ambulances on standby, what else did we learn from that clusterfuck?"

The debrief was lengthy and painful as unit after unit explained their decision-making. If that had been the actual raid, three smugglers and one bystander would be dead, one officer would have been shot in the chest and there would be a manhunt for the lone smuggler at large.

"The *Laussat* docks in six days," Aziz said as he summed up. "We have our work cut out for us, don't we?"

The sun was low in the sky by the time Ingrid sat astride her Ducati in the parking lot. She didn't much feel like putting her head inside an insulated brain bucket, but she pulled the helmet over her ears anyway. If ever there was a day when she wished for a law that made wearing a motorcycle helmet optional, this was it.

"Ingrid!" It was Ralph. He waved at her, then cantered across the parking lot, his long, spindly legs more awkward than Bambi's "Sorry. Don't want to hold you up.

Just, well, you know that thing you were asking about?" He stood beside her. "New bike?"

"Yes, it is. What do you think?"

"It's very… red."

"Well spotted."

"What happened to the curvy one? The blue one?"

"It was in an accident."

His eyebrows raised. "You never said."

"I wasn't riding."

"Oh." He looked confused. "So. You know that thing you asked me about? About your predecessor and his handler?"

Ingrid flipped up the visor so Ralph could see her eyes. "You found something out?" Her voice pitched up with intrigue.

"More a case of remembering, cos I saw him on the news yesterday."

Now Ingrid was confused.

"So," Ralph said, sinking a hand into his jeans back pocket. "His handler was SO15, that much came back to me pretty quickly."

"Counter-terrorism?" She kept her voice low, unsure who was in earshot.

"Yep. Well, the reason I was so cloak and dagger when you asked me all those years ago was because of who his handler was." Ralph looked pretty pleased with himself. "I mean, no one actually told me this, but I'm almost certain I've worked out why they couldn't say his name back then."

Ingrid had forgotten just how much Ralph liked to string out his stories. "Which was?"

"Well, because it was Andy Scott." He was beaming.

"Should that name mean something to me?"

Ralph looked disappointed. "Action Man? The Secretary of State for Justice?"

It was too hot to be having a conversation in an insulated helmet. "Help me out here."

"He left the force in 2012 and won a by-election. He's now a Tory MP. Ran on the 'strong on law and order' bollocks. Famously had an election leaflet with him in a boxing ring with his chest on display. Since then he's had a meteoric rise and now he's got a seat in the cabinet? Ringing any bells? Tipped to be a future Prime Minister."

"Ah." The man on the BBC breakfast sofa. "*He* was Mulroony's handler?"

Ralph stood a little straighter, like a kindergarten kid about to receive a teacher's gold star.

"You sure?"

"Ninety-nine percent."

If she hadn't been wearing a helmet, she could have kissed him.

14

THE MAN UP ahead had to be a copper. Short-sleeved shirt, a belly that had consumed a few too many after-work beers, wide-legged stance. He surveyed the horizon like he was scanning a crowd for trouble.

"DS Fitzpatrick?" Ingrid asked.

He turned, and a smile stretched over his meaty face. "Agent Skyberg, I presume."

"I see why you suggested meeting here." Ingrid gestured to the view.

"As soon as you mentioned David Steiner, I thought it made sense to meet at the scene of the crime, just in case it was pertinent to your inquiries." His smile contracted. "Not that there was a crime of, course." He produced a handkerchief and dabbed the sweat off his forehead.

"On a day like today, I'll take any excuse to get outside." Ingrid breathed in the sweet-smelling air and took in the view. The sun-bleached grass of Richmond Park stretched over the slope before them, bounded by a rim of broad-leafed trees punctuated at regular intervals by the triangular red roofs of the surrounding houses.

Ingrid could just make out the dome of St. Paul's Cathedral, ten miles away in the center of London, through the milky haze. *Maybe I could live out here?*

"Is this where you found him?" Ingrid sniffed. She didn't suffer from hay fever, but the high pollen count was aggravating her eyes.

"No, but it was easier to give you directions to the summit." He nodded toward a wooded area. "He killed himself in there. Shall we?"

The coroner's report into David Steiner's death had concluded he died by suicide. A single gunshot to the head. As Ingrid now knew that one of the last people to have spoken to Steiner was a Russian double agent, she had been through the report with a critical eye. She'd noted some inconsistencies, so had asked to meet an officer who had conducted the initial inquiry. DS Fitzpatrick had been a constable back in 2012 and had responded to the 999 call from a jogger who had discovered Steiner's body.

They entered the patch of woodland, and the temperature dropped from scorching to just about bearable. The wind ruffled the dense canopy of leaves, and the air smelled fresh. Ingrid inhaled deeply and sneezed.

"Bless you. Everyone's sneezing today. Not a day for a stakeout."

Ingrid gave him a smile.

"Can you imagine?" he said, his eyes crinkling at the corners. "Months of careful planning ruined because a copper didn't take their hay fever pills."

"I'd never thought of that. I'll keep it in mind the next time I plan a sting operation." Her thoughts honed in on the error-strewn training session the day before. What else hadn't Operation Pinball anticipated?

A path of dry, compacted mud curved between a carpet of crisp brown leaves and ground ivy on either side. The exuberant sounds of children climbing over fallen tree trunks, and the exasperation of their mother, rolled through the air. Fitzpatrick's breathing was heavy: his days of running after perps were definitely behind him. Maybe he was older than he looked, the extra pounds filling out lines that would otherwise be present. He stepped off the track.

"He was found just back here."

Fitzpatrick led Ingrid thirty or so yards from the path to a crater lined with a soft covering of rotting leaves. A massive tree must have fallen over in a storm, taking its entire root ball with it, to create a large, curved hollow.

"He was there." Fitzpatrick pointed to a fallen tree trunk wrapped in several years' growth of moss. "Looked like he'd sat down for a kip. Apart from the fact half his head was missing."

Ingrid took in the scene. "And it was a jogger who found him? This far off the path?"

"She was looking for somewhere to pee. That's what she said."

Ingrid pressed her lips together as she mentally transferred what she'd read in the report to the space in front of her.

"It's always joggers, isn't it," Fitzpatrick said, filling the silence. "Or dog walkers. Though mostly it's joggers that get killed and dog walkers that find the body." He waited for her to say something. "Well, obviously, it's the dogs that do the finding. Did you know their sense of smell is a hundred times more sensitive than a human's?"

Ingrid gave him a smile. "What time of day was he found?"

"A little after five, I think. In the evening."

"Would it be light at five in March?"

"Hmm." He put both hands in his pockets and arched his back. "Depends if the clocks have gone forward or not. Though it'd be a bit gloomy in the woods by then."

Ingrid positioned herself in the spot where Steiner's body was found. "And he hadn't been dead long, had he?"

"Pathologist said two to three hours."

Ingrid scrunched up her face as she thought. "You've worked out of Richmond for at least five years, I'm guessing."

"Fifteen."

"And in your experience, how busy would this place be in the middle of the afternoon in early March?"

Fitzpatrick scratched his chin. "Half decent weather? I'd say you'd have someone walking down that path a few times an hour. How many of them would venture this far from the path? Dunno. A few a day." He paused. "Has this got something to do with Mulroony, then?"

Ingrid had wondered how long it would take him to ask. She smiled at him. "What do you know about Mulroony?"

He shrugged. "Not a lot. His business card was in Steiner's pocket. It was the only card, by the way, it's not like he had a pocket full of them." His eyes narrowed. "Is it related?"

Ingrid rubbed her nose. She wished she'd brought a Kleenex.

"Did you speak to Mulroony?"

He sucked his teeth. "Eventually, yeah. Seem to remember it was a right palaver to even get him on the phone. No chance of a face-to-face." He paused. "He'd gone home to America. Redeployed. Steiner must have been one of his last meetings before getting on a plane."

Ingrid tilted her head. The FBI had obviously had an impostor take the call. "Did he say why they had a meeting?"

Fitzpatrick shrugged. "Something bland about helping him with his inquiries. In the end it didn't really matter because the coroner ruled Steiner had killed himself. Not that the verdict stopped the rumors."

"Rumors?"

He studied her face. "Come on, you must have heard them?"

"I didn't move to London till later in the year, so I didn't hear a thing."

A look of suspicion veiled his features. "Well, there was speculation, wasn't there, that he'd been killed—"

"Steiner or Mulroony?"

Fitzpatrick looked surprised. "Steiner of course, on account of he had been about to give evidence to that inquiry."

Ingrid stood very still. "What inquiry?"

"You really don't know?"

"No, but I'm getting the feeling I should." Ingrid looked at him. "You found Steiner facing this way?"

"Yes."

"Legs outstretched, torso leaning against the fallen tree?"

"Correct."

"And you never found the bullet?"

"Not for want of trying."

"Cartridge casing?"

"No, not that either." He moved toward her. "Which is probably why the conspiracy theorists moved in with their metal detectors after the SOCOs had finished up. Of course, if they had found anything they wouldn't have told us. That would have proved he died here, rather than transporting the body here from somewhere else."

Ingrid inhaled sharply. "Who do they think killed him?"

Fitzpatrick made air quotes. "The establishment."

"Ah. Well. Open and shut case." Ingrid looked in the direction Steiner must have looked before he pulled the trigger. It wasn't a bad final view. "Why would anyone want to silence a middle-ranking academic?"

He dabbed the sweat from his forehead again. "I feel like a bloody canary."

"Pardon?"

"Americans don't use that phrase? 'Singing like a canary?'"

She smiled at him. "Not since the 1950s!"

"Well, anyways, I feel like I'm doing a lot of talking."

"If it helps, you're being really helpful. You mentioned an inquiry?"

"The Hawking Inquiry." His forehead furrowed. "No, the Hawking Review. One step down from an official inquiry."

Ingrid remembered the photo of Stephen Hawking in the Snappy Snaps wallet. "Stephen Hawking?"

"Yep, the guy in the wheelchair."

Wow. Did he really just call one of the world's greatest scientists 'the guy in the wheelchair'? Her estimation of Fitzpatrick started to wobble on its axis. She didn't know what to say. Yet again, Fitzpatrick chucked words into the conversational vacuum. "Judge Hawking," he said. "A review of the Andropov case."

"Ah. Now that's something I do know about."

"You do?"

Dmitri Andropov was a former KGB spy who had been poisoned—almost certainly at the behest of the Kremlin—in a sauna at his local club. Someone had thrown something other than water on the coals.

"Why would David Steiner be giving evidence to the Hawking Inquiry, sorry, Review? He was a far-right expert, wasn't he?"

"Yep." Fitzpatrick looked at his shoes. "I'm not sure I have the answer to that. Are you going to tell me why we're here?"

Ingrid couldn't keep stringing him along. "Sorry. I thought I'd said. One of Steiner's books was found at a crime scene." It was an approximation of the truth. "Looked like it had been deliberately planted. I'm just digging around, seeing if it's significant."

Fitzpatrick looked confused. "What's the crime?"

Ingrid hadn't anticipated that question. "Corruption," she bluffed. "In Pittsburgh. Following up on behalf of the field office there."

He jutted out his jaw but said nothing.

"You were saying something earlier," Ingrid said, keen to change the subject, "about a conspiracy theory. That Steiner was murdered. Was that one of your lines of inquiry?"

He sucked on his teeth and rocked back on his heels. "Obviously we had to rule it out, especially as he used a gun. And because it was tied to Hawking, we had a lot of… how shall I put this… *oversight*."

"Ah, yes. Makes sense." He had made her remember that the Hawking Review wasn't a review of Andropov's activities in the UK, it had been a review into the Met's handling of the murder inquiry and how his killers had been able to leave the country undetected. "I imagine you would have had to dot every i."

"You're not wrong. Plus, we don't get many people shooting themselves in the leafy suburbs. Rest assured, we turned over every pebble, not just the stones."

"Was the gun his?" Ingrid asked. The coroner's report said the weapon had been made by Nagant, a manufacturer she had never heard of.

He linked his hands behind his back and stretched. "It could have been. Old guns aren't that uncommon, surprisingly enough. Lots left over from the war. Polish, mostly. Though I think this particular one was Belgian. Grandad comes home from the front with a souvenir and nobody knows about it till they clear the attic, that sort of thing." He looked at her. "It wasn't illegal then, so there was no register. With Steiner being a historian, it seemed entirely plausible he would have interviewed veterans from World War II. If it wasn't his dad's, it could easily have been a gift. Either way, untraceable. It had never been used in another crime."

"What about the ammunition?"

He smiled broadly. "Yeah, that one foxed us right enough. No other bullets left in the chamber, and as we didn't find the one that killed him, we never found out."

"Chamber?"

"The bit that spins round. Like in the cowboy movies."

Ingrid wrinkled her brow. "It was a revolver?"

"I guess."

"The report said it was a pistol."

Fitzpatrick was confused. "I realize you Yanks know more about guns than we do, but isn't a revolver a type of pistol?"

Ingrid nodded. "Yep, technically it is, but it's quite a

specific sort of pistol. Most people wouldn't confuse the two."

"Most Americans," he corrected.

One of the children fell over and started screaming. Its sibling joined in. Ingrid glanced in the direction of their mother, wanting her to do or say something to make her kids shut up. Ingrid liked the idea of having children, she just wasn't so keen on the parenthood that went with it.

"And no reports of gunshots?" Ingrid asked.

"Nope. Or gas explosions," he said. "You hear a loud bang round here, you assume it's a car backfiring."

"Any CCTV show him on his way into the park?"

"No. He only lived a few streets away. These days you might get lucky with dashcams and doorbells, but there was none of that in 2012." He stared at his shoes. "Is this something to do with Mulroony, then?"

Ingrid folded her arms. "Why are you asking?"

Fitzpatrick kicked a stone with his shoe. "Copper's hunch. Just thought it was weird that one day he's interviewing Steiner and the next day he's on a plane."

Her features softened. "Well, that's the nature of this job. Liaison agents like me, like Mulroony, make inquiries on behalf of colleagues back home. So today I'm here with you. Tomorrow a Silicon Valley founder goes missing at St. Andrews and I'm shadowing the investigation in Scotland. The day after that I'm trawling through library archives in Portsmouth." Ingrid needed to steer the conversation in a different direction. "Did Steiner leave a note?"

"Not that we found. But according to his daughter he was worried he had… what's it called? The shaking disease?"

"Parkinson's?"

"That's it. Apparently, he'd developed a tremor."

"Did he have a history of suicide attempts? Or mental illness?"

Fitzpatrick pursed his lips. "Mental illness I'm not so sure about. Maybe not diagnosed, and definitely not treated, but a few of his colleagues thought he was depressed. His last book got slated."

"Colleagues?"

"From the university. Birkbeck. In Bloomsbury." He gave her a half smile. "I suppose you'd like me to give you their names?"

She returned his half smile with one of her own. "You read my mind." Her phone rang. A London number. "Do you mind?"

"Be my guest."

Ingrid answered the call and stepped away from Fitzpatrick. "Special Agent Skyberg."

"Hold the line, please," a woman's voice said. "I have the minister for you." There was a click on the line.

"This is Andy Scott." His voice was unusually gravelly. "From the Department of Justice."

"Thank you so much for returning my call, Sir. Much appreciated. I was hoping I could come and see you." She ran a hand through her hair.

"What's it about?"

"I'd like to talk to you about your work as the FBI liaison officer, when you worked for the Met."

Scott didn't reply. Between the static on the line and the wind through the trees, Ingrid wasn't entirely sure they hadn't been cut off.

"You know that I'm now in government?"

"Yes, I do. I'd be very grateful if you could spare me ten minutes. At your convenience, of course."

Fitzpatrick paced around her, crunching the dry leaves as she waited for Scott to answer.

"I've got the Commonwealth conference next week. This isn't a good time."

Ingrid turned away from Fitzpatrick. "I only need ten minutes." She took a deep breath. "It's about Dennis Mulroony."

After another lengthy silence, Scott spoke. "Yes, I thought it might be." He sighed. "My office, Wednesday, two p.m. I have ten minutes." Before Ingrid could say thank you, he added: "Don't be late."

15

Ingrid waited patiently and let everyone else go before her. She held a slim mint green book in her hand.

"Who would you like it dedicated to?" Daisy Steiner looked up from the desk and her face instantly broadened with a huge smile. "Oh, it's you. I didn't know you were here." She looked around the bookstore, as if expecting someone else. "Have you been here the whole time?"

"I was hoping I could buy you dinner," Ingrid said.

"A date?" Daisy asked.

"Sadly not. Strictly business." Ingrid nodded at the book. "To Kathleen, please. With a K. Do you have plans?"

"Only to make sure I don't miss the last train back to Suffolk."

"What time is that?"

"Stupidly early. Ten to eleven. Can you hang around? There's a café on the top floor."

Ingrid took her signed copy and headed for the elevator. A few of Steiner's diehard fans clustered around her, suddenly able to ask questions they had been too embarrassed to put to her during the Q&A session. A young woman from her publisher also needed her attention, as did the store's events manager. Ingrid didn't expect Daisy to get away any time soon.

Ingrid flipped idly through the pages as she rode the elevator. She wasn't sure if sending Kathleen a crime novel to distract her from the trial was a good idea. There had been no point in asking Daisy to write a dedication to Svetlana. Her mother didn't even read the health warnings on cigarette packs. Ingrid couldn't remember Svetlana consulting so much as a recipe book. Perhaps it was because Ingrid had grown up in a house without books, that libraries and bookstores intimidated her. An anxiety that everyone else in the building was smarter than she was would always squat defiantly in a dimly lit corner of her psyche.

The elevator doors dinged open and the smell of coffee filled her nostrils. Bookstores had changed a hell of a lot since she was a kid. For starters they were open until nine at night, and this one was more like a department store, or even an entire mall. Floor after floor of books, brightly colored stationery supplies and gifts, sections on everything from atheism to Zionism, topped by the obligatory café. Along one wall of the café were six cubicles with computers. She presumed they were prevented from accessing Amazon.

Ingrid bought a bottle of an overpriced elderflower concoction and took it to one of the computer desks. There was something she'd wanted to look up online, and after the disappearance of the file from the bureau's database, she wasn't going to pass up the opportunity to do so with a little anonymity.

First, she checked her phone. Still nothing from Sol. If he didn't find her the name of someone to confide in soon, then she was just going to ignore his warning and involve DeWalt, or even go straight to Munsden, the Legat and chief of the FBI's London operation. She still wasn't quite sure what she should say to Munsden about the photos, but she'd uncovered enough for them to take the possibility of an active plot seriously.

The system required her to open an account, which she did using a Gmail address she had for just such tasks. Then she went into the settings and changed the keyboard preferences to Cyrillic, and finally she launched Yandex, the Russian search engine. Now she knew from Fitzpatrick that Mulroony had left London within days of Steiner's suicide, she had a timeline to narrow down, and zero in, on his new life in Russia.

"Hi."

Ingrid turned to see a twenty-something woman nervously clutching several copies of Daisy Steiner's books.

"I, um, I er, I saw you talking to Daisy. Daisy Steiner, that is," she held one of the books up to illustrate while simultaneously curtseying. "Is she, like, a friend of yours?" The woman wore a nose ring and shapeless tee shirt bearing the logo of the Harrogate Crime Writing Festival. Her long dark hair was scraped back into a ponytail. White scars crisscrossed the soft flesh of her lower arms.

Ingrid almost answered in the affirmative. It was a bit of a surprise to realize that Daisy felt like a friend. If they had met in different circumstances, perhaps they would have been friends. "No, no I'm not."

The woman's hip jutted out. Her head tipped to one side. "Oh." She couldn't hide her disappointment. She started edging away. "I thought I heard you making dinner arrangements. My mistake."

Ingrid returned to the screen and began her search. She started with social media sites, but drew a blank on all of them. She checked public records, archives, residency documentation and blogs—both favorable and critical—about the FSB. She found nothing. Most defectors ended up in one of two places: the outskirts of Moscow in a modest residential neighborhood employed by the State, or the Black Sea where they were encouraged to drink themselves to an early grave. She found no trace of Dennis Mulroony in either location. It was very uncharacteristic of the FSB not to have trumpeted their diplomatic coup of recruiting an FBI agent. Normally there was a photo of the defector shaking hands with someone high up in the Kremlin, usually done in a cryptic way that sent a message to Washington. She checked the ex-pat community forums for resorts like Sochi and Anapa. Again, nothing. If he wasn't in jail in the US, and he wasn't in Russia, where the hell was he? Ingrid got out her phone and scrolled through her contacts. She was going to need some outside help. Her finger hovered over the name of Nick Angelis. A name that made her shudder.

She had been meaning to go and visit Nick for a while. The two of them had a complicated history, but when it came to off-the-record Russian intel, she trusted Nick. He worked for a private security agency called Fortnum, which operated at the darker end of the intelligence spectrum.

Her feelings toward him had been awkward for some time—a botched assignment, a romantic misstep—but a new layer of discomfort was added the last time she'd seen him. He'd been visibly ill. A skeleton in clothes. But because she had been angry with him, she hadn't asked him how he was. Although she hadn't heard from him since, she felt sure that if he had actually died, she would have heard. Ingrid let out a sigh. She was a useless friend. She couldn't even tell Natasha when she had lipstick on her teeth. She'd had enough therapy in her life to know why she was a rubbish friend—all roads led back to Megan—but that was no excuse for not overcoming her discomfort.

Just do it, for chrissakes.

Ingrid tapped out a message. *You've been in my thoughts. Wondered if you'd like to catch up.* She didn't know how to end it. *Love, Ingrid?* No, that was wrong. *Ingrid x.*

Ingrid stared back at the computer screen. The only trace of Dennis Mulroony she'd found had been the news report of the man she assumed was his father donating his kidney. Ingrid changed the keyboard settings back to English and started searching for other Mulroonys in Cleveland who lived near the DuBois High School where Dennis Snr worked. A few minutes later Ingrid found herself staring at a list of winners of Best in Show for the local dog obedience and agility contest. Patty Mulroony had won a rosette every year from 1998, but her streak ended in 2012. It didn't seem implausible that the disappearance of her son from the face of the earth might have diminished her appetite for fun competitions.

"Shall we?"

Ingrid twisted round and blinked at Daisy Steiner. She had been so absorbed in her search she had forgotten where she was or what was supposed to be happening next. She swiveled back to the screen, then back to Daisy. "Give me two minutes?"

Ingrid carefully logged out of the system, removed her

search history and cookies, and then finally deleted her account. Are you sure, the computer asked. *Yes, I'm absolutely certain.* Out on the street, they looked for a restaurant. "The only place I know round here is The Wolseley," Ingrid said. The warm temperatures had encouraged drinkers and diners to stay out, and the sidewalk had a festival atmosphere.

"Isn't that a bit fancy?" Daisy asked. "Wouldn't we need a reservation?"

"I imagine they might have had a few cancelations with weather like this."

"What we need," Daisy said, "is one of those food trucks and a park bench."

Ingrid imagined for a second how busy the food courts of Shoreditch and Bermondsey would be on a sultry Saturday night and shuddered. Perhaps she was readier for the settled home-owning life than she was prepared to admit. "I don't think there's anywhere like that round here. We could head into Soho. Or maybe grab a takeout and go to St. James's Square?"

"Almost sounds romantic."

Ingrid was starting to feel a little uncomfortable with how often Daisy brought up dating. The next time anything related to romance came up, Ingrid needed to make it clear she wasn't interested. And even if she was, it would be deeply unprofessional.

"Gyoza? Noodles?" Ingrid asked.

"That's quite a step down from The Wolseley, but sure."

They walked down Piccadilly and chatted amiably about the book signing. Daisy was a little hyper, and Ingrid recalled those stories about rock stars coming off stage and needing to keep the buzz going with pills and liquor. Ingrid turned sharply, sensing someone was approaching them from behind. It was just a drunk who had lost his balance.

"You scared me there," Daisy said. "You're obviously trained to be alert."

They nipped into a branch of Itsu, picked up some food and a couple of bottles of Asahi then took a back street to the square, where they found a bone-dry patch of grass. St. James's Square was one of Mayfair's more genteel open spaces, and it was spared the overflowing trash cans and Bluetooth speaker parties of the garden squares in Soho. Its tall trees and well-kept borders were more like the parks of Paris or Rome than London.

"Don't suppose you've got a bottle opener, do you?" Daisy asked.

Ingrid gestured for her to hand over the beers and she popped the caps on the edge of a nearby bench. Something moved in the shrubbery, making her jump. She walked slowly back to Daisy and handed her a bottle. "We've got company," Ingrid said. "Eleven o'clock. Don't make it too obvious."

Daisy stretched her arms behind her and arched her neck. "Who am I supposed to be looking at?"

"She's about twenty-two, twenty-three. Long dark ponytail. She was at the book store. Now she's in the bushes. A little overweight."

"Is she wearing a tee shirt from Harrogate?" Daisy asked.

"You know her?"

"Ellen something-or-other. She says she's my biggest fan."

Ingrid took a pull on her bottle. "You've seen *Misery*, right? You know how that ends for the crime writer?"

"Oh, come on, she's harmless."

"Daisy, she's hiding in the goddamn bushes." Ingrid pulled a pair of wooden chopsticks from their paper sleeve. "I think she's more stalker than fan."

"Trust me, she's harmless."

Ingrid picked up a gyoza and took a bite. "You should take it more seriously."

"Well, so long as I've got an FBI agent with me I feel pretty safe." She raised her bottle. "Cheers."

They clinked bottles.

"So, I'm guessing you have more questions about my father?"

Ingrid filled Daisy in on her meeting with Fitzpatrick. "You said when I came to the farm that you thought I was about to tell you your father had been murdered." Ingrid paused to make sure she wasn't going too fast. "Until I turned up, were you happy with the verdict of suicide?"

Daisy delved around in a cardboard bucket of noodles with her chopsticks. She was in no hurry to answer. She eventually lifted out a piece of tofu and popped it in her mouth and chewed. "I wasn't unaware of the speculation he was murdered, if that's what you're asking." She rolled her lips over her teeth. "But if he was going to kill himself, using the pistol made sense."

Ingrid noted she had also failed to call it a revolver. "And was the gun his?"

"It certainly could have been. It's the sort of thing he might have had tucked behind the books on his shelves. I think he'd have quite liked possessing something illegal, something potent." She paused. "He had a flair for the dramatic." After stirring her noodles, she asked: "Is that why you wanted to talk again? Do you still think he killed himself?"

Ingrid downed another mouthful of beer. "Until I have a motivation for why someone wanted to kill him, then suicide remains the most likely option. But," she paused, taking a moment to consider the wisdom of revealing more, "the fact that a far-right specialist knew enough about the Russians to be asked to give evidence to the Hawking Review does concern me. Do you know why your father was testifying? Do you know what he knew about the murder of Dmitri Andropov?"

Daisy Steiner took a long sip of her beer, then placed the bottle down carefully on the uneven grass. "I don't think he knew very much about the murder itself."

"I sense a 'but'," Ingrid said.

"But I think he had a decent idea about why Andropov's killer was never found."

"Go on."

A commotion erupted behind them. They both turned to see a man with his hands raised, walking backwards. "You're a fucking nutter, aren't you?" The man's fly was undone.

"Jesus, it's her, isn't it?" Daisy said.

"Stay here. Get your phone out. Don't hesitate to call 999."

Ingrid scrambled to her feet and ran over to the man. "She's got a knife," he said.

Ingrid looked down at his open fly. "I was only taking a slash. Oh, fuck, it's not what it looks like." He zipped himself up and started to run. "It really isn't how it looks. I swear."

For the first time in her career, Ingrid didn't run after the man emerging from the bushes with his pants undone. She walked toward the shrubbery.

"Come out," she said. "Slowly."

There was no answer. Ingrid took a step toward the bush. The shadows were inky and dark in the twilight. Going any further was unwise.

"It's in your best interests to come out now, but come out slowly."

A rustling noise came from behind the foliage. "I thought he was going to rape me," Ellen said. "I'm the victim here!"

"Put the knife away and step out where I can see you."

"Why should I do what you say? Who the hell are you, anyway?"

Ingrid inhaled slowly. She had no powers of arrest in the UK. No authority to detain. Ingrid glanced at Daisy, who was on the phone. "The police have been called."

"Good! That man could have hurt me."

Ingrid looked at the wet patch on the dry earth. She was fairly sure the man's only crime was exercising his God-given right to urinate wherever he damn well pleased. "Then you've got nothing to fear from stepping out of those bushes."

Ingrid heard movement. And then nothing. "Are you still there?" Ingrid stepped forward, her hands parting the foliage. She couldn't make anything out between the dark branches.

The blade glinted in the orange streetlight as Ellen's fist burst through leaves. Ingrid flinched, then leaned forward, grabbing the girl's wrist and twisting her arm upward.

"You're hurting me." Ellen's voice was more of a yelp.

Ingrid gripped hard and dragged her through the bushes. "Drop the knife." Ingrid kept her eyes on the blade. Ellen's knuckles were white. "I told you to drop it." She dragged Ellen's arm down, turned her around and pressed her foot onto the girl's calf, forcing her onto her knees. She let go of the blade, and Ingrid kicked it out of reach.

"Nicely done."

Ingrid turned to see a uniformed police officer. She'd been so focused on the knife she hadn't heard him approach.

"Shall I take over?" he asked.

"Be my guest."

A second officer ran up to them. "Don't go anywhere," she said. "We'll need to speak to you."

Ingrid stepped back as they read Ellen her rights. The picnickers and sweethearts in the square stared at Ingrid as she rejoined an open-mouthed Daisy. "We need to make sure they detain her," Ingrid said. "At the bookstore, she overheard us make dinner arrangements. That probably means she also knows you're planning on getting the last train."

Daisy was too shocked to speak.

"In fact, I think you should stay in London tonight."

Daisy stared at the police as they talked to Ellen. "I… I can't," she said, obviously distracted. "I need to feed the pigs in the morning. I've got to go." She looked at Ingrid. "Did she really have a knife?"

"Uh-huh."

Daisy had turned sheet-white. "You might have just saved my life."

"The man taking a piss did that."

"I honestly thought she was harmless."

Two hours later, Ingrid waited with Daisy at Liverpool Street station for her train to leave. The concourse was a seething mass of people who'd had a glass more than they intended swaying gently as they checked the departures board for the last train to the boondocks. Ingrid wasn't letting Daisy board her train until the very last minute, when she could be sure that Ellen Methven wasn't about to step on at the last moment. Daisy couldn't believe there was a chance she could be processed so quickly, but all it would take was a big fight in Soho—not all that unlikely on a hot Saturday night—for the cops to let her go with a caution.

"And you're certain your friend will meet you at the station?"

"Yes. But it's nice you're so worried."

"And your solicitor is coming in the morning?"

"First thing."

"Because you need that restraining order."

"Oh, that is understood."

"And never," Ingrid said, "ever invite a journalist to interview you at your home, or mention where you live in interviews. Restraining orders don't always work."

"Also understood. I'm going to get cameras and alarms and a really big dog."

Ingrid smiled at her. "I'm glad you won't be alone tonight. That wasn't the night you planned, was it?"

"No, but it's been memorable for the wrong—and the right—reasons." She leaned forward and kissed Ingrid on the cheek. "I'll never forget this."

After an awkward silence, Ingrid piped up. "On the plus side, you've got a new storyline for your next book."

Daisy crinkled her mouth. "My books are set in 1930s Hollywood. It's funny, but I can't think of any movie stars back then who had stalkers. I suppose there must have been some."

All around them, passengers picked up their pace as they hurried to the platform. Daisy checked her watch.

Two minutes to go. "You think it's safe for me to board yet?"

"Give it another minute. Besides, I've been meaning to ask you."

"Oh, yes," Daisy said hopefully.

"Earlier, before the police arrived, you said you knew why your father was asked to testify in front of the Hawking Review."

Daisy looked a little disappointed. "Ah. That." She moved toward the train, holding one hand against the sliding door so it couldn't close. "He said he knew why the cops, the Met, hadn't found Andropov's killer."

Ingrid's brow puckered. "Why?"

The doors bleeped and started to close. Daisy jumped on board. "More like who. Someone deliberately scuppered the investigation."

16

Ingrid knocked on the open door of the counter-terrorism squad's office.

"You looking for me?" Sam Sherbourne asked.

"Certainly am."

"Give me two minutes."

Ingrid leaned against his desk while he finished off his email. The CT office was just as badly maintained as her own, but the big difference was the number of people. Eight agents and six civilian staff shared the space that was not quite twice the size of the criminal division office. Someone was always on the phone, conversations were always being had. Desks were decorated with family photos, potted plants and brightly colored keepsakes. Her room felt monastic in comparison, and every time she was in there she didn't know if she was relieved to have such privacy and space, or jealous of the camaraderie the CT team shared.

"Okay," he said, "what do you need?"

"You don't happen to have a copy of the Hawking Review, do you?"

"Should do." He called over to his assistant. "Ben?"

"Yes, boss?"

"Can you locate the Hawking Review for Ingrid?"

"Sure thing."

Sherbourne turned his attention to Ingrid. He wheeled his chair back and placed his hands behind his head. Sweat patches darkened his pink shirt at the underarms. It was only nine a.m. "What do you need it for? Anything I ought to know about?"

"Well, if you do, this is me notifying you," Ingrid said. "I'm following up something that may be nothing."

His nose twitched as if he was going to sneeze. "Which is?"

"The death of someone who was due to give evidence to the Review."

He pulled a Kleenex out of his pocket and held it against his nose.

"Bless you," Ingrid said, after a surprisingly delicate sneeze.

"Hay fever," Sherbourne said. "A US citizen?"

"No, but it's one of those cases where you're not quite sure you've got anything, but you can't stop digging until you're certain you never will."

He threw the Kleenex in the trash. "You have time for one of those cases?"

"Probably not. But I've got a very keen new assistant and this'll be a good task for him" She lowered her voice. "Did you ever work with an agent called Mulroony? He was—"

"Sure. Oh Denny Boy."

"That was his nickname?"

"Well, he's Irish, isn't he? I remember a few nights in the pub that ended with him singing."

Ingrid hoped she kept the surprise from her face. She had become so used to people *not* talking about Mulroony that Sherbourne's enthusiasm threw her a little. "You still in touch with him?" She tried to sound casual.

"No. No one is. He left under a big, black cloud." His eyes narrowed. "Why are you asking?"

"I think I must have his old desk. I've been getting a couple of calls for him." She jutted out her bottom lip. "What was the cloud?"

Sherbourne leaned back. "You know, I'm not sure. I'm going to go with inappropriate drunken behavior. Maybe he hit on the ambassador's daughter, something like that. Whatever it was, it was big. The sort of thing you can't come back from. One day he was at work, the next it was as if he'd never existed." He paused. "He was a sociable guy. A fun guy. But he clearly made an enemy somewhere."

Ingrid decided to test the water one more time. "Last call I got for him was a Russian caller. Any of your contacts ever ask for him?"

He pulled a face. "Nope, can't say they have."

Ben approached, carrying a bound report that was ten inches thick. "This is just the summary," he said. "I can check with the library downstairs. I imagine they have the full report. System says it's one hundred and fifty thousand pages in total."

The summary was as heavy as it looked. "They better have a damn good index," Ingrid said, adjusting her grip. "Thanks, Ben. Thanks, Sam." She passed the bulletin board on her way back to the criminal division and pulled up. Her mouth fell open. Her heart beat hard. Someone had identified the photo of the small brown bird.

"Who wrote this?" she asked. The clerks and assistants

inside the bullpen didn't even look up. "Who wrote this?" she said again, her voice quavering. She placed the report on the floor, ripped the photocopy from its pin and stepped inside the glass partition that separated the desks from the walkways. "Do you know who wrote this?" Ingrid asked. "Do you?" She was met with shoulder shrugs and head shakes. Her heart raced. The paper trembled in her hands. She looked at the unusual handwriting. The loop of the 'y' was almost theatrical. Someone would recognize the penmanship. "Listen." Her throat was so constricted it was an effort to raise her voice. She waved the piece of paper in the air. "Can I have your attention? Please!"

The chatter rolled to a stop. Their keyboards fell silent.

"Thank you." A nerve twitched in Ingrid's thigh. "Did any of you write this?"

No one answered.

"Did any of you see who did write it?"

A dull chorus of 'no' and 'huh' emanated from their mouths.

"Okay," Ingrid said, feeling a little stupid for making such a big fuss. "Does anyone know *when* it was written?"

A distant voice piped up. "A couple days ago?"

"Who said that?"

Ingrid looked around for a raised hand.

"I did."

Ingrid turned. DeWalt's secretary—her secretary until a few weeks beforehand—was sitting at her desk outside DeWalt's door at the far end of the room with her hand in the air. Ingrid smiled with relief at Penny's familiar face.

"I think it's been there a couple days," Penny said, raising her voice.

"Sounds about right," someone else said.

How had Ingrid missed it? "And no one saw who wrote it?" She looked at a sea of bemused faces. "Okay, thanks people. Thanks, Penny. Sorry for the interruption."

Ingrid picked up the report from the floor and took it into her office. She dropped it on her desk next to the copy of Daisy Steiner's book. She checked inside the flap and re-read the note she'd written for Kathleen. It was lame. She'd known it was lame when she wrote it, but so had everything else she'd thought of. 'Hope this might be a welcome distraction. All my love, Ingrid.' She pushed it away. She couldn't send it.

She was a jerk. What she wanted to say, but somehow never had, was that she loved Kathleen more than her own mother, and that she was so sorry that she hadn't been able to save Megan, or find her killer, and there was no one on earth she wanted to make amends with more than her. But Ingrid couldn't even tell a good friend to wipe lipstick from her teeth.

How could she be so brave at work, and such a coward with Kathleen? A wave of self-loathing roared through her. She closed her eyes and inhaled deeply before reaching to answer the phone that was ringing on her desk. Zeke beat her to it and picked up from his extension.

"Special Agent Ingrid Skyberg's line." His eyebrows shot up. "I'll put you through now."

Ingrid's extension started to trill. "It's the ambassador's office," he said.

Ingrid picked up. "Agent Skyberg."

"Please hold." The voice was distant. The line had an echo. It definitely wasn't a call from the sixth floor. Ingrid waited to be connected.

"Ingrid?"

"Speaking."

"It's me. It's Jen."

Ingrid's face bloomed with a huge smile. Jen was the perfect person to lighten her mood. "Hello stranger. How are you? *Where* are you?"

"Almaty."

"Is that Kyrgyzstan or Uzbekistan?"

"Ooh, so close. Kazakhstan. Jack's the new ambassador. Well, acting ambassador."

"And how is it?"

"Mostly it seems to be, like, receptions with oil workers and their wives."

"You enjoying it?"

"Oh, Ingrid, it is fascinating. Absolutely fascinating. I am loving every single second." Jennifer Rocharde was a guaranteed ray of sunshine. Or Jennifer Tucker, as she was now. Even though it had to be five in the morning where she was. "I can't believe you're still in London. I thought you wanted to get out."

Ingrid sighed. "I did. I kinda still do, but…"

"But?"

"Carolyn—you remember Marshall's sister, right—is coming back, and I promised to take care of her." Ingrid sighed. "So, I'll be here for at least another three years. I'm actually house-hunting." It was lovely to catch up with her old assistant, but Ingrid had asked Jen to call for a reason. She wanted to know what Jen remembered about the day Mulroony took a photo of her holding a birthday cake. "Listen, this is going to sound weird and arbitrary, but did you get the image I sent you?"

"You mean the one you'd labeled 'puppy63' and sent to my Gmail from some random email address you've set up? Yes, I got it. Where did you find it?"

Why hadn't Ingrid anticipated that question? "It fell out of a file," she fudged.

"Uh-huh." Jen was skeptical. "So why the secret squirrel routine?"

Fair point. Best to respond with a question of her own. "Do you remember it being taken?"

"Like, vaguely."

"Do you know who else is in the photo?"

"Sure. The girl on the right is Sacha Daniels, she was like Sol's secretary for a few months, and the girl in the middle is Missy Benoit. She was only in London a month or two. She left to start art school in Paris. I think." When Jen said 'I think' Ingrid had learned that was just self-deprecation. Jen's memory for facts and faces was faultless. "And obviously that's DeWalt to one side. I hear he got Marshall's job."

Ingrid stared at the photo. "That's DeWalt?" She was incredulous. "You sure."

"Totes," Jen said. "I remember that shirt."

He had lost a lot of hair and gain several pounds in five years. "Whose birthday was it?" Ingrid asked.

"Hmmm." Jen went quiet. "You know what, I don't think it was anybody's. Isn't that weird?"

Ingrid waited for her to continue.

"Yep, yep I remember now." She paused. "You know, it really *was* weird. The guy who, like, took the photo was Voldemort. You remember, right? The guy we were never supposed to speak about."

"Mulroony?"

"That's very brave of you saying his name out loud," Jen said. "I take it you're alone?"

Ingrid gave Zeke a big smile. "No, just living dangerously."

"Well, anyway, he brought the cake in. And the candles. He said he needed a photograph of a birthday party to send home. So, he got the three of us together and was very specific about where we stood." She inhaled audibly. "Yep, now I think about it, it was totally weird. It's like totally creepy that he kept it. What file was it in?"

Ingrid opened her drawer and took out the packet of photos. She placed it next to the torn photocopy of the bird. "Was Mulroony always like that? Always odd?"

"I didn't really know him—"

"I thought you worked with him?"

Jen was taken aback. "No, no, I worked with the CI team back then."

"So how come you were working on the criminal side when I joined?"

"You don't know?" Jen was incredulous.

"I guess I just assumed you'd worked with my predecessor."

"No, I only, like moved to that office because Voldemort's assistant… Julie Something. Julie Bairstow. Actually, it's a really horrible story. I can't, like, believe I totally forgot about this. She, um, she got attacked walking home. She was in, like a coma, for months."

Ingrid's mouth fell open as she pulled out one of the cake photos.

"I don't think she ever fully recovered, you know. I'm pretty sure at some point she was transferred back to the States and is, like, in a little hospital near her folks."

Ingrid didn't know what to say.

"She was, like, hit with a hammer. Geez, I can't believe you don't know about it. It was just the worst thing ever."

"When did that happen?"

"Right after Mul–, I mean Voldemort left." Jen breathed

in. Ingrid could almost picture her placing a hand on her hip. "Why all these questions, Ingrid? What's going on?"

This was a question Ingrid had prepared a little white lie for. "I pulled up a case file from the library, and in among his notes was this photo. I couldn't see how it was significant, but thought you might know something." Ingrid swallowed. "Plus, it's been ages, and it was really just an excuse to catch up."

"Hmm, well, if I had done that filing I would have, like, totally put the photo in the folder labeled 'Creepy Guy has secret office crush'. Maybe he needed a pretend girlfriend to show his mom?"

Ingrid was struck by how easy it was to talk to Jen. For four years they'd worked closely together and seen each other through embarrassments and hangovers and unwise dating choices and impossible bosses. She had missed her more than she'd acknowledged. They chatted for another fifteen minutes before saying their goodbyes.

"Old friend?" Zeke asked when Ingrid finally put the phone down.

"That was Jen," Ingrid said.

"Saint Jen? *The* Saint Jennifer?" He placed both hands over his heart. "Well, I feel honored to have come so close to perfection."

Ingrid pushed one of the birthday photos in Zeke's direction. He got up and crossed the office. "Don't know how much of that you overheard?"

Zeke's eyes narrowed. He had probably heard all of it but feigned ignorance.

"Apparently our mystery photographer brought in his own cake for a non-existent birthday."

"Odd." He picked up the photo. "You'd think then, he might have taken a better photograph of the actual cake, wouldn't you?" He placed it down on top of the photocopy. Then he raised his gaze and looked very deliberately at Ingrid. "Oh my God." He slapped her playfully on the upper arm. "Oh, my effing God! When were you going to tell me?"

"You mean you didn't notice before? Apparently, it's been on the bulletin board for a day or two."

"Geez, I think I would have noticed that." He swiped up the photocopy. "So, you're a skylark, are you?" he said to the image of the bird. "I don't suppose you know why someone keeps calling for you, do you?"

17

INGRID WALKED UP to the reception desk. "I'm looking for the Darwin building."

The goth behind the desk smiled at her and pulled out a leaflet. He turned it over to reveal a map of the campus of the London College of Media. "You're here." He marked their position with an X. Ingrid saw he had implants on the back of his hand that resembled an iguana's spine. "And the Darwin is out of the double doors, down the street and is the red brick building on the corner." He smiled, revealing a tattoo on the inside of his lower lip. "You can't miss it."

Most of the buildings in the street belonged to the college. Ingrid guessed that it just wouldn't have been possible to build a large university in such an ancient city, and so LCM had acquired a random collection of buildings in proximity to one another. According to the carved stone panel above the entrance to the Darwin building, it had once been a hospital for tropical diseases.

At another reception desk she got more directions and set off in search of Lecture Theater B. A network of busy corridors and noisy stairwells brought her to an internal lobby and a sign for the lecture theater. A handwritten sign on the door said, 'No entry. Latecomers must use the rear door.' Finding that door involved another maze of walkways, and two flights of stairs. Ingrid slipped in and flipped down a blue plastic seat near the back where the lighting was poor.

The projector screen behind the lecturer was a bulleted list of how to submit a Freedom of Information request, the UK's equivalent of the FOIA, and Ingrid wondered if she might actually learn something. Ingrid speculated on how many of the students knew how formidable their new journalism instructor was. Angela Tate, the Fleet Street terrier, famed for not letting go of a story until the judiciary pried it out of her jaw with an injunction. Ingrid couldn't begin to imagine how much Tate must hate being a tutor instead of pounding the streets in pursuit of rival-beating scoops. She was almost sure Tate had once told her teaching was for failures, losers and never-weres. This was not where Ingrid expected to find her.

The downsizing of media budgets had meant no newspaper was prepared to pay for a reporter of Tate's caliber, and in the past two years her byline had disappeared from the front pages. The last time their paths had crossed, Tate had been writing a book about Russian oligarchs living in London. She'd had something of a makeover since their previous encounter. The long frizzy hair was now collar length and expertly curled, and Ingrid couldn't see any of her trademark leopard print anywhere on her person. She wore knee-high boots, culottes and a white shirt under a black sweater. She actually looked smart.

At the end of the lecture, the theater emptied out and Ingrid walked slowly down the steps, catching Tate's eye.

"Well, well, well," Tate said. "As I live and breathe."

"Hello, Angela."

A few of the remaining students turned to look.

"Special Agent Ingrid Skyberg, everybody," Tate said. "From the actual FBI."

"What have you done?" one of the students asked on her way out.

Tate managed a half smile. "Knowing Agent Skyberg, I imagine it's a case of what can I do for her." She turned to Ingrid. "Am I right?"

"Nice to see you again. Can you spare ten minutes?"

Angela raised a finger, ducked her head outside the lower door, looked at something, then swung back inside the theater. "Take a seat. Nothing's on the noticeboard until this evening. Bloody poetry slam, if you can believe it." She rolled her eyes. "I'll be right with you."

Angela dealt with queries from her students, and when the last of them had left, she came and sat in the front row with Ingrid. "Some of these kids are really good," she said, almost as if she was anticipating Ingrid's pity for her fall from grace. "They're really going to cause the government some trouble when they get out of here. None of them will ever work in a newspaper office, of course, but they'll raise hell working for Greenpeace or Bellingcat or the ICIJ."

"They couldn't have a better teacher," Ingrid said.

Tate crossed her arms and her legs simultaneously. "We both know you're not here to flatter me, so come on then, what do you need?"

Ingrid leaned back against the seat. "Does the name David Steiner mean anything to you?"

Tate's forehead crinkled. "You mean the guy who 'killed himself'?" she said, using air quotes.

"So, you think he was murdered, then?"

"God, if I could have proved that I would have run it."

"So, you looked into it?"

"Yes indeedy. He'd interviewed me for his book, can't remember what it was called now, so I'd spent a bit of time with him about a year, maybe two, before he died." She waited for an interruption that didn't come. "I liked the guy, and I felt he deserved to have his death properly investigated." She inhaled slowly, narrowing her nostrils. "What the hell has this got to do with the FBI? He wasn't an informer, was he?"

Ingrid leaned forward, her elbows resting on her knees, her hands propping up her chin. "No. Or at least, not as far as I know."

Tate wrinkled her nose. "Why is an American law enforcement agency interested in a British far right specialist?"

Ingrid couldn't stop herself from smiling. "That's kind of what I was hoping you could tell me."

Tate checked her watch. "I suppose you think it's too early for a drink?"

Ingrid glanced at the clock on the wall. A little after five p.m. "I am on duty."

"Come on." Tate got to her feet. "You and I both know I work a little better when my brain is appropriately oiled."

Tate took her to a small, dark, empty pub with engraved glass windows and original oak paneling. Ingrid bought her a large gin and tonic and took it out into the small, shaded beer garden where Tate was still sitting in her sweater. It was ninety-odd degrees. Maybe she was part lizard.

"What's that?" Tate asked when Ingrid put down her own drink.

"Passion fruit and guava," Ingrid said, reading the label.

"Rather you than me. I have a policy to never drink anything pink." Tate raised her glass. "Cheers."

"Cheers."

Ingrid had never been sure if Tate was an ally or not. Her first responsibility was always to the story, and Ingrid knew that if she let anything slip, Tate would find a way of getting it into the papers.

"In *National Affront*, Steiner talks about your reporting on a group called England for the English, and this was instrumental in bringing down the William King government because he was a clandestine supporter," Ingrid said.

"Something like that."

"Did you write a lot about neo-Nazis?"

Tate drummed her fingers on the slatted wooden table. "Not as much as I should. It's shocking how few of those sorts of stories got published. The readers didn't care, so neither did the editors. If I'd been a young bloke, I could have shaved my head and embedded. Got a nice publishing deal for a memoir." She took a long sip of her drink through a straw, her lips pursing into a tight spider's web of lines.

"What did you think of Steiner's theory? That Russia was funding groups like EFE?"

Tate leaned back. A smile stretched her lips. "Ah. That's the connection. The good ole Russkies!"

There was no fooling Tate.

"And that's something else you know about."

Tate's eyebrows knitted together.

"The last time I saw you, you were working on a book about Russians in London."

Tate looked surprised. "No I wasn't. I haven't seen you in two or three years."

Now it was Ingrid's turn to smile. "Our paths crossed last year."

Tate wasn't buying it. "I might be on the scrap heap of education, but I'm not bloody senile. I'm damn sure I'd remember that."

Ingrid hesitated before filling her in. "I was undercover. There would have been a big problem if you had recognized me."

Tate's jaw dropped. "Where?"

"A recital at the Albert Hall."

She rested her elbows on the table. "You are kidding me?"

"Nope. But you had me very nervous. If you'd said anything it could have been serious. I mean, *really* serious. It could have gotten me killed."

Tate exhaled wearily. "Well bugger me. You know I hate missing out on a story." She looked up at Ingrid. "I mean, obviously it's great you're still alive and everything, but I bloody wish you hadn't told me that. I also wish you hadn't reminded me about my book."

"I noticed it's not in the stores."

"It's been stuck in legal department limbo for four months. Publishers keep threatening not to publish." She took another sip, then let out a not-so-delicate belch without making any attempt to disguise it. "In fairness to the legal beagles, if you are going to libel someone it's probably better if they're not a billionaire."

Ingrid checked the time.

"You have somewhere to be?"

"I do."

"Thought you were dressed a bit smart. Date?"

Ingrid knew she was blushing. "No, it's not like that. He's married."

Tate swirled the melting ice in her glass. "Aw, sweet. You still trying to get away with the goody two shoes act?" She tilted her glass. "I do believe I'm out of gin."

Ingrid bought her another, then returned the conversation to Steiner's book. "So, the Russians and the far right? Was he on to something?"

Ingrid's phone rang. It was Zeke.

"Be my guest," Tate said.

Ingrid answered and got to her feet. "What have you got for me?" She started pacing round the small courtyard beer garden.

"Straight to the point," Zeke said. "Very efficient."

"Sorry," Ingrid said. "Do you want to do the how-are-you-I'm-fine routine every time we speak?"

"Hey, not if you don't. Is now a good time?"

Ingrid glanced over at Tate. She hoped Angela couldn't hear what Zeke was saying. "Sure. Shoot."

"Okay then, because I found something that is so exciting I think I might explode if I don't tell someone. And the only person I can possibly tell is you."

Ingrid waited for him to continue. He sounded almost breathless.

"I went through Hawking Review," he said. "Well, the index. At first, I thought you were in it."

"Huh?"

"I know, right? But, it was just the first three letters. Guess who is in the index?"

Chills effervesced over her skin. "Skylark?" Her voice was tentative.

"Boom. It's a codename. For, get this, a Russian agent." Zeke's voice pitched between alarm and enthusiasm. "I've highlighted a passage in the report for you. It says that Skylark was a British spy, most likely inside the Met or MI5, who deliberately sabotaged the investigation into Andropov's death. It was because of his interference that Andropov's killer was able to flee the country."

That chimed with what Daisy had said on the platform at Liverpool Street. "Anything else?"

"Yep, I think so. This links back to the book, *National Affront*. The report says that the Russians recruited Skylark by blackmailing him because he was a member of an organization called England—"

"—For the English," Ingrid finished his sentence and looked at Tate.

"That means something to you?" Zeke asked.

Ingrid chewed the inside of her cheek. "It's starting to. You'll leave the report on my desk?"

"Will do."

Ingrid hung up and returned slowly to the table. Maybe Skylark wasn't in the Met or MI5 Perhaps he was an FBI agent who worked closely with the Met. It made sense, didn't it? Mulroony was Skylark.

18

INGRID HAD EXPECTED to feel nervous. But not *this* nervous. She deliberately kept her arms away from her sides to reduce the amount she was sweating. Still, she reasoned, she'd probably perspire just as much even if she was meeting him in the dead of winter. She checked her watch. Nick Angelis was late.

"Can I get you anything?" the waiter asked.

She really wanted a drink. She knew Nick would either want to order cocktails or champagne, so starting the evening off with a lone glass of Sauvignon Blanc seemed a bit too unambitious. She looked again at the wine menu. "A bottle of Veuve Clicquot, please." The waiter nodded, collected the menu and threaded his way through the tables toward the open-air bar. Ingrid couldn't remember eating outside in short-sleeves at night in London before. The terrace of the Pantechnicon restaurant was the sort of place that would be swamped with reservation requests on a warm summer evening if more people knew about it. Restaurant critics had never been invited to review its Scandinavian-inspired food. It wasn't listed on Google

Maps, or in any travel guides. Its chef wasn't a guest judge on a TV cookery program. And it most certainly did not allow its patrons to Instagram their food. It was a vast improvement on a Russian restaurant Nick had once taken her to in north London so he could keep an eye on a suspect. She looked around. On second thoughts, it was entirely possible Nick had one of the restaurant's elegantly dressed patrons on a surveillance list.

Ingrid had assumed the last time she saw Nick would be the last time she ever saw him. Not because she had been mad with him, though she had been—absolutely fuming—but because he had been so obviously ill. The firm, tanned, tattooed body she still occasionally pictured in moments of weakness had been made thin and pale either through disease, or its treatment. The swoop of his Elvis haircut had been felled by a buzz cut and his swagger had been replaced with a delicate shuffle. He had looked so ill she had assumed he was dying. However, acknowledging his illness would have indicated to him that she cared about him—she did, but she couldn't possibly let him know—or that she wasn't angry with him when she really, really was. So, to her lingering shame, she never asked what was wrong with him. That was only part of the reason she was so nervous.

As she sat, nervously fiddling with her napkin, Ingrid wished it hadn't been her need for a favor that had made her finally contact Nick. But when she had asked him about Mulroony, he had sounded more than happy to help. "Let me ask around," he had said, trying to sound nonchalant, as if she had merely asked for a recommendation for a plumber. Ingrid knew Nick's ego would mean his efforts to locate Mulroony inside Russia would have been anything other than casual. He did not like to be defeated. Which was a big part of the reason why things had always been so antagonistic with him. The attributes that repelled her—cocky, brash, egotistical, opinionated, reckless—she also found electric, a fact she wished was not the case. Her memories of the few nights they spent together still had the ability to make her catch her breath.

"Your timing really couldn't have been better." The sound of his voice raised a shiver on her bare arms.

She turned and stood. They kissed on the cheek, his new beard scratching her skin. She smiled at him. "Why is that?"

"I'll tell you in a moment, but for now I just want to look at you." He held both her hands in his as if he was about to lead her in a dance. "A sight for very sore eyes, might I say."

Nick wore a pair of dress pants and a pale blue shirt open at the collar. His hair was still cropped close to his scalp, and his beard—so black it might have been dyed—was of the statement variety: long, sculpted, deliberate.

"The beard is new," she said, taking her seat.

"It was one of the first things to grow back," he said as he shuffled his chair under the table. "After the chemo."

Ah. So it was cancer. That much she had suspected. "And treatment is over?" What she wanted to ask, but was too much of a coward to, was if the treatment had been successful. Before Nick could answer, the waiter arrived with the champagne.

"Didn't I order the Veuve Clicquot?" she said.

He was holding a bottle of Laurent-Perrier. "Mr. Angelis," he said, "prefers the Laurent."

Ingrid felt heat lick her face. This was one of Nick's ploys. An attempt to undermine her. To establish dominance. She wasn't having it. "*I* prefer the Clicquot."

"Shall we have both?" Nick said, a twinkle dotted in his eye.

"Bring the Clicquot, please." Ingrid spoke firmly.

The waiter checked with Nick, who gave him permission. She couldn't believe they had barely sat down and they were already fighting—about champagne, of all things—but she needed Nick to know he wasn't going to get away with his tricks any more.

"To be honest, I can't tell the difference." Nick leaned in, his phony upper-class accent slipping for a moment to reveal his real background as the son of a kebab-shop owner somewhere in the London suburbs. "With you, I'd be happy with a warm beer and a packet of pork scratchings."

Ingrid had no idea what they were, but she was fairly sure she didn't want to find out. "So," she said, unsure what the next word out of her mouth would be. "You said my call was well timed?"

He spread the white linen napkin across his lap. Before he could reply, the waiter returned with the champagne. He made a point of showing the bottle to Ingrid and not to Nick. He pulled off the gold foil, untwisted the wire cage, and eased the cork out of the neck with an efficient thwop. Nick and Ingrid watched as he poured their drinks into angular V-shaped flutes and then placed the bottle in a bucket of ice.

"Shall we?" Nick asked, raising his glass.

Ingrid picked up hers. "To long overdue reunions," she said.

"To fresh starts," he added, before they clinked their glasses.

"Fresh start?" Ingrid said. "You're leaving Fortnum Security?" Fortnum's was one of the best private security agencies in the world. Hired by corporations and governments to compile intelligence on rivals, and protect their strategic interests, it had a reputation for discretion and ruthlessness in equal measure.

"No," he said, squeezing an extra syllable out of the word. "I don't think they'll ever let me leave."

"Then what?" Ingrid put her glass on the table.

"About three hours before you messaged, I took receipt of an envelope." He took a long drink. "Divorce papers."

It took several seconds for Ingrid to properly register what he had said. "Nick, I'm so sorry."

He looked at his hands. "Thank you. I don't suppose it was a surprise to anyone."

"Well, it's a shock to me. You've only been married two years, two and a half." Ingrid detected a moistening of his eyes. "The shock was that you got married in the first place, but I honestly figured that if you were taking the plunge, you were deeply, deeply serious about the commitment."

"Thank you," he said again. "I was. It is not my decision."

"And to be going through this while dealing with..." her words stumbled. "With cancer. You've had a helluva time."

He looked uncharacteristically sheepish. "You can say that again."

Ingrid knew she had to say something. "And your treatment? It's over?"

"For the time being, yes. Testing every few months, checking the little buggers have been scared off."

"Oh, Nick. That's a lot to go through on your own. I can't believe anyone would leave a marriage while their partner is going through treatment."

He couldn't make eye contact. "I wasn't easy to be with."

She could imagine that. Nick was ex-Special Forces. His body had been a machine—a beautiful machine, according to her memories—and losing his physicality would have been hard enough for him. Losing his faith in his body would have been even harder.

"Besides," he said. "I rather broke our contract. She was always very clear that she wanted children. And, well, the treatment has rather put paid to that."

Ingrid exhaled, her heart swollen with sympathy for him. "I'm so sorry. I somehow had a mental picture of a future you in a house in Greece with a litter of half-feral children being allowed to camp on beaches and take boats out without adult supervision."

He raised an eyebrow. "A litter?"

She pressed her lips together. "Perhaps not my best choice of words."

"Half-feral?" They were silent for a few moments. "That does sound rather marvelous," he said, before tipping his head to drain his glass. They both knew he was blinking back a tear.

The waiter returned. "Are you ready to order?"

Nick didn't even look at the menu. "The poussin, for me."

"And the swordfish for me," Ingrid added. "Listen," she said when the waiter had left, "I need to say something."

He topped up their glasses. "Okay." He sounded nervous.

Ingrid's body was dipped in the heat of shame. She proceeded cautiously, to disguise her discomfort at such an intimate declaration. "I need to say I'm sorry." She clamped her lips together.

"You do?"

She nodded. "I knew you were ill, but I didn't say anything. That was lousy. I'm sorry." She paused. This would be so much easier if he just had spinach in his teeth. "And I'm ashamed it took me needing something from you to get in touch."

The loquacious Nick Angelis was momentarily silenced. "That is appreciated." His voice was distant. "I'll tell you one thing about cancer, you bloody well find out who your friends are."

Svetlana had once said something similar. Years after Ingrid's father had died, she mentioned the silence that followed them in the street when he was ill and how, on their fifteenth anniversary—their last—they could only summon a table's worth of dinner party guests from the hundreds who had attended their wedding.

"Another thing about cancer is people do rather tend to think you're useless, so, actually, it was nice that you still think I can help."

She had sent him a request the day before to see if his contacts knew anything about Mulroony's whereabouts. "And can you?" Ingrid asked, her voice dipping to a whisper. "Have you been able to find anything out?"

Nick leaned backward to allow the waiter to place an eggcup sized bowl in front of them both. "From the kitchen," he said, before discretely retreating.

Ingrid raised the small cup to her nose and inhaled. A pungent truffle aroma exploded in her nostrils, producing an almost simultaneous saliva response in her mouth. She took a sip, and then another. It was like the flavor of an entire meal had been condensed into a single fluid ounce.

"The chef's a genius," Nick said. "Listen, before we get to Mulroony, I need to say something too."

Ingrid was surprised. "Ah, okay."

"I also have to apologize. About Sweden. I put you in danger—I don't think I asked you to do anything I didn't know you weren't entirely capable of—and at the very least you deserved recognition of that." He looked up from his lap and held her gaze. "I should have given you an opportunity to have a pop."

"A pop?"

"Okay, more than a pop. I should have offered you my body as a punching bag, but as you can see, cancer has taken that swipe for you."

She placed a hand on his, the electricity of their touch sending a carbonated response through her veins. "I hated you Nick, but I never hated you that much."

He looked sheepishly at their entwined hands. "You had every right to." He sniffed sharply. "Now, Mr. Mulroony."

Ingrid pulled back, withdrawing her hand. "I'm all ears."

"You might want your eyes too."

"Huh?"

He reached into the back pocket of his pants and pulled out a folded sheet of photocopier paper. He placed it on the table between them. Ingrid unfolded it. In the dim golden lamplight of the restaurant, it was hard to know what she was looking at. A satellite image of a large building. A military base? She held it a little further away, trying to catch the light from the candle holder.

"That is 'Correctional Facility Number Six'," Nick said. "Somewhere near the Kazakh border."

"The Black Dolphin prison?"

"Then you've heard of it."

"It's notorious. The Russian Alcatraz."

"I think Alcatraz might feel like summer camp in comparison," Nick said, sipping his champagne. "Anyway. That's why you couldn't find Mulroony on any of your searches."

Ingrid felt a pressure on her chest. "He's in here?" She waved the paper at him.

"I have a source that says he was in 2015."

"Where is he now?"

Nick shrugged. "Presumably still there."

A shiver rippled over Ingrid's skin, despite the warm evening air. She stared into nothingness, trying to make sense of Nick's revelation. "I don't understand," she said. "If he was a Russian asset, why did they put him in jail?"

19

Ingrid considered moving the towel she'd swiped from her hotel into the shade. She had already reapplied sun lotion twice, but the cooler air under the branches of the large chestnut tree had been claimed by two mothers who were keeping their excited children close on account of the 'missing' posters stapled to the information board at the entrance to the park. Eight-year-old Mason Stebbings hadn't been seen for three days. She checked her phone. Still nothing from Sol. She had now asked him three times to get her the name of someone she could talk to about Mulroony. When she got back to the office, she was going to have to say something to DeWalt.

"Please tell me you're not thinking of buying out here," Natasha McKittrick said as she approached. She was wearing a wide-brimmed linen hat and her face was nearing beet levels of redness. "The time to buy in the Royal Docks was at least ten years ago."

"Isn't that true for all property?" Ingrid rolled over to make space for Natasha, who dumped a wicker hamper onto the parched grass. "I don't suppose you've got a parasol in there, have you?"

Natasha scrunched up her features. "No, but I have chilled water and a sarong you can drape over your shoulders if you like."

"That'd be great."

Ingrid kept her eyes on number thirty-six as Natasha spread out a picnic blanket and unpacked the hamper. "Here you go." She handed Ingrid a bottle of water that was still mostly ice. Ingrid held it against her forehead and let out a gasp. "When are we due for some rain?"

"Forecast says end of the week."

Ingrid squinted up at the dome of blue sky. The only clouds were airplane contrails.

Natasha rubbed lotion into her uncommonly pale skin. "Remind me what we're doing out here?"

"A small spot of surveillance," Ingrid said. She nodded in the direction of the house. "Number thirty-six."

Natasha peered at it over the top of her ant-black sunglasses. "Something to do with the missing kid? Aren't the local plod dealing with that?"

"No, nothing about the kid."

"Then who lives there?" Natasha asked.

"That's what we're trying to find out."

"We?" She slid her glasses up the bridge of her nose. "I have to say, Agent Skyberg, this isn't looking like an official FBI operation. No van with listening equipment, no backup. What's going on?"

Ingrid smiled at her friend. "It's one of those I-can-tell-you-but-I'd-have-to-kill-you things."

"Aye, right," Natasha said suspiciously. "More like one of those you've-been-told-to-drop-it-but-you-can't things."

Ingrid demurred. "I couldn't possibly comment."

"Well, at least tell me what I'm looking out for. I do have some experience of conducting surveillance operations." She handed Ingrid the sarong.

Ingrid took a long pull on the icy water. "Oh, you know, anything that screams criminal conspiracy, espionage and international intrigue." She looked at the sarong. "Think we can make a shade sail out of this?"

Natasha shrugged. "If anyone can, it's you. Whittle a few sticks? Bind some string out of the grass?"

The only building materials Ingrid could see were chocolate bar wrappers and what looked suspiciously like a used condom. She settled for wrapping it around her shoulders.

"I thought you Scandi types tanned easily," Natasha said, offering Ingrid a packet of potato chips.

"We do. Well, *I* do, but this much sun isn't exactly good for your skin." She was tempted to say something about not everyone wanting to resort to Botox, but her phone illuminated with an incoming message. She glanced at it briefly. Svetlana. It was 2 p.m. That meant the breakfast news would be on in Minnesota. Her mother would unleash a barrage of texts in the next half hour.

Natasha realized Ingrid's anxiety. "Go ahead. I'll keep watch."

TV is saying verdict next week. What you think?

Jones last day.

Maybe forensics this afternoon.

Svetlana's messages were pack animals, always arriving as a herd, marauding through Ingrid's phone and trampling on her psyche.

"It's the trial," Ingrid said. "My mom sends about a million updates a day."

McKittrick reached into the hamper and pulled out a

miniature bottle of wine. "I wondered if you might need this?"

Ingrid stared at the bottle. The condensation running over its curved surface made it even more appealing. "Better not." She nodded at the Ducati. "I've got the bike, remember."

McKittrick twisted off the cap and glugged a third of its contents into her mouth. "What do you think?" she asked. "Are they going to convict him? For Megan's murder, I mean? I saw he's claiming he didn't kill the first three victims. He's obviously going to the chair for the later murders. Surely?"

Ingrid tore at the wet paper label on her water. She got the impression Natasha was following the case out of loyalty to her, and not because of her professional interest in crime. "There's no death penalty in Minnesota," she said quietly.

"Oh. I hadn't realized that. I thought the whole of the Midwest was dunk 'em and burn 'em territory." McKittrick paused. "Sorry, poor taste. But, um, do you think he did it? Killed your friend, I mean?"

Ingrid glanced at more messages arriving from Svetlana. "Honestly?" Ingrid was about to say something she'd been thinking for a while but hadn't dared utter out loud. "I don't know."

"Oh." McKittrick was thrown by Ingrid's equivocation. "I guess I assumed you'd know one way or another. I mean, you'd know if he was the guy you saw, wouldn't you?"

Ingrid took a breath before answering. "Would I?" She scrunched up her face. "It was twenty years ago. It was dark. I was terrified. There's a reason they didn't ask me to testify." Ingrid's shoulders slumped. "I just want it to be over. But, I hope for Megan's mom that the jury does the decent thing and convicts." She turned to her friend. "We both know that if they don't, the police aren't going to reopen the case."

"It sounds like you think he didn't do it?"

Ingrid inhaled so deeply her entire upper body moved. "I honestly don't know. I stopped trusting my judgement about this a long time ago." She stared at the house, hoping for movement. "I've waited two decades to find out what happened to my best friend." An image of Megan in math class popped into Ingrid's thoughts. "I've lost count of the therapists who have told me I need closure on this. So..."

"So?"

"So, I hope it's him."

McKittrick pulled a sympathetic face. "What did you make of the forensic anthropologist the defense wheeled out? He looked like a character from a Saturday Night Live sketch. Was that even his real hair?"

Natasha was referring to Dr. Peter Mikkelson who had a mixed reputation. He was either a cavalier maverick with a greater regard for his own fame and power than the truth, or he was a bold outlier willing to challenge the consensus. His wild red hair and bowtie suggested the former, but he had been proved right enough times that no one could discount the latter.

Ingrid, untrusting of her own judgement, threw the question back to McKittrick. "What did you make of him?"

Natasha perked up a bit. It seemed she had missed being asked for her opinion about policing. "Well, on the one hand you can't dispute the facts. The hyoid bone in the first three victims had been broken, but not in the subsequent nine. That could suggest this Billy Starr existed and had a different way of—" Natasha paused and lowered her voice "—strangling his victims. But you and I both know the hyoid isn't always fully formed in adolescents, and given the age of the victims I don't think it's as significant a finding as it would be if the victims were in their thirties or forties." McKittrick paused and the sounds of children playing bounced through the hot, dry air. "And you'd think that if this Billy Starr really did exist, there'd be more of a trace. I mean, obviously, Starr is his stage name, but surely someone in a small place would remember the guy who used to live there. Someone who bought videos from him must currently be inside and would trade info for a shorter sentence?"

Ingrid sipped her water. "It's not a small place, it's *no* place. There isn't another building for miles. And if he was making porn and killing girls, he'd deliberately not want to see folks."

"So you think Jones isn't making it up?"

Ingrid shrugged, suddenly unable to speak. One of those girls was Megan. One of those girls could have been her.

"I'm sorry, mate. I didn't want to *not* say anything." McKittrick reached out and placed a hand on Ingrid's forearm. "I figured you'd be going through hell with it."

Ingrid looked down at Natasha's arm, surprised by the intimacy. "Thanks." She needed to change the subject. "You found any more apartments for me?"

"Nothing that beats the flat on the river, but if you'd consider Highbury something quite tasty is about to come on the market."

Ingrid had to think hard about where Highbury was. Islington, but a bit further north. She couldn't remember if she liked the area or not. "Tasty? How?"

"An old butcher's shop. You get loads for your money—four stories, four bedrooms, two bathrooms—but the ground floor is a bit awkward, cause it used to be a shop, obviously, and it's more of a yard than a garden."

It wasn't like Ingrid had green fingers. "How much?"

"About a hundred kay below your budget, so plenty left for the renovations. There's even somewhere for your bike. I take it that red monstrosity over there is yours?"

Ingrid peeked over her glasses at her friend. "Monstrosity?"

"You'll never catch me on one."

Ingrid looked over her shoulder at her bike, then looked harder. Parked beyond it, on the far side of the road, was a black SUV. There was a man in the front seat. She nodded in his direction. "Was he there when you arrived?"

Natasha turned.

"Don't make it too obvious," Ingrid said. "I thought this wasn't your first rodeo."

Natasha stretched out an arm in a theatrical fake yawn and looked again toward the bike. "Jesus, it's too bloody hot to be sitting in a car. What's he up to?"

"Keep an eye on him, will you?" Ingrid said. "See if he's interested in number thirty-six."

McKittrick repositioned herself so she didn't have to twist her neck. "As you say, this isn't my first rodeo, but if I was keeping number thirty-six under surveillance, I wouldn't park on the other side of the square where he is. It's not like he's got binoculars." She took another sip from her wine bottle. "What are we doing here, Ingrid? I mean, you must have done the basic checks. You must at least know who lives in that house."

Ingrid wiped the sweat from her brow. "Council Tax is in the name of Lisa O'Shaughnessy."

"And why are you interested in her?"

"I don't know that I am."

McKittrick let out a sigh. "Are we currently embarked on a wild goose chase?"

"Quite possibly," Ingrid said. What she didn't add, for fear of sounding unhinged, is that it was a wild goose chase that potentially pertained to American national security and Russian espionage. "I just thought you might like to sit in the sun and hang out in a park overlooking the dock with a friend."

"Don't I even get a clue as to why you've dragged me out here?" McKittrick got her phone out of her bag and toggled for the camera app.

Ingrid had been considering whether or not to tell McKittrick about the photos. "Remember the last time we met, I put those photos in to get developed?"

"Uh-huh." McKittrick sounded distracted as she propped up her phone against her handbag. "I do."

"Well." Ingrid paused, suddenly unsure of the wisdom of continuing. "They weren't holiday snaps." She looked at Natasha's phone. "What are you doing?"

"Using my spidey police senses."

Ingrid narrowed her eyebrows. "What's going on?"

"I've been looking at the guy in the car, and he keeps looking at us then turning away. So, I thought I'd film him, and then gaze at your loveliness and see if he changes his behavior when he thinks I'm not looking at him." She smiled at Ingrid. "See? Not my first rodeo."

"You think he's surveilling us?"

"Us?" McKittrick raised an eyebrow. "No, lovely. You."

Ingrid sat up. "Really?"

"Let's just see, shall we? Now," she swatted a bee from in front of her face, "you better tell me what was in those photos."

Ingrid jangled with nerves. He was probably after the bike. Maybe he was the scout and the guy with the refrigerated van would pull up shortly. Motorcycle thieves always used refrigerated vans as the insulation isolated the GPS trackers from surveillance.

"The photos," McKittrick prompted.

Ingrid told her about the skylark and the starling, the Post-its and the birthday cake, but left out any mention of Mulroony and the fact she'd found the camera in the ceiling void.

"Is this some promotion assignment?" Natasha asked. "Is this how the FBI works out who should get a corner office these days?"

A pastel-colored Fiat 500 turned onto West Park. Both women watched as is slowed and searched for a parking space.

"And you really don't know who's set you this little challenge?"

Ingrid grunted in the negative.

"It sounds like you're in an episode of the Nancy Drew Mysteries," McKittrick said. "Or whatever that show was called. You'd think I'd remember, given it was almost entirely responsible for me wanting to become a detective." She glanced down at her phone to check it was still recording. "And this roll of film was just left on your desk?"

"Pretty much," Ingrid lied.

"You think it's a really elaborate treasure hunt and at the end of it is Ralph Mills holding a diamond engagement ring?"

Ingrid couldn't be bothered to repeat that he was married, and happily so. It wasn't even worth mentioning that her romantic feelings for Ralph hadn't registered on the Richter scale for a very long time. "I don't know where it's leading," Ingrid said. "But I'm intrigued enough to follow."

A woman in her thirties got out of the Fiat, beeped it locked, and walked briskly toward number thirty-six. She reached into her shoulder bag and pulled something out. Keys, most likely. Ingrid wished she had binoculars, but they weren't the sort of thing you took to the park if you wanted to look like a regular sunbather.

"You think this might be O'Shaughnessy?" Natasha asked.

Ingrid was concentrating too hard to reply. The woman kept her head down, adjusting the strap of her bag as she walked. She glanced up at number thirty-six, then walked straight past it, opening the gate of the neighboring house before putting a key in its front door.

"Disappointing," McKittrick said, picking up her phone. She tapped the screen a few times, then pressed play on the footage she'd just recorded. "Want to look at this with me?" She held it out for Ingrid to see, and Ingrid kept switching her gaze between the phone and the house, not really concentrating on either.

"Well, honey, I'd say you've got a fan. Or perhaps a stalker."

Ingrid glanced at McKittrick. "Really?"

McKittrick picked at something in her teeth with her

tongue. "What gives, Nancy Drew? Should I be calling 9-9-9?"

Ingrid snatched the phone, zoomed in, and studied the man in the car. "I've got absolutely no idea who he is."

"You and I both know that doesn't mean you don't know why he's here."

"Well, it must be the bike, mustn't it?"

"He can keep an eye on your precious steed sitting on a park bench," McKittrick said. "There's a reason he's sweating inside a tin can on a day like today."

Ingrid knew she was right. She scrambled to her feet and handed the sarong back to McKittrick. She picked up her helmet. "Watch the house for me."

"Sod that, I'll be keeping my eye on you." She gestured with her phone. "And my finger will be hovering over the nine."

Ingrid strode across the scrubby park, gripping the chin guard of her helmet, ready to swing it at the man's jaw. She pulled her phone out of her pocket and called Zeke on speed dial. She got his recorded message. "Zeke, it's me. The moment you get a chance can you run a check on a black Nissan Qashqai, license plate GA07 PPL. Call me right back." She didn't miss a step as she slid the phone into her back pocket and approached the edge of the park. She jumped over the low wooden fence and walked straight to her Ducati. She ran a protective hand over its curves, then carried on toward the Nissan. The driver was white, male, zipped up tee, forties. Retro rockabilly hairstyle. She was close enough now to see his eyes were wide. He fumbled with the ignition. Ingrid picked up speed, crossing the road in three strides. She tapped on the passenger window. The motor thrummed into life. He glanced in the rearview mirror, refusing to look at her, and turned the wheel. The hot tires squeaked on the melting blacktop. Ingrid jumped back as he pulled away, but not before she saw what was on the passenger seat.

A photo of her. One she was very familiar with. It was the same image used on her security pass at the embassy.

20

Ingrid arrived back at the embassy, desperate for the air conditioning in her office. She mentally abandoned thoughts of an evening run—way too hot—and instead planned on doing fifty laps of the Hilton pool.

"Oh, hello." Ingrid pulled up at the sight of a forty-something woman sitting at Jen's old desk. She dumped her bike gear in her locker. "You don't look like Zeke."

The woman stood up. She had broad features that hinted at a native American heritage and there was something of the grade school teacher about her. Homely. Ingrid imagined her baking on the weekends and reading Daisy Steiner books in the evenings. "Libby Greenwood." She extended a hand. "Your new assistant."

"What happened to Zeke?" She shook Libby's hand.

"Ezekiel? I believe HR said there was an issue with his work permit."

"Really?" Ingrid couldn't believe she'd lost another assistant. She'd really liked Zeke. At least it hadn't been anything to do with his epilepsy. She tugged at the damp fabric of her tee, suddenly feeling red-faced and sweaty. "Sorry, I'm not making a good first impression, am I? It's too hot to wear anything more under the leathers."

Libby looked at her like she'd just crawled out of a swamp.

"I have a change of clothes in my locker." Ingrid pulled out a shirt and a pair of slacks. "I'm Ingrid, by the way. But you probably already know that." She emptied her pockets and placed her phone and wallet on the desk. "That sounds like a Boston accent."

"You are correct."

"With those vowels, I'm guessing you can't have been in the UK all that long."

Libby looked at the clock on the wall. "About sixteen hours."

Ingrid nodded at Libby's computer. "And you already have access to the system?"

"Correct. HR gave me a sign in."

"Did you also get the tour of the building?"

"No, ma'am."

Ingrid bristled. "Just call me Ingrid. We can arrange a tour for later in the week. Have we met before?" Ingrid yanked off her tee and quickly threw on the shirt.

"I don't think our paths have crossed." Libby perched on the edge of her desk.

"I thought we might have worked together before." Ingrid slipped out of her shorts behind the privacy of her desk. "You're slightly familiar. You work in Cleveland?"

"No, just Burlington, then Boston. Then DC."

"Ah, that's probably where I've seen you. I spent four years in DC." Ingrid zipped up her pants. She decided to stay barefoot to let her feet cool down.

"Which squad?" Libby asked.

"VCAC."

Libby winced. "That must have been tough."

Ingrid pressed the start button on her computer. "It was. I think four years is the limit for most agents working violent crimes against children."

Having taken Zeke through the role already, Ingrid didn't much relish the prospect of inducting another assistant into the labyrinthine ways of the Criminal Division. "Listen, I'm really sorry, but I flat out don't have time to take you through everything right now. I have an appointment I just can't miss." She scanned her emails and instantly saw three things that demanded immediate replies. Even they would have to wait. "Can you do something for me?"

"That's what I'm here for."

"I left a message on Zeke's phone, yours now, I guess, about an hour ago. A request for a license plate. Can you look into that for me?"

"Sure." Libby looked at the phone and its complicated console of lights and colored buttons.

Ingrid saw her confusion.

"Press the orange button then, when you hear the tone, dial eight for the messages. Then you'll need a code." Ingrid thought for a second. She'd only been through this a week ago. They chose Zeke's starting date. "Zero-seven-one-one. Then it's the regular one to repeat, two to save, three to delete."

Libby picked up the receiver while Ingrid gathered together her notebook, Dictaphone, pens and anything else she might conceivably need for her meeting.

"Oh, shoot."

Ingrid turned sharply, her eyes wide. Libby was pressing buttons on the phone's keypad. Dread rippled over Ingrid's skin.

"I'm so sorry," Libby said. "I know you said one to repeat but I must have fat fingers." She held the phone to her chest. "I can't believe I did that."

"You deleted the message?"

Libby closed her eyes slowly and kept them closed. "Yes, ma'am. Now I'm the one not making a good impression. Can I call IT? Can they recover it?"

"You can try." Ingrid tried to remember what she could about the Nissan. She really needed to get going. "If they can't, call the Met—"

"The opera?"

"The Metropolitan Police."

"Ah."

Ingrid scurried over to Libby's desk. "Somewhere here are the codes you need." She scanned the documents in a neat stack in one corner. "I think this is it." She handed Libby a laminated sheet. "You ask for the ANPR team–"

"ANPR?"

Ingrid felt herself getting wound up. She didn't have time for this. "Automatic number plate recognition. They're number plates here, not license plates."

"Okay."

"You'll be asked for one of these authorization codes."

"Uh-huh."

"And ask them to trace a black Nissan Qashqai—"

"How are you spelling that?"

"Google it."

"Okay." Libby sounded defensive; Ingrid realized she was getting snappy.

"License plate—"

"Number plate." Libby smiled.

"Number plate ends with PPL, I remember that, on or around West Park, E16 about an hour ago." Ingrid inhaled deeply. "Think of it as a little test."

"What's 'E16'?"

"A zip code. The Brits call them postcodes."

"I have a lot to learn."

Ingrid scooted back to her own desk and picked up the copy of the *Evening News* Zeke had gotten hold of. "I've got another little task for you."

"Name it."

"There's an article in here," Ingrid thrust the newspaper at Libby, "about a party at a nightclub called Mojito Joes."

Libby saw the paper was five years old, and drew her lips into a tight circle.

"Can you find out everything you can about the club, who owns it, who goes there, and then compile a report on everyone the article mentions attended that event." Ingrid checked she had everything she needed in her shoulder bag and then slipped her feet into the shoes under her desk.

"Anything in particular you're interested in?"

Ingrid slung her bag over her shoulder. "Hmm. Yes, actually. See if anyone's got any ties to Russia."

Libby smiled at her. "You need me to log this on the system? Tie it to an investigation? Or a case file?"

"Oh, wow, that would be very efficient." Ingrid was a little taken aback. She checked her phone—still no reply from Sol—then placed it in her bag. "But, um, no. Just email it to me. It's background," Ingrid said. "I'll get in early tomorrow, walk you through everything."

Ingrid checked her watch. If she could hail a cab right

outside, she had a few minutes to spare before her meeting with Andy Scott MP, the Secretary of State for Justice. It was normally a position held by an MP who was also a qualified lawyer, but he was the first former police officer appointed to the role. She now had so much more to ask him about Mulroony than when she'd made the appointment, she wasn't quite sure where to start. He had made it clear he could only give her ten minutes. In her experience, that was enough time to get answers to two questions. She had the cab ride to figure out which two.

Ingrid glanced up at the TV monitors hanging from the ceiling above the bullpen desks, her eye drawn to the feed from KEIS. The Minnesota channel was making a lot of money on the James Jones trial. She pitied the reporter who had to do live feeds to multiple news outlets every hour, especially when the court wasn't even in session and there was nothing new to report. But on the off chance he had something new to say, Ingrid lingered for a moment until she decided to visit the restroom before she left. As she turned, she saw Agent Munsden walking toward her. She did the mental arithmetic. If it was a quick conversation, and if the taxi driver knew the way, she would still make her meeting.

"Sir?"

Munsden smiled at her. "Skyberg."

"You got two minutes?"

Never one for unnecessary words, Munsden opened up a palm and indicated they should step to one side. Ingrid, suddenly nervous, realized she didn't know what she was about to say.

Peter Munsden was in his last job before retirement. His average height and unremarkable face made him the worst sort of human to place under surveillance. He blended in to every crowd. However, the very characteristics that made him so bland had also made him one of the bureau's best undercover agents. He was a chameleon who didn't look out of place in the royal box at Wimbledon, or on a construction site, and he had a reputation as a diligent and determined agent.

"I have found something that may relate to the work of my predecessor, Dennis Mulroony."

His features didn't move. Everyone else pulled a face at the mention of Voldemort's name. Either Munsden had the best poker face in history, or he'd never heard of Mulroony. He said nothing.

Ingrid searched for the right words. "I may have evidence that relates to his activities." Ingrid was trying to be discrete in such a public space.

"Okay." Munsden's tone suggested he didn't understand why she was telling him this information.

"Sir, do you know who Dennis Mulroony was?"

"Can't say I ever heard of the fella."

Ingrid sighed. "Sir, can we speak privately?"

"I'm on my way to a meeting. Is this not something for DeWalt?"

Maybe it was. At least DeWalt had heard of Mulroony. "Sure," Ingrid said. Her posture softened. She could almost physically feel the opportunity slipping from her grasp. "Sorry to have taken up your time."

Ingrid dug her fingernails into her palms and silently howled. *Could that have gone any worse?* She checked the clock. There was no time to visit the restroom. She saw the elevator doors were open so she ran down the corridor.

"Damn." They closed just as she reached them, so she turned for the stairs. The ding of the second car arriving made her turn back, and she jumped inside.

"Off anywhere exciting?" DeWalt asked, striding into the elevator behind her. He had an iPad in one hand and straightened his tie with the other in the polished steel plate housing the call buttons.

"Ministry of Justice," she said. "You look smart. Who are you meeting?"

"The deputy ambassador. You must have done this plenty of times when you covered this job." He glanced at her. "Sorry. That sounded snarky, like I got the job and you didn't. I didn't mean it that way." He pressed for the sixth floor.

"I hadn't noticed." She had, but she believed he hadn't meant any offense. DeWalt wasn't that kind of guy. "You're going up?"

DeWalt pressed six again, then ground. "Sorry. You're in a rush, aren't you?"

The car lurched upward, then stopped.

"Please tell me…" Ingrid couldn't even bring herself to finish her sentence.

DeWalt pressed the six button again. Nothing happened. "Do you think we're stuck?" he asked.

"I really need to get to my meeting. It was the only window he had." A circle of heat bloomed around her neck. "Can I?" Ingrid jabbed the button for the lobby. Several times. Then she pressed the alarm button. "What's supposed to happen when you press this?"

DeWalt's face rumpled. "I, er, I don't know. I've never had to use it. You think a light flashes on the reception desk? Or in the maintenance department?"

Ingrid pulled her phone out of her bag.

"That won't work in here," DeWalt said. "At least mine never has. Something to do with them being iron cages."

"Really?"

"That's what someone told me. Apparently it's common with buildings this old."

She checked her phone. He was right. No service. "So, what? We just wait?" Ingrid ran a hand through her hair. Her scalp was already damp with sweat. "And we can't even get a message out?"

DeWalt leaned heavily against the metal wall. "It took them four hours to rescue people last Tuesday."

"You are kidding?" There was no disguising the alarm in her voice.

"Surely you can rearrange?"

"He said it was the only slot. It's Andy Scott, the Secretary of State. He's off to some intergalactic pow wow of justice ministers in two hours."

"I remember Andy," DeWalt said. "Worked with him off and on when he was doing counter-terrorism at the Met. What are you talking to him about?"

Ingrid saw him mentally scroll through the caseload he knew she had. Was now the time to level with him about Mulroony, even though Sol had expressly urged her not to? "It's an old case," she said, vaguely. "Scott used to be the Met's point man for my division."

"What's the case?"

She pictured Sol's face and changed the subject. "Do you think the A/C has stopped working?"

"It certainly feels a little hot in here."

Ingrid checked her bag. No bottle of water. Probably no bad thing, given the fullness of her bladder. "Four hours? Really?" She pressed the alarm button again. "Should we bang on the walls?"

"I guess it wouldn't hurt."

They both pummeled the stainless-steel walls with

their fists, hoping to attract some attention. "People will have noticed the car isn't moving, right?" Ingrid said.

"I hope so. I mean, I guess so."

"Someone will call maintenance, right?"

"Unless they just take the stairs and assume someone else will make the call."

Ingrid checked her phone again. Still no service. "Any word on how long before we move to the new building?"

DeWalt untucked his shirt. "Last I heard, it wasn't good news."

She gestured for him to continue.

"Not before Christmas."

Ingrid's eyes popped. "So, the State Department has *two* buildings in London that don't work properly?"

"And both are worth hundreds of millions of dollars."

Ingrid slumped against the wall. "Sometimes I swear it's like we work for the Federal Bureau of Investigation in…" She reached for a suitably impoverished country. "Malawi. Imagine having to tell a grieving relative that you didn't arrest their son's killer because you got stuck in an elevator?" She needed to calm down. There was nothing she could do about it. If help came soon, she might still catch Andy Scott. She could rush to the airport, speak to him in the departure lounge. On the runway if necessary. "At least the deputy ambassador will work out what happened to you."

"That's what's worrying me," DeWalt said, a sheepish expression on his face. "I mean, it's only one flight of stairs. It's kind of embarrassing I took the easy route."

He had a point.

"If this were a movie," Ingrid said, "you'd give me a leg up, I'd push up the escape hatch and then shinny up the cable."

They both looked up at the access hatch in the ceiling.

"If this was a movie," DeWalt said, "the cable would be severed and we'd be about to plunge to our deaths."

Ingrid managed a smile. "So, what you're saying is it could be worse?"

"Way worse. We could be stuck in here with Mitch. You know, the maintenance guy?"

"The really big guy?"

"You mean the real *stinky* guy, right? Don't say you haven't noticed. His odor is so heavy you can see it trailing after him, like Pigpen."

Ingrid turned her head sharply. "You hear that?" A clanging sound echoed up from somewhere deep below. "You think that's maintenance?"

DeWalt slid down the wall and sat on the ground. "Or the cable fraying. I'm just glad neither of us are claustrophobic."

"You know, if this car had arrived five seconds later, I'd have been on the stairs. I'd be hailing a taxi right now."

"Not taking the bike?"

Ingrid resisted making a comment along the lines of 'can you see a helmet?'

"I heard you ride a Ducati these days."

Ingrid's brain flashed back to West Park and the man in the car. The man with her embassy ID photo on the passenger seat. The muscles at the base of her skull tightened. "You did, huh? Who told you that?"

"Little Mo," he had answered quickly. "You know, from the Agency? I think he's been eyeing your ride in the parking lot."

"His feet wouldn't touch the pedals." Ingrid stared at DeWalt's ID card, nestled in a fold of his untucked shirt and resting on his belly. Someone had accessed the embassy's security system to get the photo of her. That meant someone in the building was surveilling her. She thought back to the file that disappeared from the system, the file someone had left as a warning signal to alert them when someone approached their territory. She needed to say something. "Do you remember an agent who used to work here called Dennis Mulroony?"

"Oh Denny Boy? Sure." He made very deliberate eye contact, unnerving Ingrid. "Why are you asking?"

"I think I may have found something. Something that relates to his activities." She'd used that word again. Activities. It was both bland and sinister.

DeWalt's expression didn't change, but his breaths became more rapid. She looked at his security pass, then back up at his face. His mouth was now slightly open. Did he know? Ingrid felt the sweat pool inside her bra. *Does he know?*

"Activities?" he asked.

Sol's warning was now ringing loudly in her ears. She needed to backtrack. "You worked with him, so you'll know more than me." Ingrid kept her face neutral. "I get the impression he left under a cloud."

His nostrils flared briefly. "He certainly left fast."

"Something to do with the ambassador's daughter? At least that's what I heard."

DeWalt paused before answering. "Yeah. Sounds about right."

"You got any way of contacting him?"

"You tried HR?"

"Not yet."

DeWalt shifted to make himself more comfortable. "Shall we use our time wisely? You want to update me on the Tilbury case?"

Ingrid listened to the neighboring elevator clatter down its shaft. "Sure, makes sense." She joined him on the floor and told him about the training drill at Gravesend and how it had gone wrong. "If it had been the real thing, four people would be dead, an officer shot in the chest and one of the smugglers would be on the run." She didn't say that she had played the part of the fence-jumping escapee. "The NCA is requesting aerial support and additional manpower."

"But the boat is still coming our way?"

Ingrid rolled her eyes to the ceiling as she counted. "Three days. Currently approaching Irish waters. The important thing is I have the extradition paperwork, and as soon as the NCA concludes things here, the DEA can arrest the guys in Miami."

"You worried?"

"A little. The danger with an operation like this is that something leaks. There are so many agencies involved." She scrutinized him closely. "I mean, even you probably know enough to say something to someone."

He nodded. "There are cops all over the world taking bribes from OCGs," he said, almost wistfully.

"Thanks. That really helps." A bead of sweat dribbled from her hairline. She really wished she'd visited the bathroom. "The DEA will get their scalp, and I'll get a day out playing SWAT."

"You get to be Starling."

Her breath stalled. She pictured the photo of the bird. "What did you say?"

"You get to be Clarice Starling." He smiled. "Isn't that why you joined? It's usually either her or Dana Scully for most of the female agents I know."

Ingrid's heart stuttered. Was he testing her? First, he

mentions the Ducati, then he drops Starling into the conversation. She swallowed to moisten her throat.

"Did you feel that?" DeWalt stiffened at the sound of banging. "I think they definitely know we're stuck. I ever tell you I spent four months in the OPR?"

"You did internal affairs? I wouldn't have picked it. But guess that's why you know about cops taking bribes."

"Exactly. You'll never guess how we caught one agent," he said, glee spreading across his face. "He was taking payments from one of the Mexican cartels and he only went and left a goddamn note!"

Ingrid lifted her gaze from his name badge. She couldn't stop looking at it. "For real?"

"Yep."

"What kind of note?"

"He figured he was being real clever. It was all in code. Cryptic, you know? But what he'd actually done was leave a nice trail for us saying which drops he'd let happen, how much he estimated the street value was worth, and what percentage he thought he should get. It was like he was asking for a pay rise, diligently outlining his skills and accomplishments for his boss."

Ingrid let it sink in. Then her heart started beating a little harder. "What kind of code?"

"We're not talking 128-bit encryption. More school-yard substitutions. He never could quite get over the fact that he had prepared all this data for one set of eyes, hidden it real careful, but it got seen by someone else entirely."

Ingrid didn't hear much more of what her boss said for the next few minutes. Something about ice cream, as best she could tell. She was too intent on imagining Mulroony as he carefully photographed his treasure map, never knowing that it would be her who found his clues. But he had taken those photos for someone. Who?

The fact he was in the Black Dolphin prison meant they couldn't have been for the Kremlin. He certainly hadn't had her in mind, but maybe, she thought as DeWalt droned on about the merits of Ben & Jerry's over Häagen Dazs, they were for someone *like* her?

"You're really not listening, are you?" DeWalt said.

"Sorry, no. What did you say?"

"I think the noises have stopped." He stretched his meaty legs and flexed his feet. "We might be here a while." He waggled his iPad at her. "Suppose I better catch up on some reading. Got at least a dozen reports on here."

Ingrid shook her head, desperate to retrieve her train of thought. Someone *like* her. Why would Mulroony need someone like her? She wrestled her unwieldy thoughts and attempted to order them into a semblance of logic. She tried to picture each of the photos. The house in the suburbs, the arrows scrawled on a notebook, Stephen Hawking, the article about Mojito Joe's, Steiner's book, the birds, the fake birthday cake, the map of Scotland, the Post-its. Why did Mulroony need someone like her, someone who worked in the embassy, someone who was most likely an FBI agent, to see those images?

Ingrid's innards hollowed out as one piece of the puzzle slotted into place: there was someone in the building he couldn't trust, someone who probably worked for the bureau. *That's* why he couldn't leave a digital trace.

"What was that?" DeWalt said.

"Pardon?"

"You said something."

"Did I?"

"Kind of a gasp."

Ingrid's cheeks were flaming hot. She probably had gasped: Mulroony knew he couldn't leave a trace because he was being framed. He wasn't the spy, but he was being framed by whoever was.

And if Mulroony wasn't Skylark, then Skylark was still active.

21

It was just after eight at night when Ingrid and DeWalt were finally freed. The first thing both of them did after six hours of captivity was rush to the bathroom. They then bumped into each other on the way to the watercooler where they both filled paper cups.

"So, you want to grab that Rocky Road?" DeWalt wiped his wet hands on his pants. His face glistened from a splash of cold water.

"Hey, no. No thanks," Ingrid said, hooking a piece of dampened hair behind her ear. She drained her cup and bent down to refill it. "I better get on with a few things here."

"Don't forget to go home," he said, and headed for the stairs. Most of their co-workers had already left. A few voices on urgent phone calls drifted out of the CT and CI rooms, and at the far end of the bullpen, two assistants attacked their keyboards like they were manual typewriters. The warm, sunny evening had tempted everyone else away from their work.

The prospect of another night of room service and

cable TV made Ingrid even keener to slip into her office. Before entering, she glanced up at the muted TV screens above the empty bullpen desks. Only one was covering the Jones trial, and it was showing an anatomical sketch of the hyoid bone, which looked like a cross between a seahorse and a horseshoe. McKittrick wasn't the only person speculating about the forensics bombshell from the eccentric Dr. Mikkelson. Ingrid pulled her phone out of her pocket. Six missed calls. Four from Svetlana.

The air conditioning in her office turned her sweat-drenched shirt to ice. She shivered as she sat down at her desk. Instinctively, she moved her mouse and her computer flickered into life. Without thinking, she logged on. Seventy-one emails. Not so bad. She scanned the list for priorities, but her eyes couldn't focus. Her brain knew there was something else she should be doing. She listened to her messages. The first two were from Andy Scott's PA, then she steeled herself for the onslaught from Minnesota. "*Kroshka,* you must call me." "*Kroshka,* I mean it. Kathleen needs to speak with you." "Ingrid Anna Skyberg you call me right back, you hear?" "I email. I message. I am your mother. You don't ignore me. It's important, *Kroshka*. Call me."

Ingrid let out a deep, mournful sigh. "Mom, you're going to have to wait." The emails. The calls. Everything. They would all have to wait. Skylark was still active, and the best clues she had to his real identity were Mulroony's photographs. Ingrid leaned forward for her penholder and tipped out the contents to retrieve the key to her drawers. Her fingers pushed aside the fluff-encrusted paperclips, sticky cough drops and tangle of rubber bands. She rolled the leaking pens and broken pencils back and forth. Where the hell was the key?

Her mouth suddenly dry, Ingrid glanced over at Libby's desk. Had her new assistant taken it? Ingrid's heart thudded hard against her ribs. The pens slipped under her sweaty fingertips as she rolled them one way, then the other. She tipped the container upside down again and checked it was empty. She closed her eyes and swallowed. Ingrid tried the drawer where she kept the photos. She yanked hard, but it was locked. Heat coiled around her neck and crept up into her jaw. Desperate, she scanned her desk, looking for anything she could pry the drawer with. She checked her motorcycle gear for something that could act as a lever. She spied a pair of scissors on Libby's desk and grabbed them. When she returned to her own desk, she saw it.

"*Govno*!"

She exhaled so hard she bent forward. The key had been there all along, stuck to the underside of a fluorescent highlighter pen by the residue from an out-of-date cough drop. Feeling stupid, she slumped down hard into her chair and picked up the key. She stared at it and breathed heavily. She thought about keeping it on a chain around her neck.

She fumbled the key into the lock and slid open the drawer. She closed her eyes in gratitude when she saw the bright green and yellow packet of photographs. Ingrid checked the open office door, then got up to close it. She did not want to be disturbed. She spread out the images on Libby's immaculate desk. The photos were no longer in the order they had been taken, so she started to group them in a way that made sense.

The fake birthday photos were laid out together. Then she placed the map of Scotland, the Post-it note photograph, and the Street View image together on the basis that they shared a geographical theme. She didn't know if they really were connected. The Amazon listing for *National Affront* was slotted in next to the photo of Stephen Hawking. She then placed the photos of the notepad—the arrows, the word 'sois'—in a row with the Post-its. She couldn't link the article on Mojito Joe's, the appointments diary, the case file number, the starling or the Google image search for a yard, so she placed them randomly around the other images. She held the photo of the bird she now knew was a skylark, and tucked it in next to the image of *National Affront*.

She ran both hands through her hair and stared at the images. Her jaw twitched.

"Okay," she said out loud. She moved the photo of David Steiner's book, Stephen Hawking and the skylark to one side, as she was confident she knew why Mulroony had included them. Steiner knew Skylark's identity and had been about to testify at the Hawking Review. As the Review had been into the mishandling of the Met's investigation of the murder of the Russian dissident Dimitri Andropov, Ingrid scanned the rest of the photos for another link to Andropov. Or to anything relating to Russia.

She puffed out her cheeks and emptied her lungs in a deliberate attempt to slow her breathing. She was too tense to think straight. What she wanted was a beer, something to loosen her up and calm her down. She wasn't even going to open the door until she'd made progress, so getting a drink was out of the question.

Ingrid paced the office, circling Libby's desk to look at the images from every angle. Her eyes rested on the word sois. Her French was a little rusty—she had been fluent once—but she knew it was a conjugation of être, the verb to be. "Que je sois," she said out loud. *That I am.* Why the hell would Dennis Mulroony write out a random French verb? She kept walking, and on one circuit of the room she spotted the thick, heavy copy of the Hawking Review that Sherbourne had given her. Zeke's summary was tucked inside the cover. She scanned it quickly, reminding herself that Skylark was a Russian asset with ties to an organization called England for the English.

Ingrid held Zeke's summation in her hand and looked again at the photos. Was there anything else that indicated the Far Right? Her eyes focused on the map of Scotland. She'd lived in the UK long enough never to conflate or confuse the Scottish and English identities. Was there a Scottish far right group she needed to know about? She shook her head, attempting to forge a connection between the images.

Her restless hands flipped through the meaty Hawking report while her brain lasered in on the photos. It took her a while to make the connection between what her hands had found and what her eyes had seen. She looked down at the report, and then at the array of photographs.

"Oh, wow."

Her fingers were so sweaty it took several attempts to pick up the photo of the suburban house, but when she placed it on top of the open page of the Hawking Review she saw it was a perfect match. The Street View screenshot was of the house where Andropov had lived. He had been the spy next door, an unassuming man in an unassuming house. When she'd read that he'd been killed in a sauna, she had pictured an exclusive country club with a member list of the rich and powerful. She'd somehow forgotten that he was a former KGB agent and that not every Russian in London was a billionaire. She pushed the photo of the house next to Stephen Hawking, then promptly let out a sigh. Nice as it was to make a connection to another photo, finding out the suburban house was Andropov's home didn't appear to move the needle on Skylark's identity. Maybe her theory about the photos was wrong?

Ingrid wandered back to her own desk and looked again at her unread emails. There were now seventy-nine of them. She scrolled her mouse and clicked on the one from Libby. She had compiled the list of people who had attended the gala event at Mojito Joe's. Based on reports from other newspapers and gossip magazines, Libby had come up with a list of twenty-three named attendees, mostly a meaningless tally of British TV celebrities and international businessmen with wealth and influence. The names that stood out were Karlos and Serena Ivanov, the owner of the *Evening News* and his wife. According to Libby's research, the nightclub was a venture of their playboy son, Alexei. It explained why the newspaper had written about the event, but not why Mulroony had photographed it. Tomorrow she would ask Libby for more than just the names of the people at the gala. She wanted their full biographies, who they worked for, who they socialized with, who they had dirt on.

Ingrid returned to Libby's desk and placed her forefinger on the photo of the newspaper article. She moved it in small circles, like an attendee of a séance might move the upturned glass. Did it belong with the collection images that related to the Hawking Review? The Russian connection was enough. She pushed it over to join the growing cluster.

Her cell rang on her desk, making her jump. Her hand jerked, flicking a photo away from its allocated position, as she scooted over to her desk. She looked at the phone. A

Minnesota number, but not Svetlana's. Maybe her mom was at Kathleen's? Ingrid mentally calculated the time difference and swiped to take the call.

"Mom? Is that you?"

All she could hear was transatlantic static. "May I speak with Miss Ingrid Skyberg please?"

Miss? Ingrid's blood turned to ice. Was her mom in the ER? "This is Special Agent Ingrid Skyberg." Her voice cracked as she spoke. "Who is this?"

"Good afternoon. My name is Xander J. Carroll. I work for Leander and Spicer in Minneapolis."

Ingrid held her breath as she waited for him to explain why he was calling.

"I am working with James Jones's team in Jackson."

Ingrid placed a hand on the back of her chair for support. She felt like she might collapse.

"Miss Skyberg, would you be willing to testify?"

Ingrid still hadn't recovered from the thought her mom was in danger. "I, er—" she struggled to find the words. "I mean… You're not from the DA's office?"

"No, Miss. Leander and Spice are defending Mr. Jones."

Ingrid's thoughts slammed into a brick wall. "I, ah, I." She thumped the chair.

"Miss, did you hear me? I am calling to ask if you would be willing to testify."

Ingrid's vision blurred. The room softened at the edges. She needed the chair to steady herself. "I can't," she managed. "I mean, I *couldn't*. I could never look my mom in the eye. I could never look at Kathleen Avery without dissolving into a pool of…" Ingrid's jaw hung loose. "I… I can't be a witness for the defense. I could never go home."

Carroll didn't miss a beat. "Miss, I appreciate you were not expecting me to call—"

"I thought the DA might. But I never for one second thought the defense would. I mean, why would you?" She knew damn well why. The same reason the prosecution hadn't listed her to testify. It was dark. It was a long time ago. She was young. If the prosecution can make an FBI agent sound unsure about what she'd seen, it was a damn good way to create reasonable doubt in the jury's mind. "No, no I won't do it."

"Miss, you are an FBI agent. You spend your life in the pursuit of justice." He sounded like he was smiling. "James Jones deserves your service as much as any other citizen."

"He killed twelve women!"

"Miss, as I am sure you are aware, he has only admitted to nine counts of murder."

Ingrid's hand was shaking. "He killed my best friend."

"He denies the murder of Megan Avery."

Ingrid breathed heavily, audibly. She knew what would happen next. She understood the legal process, but she wasn't going to make it easy for him. "My answer is no."

"Miss, you will be aware that you will be subpoenaed and you will be obligated to testify." Xander Carroll had a laid-back Southern lilt to his voice, like a New Orleans bartender.

At least he had credited her with knowing the law. "I'm not in Minnesota. I'm not even in the States." She thought of the months of planning for the Tilbury drugs bust. "I can't just drop everything and cross the Atlantic."

"We can swear you in via video link, that is not a problem." Ingrid could picture the smirk on his face.

"You will have to list me as a hostile witness."

"We are aware of that, Miss." She did not like being called 'miss', ergo she did not like Xander Carroll with the pretentious middle initial.

Ingrid's lower lip trembled. The floor beneath her feet softened. She felt it would not support her weight. Ingrid leaned forward over her chair. Her empty stomach convulsed.

"Do you still need me to subpoena you?"

Her nostrils flared. "Hell, yes. I won't talk unless you make me."

Ingrid dropped the phone onto her desk and when she saw that Xander J. Carroll had ended the call, she let out a small, soft howl. How could they do that to her? The cruelty of it slammed into her chest and made it hard to breathe. Megan's abduction was the most painful event in her life. Not only was the firm of Leander and Spicer trying to deny her the justice she needed—the justice she had craved and fought for—but they were going to use her own testimony to do it.

Ingrid paced the room. She knew she couldn't lie under oath, and she knew her testimony would not help secure James Jones' conviction. All the defense had to do was ask her, 'Was this the man you saw' and the seed of doubt would be sown. The words they would force her to say would inflict so much pain on Kathleen Avery that she may as well aim a gun at the woman's heart.

Ingrid's phone illuminated on her desk, but she didn't even bother to see if it was her mom. She knew she had to be the one to tell Svetlana she was being forced to testify, but she also knew she would never make her mom understand.

"Oh, God."

It dawned on Ingrid that her mom would see it as such

a betrayal she could even cut off contact. Svetlana wasn't known for her shades of gray or understanding of nuance. Even with the subpoena, she would expect Ingrid to remain silent on the stand, or to lie. Kathleen was not a well woman, and all her mom wanted was for Kathleen to live to see justice for Megan. Ingrid yearned for that too, so much so that her swollen heart pressed against her ribcage, making its anguish felt.

"Always better to rip off the Band-Aid," Ingrid said out loud. Delaying talking to Svetlana would only make the next few hours even more unbearable. She marched over to her phone and brushed against Libby's desk, sending several photos over the edge. She watched as they tumbled, then bent to pick them up.

"Oh." Ingrid shifted from the balls of her feet onto her knees. "Oh, my."

She stared at the photos for many seconds, her heart pulsing violently as she assessed what she was looking at. The phone continued to trill. The photo of the arrows on the notepad had overlapped one of the birthday cake photos. The three arrows clustered at one side of the notepad pointed to Jen and the other women holding the cake. The fourth, heavier, arrow at the other end of the pad, pointed to a figure in the background.

Shaking slightly as her phone kept demanding her attention, Ingrid picked up both photos and examined them more closely. Then she looked at the other birthday cake photos with the three women awkwardly positioned at the edge of the frame. She thought about what Jen had told her, how Mulroony had brought in the fake cake, only to take these bizarre images. The phone went to voicemail and Ingrid winced: not answering would only anger Svetlana further.

Inside the plastic photo wallet were the strips of negatives. With trembling fingers, Ingrid held them up to the light. She swallowed several times to lubricate her mouth. The photograph of the arrows came straight after the birthday cake snaps. It was as if Mulroony had captured the image he needed, and immediately sketched out the positions of the people in the photo. The reason he had taken three photos of the cake was because he was waiting for the right person to be in shot behind Jen and the other women.

Ingrid put the negatives down and inhaled hard. Her nose tingled and she pressed her lips together. After another deep breath, she walked over to the window and looked down at Grosvenor Square where coworkers and sweethearts gathered in groups on the grass. Her cell bleeped to tell her she had a new message. She realized she was shaking her head.

Was that really what Mulroony had intended?

She went back to Libby's desk and stared at the photos. The arrows lined up with the four figures almost perfectly. She was sure it wasn't a coincidence. She was certain Mulroony wanted anyone who saw these photos to look at the man in the background that the thicker arrowed pointed to. That man was Jacob DeWalt.

Was he Skylark? Had he framed Mulroony?

22

Ingrid couldn't stop checking her cell. She knew looking at it wouldn't make it ring, but Sol had promised he would call her back within the hour, and that was over ninety minutes ago.

She'd had no choice but to call him. She needed help, and if DeWalt was Skylark there was no one in the bureau she could trust. He had promised to make some calls and get back to her.

Ingrid also called her old buddy from Quantico, Mike Stiller. He'd moved from Washington, DC, to Washington State since they'd last spoken and now worked as a case agent in Seattle. That was fortunate, because it meant that although it was midnight in London, Mike would still be at his desk on the West Coast for another few hours. There was still plenty of time for him to come good on his promise of intel.

The TV on the wall of her hotel room silently showed a report about identical triplets getting identical grades. Ingrid's eyes glazed as she stared at the establishing shots of their high school, sending her mind in the direction of last time she'd looked at an image of a US school. She thought about Dennis Mulroony Snr and his lone kidney, and then about his wife who no longer took her Afghan hound to dog shows. What did they think had happened to their son?

She closed her eyes. She pictured the Black Dolphin prison, her mind swarming with visions of rats and fleas and cockroaches and excrement. And blood. It was a violent cesspit where murderers learned new skills from each other. Ingrid didn't know if Mulroony even spoke Russian. She could barely imagine the hell he had endured. It would be one thing to be in the Black Dolphin as a guilty man, but as someone who had been framed? She let out an involuntary gasp. The FBI was a family, and one of her brothers needed her. Acid swirled under her tongue. Her head nodded slowly. If DeWalt really had put him there, she was not only going to bring him to justice; she was going to punish him. She checked her cell again. Still nothing from Sol.

The phone on the nightstand rang. "Hello?"

"Good evening, this is Jerome on reception."

Hairs rose on the back of Ingrid's neck. "Yes?" Why the heck was reception calling her room at half past midnight?

"We have received a fax for you."

"A fax?" Had she time traveled to the nineties?

"I would like to bring it to your room, but the night shift is short staffed tonight."

"No, that's fine. I'll come down."

Ingrid pulled on some sweat pants and jogged down to the lobby. When she collected the sheaf of paper from the bemused Jerome, she smiled. She needn't have been nervous: the handwritten note on the cover sheet read Beachfront Properties available from June onwards. The fax was from Mike: he had spent the first ten minutes of their phone call telling her she should move to Seattle. On her way back to her room, she detoured to the ice machine to stock up on London's most in demand commodity.

In amongst the real estate details Mike had hastily printed off from the web were the documents she'd asked him to send over. Worried that her own searches might be monitored by DeWalt, she had delegated the task of pulling up DeWalt's personnel file to the ever-faithful Mike. As she propped herself up on her bed, Ingrid had to admit she was a little impressed with Mike's ingenuity. She couldn't remember the last time she had traced contact between two perps via fax, and the fact that he hadn't emailed the findings meant their communication was unlikely to be traced. It was building to building contact, not person to person. She made a mental note to look for fax links between suspects in all future investigations.

Ingrid scanned DeWalt's record, looking for any cases or any postings that hinted at a connection to Russia. His file showed that before joining the bureau, Jacob DeWalt had worked for AT&T designing automated call center systems. He was an electrical engineer by training and had joined the bureau at twenty-eight. He was married with two kids who were now twelve and fifteen and had a solid case to conviction ratio. No commendations or medals, but no warnings or reprimands either in his seventeen years of service. Ingrid suddenly understood why he had gotten the promotion to SSA: DeWalt was a diligent, hardworking, white, straight, middle-aged male who had never pissed anyone off. It was the magic formula for success in an organization like the Federal Bureau of Investigation.

The blandness of his resumé indicated one of two things. One, this all-American sitcom dad figure was the least likely man on the payroll to be a Russian asset. Or two, it was a genius cover for a spy who planned to rise high and go deep within the organization.

According to the files, DeWalt didn't speak Russian, or any other language apart from English, and he had never worked in any former Soviet territory. Nothing in his financial records showed unaccountable wealth, and the holidays his kids posted on Instagram were in the range of what an FBI agent on a GS-14 pay grade could afford. His passport had only been used to fly between the UK and the US for the past two years, and his personnel record in London didn't have any absences for illness or undeclared travel. The very fact that he had just been promoted suggested he had aced all his background checks. If he was a Russian asset, he was damn good at hiding it.

The only red flag—and if she was honest, it was more of a pale pink one—was that Ingrid couldn't find out much about his wife. She didn't appear to have any social media accounts, and the only images Ingrid found of her were in the background of her sons' Instagram photos. Mostly she was too far from the camera, or hiding behind her hands, for Ingrid to perform a reverse image search. The only thing she could surmise about Mrs. DeWalt was that she was Irish, or at least of Irish heritage, judging by the parties the boys attended every March on St. Patrick's Day. With a name like DeWalt—was that German? South African?—Ingrid was guessing the Celtic connection came from their mom.

Ingrid cracked open a small bottle of vodka from the minibar and took a pull. The sting of the liquor immediately brightened her eyes and suppressed the urge to sleep. She checked her phone in case a glitch meant Sol's call had gone straight to voicemail.

She returned her attention to the fax printout. The details of a five-bedroom property with a double garage and a home gym caught her eye. It was half the price of her budget for an apartment in London. Ingrid glanced around at her hotel room. Everything she owned didn't just fit into the 250 square feet of a Hilton mid-range room, it packed down to fit inside two suitcases. She didn't need a double garage, and she never would.

Enflamed by the vodka, Ingrid looked again at DeWalt's career history. After Quantico, he'd spent two years in San Diego, then Vermont, then St. Louis before transferring into the Legal Attaché Program where his easy-going personality was well suited to international cooperation. He'd spent a year in Ottawa before moving his family to London.

One of those locations was standing out, and she stared at the list to figure out why. *That's it.* In the elevator, DeWalt had gone on about ice cream and extolled the virtues of Ben & Jerry's over every other brand. Now she understood: his posting in Vermont had been to the Resident Agency in Burlington. The only thing Ingrid knew about the Vermont capital was that it was famous for being the home of Ben & Jerry's.

She dialed Mike in Seattle.

"At your service, ma'am," he said by way of a greeting.

"I have to tell you, Mike," Ingrid said, taking another sip of vodka, "I thought the fax was a genius move."

"Why, thank you. Wish I could tell you it was my own idea, but I have to say I kinda borrowed it."

"Please don't tell me a drug cartel has been sending faxes undetected for the past couple years."

"Make it a decade. They've been using copy shops to send orders from coast to coast. It was only when one copy shop couldn't get their fax machine repaired any longer that the whole thing crumbled."

Ingrid took a beat. "And we work for the finest criminal investigation organization in the world."

"No wonder so many crooks think the cops are dumb. Sometimes, we are just plain dunces. So, did that stuff I sent have what you need?"

Ingrid finished the bottle. "It was super helpful, thanks."

"But you need something else?"

"Something real quick. I don't want to log on to the embassy systems from here. Could you look one thing up for me?"

"Is there any point in me saying I'm too busy, or asking what I'm going to get in return?"

"Is there any point in me answering that?"

"Nope. What is it, Skyberg?"

Ingrid sat on the edge of the bed, her fingers drumming on the nightstand. "Can you look at the database for the RA in Burlington, Vermont?"

"Sure. What do you want to know?" Ingrid heard Mike's fingers stabbing his keyboard.

"How many agents work there. How many civilian staff."

Mike made a lame attempt at humming hold music. "Okay. Got it. Two agents. Nothing about civilians, but what do you reckon? An office manager, a couple of clerks?"

Ingrid's nostrils flared as she sucked in air. "Sounds about right. Thanks, Mike."

"What, that's it?"

"Uh-huh. That's all."

"How disappointingly straightforward."

"I can only apologize."

They said their goodbyes and Ingrid got to her feet. She pushed aside the net drapes and looked out at the black expanse of Hyde Park, hemmed in by the orange streetlights of the surrounding thoroughfares. Her breath misted briefly on the glass. She didn't even feel the need to check that DeWalt's posting to the tiny Burlington RA coincided with Libby's tenure in the same five-person office. She knew it did.

DeWalt had been the one who'd left that file on the system. He had set the trap, and as soon as he knew she was digging around into Mulroony's disappearance, he had installed his old contact from Burlington to spy on her. Ingrid shuddered: Libby's deletion of her voicemail about the license plate hadn't been accidental.

Ingrid looked at her phone. Sol still hadn't called.

23

Sunrise was at five thirty-eight. The high-rise Hilton cast a rectangular shadow over the greening expanse of the park. Overhead, the lights of descending passenger planes tracked west to Heathrow, crossing the milky sky at regular intervals. Ingrid blinked at the view. She had barely slept. But on the plus side, she had come up with a plan.

She opened the closet and pulled out her running gear. She had eight miles to figure out if her plan was any good. Ingrid secured the arm band that held her phone tight over her bicep, then stopped. If DeWalt was Skylark, *and* he knew she was onto him, the phone was a bad idea. She glanced over at her fitness tracker charging on the dressing table. That was probably a bad idea, too. She swiped a bottle of water from the minibar and slid a bank card and the rectangular plastic room key into the waist pocket of her running shorts.

A copy of that day's *Sun* newspaper was on the hallway floor. Ingrid hadn't ordered a paper, and if she had, it wouldn't be a tabloid filled with celebrities she didn't know and sports she didn't follow. She bent down to check which room really had requested it, and saw the handwritten note.

Tonight. Connaught bar. 9 p.m.

Whoever had written it had circled the word 'Sun' in several heavy rings of ink. Ingrid checked the corridor, made sure it was empty, then headed for the stairs. She left by the tradesman's exit and slipped into the back streets of Mayfair. When she came to a trash can a few blocks away, she ditched the newspaper, but not before taking one last look at the message.

With no phone and no watch, Ingrid had no music to accompany her run. Instead, she paid attention to the city as it yawned into life. Garbage trucks prowled the alleys as shutters were rolled up and doors unlocked. She ran east, past an almost empty Trafalgar Square, past the High Court toward St. Paul's cathedral, and then on to the Tower of London. For the first two miles, she checked behind her, making sure she wasn't being tailed. Satisfied the early start and the lack of a phone meant she was on her own, she powered on. When the fatigue entered her legs at the five-mile mark, she started smiling. Pushing her body, knowing it could still do what she asked of it, was an endorphin kick like no other. She was going to be in great shape when the *Laussat* docked in two days' time.

Ingrid wasn't entirely sure of her route, but an occasional glimpse of the river between the buildings reassured her she was heading in the right direction. When the corporate skyscrapers of Docklands loomed over the low-rise Victorian housing stock, she knew she only had another couple of miles to go.

By the time she reached the Royal Docks, it was six fifty-five. A coffee cart outside a Docklands Light Railway station had just opened up, and she stopped for a long black and a pain au chocolat. She walked the rest of the way to West Park, keen for her body to cool down before she took up residence on the dewy lawn.

Ingrid circumnavigated the small park as she sipped her coffee. The posters for Mason Stebbings were now a little sun-bleached, and it seemed they had multiplied either out of desperation or hope. Almost certainly the former: it was now four days since the lad had gone missing, and the odds weren't good for his safe return.

Ingrid walked slowly past number thirty-six. The drapes were still drawn at the upstairs bedroom window, but the light was on downstairs. The house occupants were just waking up. She hoped her timing would coincide with the school run.

During her restless night, Ingrid decided to assemble as much evidence as possible before accusing DeWalt of being Skylark. His blemish-free resumé and recent promotion meant she'd need concrete proof before she would get anyone in the bureau to listen. Her plan was to find a link between DeWalt and each of Mulroony's photographs. She was starting with the image of the three colored Post-its.

West Park was no bigger than a third of a football field. Along its southern edge was a road separating the grass from the dock, and on the other three sides were rows of almost identical houses clad in charred timber set at different distances back from the sidewalk. It looked almost haphazard, but their front gardens with raised planters burgeoning with big-leaved statement plants gave the houses a unified look. The gardens were so uniform they must have been planted by whoever built the properties. The whole place had a corporate but slightly hipsterish vibe, as if Starbucks designed homes.

The sun nudged above the roofline and thrust its first morning rays onto the far corner of the park. Ingrid's sweat-cooled skin needed the heat: it might be an hour or two before anyone emerged from number thirty-six. To avoid suspicion, and getting cold, Ingrid started a body-weight workout in the growing triangle of sunshine. Tricep curls against a wooden bench, chin-ups using the branch of a cherry tree, bunny jumps over the low perimeter fence. She was on her fourth repetition of reverse angle press ups when she sensed movement at number thirty-six.

The front door opened inward. Whoever was leaving was obscured by the dramatic shrubbery. She waited, arms straight in a plank position, for them to take the handful of steps to the sidewalk.

A mixed-race male. Thirties. Six feet or thereabouts. Suit. A bounce in his step.

Ingrid's eyes widened, then she looked down at the grass to hide her face. She was so shocked she couldn't maintain the plank. Her elbows buckled and she collapsed onto the lawn. She craned her neck to make sure.

It was definitely him.

What the hell was Sam Sherbourne doing there?

Ingrid took her time getting back to the Hilton. She lingered in West Park for another hour and watched as two teenage boys left for school and a woman she presumed was their mother jump in a Tesla and drive off in the direction of the city. Then she picked up another coffee from the same vendor and started walking back toward Central London. When the roads snarled into a busy intersection that resembled spilled spaghetti, she flagged down a black cab.

She stared out of the window at the blur of streets, computing the significance of Sherbourne's departure from number thirty-six. Ingrid was sure Sherbourne had said he had a young baby. She could almost visualize the photo of the little boy in a frame on his desk. Hadn't he even said something the other day about the baby having had a bad night? She was damn sure that when the final occupant had left thirty-six West Park earlier that morning, a baby had not been abandoned inside its walls. What was his relationship with Lisa O'Shaughnessy? It wasn't just Sherbourne's ethnicity that made it unlikely the white-skinned teenagers she'd watch slope off to school were his. He would have barely been out of high school himself when those boys were born.

Sam Sherbourne was the bureau's Russian intelligence specialist in London. If he was Skylark, not only did it mean the Kremlin had a well-placed asset, it would call into question all the advice he had given the bureau during his tenure. It would be devastating for US counter-intelligence.

After a long shower at the Hilton, Ingrid arrived at the embassy a little before nine thirty, intent on gathering evidence on Sherbourne. She marched through the lobby heading for the stairs, but something pulled her back. Curious, she returned to the bank of elevators. A sign had been taped next to the call button.

Circuit fault identified

Do not press 6 and then a lower floor.

If you need the 6th floor, wait until all other levels
have been selected before pressing 6.
Press 6 last.
Specialist attending soon.

Ingrid read it several times, then headed slowly for the stairs. So that's why she had missed her meeting with Andy Scott. That's why they had been trapped for six hours. Had DeWalt known about the fault? Why would he deliberately stop her from meeting Andy Scott?

Ingrid leaned against the wall in the stairwell, unready to enter the Attaché Program offices. She had to think. She couldn't trust Sherbourne, she couldn't trust DeWalt and she definitely didn't trust Libby Greenwood. Ingrid glanced up at the door to the fifth floor. She needed to walk in there calmly, she needed to do her day job, and she needed to gather evidence.

The lack of sleep was already catching up with her. It was possible the run and the workout were too much. She was mentally and physically low and the prospect of testifying for the defense was weighing on her more than she had realized. She breathed in through her nose and pressed her back into the cool wall. *Dig deep, kiddo. Dig deep.*

Ingrid pushed herself to standing and climbed the remainder of the stairs. She walked the short corridor toward the bullpen where Sam Sherbourne appeared to be waiting for her.

"Can we talk?" He seemed nervous.

Ingrid popped her head inside the Criminal Division office. She smiled at Libby.

"Not in there," she said.

"I agree," he said, his voice barely louder than a whisper. "After work? The Golden Lion? On King Street?"

Ingrid nodded. She had to be at the Connaught at nine. "Eight o'clock?"

He pressed his lips together sheepishly. "See you there."

Ingrid watched as he slunk off to the CT office, then rolled her shoulders back, filled her lungs, and plastered a smile on her face. "Morning, Libby. Sorry I'm late." She threw her bag under her desk. "What have you got for me?"

"Good morning, Ingrid." Libby picked up a notebook and stood up. She leaned against the edge of her desk. "Okay, let me see." She reeled off a list of requests from field offices around the States as Ingrid logged on and scrolled through her emails. One from Deputy Director Aziz at the National Crime Agency marked URGENT made her heart beat in double time. Ingrid didn't hear anything else Libby said as she scanned it quickly, barely daring to breathe. She made a fist and punched the air with relief. Nothing had gone wrong. Aziz was merely informing all participants of Operation Pinball that the Secretary of State for Justice would be present for a photo op. Perhaps the macho Andy Scott thought an image of him in SWAT gear could replace the boxing photo in his next election leaflet.

The good news was that, if it was like every other sting operation Ingrid been part of, there would be plenty of sitting around doing nothing. And that meant she would get her ten minutes with Scott after all.

24

INGRID SMILED as she entered and looked around. No one appeared to be waiting for her, so she took a stool at the bar. The Connaught was one of those five-star, maybe even six-star, hotels that you only found in European capitals. Unobtrusive, elegant, demure. Low, soft lights and a dark interior of leather and satin made walking into the hotel's bar like walking into a black and white movie.

Ingrid wore a ruched black silk blouse, figure-hugging slacks that were a little warmer than was ideal, and open-toed sandals. She had been slightly overdressed for her drink with Sam Sherbourne in the Golden Lion pub, but was now a notch or two below the Connaught standard. She pushed her hair behind her ear and caught the eye of the bartender who was fixing a pair of whisky sours.

"Excuse me."

A man on a stool halfway down the bar turned to her. He had the taut, tanned skin that only money can buy.

"Have you got the time?"

He was annoyed to have been asked and twisted his arm to reveal a Breitling timepiece. "Five to nine."

He had already returned to his younger, female consort by the time Ingrid said 'thank you'. She had left her watch and her phone in her hotel room as a precaution against surveillance. She was relieved she wasn't late for her rendezvous.

"What can I get you?" The bartender had a thick Spanish accent and a tiny splash of something—Angostura bitters? Campari?—on the cuff of his otherwise immaculate white shirt.

Ingrid had already had a beer with Sherbourne, but ordering another in such elegant surroundings seemed almost disrespectful. "Dirty vodka martini, please. Dry."

She watched him work while she processed what she'd learned from Sherbourne, replaying their conversation word for word. His opening gambit had been: 'Did DeWalt send you?' and that had thrown her. Sherbourne told her he had noticed someone exercising in the park as he'd left number thirty-six, and after he'd rounded the corner in the direction of the station, he'd doubled back. His girlfriend, Lisa, was looking for a personal trainer and he assumed the woman he'd seen in the park was waiting for a client and planned to ask for a business card. When he'd realized it was Ingrid, he'd been too shocked to say anything.

Ingrid had played dumb. "Why would DeWalt send me?"

"Come on, don't pretend you don't know."

"I'm not pretending."

In the ten minutes that followed, Ingrid reassessed her prediction that Sherbourne was a future director of the FBI. Not only was he cheating on his wife with whom he had just had his first child, but he was cheating on her with his boss's ex. Lisa O'Shaughnessy had reclaimed her maiden name after her divorce from Jacob DeWalt.

Ingrid tried not to make moral judgements about other people's marriages—there was always another side to the story—but the six-month-old baby thing, and the boss's very recently ex-wife thing, seemed like two dubious moral judgement calls from the man who had downed a whisky at the bar before bringing their beers to the table.

"I had no idea." She sounded genuine because she really hadn't had a clue. "And if DeWalt suspects—"

"He *knows*."

"Well, he wouldn't ask me to spy on you. He'd get one of his golf buddies." She looked him square in the eye. "I promise you, I didn't know. DeWalt never said a thing."

Sherbourne's dark brown eyes narrowed. "For real? I thought you two were tight. Not tight tight, I didn't think there was anything going on, but I thought you were friends."

"What gave you that idea?"

Sherbourne's mouth crinkled. "Dunno. Guess he's been talking about you a lot lately."

That was new information. "Must be because I left him such dreadful handover notes."

Sherbourne wasn't buying it. "Maybe he's sweet on you."

"Ew." It was an involuntary reaction.

"I mean, you could do way better."

It was the kind of intimate talk Ingrid tried to avoid with co-workers.

"So, what were you doing there?" Sherbourne asked to fill the silence.

Ingrid had prepared a cover story for that question. "You're not the only one who's dating, you know."

"You're also seeing someone who lives on that

square?" Sherbourne was incredulous. "What are the chances?"

"No, not the square. The other side of the dock." She hoped she sounded convincing. "I just ended my run there. Perfect spot for a warm down."

Sherbourne's forehead crinkled. "Which complex?"

It was a question Ingrid hadn't anticipated. She tried to picture the buildings she had seen from the dockside. "One of those warehouses on the water."

He jutted out his lower jaw. "That's where DeWalt lives. He says it's to be near the boys, but he could almost have a telescope aimed at Lisa's bedroom window."

"Well, I promise you I am one hundred percent not dating DeWalt," she told him.

The bartender placed an ice-cold martini glass in front of Ingrid. The olive brine swirled through the vodka, making the transparent drink seem gelatinous. She took a sip and let the salt rest on her lips before swallowing. She checked the paper coaster under her glass, half expecting a message. There was none. She looked around the bar, but no one was looking back at her. She would have to be patient. In the meantime, she had the consolation of having connected DeWalt to one of Mulroony's photographs. He had lived at 36 West Park at the time the photographs were taken.

A bowl of complimentary almonds was placed next to her glass, though she was aware the price of the cocktail had been sumptuously inflated to absorb the cost of the 'free' bar snacks. Ingrid was never sure if it was the done thing to eat an olive in a dirty martini, but as she got closer to the bottom of the glass, it became more and more of an impediment to draining it. She eased it off the cocktail stick with her teeth and pressed it against the roof of her mouth with her tongue, pressing out the tangy brine.

"Another?" the bartender asked.

Ingrid looked at her glass. It was two-thirds empty. "No, thank you." She'd been drinking too fast for the vodka and vermouth to have made their way to her cognitive function, but after the beer she'd already had, it was wise to slow down. "But a glass of ice water would be wonderful."

The bartender swiftly placed the water in front of her before answering a phone call. Ingrid had just popped another almond into her mouth when the bartender handed her the phone. "It's for you."

Ingrid was impressed, and a smile of appreciation stretched her mouth. "Hello?"

"Hi."

"Hey, Sol. I thought it'd be you."

"I knew you'd figure it out."

"Whoever delivered the paper had circled the word 'sun' rather excessively. Sol, sun. Sun, Sol. It was a decent sized clue."

"I figured it wasn't too big a leap for a linguist like you. Listen, I'm sorry I didn't call last night. I couldn't."

Couldn't?

"I had to buy a burner. I had to drive fifty miles. They're probably listening to me too." Too? Wind created interference on the line. Where the hell was he?

"And you send me to a hotel. That's quite an elaborate plan to make sure this call can't be traced. Should I be scared?"

Ingrid didn't like the length of his pause. "Ingrid, I'm real sorry, but I don't think I can help you." Another pause. "But I can level with you."

Ingrid picked up the cocktail stick and jammed it onto the counter. "Okay." Her voice was tentative. She knew she wasn't going to like what he had to say.

"Last week, I wasn't in London for Madeleine's work. I was there to see you."

The skin prickled on the back of her neck. A shiver washed over her scalp.

"More accurately, I was asked to go and see you."

"By who?"

Sol ignored her question. "You were right about that file on the system. There are several of them, and whenever anyone accesses them, a little flag is raised. When they saw you were the one who had pulled it up, they were confused. You hadn't been in London when Mulroony disappeared, so you weren't a suspect, but your Russian connections spooked them. They looked around for someone to find out what you knew. They asked me."

"Who's 'they'?"

"People real high up."

"Director Leery?"

"High high."

The Secretary of State? The White House? "But you're not going to tell me?"

"I can't."

Ingrid's jaw tightened. "Why are you calling me in a bar from a burner phone?"

"I'll come to that." It sounded like Sol had taken up smoking again. After a long exhale, he continued. "The best I can tell you is that, when Mulroony disappeared, someone somewhere wasn't convinced he was Skylark, so they laid a trap. Several of them. They figured the only person who would access those files was the real Skylark."

"And now they think I'm Skylark?"

"Correct. At least, they think you *could* be. It's your mom. It's always been your mom, hasn't it? The Soviet defector thing always made them uncomfortable."

Ingrid recalled several conversations she'd had with Sol about the bureau's lingering suspicions over Svetlana, a woman who was so grateful for the sanctuary of the United States that she hosted Minnesota's biggest Fourth of July party.

"Ingrid?"

"Yes?"

"I know, deep in my heart, I know you are not a traitor."

"So why the burner?"

"Because tomorrow I'm going to call you on your cell and tell you I can't help you."

"And they're going to be listening in?"

"Count on it."

Ingrid's head started to spin. The lack of sleep suddenly made her feel weak. "And this call? This is to say that you can help?"

"It's to say I want to. I'm going to try to. But I'm on the outside now and I don't get the access I used to." A long drag confirmed he was definitely back on the cigarettes. "Listen, I worked with Mulroony. If he's in the Black Dolphin and he has been set up, then I want to see him freed. I didn't rate him that highly as an agent, but he doesn't deserve this."

In the pause that followed, Ingrid figured out why Sol couldn't say this on a line that was being listened in to. "But the bureau, or whichever part of the government asked you to get on a plane last week, would rather he stayed where he is?"

Sol exhaled audibly before answering. "Right now, the

public and the press do not know the FBI harbored a double agent for many years. If there is any attempt to free Mulroony, not only will the story get out that we had a Russian asset in our midst—"

"But it would expose the fact we still have a double agent on the payroll."

They were both silent for several moments. "Yup. That's about the size of it."

"So Mulroony suffers to save the bureau's reputation?" Ingrid asked.

"Not quite. If you blow the Mulroony situation open, then those traps that have been left for Skylark will never ensnare him."

"So, we do nothing?"

"You might call it nothing, but officially it's called waiting."

"And right now they're monitoring me?"

"Correct."

Six months ago, she had been the bureau's poster girl. Now they thought she was a double agent. "How worried should I be?"

Sol exhaled. "If I were you, I'd take it as a good sign that I'm having trouble getting answers out of anybody. That tells me the Mulroony thing is on the back burner, that it's no one's priority. If you don't rock the boat, you'll be fine."

The stick snapped as Ingrid increased the pressure. "Every day I don't rock the boat, is another day Skylark collects intel to share with his masters. Every day I don't rock the boat, is a day a brother agent unjustly spends in a foreign jail."

"I don't know how they could doubt you." The wind

howled through the phone line. "Listen, I better get home. I'm going to keep trying, okay?"

Ingrid didn't answer.

"I'll call you tomorrow."

Ingrid sighed. "And I'll make sure I say the right things when you do. I appreciate the heads up."

She handed the phone back to the bartender and nodded at her empty glass. "I think I'm ready for another one now."

25

"Okay, Sol, I appreciate the heads up." Ingrid ended the call and placed her cell into the outstretched palm of a Department of Justice employee. "Sorry," Ingrid said. "I needed to take that."

"Sounded real important," the woman said. Ingrid wondered if it might be helpful that a representative of the DoJ had witnessed Sol officially tell her that he couldn't help. It was even possible the lapel mic she was wearing had recorded their conversation. "It looks like they're ready for you now." The woman nodded at the screen on the wall.

Ingrid gulped. It was show time.

"Raise your right hand." Judge Isaacs' voice was crystal clear, a fact no doubt helped by the embassy's secure line normally reserved for intelligence and State Department briefings. "Do you promise to tell the truth and nothing but the truth, so help you God?"

"I do."

The Justice official from the third floor took the bible from Ingrid. There was another DoJ representative in the conference room, and they had both been sworn in as officers of the court for the occasion. They were there to check Ingrid was not testifying under duress and without outside interference. While that was technically true for the purposes of the trial, the duress and interference of the defense team weighed heavily on her.

Ingrid looked up at a screen that gave her a different view of the courtroom than the limited three angles of TV coverage. She could see the two desks where the defense and state's attorneys sat, and beyond them were the public benches. She couldn't see the jury, but she spotted Sheriff Stanton, her first boss. His complexion suggested his retirement involved a good deal of golf and an even greater amount of red wine. He stared at the camera, and Ingrid felt exposed under his gaze.

She knew he wasn't the only person looking at her. According to media reports, over three million people worldwide were watching the livestream at any one time. Ingrid only cared about two of them: Svetlana, and Kathleen Avery.

The defense attorneys had their heads together in a last-minute discussion of tactics. SuAnn McConnell got to her feet and smoothed out the creases in her dark orange skirt. McConnell was a well-presented woman in her fifties, with expert highlights running through her luxuriant chestnut hair, professionally manicured nails and unnaturally white teeth. Her fashion choices were bold and expensively tailored. As the second chair, she had often cross-examined the female witnesses in the trial. She smiled into the camera. "Miss Skyberg, thank you for agreeing to testify today."

It was the sort of opening move designed to trick Ingrid into saying 'no problem' or 'it's a pleasure' or 'anything to help the court' to make her seem like a compliant witness. Ingrid simply nodded.

"For the benefit of the jury, would you please tell the court about your current employment?"

"I am an FBI Special Agent." Ingrid was going to leave it at that, but did not want the jurors to think of her as deliberately obstreperous. "I work at the embassy in London, which is why I cannot be there in person."

"But you grew up here in Jackson?"

"Near enough, yes. About a half hour drive north." Ingrid took a sip of water and glanced at the clock on the wall. The *Laussat* was due to arrive in Tilbury within the hour. Over four months of planning and she wouldn't be there when it docked.

"Why did you want to become a federal agent?" McConnell had the warm persona of a daytime talk show host. She tilted her head to make a show of listening intently to Ingrid's reply.

Ingrid breathed in deeply through the nose. She decided to take the bait. "My best friend was abducted when I was fourteen. I wanted to find her."

"And your best friend was…?"

"Megan Avery. We attended Middleton High together."

"Go Wildcats," McConnell said with a small fist pump.

Somehow Ingrid managed to stop herself from saying 'Go Wildcats' in response. She did not want to get drawn in to McConnell's folksy exchange. The fact she refrained made McConnell miss a beat, and Ingrid's confidence grew.

"Now, as we all sadly know, you did not find your friend. Her remains were among those recovered from the Fielding ranch in 2013, but I am curious to know why your noble ambition was not to join the local police, but the Federal Bureau of Investigations."

"Investigation," Ingrid corrected. She instantly bit the inside of her lip. McConnell was deliberately trying to make Ingrid seem like a smartass. "It's singular."

McConnell nodded. "Of course. But, I'd still like an answer to my question."

Ingrid narrowed her eyes. "Well, for the first few months after Megan went missing, we—and by 'we' I mean her family, my family, local law enforcement—thought she was the only victim." Ingrid sipped her water from a paper cup. "As the months turned into years, I became aware of other girls who had gone missing at traveling carnivals in several states across the Midwest."

"So, it was a federal crime, not a local one?"

"Potentially, yes. But it had been investigated as a local one. I always thought it needed federal resources."

"And you thought this even though you were just a teenager?"

"We're talking a few years later, but yes, I was still in college."

McConnell moved to stand directly in front of the camera, obscuring Ingrid's view of the rest of the courtroom. "And where was college?"

Ingrid couldn't see how it was relevant, but she answered. "Chicago."

"And what did you do after college?"

"I joined the Jackson County Sheriff's Department."

McConnell tilted her head again. "The same Sheriff's Department that had failed to find the man who abducted your friend?"

Ingrid wasn't going to let her sow the seed of doubt about investigatory competence in the jury's mind. She pictured Stanton's ruddy face. "The same Sheriff's Department in the county where my mom lived. Lives," she corrected.

"Of course." McConnell tried to sound conciliatory. "How long were you with the Sheriff's Department?"

"A little over two years."

"And in those two years, did you attempt to re-investigate your friend's disappearance?"

"By the time I joined, nine years had passed since Megan's abduction. Like any new recruit, I had a very full caseload. But when I got a chance, I did look at the records relating to Megan, yes."

McConnell nodded before walking away from the camera. This was far from Ingrid's first time giving evidence, and in her experience, the closer the lawyer is, the softer their questions. Ingrid steeled herself for a zinger. Much easier to lob a grenade from twenty feet. "What did you make of the investigation? Professionally?"

Ingrid thought the defense had called her to create doubt that Jones had abducted Megan. She hadn't considered they would ask her to discredit the entire investigation. She inhaled, steadied herself, and answered. "I found it strange." Ingrid didn't wait for McConnell to ask her to elucidate. "One of the first things I looked at was the transcript of my interview, the one I'd given as a fourteen-year-old. It was strange to see my recollections written down in black and white. It made them feel different, slightly removed."

"There were discrepancies?" McConnell butted in.

"No." Though actually Ingrid remembered that by the time her twenty-three-year-old self read the transcript, her memories of June 17, 1995 had warped and tilted. Certain images were bright and sharp, like neon, while others had become blurry and tentative. She hadn't known which was more accurate; the account she had given Deputy Hanlon in 1995, or the truth her brain had held on to and forged into something more immutable. Throughout her career, that experience had shaped how much weight Ingrid had given to witness testimony delivered years after a crime had taken place. "And I was pleased to see that the Sheriff's Department had interviewed everyone I would have expected them to. So, no, I thought the file was a very fair representation of the night Megan was taken."

McConnell started to speak, but the delay on the line meant Ingrid inadvertently cut her off.

"When the carnival returned in 2004, I set up an incident station and we looked for new witnesses. On the tenth anniversary of Megan's abduction, we were able to interview a handful of people who had been missed from the initial investigation."

"But you still had faith in that investigation?"

"Carnivals, by their very nature, are transitory. People who work for them,"—Ingrid was determined not to use the pejorative 'carnie people'—"tend to be wanderers. It wasn't a surprise a few folks had slipped through the net." Ingrid paused. "Anyway, these new interviews did give us a few new names, and that meant we briefly reopened the investigation."

"And at any point in the ten years after Megan disappeared, was my client a suspect?"

Ingrid looked down at the table before answering. "No. James Jones's name never came up."

McConnell approached the camera. She was about to throw a soft ball. "Agent Skyberg, I appreciate this will be painful for you, but can I ask you to please tell us about the night Megan was taken."

"Sure." This was what she had been anticipating. She had relived the darkest night of her life for so many therapists over the years that it was wrapped in titanium and stored in a box she had learned to open without triggering detonation. "Where would you like me to start?"

McConnell smiled. Please, not the head tilt again. "Why don't you tell us something about Megan, the kind of girl she was."

Ingrid nodded. "Of course." She closed her eyes and an image on Megan's smiling face surfaced. The deep brown eyes, the constellations of freckles, the look of surprise as she learned about everything from the commissary menu to the birds and the bees. She had been a girl who expected little and was consequently delighted by everything. "Megan was an exceptionally—and I really do mean exceptionally—kind girl. She had a capacity for compassion and empathy beyond anyone I have ever met. She couldn't pass a kid crying in the corridor or leave a bird with a broken wing to figure its own way back to its nest. If you stamped on a spider in her presence, she wouldn't look at you for a week." Ingrid needed another sip of water. She knew Kathleen was watching, and she wanted to be sure she said as little as possible to hurt her. "My father died when I was ten and Megan didn't leave my side for three months. She honestly had to know that I was asleep before she could go to bed. It seems impossible from one so young, but she was a cross between a guardian angel and a St. Bernard." Ingrid smiled at the memory. "I spent a lot of time at the Averys's house that year. Kathleen became a second mom." In fact, it had been Kathleen who showed Ingrid what a mom was really like: Svetlana had always been more of a distant aunt or a fairytale stepmother, either cruel or indulgent, but never loving. "Megan wasn't just my best friend, she was the sister I never had." Ingrid instantly knew Svetlana would take that as a criticism. She couldn't retract it now. "We were incredibly close. We did everything together."

"And so, one June night in 1995, you went to the carnival. Just the two of you?"

"June seventeen," Ingrid said. The date her whole life changed. "Megan and I were the square kids in school. Our assignments were always delivered on time, we were never in trouble and I guess our parents trusted us to behave ourselves, so yes, we went to the carnival on our own. Kathleen, Megan's mom, gave us a curfew of ten, which was a whole half hour later than our curfew the previous year. We were a little giddy at being so grown up we could stay out until ten." The next words stalled in Ingrid's throat, and she had to fight to get them out. "It was one of those balmy summer nights." Ingrid had to blink back tears. "Sorry."

"Take your time." McConnell did her best Oprah impression.

"Anyway, we had a lovely evening, but then it got late. In our heads we knew we needed to leave by ten, but then we realized we needed to be *home* by ten and we'd left it too late." The air had left Ingrid's chest. This was so much harder than she had anticipated. The DoJ official sitting a few chairs away on the side of the conference table looked down at her hands, as if to give Ingrid some privacy. "So, we took a shortcut home from Baxter's Fields and headed back through Simpson's Cut. It's a cycle route now, at least it was the last time I was home, but back then it was just a firebreak between the trees. The sort of path everyone used during the day, but it was a little spooky at night. The carnival meant there were lots of people around, so we thought we'd be safe." Pressure constricted her sternum. It was hard to breathe.

Sensing Ingrid's discomfort, McConnell asked another question. "You said there were a lot of people around. So any one of them could have taken Megan?" She knew that all she had to do was create reasonable doubt in the jury's mind.

Ingrid shook her head. "When I went through the initial investigation reports, one of the things I was pleased about was that every name I had given to the deputies had been interviewed. They were other kids from school and their older brothers and sisters. Couples making out. None of them were the man who chased us and who took Megan." Ingrid stopped, suddenly unable to continue.

"So you saw the man you claim abducted Megan?"

Ingrid exhaled hard, flaring her nostrils. She knew where McConnell was leading her. "Some of the boys from school, they started teasing us. Name calling. We got a lot of it. Just because we were used to it, it didn't mean it didn't hurt. For the first few times, we ignored them as always, then they started to come after us." Ingrid dug her fingernails into her palms and looked right into the camera. "Megan and me, we were the fat kids. The boys were teasing us, telling us that we couldn't run." Ingrid shuddered, the inside of her skull reverberating with the school yard taunts of Mega Megan and Ingrid Fatberg. "They started throwing things at us, food mostly. We were used to it, and as long as we were together, we could cope. I hope those boys feel bad about it now, but they were throwing hot dogs, thinking we would do anything for food. It was childish, but it was still cruel. Maybe some of the older boys had drunk a beer... anyway, the mood changed. Corey Peters was there, Shaun Trimmins, Pauley

Shearwater. We started to feel scared, and they sensed our fear so the taunts escalated. Then they got nearer." Again, Ingrid hit a roadblock. The words simply could not steer a path around the lump in her throat.

"Then… then this man appeared and asked us if everything was all right. We just wanted to get away from him, away from anyone, so we kind of ignored him and carried on down the Cut, though maybe a little faster than before. He shouted after us, telling us we were little bitches, but he must have said something to the boys too, because they left us alone after that. I think they turned back to the carnival because, suddenly, there was no one else around. Then I guess it was another hundred yards or so, I mean, we were almost back at Cooper's Crossing by this point, practically back into town, when he shouted at us, this man. We turned back and saw him striding toward us, so we sort of stopped talking and started walking real quick. Then we heard his footsteps, so we started running. He shouted again, told us to stop, but we just knew we had to get away from him." The familiar dread pulsed through her in time with the memory of his footsteps. That primal fear of being chased, knowing she was running for her life.

Beyond McConnell, the people in the court looked to one side where the monitor showing Ingrid was. They were still and silent, waiting for her to continue.

"So we ran, but like I said, we were fat kids. We couldn't run far, or fast, and he caught up with us in about thirty seconds flat. One moment I looked behind and he was a hundred yards back, the next I felt him behind us. Out of the corner of my eye, I saw his arm reach out to us." Ingrid stifled a sob. "Megan was only a stride behind me, but he grabbed her wrist and—" That was all she could manage. Ingrid still felt the pain of separation as she ran on and Megan was pulled backward. It was several more strides before she realized Megan wasn't going to break free. She twisted her neck and saw the man's other hand clamp over Megan's mouth. Her eyes were wide with terror. Ingrid's insides deflated as she remembered that she kept running, that she didn't turn back to save her friend, she kept running until she reached Cooper's Crossing where she waved at cars that didn't stop as the carnival music and the scent of cotton candy skulked over the treetops from Baxter's Fields.

Ingrid had relived that night so many times and interrogated her choices in so many therapy sessions. If she had stopped running. If she had turned back. If she had called out to Corey and Shaun. But she didn't. She hadn't. Instead, she had walked back into town because it was already past the curfew and she didn't want to be any later. Ingrid felt weak at the memory of Kathleen's face as she opened the door and saw that Ingrid was alone.

"Thank you," McConnell said, a half-smile softening her face. "What can you tell us about the man you encountered in Simpson's Cut?"

Ingrid wasn't sure if what she was about to say was what she remembered from June seventeen, or what she recalled from the interview report Deputy Hanlon had written up. "He was white, taller than us, at the time we thought—sorry, I thought—he was old, but he might only have been twenty. Kids think all adults are old, don't they?" It was one of the things she had learned working in the FBI's VCAC unit that you could never rely on a kid's guess at an adult's age. "He was lean, dirty. I mean muddy. His jeans were filthy. He had a cowboy buckle on his belt, and a bandana."

McConnell walked over to the defense's desk and

picked up a piece of paper. "Agent Skyberg, would you please look at this photograph." The image in front of the camera was a mug shot, clearly of a younger James Jones. "Was this the man who abducted Megan?"

Ingrid studied the photo. "It could be, yes."

McConnell smiled at the camera. "Could? Interesting." She was going to leave that there. "Agent Skyberg, you have said you wanted to join the FBI to find the man who took Megan. When you graduated from Quantico, did you get the opportunity to investigate your theory about a carnival killer?"

Ingrid's forehead furrowed at the unexpected question. "Yes, yes I did. I joined the Violent Crimes Against Children unit and I was able to investigate many crimes that took place in and around traveling carnivals."

"I'm sure you can anticipate my next question." McConnell squeezed a half smile onto her lips. "Did you find other abductions similar to the one you have just described."

"Yes, yes I did, though in all cases the girls were found, or were abandoned soon after."

"And did the suspect in any of these cases fit the description of the defendant?"

Ingrid wasn't sure where McConnell was headed with this line of questioning. "It's quite a generic description—white, lean, jeans, bandana—so yes, oftentimes."

"Thank you, Agent Skyberg. No further questions."

Ingrid hid the surprise at the sudden curtailment by looking down at her hands. Red crescents had formed in her palms from her fingernails. An unbidden tear dropped onto her fingers. She wiped it away before the next one could fall. The DoJ officials shifted uncomfortably in their seats.

"Agent Skyberg." The DA's voice came down the line from Minnesota. "Thank you so much for appearing today and for letting us know some more about Megan. She sounds like the most wonderful girl. It must hurt so hard that she is no longer at your side."

Ingrid looked up at the screen showing Merritt Danver and smiled at him.

"I remember you when you were with the sheriff. I'm sorry we're meeting again in these circumstances," he said. Merritt was a youthful fifty and the extra pounds he had gained since Ingrid was last in a courtroom with him were filling out any wrinkles. "I just have one question for you."

Ingrid blinked hard, unable to anticipate what he was going to ask.

"When you worked with the Violent Crimes Against Children unit, you must have encountered several monsters who preyed on teenage girls. In your experience, what is the average age of an offender when they commit their first offense?"

Ingrid's eyes widened at Danver's curveball. She nodded to herself as she prepared her answer. "It was very common for there to be a pattern of behavior in early childhood of bullying, petty cruelty and committing offenses like shoplifting and stealing cars. But there is actually a good deal of evidence that men who go on to be persistent sexual offenders against young women commit their first rape around the age of seventeen. Very often this won't be reported because their victim was known to them and she feared friends and family finding out, but when a perpetrator's history was investigated, we frequently found evidence of the first serious assault being committed as a late teenager."

"So that would fit perfectly with James Jones's age in

1995. Thank you for your time, Agent. I have no further questions."

Judge Isaacs released her, and Ingrid unclipped the microphone. The younger of the DoJ officials turned off the camera and the screens while the other one handed her cell to her.

"Well done," he said. "That can't have been easy."

Ingrid nodded. She looked at her phone. A message from Ralph. The *Laussat* had docked early.

26

INGRID ARRIVED at the Napier Yards complex a little after seven. It was less humid than the previous week, but the hot day nevertheless promised to stretch into a pleasantly warm evening. The stench of rotting fruit suggested the C&C wholesalers in the big warehouse had fought a losing battle against refrigeration.

On an evening like this, it was just possible, if Ingrid squinted, to visualize the haphazard Victorian buildings surrounding the courtyard as craft breweries and vegan cafes. Tilbury was probably too far out of the city ever to be gentrified in the same manner as similar industrial buildings in Hackney and Kings Cross had been, where former factories and coal stores were now duplex apartments and farm-to-table restaurants. *If McKittrick was here she'd be telling me to flip my way to a fortune.*

Ingrid tried to avoid eye contact with anyone. As Jayne Andrews, the security director of Shoreham Medical, she wouldn't be on friendly terms with the occupants of the warehouses, several of whom were undercover Met officers waiting for one particular shipment of bananas from

Costa Rica. Ingrid gathered the keys from her bag and walked past the parked cars on one side of the yard, most of which were probably unmarked Met vehicles, through the alleyway between the fruit importers and the shipping company, then down toward the yellow warehouse.

She had chosen her outfit carefully and gone for the blazer, jeans and sneaker combo that suggested a woman called into the office at the last moment. The blazer was to conceal a sidearm; the sneakers were in case she had to run. She heard the beep-beep of a forklift truck coming out of a side alley before she saw it and had to press herself into a wall to let it pass.

The shutter to the yellow warehouse was already up, but the door was locked. She found the key and let herself in. There was no sign of anyone in the ground floor storage area, so she slipped between the racks of blue metal shelving stacked with supplies and headed for the stairs. She clanked her way noisily up to the upper level.

"Hi," she said, opening the office door, "sorry I'm late, I—"

"I know," Ralph said, getting to his feet, "I was watching you. You okay?"

She gave him a kiss on the cheek, only considering if it was unprofessional afterwards. "Yes," she said, dumping her bag on a desk. "Absolutely fine."

Ralph tilted his head, McConnell style. "Really?"

Ingrid pressed her lips together. "I'm glad it's over." She went to stand next to him so she could see what he was looking at. On his laptop was a grid of CCTV images covering the dock where the *Laussat* was newly moored, the main gate to Tilbury, the entrance into the Napier complex and the yard where Ingrid had just been. Beside the laptop were two radios relaying the same coded messages from the team in their various surveillance positions. "Have I missed much?" she asked.

"Nah. You might actually have timed things perfectly." He offered her a bottle of an orange-colored soda with a monster on the bottle. A holster pinned an olive-green tee against his pecs, making him look surprisingly muscular. All that home improvement activity had created unexpected definition.

"No, thanks."

"You don't need to turn your nose up," he said. "It's not as bad as it looks."

"I'll take your word for it."

Ralph pointed at the laptop. "The boat arrived a couple of hours early, but there's been a slight delay in unloading. Don't know why. Guess it happens sometimes." Ralph leaned over the laptop and jabbed the screen. "The container we're interested in is, I believe, that one."

"How can you tell?"

"Aziz has eyes on. It's the right serial number."

"He's at the dockside?"

"The guvnor is posing as a customs official. Anyway, if they carry on unloading in the same order, our container is next." He turned to her. "You sure you're up for this. You've already been through quite a lot today."

Trust me, Ingrid thought, *giving evidence was nothing compared to the phone call she'd endured with Svetlana on the cab ride over.*

Ingrid pulled up a chair next to Ralph's and sat down. "And everything else is going according to plan?"

"Seems so. We're expecting that container to be transferred to a lorry, sorry, truck, in about twenty minutes and then it'll be brought into the yard for unloading."

"And is that when we move in?"

He shook his head, revealing a flash of white paint masquerading as gray hairs. "Plan A is still to wait and observe. See what they do with the pallets. This could just be surveillance instead of intercept."

Ingrid scanned the office but didn't see what she was she was looking for. She indicated the semi-automatic strapped to Ralph's side. "I miss out on the toys?"

"Afraid so. I did ask if I could sign for one for you, but the quartermaster wouldn't let me." He pulled an apologetic face. "I doubt we'll need them. We'll probably just spend the next three hours watching a screen and then the lorry will trundle off to..." He trailed off. "Skegness."

"Is that even a real place?"

"Oh, yes indeed. But trust me, there's no reason for you ever to go there."

Ingrid's gaze lingered on the Glock 23. Or maybe Ralph's chest. "After the mess we made of the dry run last week, you'd think they might have issued a weapon for me in my absence."

Ralph swallowed a mouthful of his monstrous concoction. "As you well know, our gun laws are a little tighter than yours. Hungry?" he asked. "I brought snacks." After the orange soda, Ingrid wasn't hopeful as Ralph dug around in his bag before pulling out an assortment of small meat pies, chocolate bars and Peperami sausages. Ingrid was generally omnivorous, but Ralph's choices weren't getting her saliva flowing. He saw the disappointment on her face. "It was all they had at the Esso."

"If we're here for hours, I'll be very grateful. Listen," she stalled, considering if what she was about to say would be welcome or not. "Should I take the Glock?"

Ralph's features narrowed. "I've had the training. I've got the certificate."

She smiled at him. "I wasn't impugning your credentials, macho man. I was just thinking about Shelbie. You're going to be a dad in a few weeks—"

"Next week."

"See. It's not really the right time for you to be taking risks."

He scrunched up his lips. "I appreciate the offer, but a) I signed for this, and b) perhaps that means I need it more? Gives me a chance to defend myself."

Ingrid shrugged. "Just, you know, offering."

"Thanks."

They slumped into a slightly awkward silence and watched the screen until Ralph manufactured a topic of conversation. "Did you see Andy Scott when you arrived?"

"No. Is he out in the yard somewhere?"

"Yep. He's with the team in the big blue warehouse. The one with all the machinery."

"Please tell me he didn't bring a photographer and a press officer."

"Nah, I think he's still too much of a copper to do that. But," Ralph drained the bottle of its vivid contents, "you can bet that somewhere on the perimeter of Tilbury is a government photographer sitting in a car ready to get tomorrow's front-page snap." He waggled the empty bottle. "Apparently he was a total effing disaster at the Commonwealth shindig and he's desperate for a good headline." He ran a hand over his collar length hair, sweeping it out of his eyes. "Still, it's a good sign you didn't spot him. Hopefully he won't screw this up as well as our international relations."

Ralph got to his feet. He had never been very good at sitting still. It was as if his limbs were slightly too long for his body and he never quite knew how to fold his arms or cross his legs. "So." His voice was suddenly serious. "I thought you were excellent today. On the stand." He deliberately looked at some empty boxes on one of the abandoned desks to avoid the intimacy of eye contact. "Can't have been easy."

Ingrid didn't know how to respond.

"I mean. I *know* it wasn't easy. I know how much Megan meant to you."

One of things Ingrid still loved about Ralph was his willingness to say the things he knew he ought to say, even if they made him uncomfortable. Most people would rather talk about any other subject. "Thanks," she managed. "According to my mother, my testimony has not gone down well in Minnesota."

He turned and looked at her. "According to your mother, you haven't done anything right since you left home."

Affection surged through Ingrid. His attempts to wander into areas of conversational discomfort were truly heroic. "A good point, well made," she said. "It would have been so much easier if I had been called as a state's witness."

Ralph perched on the edge of the desk. "You think he'll get off? For Megan? For the two other girls?"

Ingrid twisted off the top of her water bottle. She lifted her eyebrows. "I think it all depends on how much the jury likes him. We both know that a charismatic killer holds a weird appeal for a lot of folks. The defense's strategy might be good enough."

"But if he's going to jail for the others, won't the jury think he's going down for nine, he might as well go down for all twelve?"

Ingrid pulled a face. "It'll come down to the forensics. The hyoid thing is inconclusive, but who knows how much a jury understands. He says three bodies were already in the yard when he got to Fielding Ranch, but again, how much do jurors really take in about soil samples and pollen residues?"

Ralph shrugged. "I guess. Must be agony for you, waiting for the verdict."

Ingrid didn't answer.

"You think this Bill Starr character really existed?" Ralph asked to fill the silence.

Ingrid took a slug of water, then wiped her lips. "I've heard some crazy defenses in my time. Voices in my head. My father's ghost. Iron Maiden lyrics. My non-existent twin brother. But inventing a man that no one remembers," she sighed. "That's a bold move."

"But do you think he actually existed, or did he totally make him up?" Ralph kept both eyes on the screen.

Ingrid nodded. "We know he did. Sadly, there is plenty of video evidence in seized porn collections of a man who isn't Jones abusing Ellen McDormand, the first victim to disappear. And Jones would only have been sixteen when Ellen was taken. So, yes, I think there's a chance the jury will believe he was coerced by an older man into making snuff movies. But." Ingrid couldn't continue. Just talking about the trial exhausted her. "But, his claim he's just another of Starr's victims won't have gone down well. My guess is they'll want to punish him for that."

Ralph picked up a pen and rotated it between his fingers. "Look. That's our container. It's on the move." He leaned in for a better look, then checked his watch. "It should be here in, what, eight minutes? Ten?"

An unexpected chill snaked up the back of Ingrid's

neck. "Let's hope all these months of planning don't blow up in our faces."

Ralph looked to his shoes. "It'll be all right. Whenever the rehearsal is a disaster, the opening night is a five-star triumph."

Ingrid raised an eyebrow. "And that's based on your extensive experience of theater?"

He blushed. "I must have read it somewhere." He opened a packet of chips that smelled like farts and offered her the bag. She didn't even have to say no before he withdrew his hand. "So, um, is anyone looking for this Bill Starr?" He really had been paying attention to the trial.

Ingrid inhaled slowly. "Think a manhunt will wait for the verdict. If Jones is convicted of all twelve murders, no police department is going to spend resources looking for him. Would you?"

Ralph leaned back in his chair. "It's the sort of thing you take on when you retire, isn't it? One last case." He was suddenly distracted by something. "Look." It was a bee. "I was too scared to check on the room at the end when I got here. I just kind of assumed they'd have moved on by now. The alarm hasn't gone off since."

The bee settled on top of a file cabinet. Ingrid peered at it. "No," she said, "that's from a different hive."

Ralph's eyebrows shot up. "You can tell?"

Ingrid smiled. "I grew up on a farm."

Ralph stood up to inspect the bee. "So, go on then, how can you tell?"

"Well," Ingrid said, "you see this wing here?"

"Yes."

"Well, it doesn't have the logo on it."

"Logo?"

She pulled back from him and folded her arms. "Yes, Ralph, the team logo."

He grimaced. "Ah, I see. Very funny. Ha bleeding ha."

On the screen, the shipping container was lowered onto the flatbed of a truck. Aziz's voice crackled over the radio. "Target on the move. All units prepare."

Ingrid looked at Ralph. "You okay? Nervous?"

"A little."

"We need to run through things one last time?"

"Sure," he said. "Might as well."

"All right then. Truck pulls into the yard. Crane lifts it on to a flatbed trailer."

"It gets yanked into the C & C building where Danszak and his team are—"

"That's the thing I don't like most about Aziz's plan, that Danszak is the one inside C & C. He's a loose cannon."

Ralph twitched his nose. "He's not so bad. Okay, so they start to unload the boxes. That's when I go out and move my car—"

"You sure your tire's flat?"

"I stuck a really big blade in it when I arrived, so I won't be going far."

"Okay, so you block the rear exit, and then?"

"Then we wait and see what happens to those boxes of bananas."

They both bit the inside of their lip and smiled as they noticed the other doing the same thing. "Be a bloody big cock-up if there's only bananas in them boxes, won't it?"

"Oh yes," Ingrid replied. "I do not look forward to the paperwork on that." She pointed at the laptop. "Is the top left image Danszak's bodycam?"

Ralph narrowed his eyes to check. He was on the cusp

of needing reading glasses. "Yep. Look, that's Desi behind him. That's definitely inside C & C."

Ingrid looked up through the high windows to the sky. "It's still really light, isn't it?"

"Guess the floodlights at the docks mean it never gets dark round here. It's a twenty-four-hour operation, innit." He nodded in the direction of the laptop. "It's weird to think those images are coming from less than a hundred yards away."

"Listen."

"What?"

"Isn't that the truck arriving?" Ingrid said.

On the laptop, the camera in the courtyard showed the truck approaching. "Your hearing's good," Ralph said. "That took less time than we thought. I suppose it is only over there."

They watched the operation to get the shipping container onto the flatbed trailer in silence. Ingrid switched her view from the courtyard camera to the bodycam as Aziz's voice gave out the standby command for Ralph.

"You definitely don't know how to change a tire?" Ingrid checked as he got to his feet.

"With this face?" He asked. "All I have to do is ask nicely."

Ralph picked up his jacket from the back of his chair and slipped it on to cover the holster and the Glock.

"Very smart," Ingrid said. "Light gray was a good choice."

"Thank you. That's what I thought. Makes it more believable that I wouldn't want to get dirty and change my own tire." He smiled at her. "Right. See you on the other side."

"Don't say that. It makes it sound like you're dying."

"Oh." He looked perplexed. "Does it? How about see you in the Jolly Sportsman in a couple of hours?"

"Much better."

Ralph scooped up his car keys and turned to leave.

"Hey." Ingrid held out one of the radios.

"Thanks." Ralph took it from her. He looked nervous.

"Switch it to silent."

"Yep, of course."

Ingrid heard his footsteps on the metal gangway. They were even louder when he bounced down the stairs into the cavernous storage area. Then there was the faint clunk as the front door closed behind him. Two minutes later, Ingrid watched Ralph cross the yard toward his BMW X-5.

She felt the explosion before she heard it, rattling the high fragile windows but not shattering them. Several seconds of deep, throbbing silence followed.

And then all hell broke loose.

27

THE FEED from Danszak's camera was black. Three more detonations followed in quick succession. Ingrid heard them twice, first through the air and then their electronic echo over the radio. Then the alarms started. Sirens tripped by the explosions overlaid each other in an unbearable cacophony.

Ralph.

The radio erupted with so many call signs they cut out over each other as everyone tried to report their position. Ingrid got to her feet and staggered as if her body were belatedly absorbing the shock. She pushed on out into the corridor, ran along the metal walkway, and tore down the stairs before racing out into the alleyway outside. She had to get to Ralph.

Ingrid ran between the warehouses. The air was thick with cordite and shouting. She turned left and accelerated between the buildings. The yard was strewn with broken glass. Smoke funneled out of the C & C warehouse. Stunned workers staggered outside, unable to speak, looking blank.

She ran toward the parked cars in search of Ralph. Where was he?

"Ralph? Ralph?" Her voice sounded distant over the ringing in her ears. She doubted he could hear her. "Jesus."

She found him lying flat on his back between a Jaguar and his BMW with its door open. He was unconscious and had a large welt on his forehead. She crouched down as the yard filled with men and shouting.

"Ralph?" She stroked his face. "Ralph. Wake up." She shook his shoulders and he let out a moan. "Ralph. It's Ingrid. Wake up!" She slapped his cheek and his eyes flickered, then opened.

"What the—"

As best Ingrid could make out, he must have just opened the car door when the first explosion happened, thrusting the metal forcefully into his skull. He'd either passed out standing up, or had been knocked unconscious when his head hit the cobbles. The muscles in his face tightened, he looked at her then gave up, closing his eyes and letting his body go limp. She slapped his face again.

"Ralph, wake up. Come on, buddy."

The ground shook with footsteps. Ingrid glanced over her shoulder. A small army gathered outside the C & C warehouse. She couldn't tell how many were Operation Pinball colleagues and how many were local workers.

"Come on, Ralph." She was desperate to be heard over the sirens. "You can't stay like this."

His hand reached for hers and he held it against his face. Ingrid was shaking. She didn't know if it was from adrenaline or relief. For several terrible seconds, she had envisaged having to tell Shelbie that the father of her unborn child had been killed. But he was squeezing her hand. Ralph would be okay.

"Come on, sit up. I need you to sit up." She pushed her other hand under his shoulder, encouraging him to move.

He pursed his lips. He understood.

"Come on, now." She forced her arm under his neck and helped him to a seated position. When she took her hand away, it was covered in blood. There was a pool of it where his head had been. "Let me look."

Ralph's eyes swam in their sockets. She feared he would pass out again, so she leaned him up against the car door. The gash wasn't too bad, but he would probably need stitches. Ingrid took off her jacket and pressed it against Ralph's head. She knew it wouldn't be long before ambulances arrived, but she also knew whatever had happened inside the C & C warehouse would mean Ralph wasn't the only casualty. She kept the jacket against his scalp and stared into his eyes. "You're going to be okay, buddy. Help is c—"

A bullet tore through the air and ripped into the Jaguar. Ingrid turned. "*Govno*!" The air fizzed with semi-automatic gunfire. The open driver's door was their only protection. "Ralph, I've got to move you. We need to be behind the car."

His body softened against the car as he moaned. His head started to loll. "Go," he said.

"I'm not leaving you."

His breathing was heavy. Speaking was an effort. He grabbed her hand and squeezed it. "Go."

"No!" She wasn't going to leave him. She reached inside his jacket for the Glock and climbed into the BMW. She lay across the front seats and rested the muzzle in the V between the open door and the side of the car. She raised her head tentatively and surveyed the yard. Shots were coming from the second floor of the C & C warehouse. Met officers in the engineering factory were returning fire. Smoke escaped from C & C's doors. Stunned workers ran for cover.

A gunman appeared at an upper window of C & C. It was a long-range shot for the Glock. Ingrid breathed in deeply, steadied herself and pulled the trigger, sending a bullet across the yard. It shattered the glass next to the gunman who retreated briefly, then rolled back into view and returned fire, obliterating the windshield. Ingrid ducked. Ralph's head was protected by the open car door, but his legs and lower torso were vulnerable to a bullet that raked low. If she fired again, she would put Ralph in too much danger.

"You okay, Ralph?"

He didn't answer.

"Ralph?"

Garbled commands were audible over the radio in a lull between shots, but Ingrid couldn't make out their instructions. Lying flat across the front seats, she stuck her head out and checked on Ralph. He turned to look at her and mouthed the word 'go' just as the car shook with the impact of another round.

Ingrid scrambled out of the car, looped her arms under Ralph's shoulders, and hauled him up into the BMW. She laid him flat on the front seats so he was shielded by the hood and the dash, then crouched down in the passenger footwell. Her chest hurt with the urgency of her breaths, the cordite searing the insides of her lungs.

"What do you think happened?" she asked Ralph. "Were the bananas booby-trapped?" He didn't answer. "Okay, listen. Your job is to stay awake. Looks like you've had two big blows to the head, one from car door the other from the ground, but other than that I think you're okay."

He said something.

"What was that?"

"Other than that," he said through a half smile.

She placed a hand on his and gave it a squeeze. "I think you're going to be okay, Ralph Mills."

He closed his eyes slowly, then opened them to make deliberate eye contact. "Go."

Ingrid reached over and opened the passenger door with her left arm. The movement immediately drew fire. She waited thirty seconds, then climbed out and scampered to the back of the BMW. She raised her head and looked through the rear window at the yard. Most people had taken cover or gone back inside the warehouses. The sirens drilled into her ears, making it harder to think. She glanced left and right and saw people crouched behind the other parked cars. They stared wildly at the Glock in her hand. "Police," she said. But as she was only wearing jeans and a white tee shirt, they seemed skeptical. Ingrid twisted round and looked through the car windows at the C & C warehouse. A figure was on the fire escape with a carbine rifle. He wasn't part of Operation Pinball. He was one of the drug gang. He turned and ran. He was trying to get away.

The fire escape led down to the alley alongside the fruit importers. Ingrid kept low and scurried behind the line of cars, aiming the Glock at the ground. She reached the end of the cars and ran as hard as she could across the yard, then darted into an alley on the other side. Now out of the line of fire, she took a moment to look up to make sure there was no one on the roofs above her. She powered down the alley to where the fire escape descended. At the end of the building, she pressed herself into the wall and raised the Glock. She took a deep breath and turned the corner with the gun out in front of her. There was no one there.

Was he still on the roof?

Ingrid felt the bullet as it passed her head and zeroed into the wall in front of her. It had come from shoulder height. There was no way it had been fired from the roof. Someone had followed her from the yard. She accelerated away from the shooter as he fired another shot. Her eyes darted left and right, searching for an escape.

The smell of something prickled her nose. It wasn't cordite. It was cotton candy. She was back in Cooper's Cut, running for her life. The swirl of sirens and gunfire coalesced into the carnival music of a clockwork pianola. Her mouth was dry. Fear tugged on her skin. She could barely keep her eyes open. It was only the closeness of the next bullet that yanked her back to reality.

Ingrid turned sharply into another alley, giving her respite from the threat of getting shot. She didn't recognize the buildings. They were all starting to look the same. None of the doors were open. Any second now he would turn the corner and fire again.

Ingrid risked a glance over her shoulder but turned back just as he came into view. Tall, white, close-cropped hair. She kept running as she tried to lock down his description. The only face she could picture was James Jones's. Her breaths were short and heavy. Her ankle twisted on the cobbles, but she knew she couldn't stop. Not until she had somewhere to hide.

She recognized something up ahead. The warren of alleys had somehow led her back to Shoreham Medical Supplies. Ingrid ran for the yellow warehouse, knowing she had left it unlocked. She ran inside and slammed the door behind her, muffling the alarms and sirens. She darted between the long rows of metal shelving and headed through the unlit warehouse toward the metal staircase.

The door opened and she froze. The muscles in her neck constricted. She almost couldn't breathe. Every fiber of her body understood that she was now the prey, and he was the predator. Her jaw went into spasm. She raised the Glock and aimed it at the end of the row of shelves, waiting for him to appear.

"I'm with the Metropolitan Police," she said, her voice weak under pressure. "I am armed."

He did not reply. She sensed his movement on the other side of the shelving rack. He was stalking her. She caught a flash of him in a gap between boxes and she tracked him, moving her shoulders in an arc. It was one on one. It was him or her.

Ingrid clenched her teeth to stop them from chattering and locked her arms, aiming them at where she thought he was in the other aisle. Blood pulsed in her ears and the wailing of the alarms was joined by a humming noise. Her arms began to shake, the Glock suddenly heavy and hot.

Something moved through a gap. Rapid movement. She tried to keep her aim steady as the humming noise got louder. The gunman moved quickly.

"Fuck," he said. "Fuck off." A London accent. Then louder. "Fuck the fuck off."

He was on the move again, back toward the door. Ingrid rotated her shoulders, keeping her aim on where she was betting he was.

More movement. "Fucking hell." A bright flash from his gun illuminated his silhouette between the boxes, his bullet pinging off the metal shelves. Ingrid returned fire and he stopped. Stock still. She had shot him. Why hadn't he fallen?

For what felt like a minute she kept her aim on the sliver of stationary torso she could see.

She flinched as a bee landed on her hand. Then another. She instinctively shrugged them away. The hum was permeating her skull, boring in through her ears. The swarm was on the move. The explosions had unsettled them. Her arms trembled. Her aim wavered.

He moved suddenly. A lurch toward the door. One stagger then another. Ingrid winced as several bees circled her head. She lost sight of him through the boxes. She took several slow deliberate steps toward the door.

"You fuckers," he said. "You fucking fuckers." The bees were stinging him. The more he swatted them, the more they stung. He started to run. She heard him clatter against the door as he left the building.

Ingrid blinked hard and took a breath. She ran to the open door and looked both ways down the alleyway. She saw the man disappear around the corner into the yard. He was wearing a bullet-proof vest. That explained why her shot hadn't floored him. But it wasn't one of the drug gang. It was a cop.

A cop had tried to kill her.

28

"Hey."

Ingrid lifted her head out of her hands and looked up to see Sam Sherbourne in the doorway of her office. "Hey."

"I thought I'd see if you needed a drink. You've had a helluva day."

Ingrid was almost too tired to appreciate the gesture.

"You had a helluva day yesterday, too. You must need a drink."

"Thanks, but I now have to catch up on everything I wasn't able to get done today."

Sam nodded. "Every time I left my room, there were either people coming in here, or you going into another meeting." He leaned against the door frame. "Still, looks like the Tilbury thing was a huge success?"

Ingrid clenched her lips between her teeth and gently shook her head. "Certainly looks that way."

"Don't stay too late." Sam rotated away from the door and disappeared into the bullpen. Ingrid checked the clock. Six forty-six. She had spent seven of the last eight hours in meetings debriefing the Legat, the DEA and the ATF and signing off on paperwork that allowed the Miami drug wholesalers to be indicted on the evidence gathered at Tilbury. Everyone had congratulated her on a job well done. It wasn't the reaction she had anticipated.

When Ingrid had left Tilbury at two a.m., the consensus of Operation Pinball participants was that it had been a clusterfuck of a disaster. Danszak had moved too early, activating the booby-traps. Her DEA counterpart told her it was something they were seeing more and more; a new and lethal trick to make both rival gangs and law enforcement think twice before wading in. When the first charge detonated, it had triggered a chain reaction. In the chaos that followed, no one was in control, shots were fired indiscriminately and ambulances could not attend because the police could not secure the Napier Yards complex. It was a miracle no one died.

By the time the breakfast news bulletins aired at six a.m., the media was reporting how Met and NCA officers had heroically arrested seven men and seized over £50million worth of cocaine despite a gunfight and a series of explosions. No members of the public had been hurt, and the only serious injuries had been sustained by Met officers, one of whom was Danszak who had lost part of his arm in the initial explosion. Ralph was one of six officers taken to hospital and had already been discharged. When they'd spoken at lunchtime, he'd been well enough to joke that it was excellent timing as he had been given two months sick leave, which was way more than his official paternity allocation.

When the *Evening News* hit London's streets at midday, there was already talk of movie rights and who would play Danszak. The Met's press office had done an exemplary job in glossing over the fact that the Tilbury raid had not gone to plan and that the opportunity to gather evidence on the rest of the network had been squandered.

Also missing from the media coverage was Andy Scott MP. He had apparently fled in the middle of the gun battle to distance himself from what looked like reputational disaster. There were no photos of him in the SWAT gear, though the *Evening News* ran a quote from his office in praising the heroism of the Met and citing the raid as an example of all that was best about British policing.

Despite all the meetings, the one person Ingrid hadn't seen all day was her immediate boss, Jacob DeWalt. He hadn't asked for a debrief on Tilbury, he hadn't sat in on Munsden's debrief, he hadn't even called or popped his head in the door. Ingrid took his absence as an indication that not only was he Skylark, but that he knew she knew. His first attempt to kill her had failed, and he was now planning another method of dispatch.

Ingrid was tired. She was exhausted. But she didn't think she was delusional. DeWalt's work in counterterrorism meant he would have plenty of contacts in the Met. Was it too much of a leap to think he had leaned on one of those contacts to take her out at Tilbury? He had stopped David Steiner from unmasking him; now he was making sure Ingrid didn't either.

Ingrid's head dropped. On the one hand, it did seem plausible that DeWalt was Skylark, but on the other it was utterly preposterous. She had worked with him for four years. She would know, wouldn't she?

An involuntary sigh left her chest and drained out from between her lips. Speculation was useless. What she needed—what every case needed—was proof. Hard, concrete evidence that Jacob DeWalt, a Supervisory Special

Agent with twenty years' service in the Federal Bureau of Investigation, was a Russian asset. Only then would the diplomatic process to free Mulroony begin.

Mulroony.

Ingrid had never met the man whose desk she'd inherited, but she hoped to God that whoever followed in her footsteps would do the same for her. There was a code. There was a brotherhood. Her lip curled with disgust and her nostrils smarted at the thought the bureau had let Mulroony languish. She shook her head. Languish wasn't the right word. Fester. Rot. Perish.

Sol had said some people in the organization doubted Mulroony's guilt enough to leave traps in the system for the real Skylark. The bureau had been willing to sacrifice Mulroony to avoid a PR calamity. Resentment flooded her veins. Heat rose in her neck, making her head fizz. How dare they? How fucking dare they? Her sense of injustice raged like a wildfire: she didn't just want to rescue Mulroony, she wanted to expose the sniveling cowards who had made the decision to hang him out to dry. Their decision had left DeWalt in place. Their decision had nearly gotten her killed.

What she was about to do would cause one of the biggest scandals in the bureau's history: she was not going to get any support for what she did next. Not that it mattered. It was her life in danger, not theirs, and that meant she would do things her way.

The longer she waited, the more opportunities DeWalt had to make another attempt on her life. She needed a plan that was quick. Quick and dirty was fine, just so long as it was quick. Ingrid leaned back in her chair and stared up at the ceiling tiles. None of this would have happened, she thought, if we had moved to the new building on schedule. She emptied her lungs. "Okay," she said out loud. "Think."

Putting together a meticulous case on her own would take time. Weeks, probably. And every hour she waited was another hour DeWalt had to plan a new way of killing her. That wasn't an option.

There was one way she knew to speed things up. Cops did it all the time when the deadline to charge drew near. You tell the suspect you've got more than you have, and he spills his guts and—bam—confession. To save her own life, to save Mulroony's, Ingrid knew she had to get DeWalt to confess.

She had enough to at least make DeWalt talk, didn't she? And she was a skilled enough investigator to make him say something incriminating, wasn't she? All she had to do was record their conversation, right?

Right?

Ingrid sat very still for several minutes. It wasn't a crazy idea, was it? She knew she was exhausted. She knew she had barely slept. But it could work, couldn't it? She pushed back her chair. It really could work.

Ingrid was back at the Hilton inside ten minutes. She used one of the lobby phones to make a call, then showered and changed. She looked at herself in the bathroom mirror to check she was really going to go through with her plan. She nodded at her reflection. Yes. Yes, this was the right thing to do.

The doorman flagged down a taxi for her. She asked to be taken to Kings Cross, with a short detour via a phone repair shop. At the station, she hurried through an underground network of ticket halls and corridors to emerge from another exit, where she hailed a second taxi. At ten past nine, she paid the driver in cash and looked up at the looming block of warehouse apartments in front of her.

Century Mills was an enormous building. Eight, maybe ten, stories high with a footprint of two football fields. In the Victorian heyday of the British empire, the entire dock would have been surrounded by warehouses just like it, importing and storing goods from across the globe. Now it had been converted into seven hundred apartments offering 'dockside views' and 'urban living'. Recently added wrought-iron balconies studded the massive brick walls at regular intervals.

Ingrid turned toward the water as a propeller plane came into land at London City Airport. The runway was in the middle of the dock and the jet was so close she could see the passengers through the oval windows. The noise was deafening. *I bet that didn't make it into the realtor's brochure*. On the other side of the Royal Albert Dock, just as Sam Sherbourne had said, Ingrid saw West Park and could just make out Lisa O'Shaughnessy's house.

"I hope you heard that, Sol," Ingrid said into the tiny lapel mic she had hidden inside her jacket. "Because then that means you can hear me. I'm going in." Ingrid had no earpiece to hear what Sol said in reply. She'd had to make do with the kit she had in her desk drawer. "Approaching the building now."

The door was recessed inside a cowled entrance. Ingrid checked the apartment numbers on the panel adjacent to the door. She was outside the wrong entrance. She walked hundred and fifty feet to the next entrance and checked the numbers again. With seven hundred apartments, and only fifty numbers per door, Ingrid figured DeWalt lived on the side of the building facing away from the water. He didn't have a sight line across the dock to his ex-wife after all.

"Bear with me, Sol. This might take a while."

A few minutes later, Ingrid walked up the short path to the correct entrance. As she stepped into the cowled recess, something moved at the edges of her vision. Something fell from above. Ingrid flinched as the ground shook. She turned, her breath trapped in her chest.

"Oh my, God."

It was a body. It was DeWalt. Ingrid ran the few steps to reach him, his arms and legs splayed and crumpled. She crouched down and checked his pulse. His head was twisted to one side in a way that suggested his neck was broken. Blood bloomed from the underside of his skull. His eyes flickered.

"Dear God." His pulse was weak, but he was alive. "Sol, I need you to call an ambulance. DeWalt's injured. He fell from his balcony." A noise from above made Ingrid look toward the sky. "Or he was pushed."

Sensing there was little she could do to help DeWalt, Ingrid got to her feet and pressed every number on the door panel until someone let her in. The elevator was open and she rode it to the fifth floor. She ran down the cream-colored corridor until she located apartment five-ninety. She didn't even bother knocking, instead she aimed her right heel at the lock and kicked hard. The door flew open with such speed it was as if it was being sucked inwards.

"Sol, I can't hear an ambulance."

A stiff breeze funneled through the doorway and she stepped into a hexagonal vestibule with an identical oak door on each side. The apartment was bland and hotel-like. Shades of beige and concealed LED lighting. A set of keys and a wallet were on the console table. Through the open doors she could see a bathroom, a bedroom and a short hallway that led to the living room.

"Hello." Her mouth was dry and her voice was scratchy. She cleared her throat. "Hello," she said again, this time more firmly.

In the living room, long sable-colored curtains framed the open balcony doors. Ingrid ran to the balcony and looked over. Two people stood over DeWalt, mobile phones attached to their ears.

Ingrid made sure not to touch the handrail, then turned to go inside. DeWalt's golf bag rested in a niche between the windows as if it were a piece of sculpture. The pictures on the wall were framed tickets to sporting events and signed memorabilia. The TV was showing a video game. A beer bottle on the kitchen counter was half full. It looked like a regular guy's apartment on a regular guy's night in. There was no upturned jar of pills. No empty whisky bottle. No note for his kids.

Either the breeze got a little stronger, or a chill swept over her skin. "Sol, I don't know if you're still there, but there ain't a snowball's chance that this was suicide."

29

INGRID WAITED for the cops to come and answered their questions. No, she didn't think he was suicidal. No, she didn't know who might push him. No, she hadn't seen anyone acting suspiciously. No, she had no reason to think the timing of her arrival and his exit was anything other than a coincidence.

The uniforms immediately called in CID. Even though there were no signs of a struggle or a break-in, they had to rule out a grudge from either his ex or a connection to a case he had worked. As DeWalt was a federal employee, his death fell under the bureau's jurisdiction, so Sergeant Paphides agreed that someone from the embassy could be attached to his inquiry. "Just not you," he said. "You're a witness. You can't also be part of the investigation."

At least he hadn't said she was a suspect.

"I'm going to ask you again," Paphides said as the forensics team arrived. "If he was pushed, do you have any idea of who might want to kill him?"

Ingrid didn't like that this was the question he asked twice. It suggested he hadn't liked her first answer, or that he expected her to change her story. She felt confident in her decision to not mention Skylark. If the bureau would disapprove of her investigating, they sure as hell didn't want the Met sticking their noses in. Detective Sergeant Alexis Paphides was disheveled, hesitant, and dressed like a man twice his age, which Ingrid estimated to be early thirties. He did not impress her, and that was a good thing: she hoped she could rely on him to do a less than thorough job.

"I don't, no," she said. "I think things were a little tense with his ex, but DeWalt's a big guy… *was* a big guy. If he was pushed, it would have been by someone very strong."

Ingrid told Paphides that DeWalt's ex lived on the other side of the dock and persuaded him to let her accompany him when he broke the news. Ingrid knew it would count for something if a representative of the FBI was there when Lisa O'Shaughnessy learned that the father of her children had died. She also thought Paphides' interpersonal skills would add to the woman's trauma.

Lisa O'Shaughnessy didn't seem too surprised that the police were on her doorstep.

"Can we come in?" Paphides asked.

"I was literally just speaking to your colleague." O'Shaughnessy's long, dyed blonde hair was scraped back into a ponytail. If she had worn make-up, she had already taken it off. She had the harassed look of a single mother who was fighting to get her sons to bed and looking ahead to a glass of wine on the couch before zonking out before the clock struck eleven.

Ingrid stepped forward. "This isn't about the boy who's gone missing."

"You're American?" O'Shaughnessy was confused.

"I work with Jacob at the embassy."

O'Shaughnessy's eyes widened. Her body softened slightly. "Right. Yes. You better come in."

Lisa O'Shaughnessy took the news stoically. Ingrid suspected the magnitude would hit her in a few hours. Perhaps when she woke up the following day. She answered their questions fully and didn't know of anyone with a grudge against her ex-husband. She was also doubtful that he would take his own life. "In fact, he seemed a little happier lately. I think he had a girlfriend." *That* was new information.

Ingrid asked if there was anyone she could call for her, and was relieved when she said no. None of Ingrid's contacts were in the burner phone she had on her, and she had managed to keep that fact from the Met up until that point.

"Can I give you a lift somewhere?" Paphides asked when they left Lisa's house.

"No, thanks. I might just walk for a bit. And then I better start calling my co-workers."

"I'll be in touch tomorrow," he said.

"Let me know if forensics find anything. Or the CCTV produces the goods."

"Will do."

Ingrid stepped over the low wooden fence and into the park where a man walking his bull terrier had stopped to read the missing poster for eight-year-old Mason. For the first time in weeks, Ingrid felt cold. A breeze suggested the weather was finally going to break. She sat on a bench and looked at number thirty-six. She saw a light go on in an upstairs window and knew that Lisa was telling her sons that their father was dead. Ingrid slumped forward, her elbows on her knees, her head in her hands.

The thought that she was responsible for DeWalt's

death made her feel hollow. Like a tree being gnawed by a beaver, she felt her core weaken and sway. It took her a while to realize the unfamiliar ring tone was the burner phone in her bag.

"Sol?"

"How are you doing?" His gruff voice was comforting and reassuring, like a camp fire.

"Pretty shit right now."

"Yeah, well, that's to be expected."

Ingrid leaned back, tilting her face to the dark sky and silently screamed.

"What's your hunch?" Sol asked. "You still think DeWalt's the real Skylark? Or do you think Skylark has killed again?"

She looked over at the spot where the black Nissan Qashqai had been parked. Her head rocked slowly with disbelief. She thought she had figured it out, that DeWalt was Skylark, that he'd framed Mulroony, and that he'd given her embassy ID photo to someone who would silence her, then used his Met contacts to ensure she got shot. "I don't think I know anything anymore, Sol." She wiped away a tear—she hadn't even realized she'd been crying—and sniffed hard. "I mean, if he is, was, a Russian agent, then who killed him? The CIA? MI5?"

"Or maybe the Kremlin?" Sol offered. "Perhaps they sensed the heat you'd generated and thought he'd served his usefulness? Better to silence him than have him confess."

"Oh, don't worry, I've already been thinking that it was me who got him killed."

"Well, if you did," Sol said, "it was because he was a Russian spy."

Ingrid sighed. "Right now, he was mostly a dad." She looked at Lisa's house and felt a stab of pain in her chest.

"So," Sol said.

"So?"

"So, I'm sending you something."

She really didn't need flowers.

"Don't worry, it isn't flowers. It'll be in the office in the morning."

It took Ingrid three hours to walk back to her hotel. Ten miles through London streets she'd never been down before and would likely never see again. She was at St Paul's when the first drops of rain fell, releasing a sweetness from the leaves that the trees had been holding onto for weeks. Rain was such a novelty that people stood under store awnings and gawked at the water like tourists staring at the aurora borealis.

By the time she made it to Trafalgar Square, even her bra was soaked through, but when she finally reached the lobby of the Hilton at twelve fifteen she was almost dry. A brief summer shower that most people in the city would never know a thing about.

When she woke, her calves ached. Running ten miles would have done less damage—she'd have worn the correct footwear for starters—so she joined the hotel's morning yoga class and arrived a little later than usual at the office. When she emerged from the stairwell into the FBI's suite of offices, the silence told her everyone already knew about DeWalt. As she walked the short corridor to the bullpen, she only heard one voice, and it was one she hadn't heard in years.

The entire Legal Attaché team was in the bullpen listening to Marsha Gibson, one of Ingrid's instructors from Quantico, give a speech. Marsha noticed Ingrid's arrival and smiled at her.

Ingrid almost had to catch her breath at the shock of seeing Marsha again. She'd always known it would happen sometime, but Ingrid had thought they would meet at a training retreat or refresher course. Seeing Marsha in London was so… Ingrid reached for the right word. Unexpected? Unsettling?

The rest of the team seemed as captivated by her as Ingrid had been at Quantico, listening to her talk in virtual silence. Marsha had always been gorgeous, but the extra years suited her. She had more definition in her face than Ingrid remembered, and more definition in her hips too. The muscularity she'd displayed in her thirties had become sinewy in her forties, and she wore a simple white blouse and tailored black pants with catwalk grace.

"I know you're all hurting today, so be kind to yourselves, okay? The Metropolitan Police are going to be here at nine a.m. and they're going to want to speak to as many of you as possible. Some of you might know something that will help their inquiry, or something that would be of comfort to Jacob's kids."

Ingrid looked over at Sam Sherbourne. He looked like he'd just been given a terminal diagnosis. Clearly, Lisa hadn't called him last night. If Ingrid had been carrying her regular phone on her, she would have done so, and now it looked weird that she hadn't. Ingrid scanned the ashen faces of her co-workers until her gaze rested on one in particular. Libby's. She dabbed at her streaming eyes with a handkerchief as her bottom lip quivered. Ingrid took her anguish as confirmation that Libby had not only worked with DeWalt in Burlington, but was the girlfriend O'Shaughnessy had mentioned.

"If any of you want to come and talk to me, my door—Jacob's door—will be open," Marsha said. "I'm going to do my best to get up to speed on your assignments and investigations, but I'll end by saying that I would have been delighted to have been posted to London under any other circumstances. I look forward to getting to know you all."

The crowd dissipated, their chatter rising like steam from coffee, and they slunk away to their rooms and cubicles. Half the team headed for the commissary. Ingrid followed Libby into the criminal division, but before she got there, Marsha called out. "Ingrid!"

Ingrid turned back to see that Marsha was smiling nervously.

"I have something for you."

The closer Ingrid got, the harder she found it to maintain eye contact. How was it that Marsha still made her feel awkward after all this time? Ingrid didn't know how to say hello. Did they shake hands? Kiss on the cheek? Embrace? They settled on a mutual nod. "Well, this is a surprise," Ingrid said.

"A good one, I hope."

A memory of a hotel room in Virginia danced through Ingrid's thoughts. "Of course. You're replacing DeWalt?"

"Temporarily." She was holding an envelope. It had been folded several times and the corners were turned and scuffed. Their hands touched as Ingrid took the letter, sending fire leaping up her arms and into her chest. There was a single handwritten word on the envelope: Skyberg. The tail of the Y had a distinctive loop. She looked up at

Marsha's soft brown eyes and her mouth opened slightly. Ingrid ripped it open.

She knows everything. You can trust her.
Sol

"Later?" Marsha said. "Tonight?"

Ingrid's mouth was parched and she couldn't answer.

"Tonight?" Marsha repeated.

Ingrid nodded. On her way back to her office, she passed the bulletin board where she had pinned the photocopy. She looked down at the envelope. Skyberg. Skylark. It was the same loop on the Y. Sol had identified the skylark. The room seemed to melt, the floor to undulate. He told her he had been sent to dissuade her from investigating. Yet, by naming the skylark, he had ensured she kept pushing. Ingrid held a hand against the wall to steady herself.

When the room stopped spinning, she returned the note to the envelope and put it in her pocket. She stood in the doorway to her office and observed Libby, who sat looking straight ahead, tears falling. Ingrid closed the door behind her and approached Libby's desk. "You were close, huh?"

Libby looked up at her, the movement of her eyes releasing another cascade of tears.

"You worked together in Burlington?"

Libby nodded.

"You know, that's Jen's old desk. I'm willing to bet a hundred bucks there's a box of Kleenex in the bottom drawer." She walked around to Libby's side of the desk and crouched down. "I think they're in here." She handed

Libby the box then leaned against the edge of the desk. "When did you last speak to him? To DeWalt?"

Libby wiped her nose. "Yesterday afternoon. We had plans to catch up, but he called to cancel."

"How did he seem?"

Libby glanced toward the ceiling to blink back her tears. "Not suicidal, if that's what you mean."

"You don't think he killed himself?"

"I don't think he could have." Libby dabbed her eyes. "You know much about his divorce?"

"No, can't say I do."

"Well, I don't know another man who fought so hard to stay close to his kids." She shook her head. "There ain't no way he'd walk out on those boys."

Ingrid crossed her arms. "Or you?"

Libby's head whipped round and she studied Ingrid.

"Isn't that why you came to London? For him?"

Libby let out a gasp. "It was that obvious?"

Ingrid shook her head. "No. I only guessed because he said something about ice cream."

Libby smiled. "Rocky Road?"

"Yep, that's the one."

"Man, he loved him some Rocky Road." Her lip trembled and then the tears came again. Ingrid let her cry. Touching Libby's shoulder felt too intimate. Instead, she chose proximity to demonstrate her solidarity and stayed at Libby's side like a Labrador. "We dated way back when. Past couple years we've been talking a lot on the phone. And now my youngest is starting college—"

"Your youngest?"

Libby managed a smile. "I had my two early. So, me and Jacob thought we'd see if we had what it took."

Libby's chest seemed to empty out, and she fell forward. Her head dropped.

"Oh, Libby, I am so sorry." She probably wasn't even over the jetlag, and the reason she had come to London was in a police morgue. "When the Met get here, you do know they'll want to talk to you. They'll have a record of the call between you yesterday afternoon."

Libby nodded and wiped her nose again.

"Did DeWalt say why he was canceling your meetup yesterday?"

Libby shot her a look. "He wasn't canceling. He was rearranging."

"Of course. That was thoughtless of me."

Libby knew she had snapped. "He just said it was work." She sat a little straighter. "Work seems to have been real tough for him the past two weeks. You used to do his job. Do you know why things suddenly got so bad for him? I was going to move into his place, but the day before I flew, he said he'd asked the relocation team to get me a hotel. Said he was working all hours and with the jetlag and everything, he said a hotel was a good idea." Libby looked up at Ingrid. "I know what you're thinking. That he had someone else, but I've been to his apartment several times. There was only one toothbrush there. No long blond hairs on the couch."

Ingrid grimaced. "I promise you, I wasn't thinking that. And, no, I don't know why things might have been different for the past two weeks." *Apart from the fact he seemed to know I thought he was a spy.* Ingrid looked at her hands. "He might have mentioned something about Russia," she ventured, hoping Libby might take the bait. "He say anything to you?"

Libby's eyebrows knitted. "Russia? No. He said he was getting a lot of pressure from 'the powers that be'."

"Washington?"

Libby wrinkled her nose. "No, no. Someone in London." Libby pulled out another tissue from the box. "You think he was caught up in something?"

"I, er." Ingrid didn't know what to say.

"He said he had to do what he was told." Libby's Adam's apple moved as she swallowed. "One thing about Jacob DeWalt, if you know him well, is you should never tell him what to do. Stubborn as a goddamn mule."

The phone rang on Ingrid's desk. She crossed the office and picked up. "Agent Skyberg."

There was a delay on the line. "Sky*berg*? I was expecting Skylark."

30

Ingrid needed to think fast.

"Where are you?" she said.

"Um, ah. The Sofitel. At Heathrow." He sounded confused. "Who is this, please?"

"You called me. You know what number you dialed?" The change in her tone had stopped Libby's tears.

"The US embassy? Correct?"

"You know who I am?" Ingrid grabbed a notebook and pen.

"You said your name was Sky-something." He had an Australian accent.

"And you are?"

"James McAvenny. I'm a journalist with the Sydney Morning Herald."

"Well, James, I'll need verification of that. I'm sending a car for you. Make sure you've got your ID and paperwork and I'll see you in an hour." Ingrid ended the call, then dialed the garage. She ordered a car to collect McAvenny before phoning the front desk and requesting access to the immigration interview rooms.

"What's happening?" Libby asked.

Ingrid wasn't sure if she should level with her. "An informant just made contact. I need to set up a secure interview."

"Anything I can do to help?"

Ingrid tipped her head to one side. "I think you've got enough to deal with right now. Maybe you should take the rest of the day off?" Ingrid realized she didn't want Libby around. After the deletion of the phone message, and her loyalty to DeWalt, she wasn't sure if she could trust her.

Libby shrugged. "And spend the day in my hotel room? I'd rather be here."

"Of course." Ingrid attempted to keep the disappointment from her voice. "Is there anyone I can call for you? Anything you need?" She knew her tone sounded artificial.

Libby looked blank. "I have no idea."

"Well, if you think of anything…" Her priority was now the arrival of Mr. McAvenny, but something Libby said had sunk its teeth into her and was rattling her like a dog with a chew toy. "Listen, what you just said about DeWalt, about Jacob, getting pressure from 'the powers that be', you know the Met are going to want to know details?" Ingrid leaned forward, propped up an elbow on her desk and rested her chin in her hand. "Do you remember anything else?"

Libby closed her eyes and kept them shut for several seconds. When she opened them, she focused on Ingrid, assessing her. Her head began to nod slowly. "You want to close the door?"

Surprised, Ingrid got to her feet and gently pressed the door shut. She returned to her own desk. "What is it?"

Libby's face hardened. "How do I know I can trust you?"

Ingrid was a little taken aback. "I'm an FBI agent. I've taken oaths."

"People break promises all the time." Libby shredded the Kleenex and rolled the shreds into tiny white balls. "Two weeks ago, I was at home in Boston getting on with my life. Ten days ago, he says he needs me. A week ago, I'm on a plane. I thought he couldn't live without me." She ran a finger under an eye. "Now it turns out I'm just an old fool who thought he still loved me."

Ingrid wasn't following. "Libby? What did DeWalt say, exactly?"

Her features were cold. "He wanted me to spy on a spy."

Ingrid took a sharp intake of breath. "Me?"

Libby nodded very slowly. "Yes." The final 's' hissed like a snake's. "So now I'm thinking you got him killed. So, Agent Skyberg, what do you think I should say to the police now?"

Ingrid maintained eye contact as she picked up the phone. She dialed an internal number. "Hi, it's me. Can you come to my office?" Ingrid replaced the receiver slowly, then stood up. "First things first, you're going to find out soon enough that I was at DeWalt's building when he died. I saw him fall."

Libby gasped. She covered her mouth with her hand.

Ingrid leaned against the edge of her desk "I was there because I thought *he* was the spy. I've been working on something and he's been stalling on me."

Libby's face crumpled. "I- I don't understand."

Ingrid folded her arms. "The night before last, at the

Tilbury raid, I thought he had tried to get me killed. I went to his home to confront him, but I never—"

"Got the chance." Libby finished Ingrid's sentence. "Is that why you asked about Russia?"

There was a light knock on the door, and it opened slowly. Marsha Gibson popped her smiling face through the gap. She had reapplied her lipstick and tidied her hair. When she saw Libby's tear-stained face, Marsha's smile contracted. "What's going on?"

Ingrid turned her attention to Libby. "Did he say something about Russia?"

She shook her head. "No. Never."

Marsha closed the door. "I'll say it again, what's going on?"

Ingrid's mouth slanted into a half-smile. "You want to take a seat?"

Marsha sat in Ingrid's chair. "I'm listening."

Ingrid paced as she talked. "Have you two met, by the way?"

Marsha raised a shoulder. "No, no, I don't think so. I'm Marsha Gibson."

"I heard as much when you gave your little speech." Libby sounded hostile. "Libby Greenwood."

Ingrid picked up pen and started twiddling it between her fingers. "First things first," she said, "Libby's only been here a week. DeWalt asked her to come work with me."

"Okay." Marsha watched Ingrid as she walked.

"To *spy* on me. Libby was in a relationship with DeWalt."

Marsha's eyebrows shot up. "Okay," she said again.

"Libby thinks I'm the spy. And, she thinks I got him killed."

"Ah." Marsha turned to Libby. "Please excuse us for one second." She gestured for Ingrid to join her in a corner of the room. "Shall we?"

"You trust her?" Marsha whispered, her head bowed next to Ingrid's.

"Nope, not really." Ingrid felt Marsha's breath on her cheek. "I don't think we like one another very much. But she thought I was a spy, so go figure."

"You think she knows who killed DeWalt?"

"I honestly don't think so." Ingrid looked up into Marsha's wide brown eyes. "There's something else."

"Yes?"

"I need you to second chair an interview in about forty minutes."

"Who's the suspect?"

"Someone who just called and asked for Skylark."

Marsha's eyes widened. She took Ingrid's hand and gave it a squeeze. "Okay, then. Let's deal with Libby." Marsha straightened up and turned. "Libby, I'm very sorry for your loss. I appreciate that today you're going to find it hard to focus, but I think there's a good chance you may know why Jacob DeWalt died yesterday." She perched on the edge of Libby's desk. "I want to ask you some questions. Is that okay?"

Libby looked scared. "How do I know I can trust you? I just saw the way you were together over there. You just show up. Within *hours* of Jacob dying. How do I know you're not here to cover things up and keep your pal in position?"

Marsha's nostrils flared. "I don't know of a single double agent in the bureau's history who has had an accomplice. The idea that both Agent Skyberg and myself might be foreign assets is fanciful. To say the least." There was an edge of anger in her voice. She tapped the side of the desk with impatient fingers. "Libby, do you realize that your boyfriend was under suspicion himself? If he killed himself, it could be because he feared he was about to be found out. And if he was killed, it could have been to prevent him from switching sides."

Libby blinked rapidly.

"How well did you know him?" Marsha asked.

Libby cast her eyes downward, then made deliberate eye contact with her new boss. "Well enough to know he was not a traitor." Her bottom lip quivered.

While Marsha and Libby were talking, Ingrid had been thinking about the photos in her drawer. She had been sure they identified DeWalt as Skylark, but she now realized all they indicated was that Mulroony *thought* DeWalt was Skylark. She took a step toward Libby. "Do you know any reason why someone would think DeWalt was a spy?"

Libby's eyes darted from Ingrid to Marsha and back again. "No."

"Because someone did. Someone *really* did."

"I, ah, um." Libby was flustered.

"I appreciate you and I haven't got off to the greatest of starts," Ingrid said, "but if you know some reason why anyone would think Jacob DeWalt was a spy, then we can figure out why he died yesterday."

Libby's face flitted between aggression and confusion. She looked at Marsha, then back to Ingrid. Her shoulders rose and fell. Then she nodded. "The only thing I can think of, and I mean the *only*, was that he was a people pleaser."

"Go on," Marsha said, her tone conciliatory.

"He was a scratcher of backs. He liked to help out. Whether it was his drinking buddies or his golf buddies." Again, her eyes switched between the two of them, searching for support. "He bent the rules occasionally. I'll admit he didn't always do things by the book, but he took care of his friends. He was always balancing the favors. Maybe..." She paused. "Maybe someone thought he owed them?"

Marsha and Ingrid exchanged looks.

"Which fraternity was he in?" Ingrid asked.

"Phi Gamma Delta."

"Was he a freemason?"

"I, um, I don't know. I don't think so." Libby's head turned at a knock on the door.

"Come in," Marsha said.

It was Penny. Ingrid would always think of her as Marshall's gatekeeper, but her ashen face was a reminder that—until the day before—she had been DeWalt's right-hand woman. "Hi." She pushed a piece of dark hair behind her ear.

"Penny, right?" Marsha asked.

Penny bobbed her head. "It's the Met."

Marsha checked her watch. "They're here already?"

Penny pursed her vermillion lips. "Nope. They say they don't need to come."

Ingrid and Marsha checked in with one another. "Huh?" they said in unison.

"They told me they're satisfied it was suicide."

Marsha jutted out a hip and rested a hand on it. "Please come in and close the door."

Penny did so, then leaned against the door, holding her hands together in front of her tightly fitted skirt. She looked anxiously at Libby's red eyes, then at Ingrid and Marsha's serious faces. "What's going on?"

Marsha moved in Penny's direction. "You have worked

closely with Agent DeWalt for a few months now, is that right?"

"Yes."

"You knew him pretty well, right?"

"He was my boss. We weren't friends."

"But you spent a lot of time in his company?"

"I guess."

"If anyone would have seen something, either in his behavior, or his correspondence, that indicated he would take his own life, it would probably be you, right?"

"Um, I guess."

"And did you?"

Penny exhaled and gazed into the middle distance. "No, nothing. Nothing that's come to mind, at least."

Marsha moved over to the window and looked down at the view. Her fingers steepled under her chin, giving the appearance of being deep in thought. Ingrid took over the role of questioner.

"You coping okay?" When Ingrid was acting SSA, she had worked closely with Penny. She was very well aware that, after Marshall, DeWalt was the second boss to have died on Penny inside a year.

"No one's going to want to work with me ever again, are they? I'm like the black widow."

Ingrid placed a hand on her shoulder. "Hey, I didn't die when I sat in that office, did I?"

Penny let out a little snort. "Everyone knows you're indestructible, Ingrid."

"Oh great, so you're the black widow and I'm, what, a cockroach?"

Penny was smiling now. Ingrid smiled back. "Obviously Agent Gibson is going to need your help a lot over the next couple of days, but maybe you should schedule a little down time for next week? Take a day off?"

"Thanks." Penny's eyes brimmed at Ingrid's kindness. "I better…" She pointed her thumb at the door behind her. "Get back to it."

Marsha turned her head toward Penny. "Would you mind pushing back everything else until…" She checked her watch. "Say, ten-thirty?"

"Sure thing."

When Penny had left, the three women took a moment. It was Ingrid who spoke first. "I was in his apartment. There's just no way it was suicide."

"So," Marsha said carefully, "the Metropolitan Police either have budget constraints and know we'll investigate anyway. Or?"

"Or?" Libby said.

Ingrid looked her right in the eye. "Or someone is leaning on them not to investigate."

Libby looked confused. "Why wouldn't someone want it investigated?"

Ingrid didn't miss a beat before answering. "That's exactly what I intend to find out."

31

Ingrid lingered outside DeWalt's office for Marsha to appear. She fiddled with her watch, scrolling through her fitness stats in a bid not to look like a faithful puppy waiting for its owner, which was exactly how she felt. Seeing Marsha after all this time—how long was it? Twelve years? Thirteen?—was like hearing the song you haven't danced to since high school but still know all the words to.

"Okay," Marsha said, striding out of the door. "Let's do this." There was nothing in her appearance or demeanor that suggested an abrupt uprooting from whatever her previous posting had been, or a transatlantic flight at extremely short notice, yet it was only fifteen hours since DeWalt had landed in the parking lot of Century Mills. What had Sol said to her to make her drop everything and come to London? "You speak to the Met?"

"Interview room is this way." They started walking. "Yep. Spoke to DS Paphides. He said his DCS—"

"DCS?"

"Detective chief superintendent. He reallocated the

team to the major incident squad. There's been a missing kid out there for the past week. There are posters everywhere. Anyway, there's been a sighting and they need officers on the street for the optics. Because if the kid dies and they hadn't thrown everything at it..."

"Obviously you told him we'd be continuing our own inquiries?"

"Obviously. Requested all files to be sent over immediately." Ingrid led her through a series of corridors to another bank of elevators. "You ever worked out of an embassy before?"

"No, this is my first."

"Well, there's a suite of interview rooms Immigration Services use for citizenship applications. They're designed to intimidate."

"Sounds ideal." Marsha lingered outside the elevator, clutching her iPad and files. "We're not taking this?"

Ingrid was already halfway through the door to the stairs. "Um." She thought about getting stuck with DeWalt and did not want to risk being alone in an enclosed space with Marsha. Marsha pointed to her shoes. She wasn't planning on running after any perps today.

"Ah, understood," Ingrid said. "Third floor."

Marsha pushed the button, and Ingrid noticed a wedding band. Ingrid was suddenly engulfed by questions. Was she married to a man or a woman? Who on earth would be worthy of the magnificent Marsha Gibson? She wanted to know. She *really* wanted to know. The elevator doors opened almost immediately. Three people were already inside. Marsha and Ingrid looked at each other, then at their feet. Another opportunity to ask about the ring would present itself.

"It's down here," Ingrid said, leading the way through

the third-floor warren. She handed Marsha a printout of the background information she had pulled on James McAvenny. It ran to several pages. "I haven't had a chance to read it all. There's a lot about this guy online."

"He's legit?" Marsha asked.

"Let's find out."

They reached the interview suite where a receptionist guided them to the room where McAvenny was waiting. Marsha stretched out an arm and touched Ingrid's. "Before we go in, I just wanted to say, it's so nice to see you."

Ingrid demurred. "You too." She couldn't quite manage eye contact. "We must, like, have dinner or do something fun while you're here."

Marsha smiled. "Perfect. Shall we?"

Ingrid pushed down the lever and opened the door. "James McAvenny?"

A crumpled middle-aged man with lank hair and heavily stained teeth looked up at them.

"I am Agent Skyberg. This is my colleague, Agent Gibson. Don't get up."

McAvenny shuffled back into his seat on the other side of a stainless-steel table that reminded Ingrid of a mortician's slab. Rectangles of diffuse bright light created the illusion of windows in the completely white room. An air conditioning unit purred above them. Buttons underneath the table allowed the brightness, the temperature, and the noise levels to be manipulated. Ingrid pulled up a black plastic chair and sat down, spreading her paperwork in front of her. Marsha stayed standing.

"Did you say 'agent'?" McAvenny asked.

"Special Agent. We're with the FBI."

McAvenny's eyes popped, and then he leaned back in his chair and smiled. "Well, well, well."

"What does that mean, Mr. McAvenny?"

"It means I've bloody well got myself a story, doesn't it?"

Ingrid opened the folder in front of her. Without looking up at him, she asked, "And where will you be publishing this story of yours? On the phone, you mentioned you work for the *Sydney Morning Herald*." She eyeballed him. "I called them. They said you haven't worked there for eight years."

He looked slightly less pleased with himself.

"The most recent article of yours I found was published on a website called Brighton Beat. As far as I can tell, it's a website for a suburb of Melbourne that mostly features restaurant openings, beach combing finds and missing pets." She gave him her best smile. "Why are you in London, Mr. McAvenny?"

He yawned. His plane had landed at six fifty-five. He hadn't wasted any time before putting a call into Skylark. "Have I done something wrong?" he asked.

Marsha flipped through the slim dossier behind Ingrid, and made the kind of 'a-ha' and 'h-hmm' noises that made interviewees nervous.

Ingrid looked at the printout. "Let's see. Kidnap—"

"My wife wouldn't let me see my kids!"

"Possession of cocaine—"

"I'm a journalist!"

"So, what, it's a tool of the trade, like a notebook or a Dictaphone?" Ingrid returned to her list. "Two speeding tickets and a caution for gross indecency—"

"I was taking a slash!"

"So, yes, to answer your question, you have done something wrong, but, ooh," Ingrid tapped the file, "not for the past eighteen months or so."

He folded his arms indignantly over the dome of his belly.

Ingrid examined the controls beneath the desk and increased the air-conditioning. McAvenny had the sour aroma of someone who hadn't changed their clothes for two days. "Why do *you* think you're here, Mr. McAvenny?"

He pulled off his horn-rimmed spectacles and rubbed the bridge of his nose. He palmed his hair over his scalp. If he had gone gray, you could generously say he was going for the Einstein look, but there was something sleazy about his thinning, long hair; like an old rocker reliving his glory days. It didn't help that it was unwashed. McAvenny popped his glasses back on and sighed heavily. "Saskia Cole," he said. "That's why I'm here, right?"

Ingrid had no idea who Saskia Cole was. She glanced at Marsha in case she'd seen the name in the dossier. Marsha shrugged and Ingrid returned her attention to McAvenny. "Well done, Mr. McAvenny. You've stumped us. Who the heck is Saskia Cole?"

He looked surprised. "Who *was* Saskia Cole, more like." He stared at each of them in turn. "Bloody typical. We swallow a bucketful of US news, about your stolen election and oil spills, but you guys don't have a clue what's going on in the rest of the world."

"You may have noticed that we are in the rest of the world," Marsha pointed out.

"Fair point." He inhaled at length, then continued. "Saskia Cole was murdered five years ago. They tried to make it look like an accident, but she was definitely murdered."

"They?" Ingrid asked.

"The Russians. Jesus, you really don't know this story, do you?"

Russians? Ingrid sensed there were some dots in danger of joining up. "Any particular Russians?"

"Two FSB operatives. Evgeny Poliakoff and Josef Polinin. Though those probably aren't their real names."

Marsha placed her iPad on the table in front of Ingrid. It displayed a report from an Australian newspaper dated March 7, 2012. *Woman killed in robbery was former Herald journalist*. It was accompanied by a photo of a woman in her fifties wearing a helmet and flak jacket emblazoned with the word 'press'. It looked like she was reporting from Afghanistan. "Was Saskia Cole a friend of yours?" Ingrid asked.

"More of a mentor. She was my first editor when I worked at the ABC. A bloody brilliant journalist. Didn't give a flying fuck about anything other than the truth. She never took any bullshit or flannel from anyone. Second sourced everything."

Ingrid scanned the report. She felt the heat from Marsha's body just inches behind her own. "I can't see anything in this report about Russia." Ingrid locked eyes with him. "So, what do you think is the real story?"

He looked at one then the other. "Can I get a glass of water?"

Ingrid pushed her chair back slowly. "Sure." She ducked out into the corridor and filled three mugs from the tap in the small, filthy kitchen area. She paused outside the door before going back in to remind herself that no matter how unlikeable McAvenny was, he wasn't a suspect, he hadn't done anything wrong, and the most important thing was to keep him talking. She plastered a smile on her face and pushed the door open. "Here you go." She distributed the mugs and sat back down. "Did I miss much?"

"We were discussing what the British English term for liquor store is," Marsha said.

Ingrid wrinkled her nose. "They call it an off-license. Why?"

"Because Ms. Cole was killed in what Mr. McAvenny calls a 'bottle shop'."

Ingrid didn't want to get distracted by semantics. "Do you want to tell me the story?"

McAvenny nodded. "It's pretty simple, really. There was a hold-up in a bottle shop. Gunmen asked the guy at the cash desk for money. Saskia got a bullet in the neck. Masked men ride off on a motorbike and are never seen again."

Ingrid rubbed her nose. "Where do the Russians fit in?"

McAvenny yawned before answering. "Sorry. I've been awake for what feels like a week. I don't know what time zone I'm in but I could murder a beer."

"It's ten a.m.," Ingrid said.

"Is that too early?" When neither of them answered, he carried on. "Yeah, right. So normally when there's a stickup at a store, it's some local kid who's high on meth, nicked a neighborhood bike and the cops know who it is before they get a chance to look at the CCTV, right?"

He wasn't wrong. Ingrid shrugged. "Go on."

"Well, these armed robbers arrived on a brand-new Honda with fake plates, fired a gun that had never been used in a crime before, according to the ballistics report, and the money they took has never gone back into circulation."

Ingrid raised her hand. "Let me stop you there. Are you saying that the target of the holdup wasn't the liquor store, it was your friend, and the holdup was the cover story?"

McAvenny smiled. Color reddened his cheeks. "Yes. Thank you! You get it."

"I might get it, Mr. McAvenny, but I'm not sure I buy it. Just to be clear, you're saying the robbers were actually Russian agents committing an assassination on sovereign Australian soil?"

He leaned forward and raised his eyebrows. He peered at Ingrid and then Marsha. "Yeah, like duh. That's not what I'm saying, it's what bloody happened."

The Russians had certainly murdered people on UK soil, hence the Hawking Review into Andropov's death. "And what do the police in Australia think?" Ingrid asked.

"They think it was an out-of-town holdup. That's why they've got no leads."

"And you think it's the Russians because?"

McAvenny reached down to his bag. Marsha and Ingrid both leaned forward to see what he was doing. He dived into a carryall and yanked out several cardboard folders of files. "I can't believe I have to travel half way round the world to get someone in law enforcement to take this seriously." He spread out the files into four piles on the stainless-steel table top. "These are Saskia's notes. She was working on a story about illegal arms deals. I think she found something out no one wanted her to know and..." He made a pistol from his fingers and pointed to his head.

"May I?" Ingrid asked, leaning for a blue folder.

"Just keep them in order, okay. I know it doesn't look like a proper filing system, but I can take you to any document, in any folder, so don't mess it up."

Marsha cut him a look.

"Sorry," he said. "But, please, respect the piles."

Marsha kept up the pressure while Ingrid flicked through the dead journalist's research, her mind wandering to thoughts a little closer to home. "I just want to check I understand you correctly," Marsha said. "You believe your friend and mentor was killed, what, five years ago, in Melbourne by Russian assassins because she got too close to knowing something about an arms deal?"

"Broadly, yeah, that's right?"

"Then why are you in London?"

He leaned back and put his arms behind his head to reveal two enormous sweat patches. "Because I'm a bloody good journalist and I need to prove it. I used to work for the ABC, I was on their nightly news, I worked for the Herald, but the last time I made the national news it was because I *was* the story." He ran his tongue over his gums. "'From the headlines to the bread line' was the angle the tabloids took. They had a photo of me living under the boardwalk looking like Robinson fucking Crusoe. My life had fallen apart. I'd started gambling, my wife had kicked me out, my kids were ashamed of me, and the only work I could get was freelance, and that doesn't pay like it used to." He took his specs off again and rubbed his eyes. "So, I'm a failure, right? My wife hates me, my kids are ashamed of me I'm as broke as quadriplegic's spine—" He stopped suddenly. "I'm guessing from your faces that was poor taste? Anyway, I'm here for the scoop of a lifetime and I've got a wonderful feeling that you lovely ladies are going to help me get it."

Ingrid looked up briefly from one of Cole's notepads. "Lovely ladies? Really?"

"What, that's bad taste too?"

"Yep," Marsha said. "So, if you're so broke, who paid for your flight?"

"Saskia's dad." McAvenny seemed quite pleased to have a comeback. "I want answers, but that poor bugger *needs* them. He's given me ten thousand dollars and, in exchange, I'm going to get him the truth. Several other people have tried, but I promised him I'm going to deliver."

Ingrid's attention was divided between watching Marsha get the upper hand over McAvenny, Saskia Cole's notebook and a nagging feeling that was tugging at the edges of her brain. If Saskia Cole's murder was somehow related to Skylark, it was a completely different MO from pushing DeWalt off a balcony.

The corners of spiral-bound pad were worn and torn and some of the pages had press clippings and business cards stapled into them. Ingrid flicked through them, unsure what to make of them or the disheveled man who had brought them to her.

She thought back to the woods in Richmond and imagined David Steiner, a fit man in his sixties, being frog-marched to the place of his execution. Whether Steiner was forced to pull the trigger himself, or the gun was placed in his hand afterwards, it was likely the work of a killer working alone. Saskia Cole's murder, on the other hand, was a team effort. Ingrid wasn't sure there was a connection. She studied McAvenny. He was simultaneously cocksure and desperate. For a man with a gambling addiction he totally lacked a poker face.

"Who else has looked into this?" Marsha asked.

"When the police gave up, old man Cole was sure Saskia's notebooks would identify her killer. And they did." He took a gulp of water, some of which dribbled down his chin. "A couple of journos at the *Age*, ex-colleagues, identified the Russia thing, found Polinin and Poliakoff on flight manifests. That's pretty much proven now. What no one's figured out is why."

Ingrid leaned forward and picked up a ring binder marked 'interviews'.

"Let me guess, except you?" Marsha said.

"I reckon I'm close. Reckon I'm a damn sight closer since you sent that car for me."

He was laying all his cards on the table face up. Now they just needed to find out if he was holding an ace.

"And you dialed my number because...?" Ingrid tapped a pen as she scanned a list of interviewees.

"I'm looking for Skylark." He stifled another yawn.

"And what is Skylark?" Marsha asked.

"Oh, you're being cute, aren't you? You mean *who* is Skylark."

Marsha narrowed her eyes. "Okay then, who is Skylark?"

"Someone who must work in this building, given this is the number Saskia had for him."

"Him?" Ingrid said without looking up from the notebook. A name on Cole's list was leaping out at her. Sidney Baxter.

"Or her."

"It's an unusual name, Skylark," Marsha said.

"Well it ain't a real name, is it?"

"What sort of name is it?"

"Well, duh, obviously it's a code. And it's one you bloody well know because you sent a car for me. So, you tell me, who is Skylark?"

Ingrid had turned to the transcript of Sidney Baxter's interview. The moment she started reading, she understood why his name had rung a bell the size of the Big Ben: Baxter was the real name of a man she had helped arrest when she first arrived in London. An arms dealer she had known as Greg Brewster. Ingrid blocked out the discussion between Marsha and McAvenny as she tried to remember everything she could about Brewster. Arrogant. Red faced. Boorish. Pompous. But the real reason she hadn't taken to him was because he insisted on dealing with the agent he was familiar with: Dennis Mulroony. Ingrid's vision started to swim. The sounds of Marsha's voice drifted like fog through her ears.

Everything came back to Mulroony, didn't it?

She was snapped back into the room by the harshness of Marsha's voice. "Mr. McAvenny, let me ask you again, why are you looking for this Skylark?"

"Because he knows why Saskia was killed."

32

JAMES MCAVENNY DIDN'T SNORE, but he did dribble. He lay with his head on the table, his glasses askew on his face. Marsha and Ingrid pored through his treasure trove of documents.

"What do you think?" Marsha asked, her chin propped on a palm. "If these papers identify the person who ordered Saskia Cole's murder, will it be linked to whoever pushed DeWalt over his balcony?"

Ingrid grunted rather than answered. She was too deep inside the transcript of the interview with Sidney Baxter to form any actual words. It was dated November 16, 2011. That meant Saskia Cole had interviewed him before his arrest in 2012, when Mulroony still worked at the embassy. As best she could tell, Cole interviewed Baxter thinking he was a legitimate arms dealer to get his insights into the illegal trade.

SB: It usually starts with blackmail. They find some dirt on you, ask for a favor to keep things quiet, then threaten to tell your embassy, or your rival's embassy, if you don't

do them another favor. Suddenly you're five indiscretions down and you've got no way out.
SC: And you know this because?
SB: You hear stories. At conventions and conferences.
SC: So you don't have any proof?
SB: No, just twenty years in the business. Trust me, that's how it happens. They get you to supply arms in breach of sanctions, or share technology.
SC: You mean—
SB: Or, alternatively, they show you pictures of your kids or your wife at the shopping mall. They can be pretty persuasive, and of course the first thing they ask you to do seems trivial. [throat clearing] Blackmail and persuasion is a heck of a lot cheaper than the kind of R and D operation we have.
SC: And this is state sponsored?
SB: Hell yes. The Russkies, the Koreans, Chinese, the Iranians, of course. Now, I know what you're thinking, you're thinking, how could anyone fall for it. Let me tell ya, it's because the guy who approaches you doesn't look Chinese, he doesn't sound Russian. They've recruited sleeper agents. He'll have an American accent, maybe he'll be an Aussie like you. Chances are, he'll be a Brit.
SC: Why's that?
SB: Oh, no reason, just, you know, experience. [Pause.] And I tell you what, he won't be working for the intelligence services, at least not directly. He'll be a middle-ranking official somewhere, so you think, 'What harm can this do? It's not like he's one of the swinging dicks or he works for the Kremlin or anything.' But one way or another, he does. He was probably blackmailed, too. It's a goddamn pyramid scheme.

Baxter was describing his own recruitment. Ingrid walked over to a console desk in the corner and picked up the phone.

"Criminal division, Libby Greenwood speaking."

"Libby, hi, it's Ingrid. How are you doing?"

"Okay. A bit shaky."

Ingrid wished that Zeke was still her assistant. Or Jen. But Libby was who she had. "You up for some work?"

"Will it help figure out who killed Jacob?"

"Absolutely."

"Then fire away."

Ingrid asked her to find out everything she could about Sidney Baxter. The transcript proved that Baxter liked to talk. She couldn't get his sentence for breaching sanctions reduced, but she hoped the promise of a transfer to a prison closer to his family would make him want to carry on the conversation with her.

"You're quiet," Ingrid said to Marsha when she finished the call. "Finding anything interesting?"

Marsha looked up at her with bleary eyes. "There's too much here. We need to impound this cache. I'm trying to work out under what law we can seize an innocent man's assets because," she tapped her watch, "I need to put in an appearance upstairs."

"He's a journalist," Ingrid said, thinking of Angela Tate. "He'll do anything for a scoop. What he wants is to get his old job back and make his kids proud. So, we let him sit in on a few meetings. Promise him something on the record. I bet you he'll play ball like a trained seal."

Marsha glanced over at him. "Do we wake him up?"

"No," Ingrid said. "Let's leave instructions with the receptionist outside. He can come and find us."

They were collecting up the folders when the phone rang on the console desk. McAvenny briefly stirred.

"Skyberg."

"It's Libby."

"That was quick."

"It's because I have a definitive answer for you."

That didn't sound good. "Go on."

"Sidney Baxter died in December 2012 in the federal penitentiary at Allenwood."

Ingrid blew out her cheeks. "Let me guess, it wasn't natural causes?"

"Suicide. Hung himself."

Ingrid's cell vibrated in her pocket. "Okay, thanks Libby. We'll be up soon." She switched phones and saw that Nick Angelis was calling. "Nick, hi."

"How marvelous to hear your voice."

Why was he always so over the top? Surely part of the job description for work in the private security services was the ability to blend in? "Likewise," Ingrid found herself saying. "What can I do for you, Nick?"

"It's rather what I can do for you. I have some information that I'm not sure you'll like."

Ingrid gestured to Marsha to stop packing away McAvenny's files. She needed to concentrate on what Nick had to say. "Sounds ominous."

"I'm afraid to say it's not good news."

Ingrid's brow knitted. "Go on."

"I've heard from my source with eyes inside the Black Dolphin."

A shudder of dread scattered over Ingrid's skin. He wasn't about to tell her about another prisoner suicide, was he? "Mulroony?"

"He's been moved."

"That's bad news?"

"Yes, I fear it is. He's been moved to their *pūkūl* block." He paused. "No one ever leaves *pūkūl*. I don't need to tell you what it translates as."

What was he trying to say? "It's an extermination camp?"

"Oh, gosh, I wouldn't have used that phrase, but I suppose in its own sick way, it is. They barely feed people. They don't let them wash. The conditions are horrific. Skin crawling with lice, perpetual dysentery, untreated wounds from all the fights that break out."

Ingrid was still trying to process her last conversation while taking onboard what Nick was saying. "Do you know why they've moved him?"

He sniffed sharply. "I think I do, yes. He's no longer useful. If they were keeping him to trade with your Skylark, then they no longer feel they need the leverage."

Marsha could see the consternation on Ingrid's face and was looking puzzled.

Ingrid's brain tried to compute the new information. "They think Skylark's dead?" Was it DeWalt after all?

"That's not what I'm hearing. They think Skylark's been compromised and they're planning an extraction."

She scrunched up her face. "Why? Why do they think he's been compromised? What's he done?"

"It's not entirely clear," Nick said. "I hear that the Russians feel either the stress or the power has got to him. There aren't many who can handle it. And before he melts down and exposes their entire operation, they are going to quietly make him disappear."

"How?"

"Lord alone knows."

"Will he know? Will Skylark know he's being recalled?"

Nick made a tutting noise. "I don't have that information."

"What's your hunch? Is that usual practice?"

"It can work both ways. If they tell him, they risk him unraveling in position as he tries to prove them wrong. If they don't, they risk him not covering his tracks and leaving unnecessary loose ends."

Ingrid placed a hand against the wall and closed her eyes as she took in Nick's revelations. "Let me get this straight. To free an FBI agent from the 'hell' block of the Black Dolphin prison, I have to find Skylark so I can trade him for Mulroony?"

"Yes, yes, I think so. I am, of course, willing to help."

"So." She sighed. "I need to get to Skylark before the Russians do."

"I'm rather afraid that's the case, yes."

"Okay," Ingrid exhaled loudly.

"Listen. This is highly confidential. I shouldn't really have access to this, but..."

"But what?"

"We have been monitoring Spetsnaz activity—"

"Special forces?"

"They're planning something in London. Ingrid, it's got to be the extraction."

Ingrid's skin turned cold. "When?"

"Tomorrow night."

33

"I HAVE ABOUT sixteen meetings I need to be in," Marsha said outside the door of the Criminal Division. She passed the files she'd carried up from the immigration suite to Ingrid.

"Understood."

"I'll swing by the moment I get a chance."

Ingrid bobbed her head. "Thanks. Um. Listen, can you spare Penny?"

"My PA? On my first day?"

"It's just," Ingrid lowered her voice. "Libby. I'm not one hundred percent there with her. I just don't feel comfort—"

Marsha raised a hand. "Say no more." She popped her head into Ingrid's office. "Libby, right?"

Libby looked up from her screen. "Hi."

"Congratulations, Libby, you're now the executive assistant to the SSA."

Libby stood up. "Okay." She sounded uncertain.

"You want to gather up your things and come to my office?"

God, Marsha was magnificent. No dilly. No dally. Just action.

"Sure, I guess." Libby looked confused.

"In five?"

"Yes. Yes, I'll be there."

Ingrid mouthed a 'thank you' to Marsha.

"Keep me in the loop."

"Of course."

Ingrid avoided looking at Libby as she entered—she felt awkward about kicking her out—and dumped McAvenny's notebooks and folders on the spare desk.

"What are all those?" Libby asked.

Ingrid explained about Saskia Cole.

"And you don't need my help to go through them?"

Ingrid took a centering breath. "I think I've got this."

"Are you sure, because the Met's info dump just landed."

"The crime scene stuff from Century Mills?"

Libby nodded.

"That was quick." Ingrid wrinkled her nose. "It's almost like Paphides wants me to investigate this."

"And I want to help you. If someone killed Jacob, I'm onboard."

Ingrid plunged both hands into her pants pockets. She didn't want to sound too hostile, but she really didn't want to be working with Libby anymore. "I know. But today, the best way you can do that is by running Marsha's desk. Stall as many people as you can, reschedule everything that isn't level five, and let her come back to me as soon as possible."

Libby looked dubious. "If you're sure."

"I am."

Libby scooped a few things into her leather tote bag. "You need anything before I go?"

Ingrid thought for a second. "You'll only be on the other side of the bullpen. But can you ask Penny to bring DeWalt's desk diary, any unfiled expenses, receipts shoved in bottom drawers, anything that isn't on the system."

"Yes, of course."

Libby had reached the doorway when Ingrid turned to her. "I will find who did this, I swear."

Libby managed something approaching a smile and slung her bag over her shoulder. Ingrid sat down at her desk and logged into the system. She stared blankly at the screen, then closed her eyes. *Think. Prioritize*. She only had a day before Skylark was extracted so she couldn't waste even a minute on the wrong path.

She got back to her feet and pulled a sheaf of copier paper out of the printer's feeder tray and took it to the empty intern's desk. She picked up a pen and sat down. At the top of one sheet of paper she wrote the heading, Things we know about Skylark.

1. People have been calling my number for him
2. The following people have been killed to protect his identity. David Steiner. Saskia Cole…

Ingrid's pen hovered over the paper before she continued.

… Jacob DeWalt.

She felt sure there were others. Mulroony would be added to the list if she didn't find Skylark. Then she remembered another victim. One that Jen had told her about.

Mulroony's assistant (coma)

She paused before continuing with her list.

3. Before Mulroony was extracted, Skylark was a code-name for a suspected double agent inside MI5 or the Met.

Ingrid stopped. That felt significant in the light of what Sidney Baxter had said. In his interview with Saskia Cole, he'd said the approach often came from someone with a British accent.

4. Until his death, I thought it could have been DeWalt.

She paused again and attempted to recall all the reasons why she had thought it was DeWalt. There were the arrows in the photograph. There was the fact he had jammed the elevator. That his former address was 36 West Park. More importantly, Mulroony thought he was being framed by DeWalt. She made a note on another piece of paper.

Why would DeWalt frame Mulroony if he wasn't Skylark?

She needed to look again at the photos. Ingrid crossed the office, tipped up her penholder, located the small steel key and opened her top drawer. The photos weren't there. She bent down, pulled the drawer out further, pushed her hand in deeper.

Where were they?

Ingrid swallowed, her mouth painfully bone dry. She glanced over at Libby's desk. Had she? Ingrid's temperature spiked, her palms became moist. A droplet of sweat rolled down between her shoulder blades, making her shiver. Ingrid crouched down and looked inside the drawer. Exhale. The wallet of photos had slid to the back. She took a moment to center herself before standing. *Calm down. Think straight.*

Ingrid tipped out the images and scattered them on the spare desk next to her notes and Saskia Cole's notebooks. She created a pile of the photographs she had figured out —the house where Andropov had been killed, Stephen Hawking, the Post-its, the file number, the skylark, David Steiner's book, the cake and arrows—and looked again at the ones she had failed to identify. The map of Scotland, the diary, the word 'sois', the Google image search for yards—

"Oh, duh." She slapped her palm into her forehead, then moved the photo of the map of Scotland next to the one of all the yards. Scotland Yard. "How the heck did I not make that connection?" She flamed with embarrassment as she shook her head in disbelief. "How stupid are you, Skyberg? I mean, seriously."

Ingrid took a deep breath and exhaled slowly. She nodded, her head movement affirming her thoughts. Skylark being in the Met made sense. It explained why Mulroony—the Met liaison agent—had been relatively easy to frame. And it explained why Paphides' investigation had been shut down. Someone high up must have leaned on him. Ingrid rose powerfully to her feet and strode over to her own desk. She needed to examine the documents Paphides had sent through.

She clicked on the folder on her screen and saw a clutch of files. The initial 9-9-9 call, the report from the uniformed first responders, notes from door-to-door interviews with neighbors, CCTV logs, Paphides' own report. She scanned the list again: no forensics. That wasn't a surprise—DeWalt hadn't yet been dead for a day—but she had hoped for a provisional assessment of the crime scene and working assumptions. There was nothing on DeWalt's phone records.

Someone cleared their throat. Ingrid turned to see Penny standing in the doorway, her arms full of notebooks and folders.

"Hi," Ingrid said. In the four months Ingrid had been the acting SSA, she had found Penny to be aloof, but also efficient, trustworthy and discreet. "We get to work together again. Come on in."

Penny almost always wore the same clothes. Ingrid didn't know if her librarian appearance—tweed skirts, pussy bow blouses, sensible shoes and tortoise-shell glasses—was archly retro, or genuine geek. The parting in her severe bob was a white chalk path between neatly plowed fields of dark brown soil, and her lips were always a shade redder than Ingrid remembered. It was hard to tell if Penny was closer to twenty or thirty, lending her a sense of mystery.

Ingrid's private joke was that Penny was some kind of secret superhero. She was so demure, so reserved, so aloof, that Ingrid felt she must lead a double life, like Kate Kane or Diana Prince. And if Penny *wasn't* secretly saving the world in her spare time, then Ingrid was convinced she was quietly writing a future Pulitzer Prize winner.

Ingrid installed Penny at Libby's desk and pulled over the chair from her own. "How are you doing?"

"A bit shell-shocked, but okay I guess." There was even less color in Penny's face than usual.

"Did Marsha tell you why you're swapping jobs with Libby today?"

"No, not really. Only that you needed me, and you needed all this." Penny gestured to the documentation she had brought with her.

Ingrid nodded. "As you know, the FBI has a mandate to investigate the death of all federal employees, and that's what we're doing for DeWalt."

"Without the Metropolitan Police?"

"Correct. They've sent over their initial findings, and I'm working my way through those just now." Ingrid nodded in the direction of her monitor.

"What are those?" Penny asked, pointing at the spare desk.

"They're research files we've, um, borrowed from an investigative journalist."

"Okay." Penny seemed to be taking it all in and computing everything Ingrid said. "What do you need from me?"

Ingrid paused for a second. "First off, you're sure you're okay to work?"

Penny closed her eyes briefly, revealing perfectly applied eyeliner on her top lids. "I'm good to go. How about you? I mean you actually saw him fall."

Ingrid squirmed. "Also good. So, first things first, I want to ask you some questions."

"Fire away."

Ingrid leaned forward in her chair, placing her elbows on her knees. "Are you aware of any stresses DeWalt was under, bar the usual, in the past few weeks? I know he was recently divorced. Were things escalating with Lisa?"

Penny stared into the middle distance as she concentrated. "No, no, things with Lisa seemed okay. I usually spoke to her a couple of times a week. Childcare arrangements, mostly."

"And how did DeWalt seem after he had spoken to his ex?"

"Maybe a bit snarky, talked a little quicker." Penny shrugged one shoulder. "But actually, I think that's me reading something into nothing just because you asked me about her. He was fine. Let's just say he was fine."

Ingrid nodded. "Okay. So, what about work? Was he still running any cases?"

Penny shook her head. "No, you did that job for long enough to know you don't really get your hands dirty."

It was true. Four months riding a desk had convinced Ingrid never to put in for promotion. "Pressure from above? Any contact with the Legat or the ambassador?"

Penny smiled. "Not the ambassador, no, but quite a lot with 'Pete'" She made air quotes around the Legat's first name. "You, and Marshall, always called him the Legat, or Munsden, but DeWalt called him Pete."

Ingrid thought about what Libby had said about DeWalt being the kind of guy who did favors for other people.

"You think they knew each other socially?"

"Maybe they worked together way back when."

"Okay," Ingrid said. "Can you tell the Legat I need to speak to him. ASAP?"

"Of course."

"Then I need you to pull up DeWalt's diary. I want to know every meeting he had, every meal he ate, every taxi ride he took in the past week. Then call the doctors on the second floor and ask for his latest medical report. I want to know if he was on any medication, or had any diagnoses that could have impacted his health."

Penny scrutinized Ingrid. "That sounds like you think he might have killed himself?"

Ingrid tipped her head to one side. "For the record, until an hour ago, I thought he was pushed. But, now I'm investigating his death, I need an open mind. So, do you."

"But he wasn't the suicidal type."

"You know that for sure?" Ingrid asked. "In my experience, it's the jocks and the alpha males who suddenly do something out of character. They're all action and no talking. They have no outlet for their feelings and—" she stopped herself. "And then they do something like this." Ingrid swiveled in her chair, then turned back to Penny. "And presumably you've seen all his emails?"

"All his work ones. He has a Gmail."

"Know the password?"

"Nope."

"Can you guess it?"

"I'll try."

Ingrid wondered if Libby would know it. "And let's put in a request for his bank statements."

Ingrid wheeled back to her own desk feeling a surge of energy. She returned to the paperwork Paphides had sent. As she had been there when DeWalt fell, she skipped the initial reports from the uniformed responders and opened the file on the door-to-door inquiries. Most of the neighbors hadn't been in, so only three interviews had been recorded. There was an unwritten rule in investigations: the bigger the city, the fewer the witnesses.

The first interview was with a woman whose front door was directly opposite DeWalt's apartment. The staccato notes revealed the neighbors had spoken precisely three times, once when the fire alarm had gone off, once when she had complained to him about muddy golf gear left in the hallway, and a third time in the sauna in the gym in the basement. The constable who conducted the interview wrote:

Had radio on, did not hear anything, did not see anyone. Sound insulation good between flats.

The next interview was with someone else on the fifth floor who only knew DeWalt as the 'guy with the golf clubs'. The third interviewee had heard the body fall but had thought someone was throwing out a bag of clothes.

Useless.

Ingrid flipped through to find eye-witness interviews from the people in the parking lot, but of the people who had gathered around DeWalt's body, none had actually seen him fall. She was about to turn to the CCTV report when she stopped. Something in one of the eye-witness accounts made her look twice.

Witness heard scream (she doesn't know from which balcony/flat). Did not see body fall. Two other people approached the body (interviews 6-11 and 6-12) and together they called triple 9. Witness reports black Nissan 4x4 leaving the car park at speed.

Ingrid stared at the report. A black Nissan 4x4? The British term for an SUV. Ingrid immediately turned to the CCTV dossier and found a list of license plates and models. GA07 PPL. Black Nissan Qashqai. The same car that had been in West Park.

34

Ingrid tore over to Penny's desk and grabbed the folder with the Met access codes.

"What's happening?" Penny asked.

"Think I've got a lead." Ingrid snatched up the phone and went through the automated system, pressing the relevant code, saying her name for the database and finally being put through to an actual human. "Could you please give me the ownership details of a Nissan Qashqai, license plate Golf Alpha Zero Seven Papa Papa Lima."

"One moment, please."

Ingrid drummed her fingers on the desk as she waited.

"Could you repeat that, please?"

Ingrid did.

"Ah, okay, here it is. Black Nissan Qashqai, registration GA07 PPL, is registered to Wayne John Burridge. You got a pen for the address?"

Ingrid wrote down the details and hung up. She put the location into Google and looked at Burridge's home on Street View. It was an apartment over a chicken shop on

Uxbridge Road, one of the major thoroughfares heading west out of London. His car was a lot nicer than his residence.

Without the power of arrest on UK soil, Ingrid needed Met assistance to take Burridge in for questioning. She didn't like the chances of Paphides playing ball, so she decided to call Cath Murray, a friend who was also a detective sergeant at Belgravia police station. The phone rang before she could dial.

"Skyberg."

"This Immigration Services on the second floor."

"Hi."

"We need the interview room and your friend is still asleep."

"Ah." Ingrid checked her watch. McAvenny had been under for over ninety minutes. "Okay. Can you keep him there for, like, fifteen minutes? I'll send someone down to escort him."

"We need the room at one p.m."

"Understood."

Ingrid stood and turned to Penny.

"Yes?"

"Slight change of plan," Ingrid said. "Those documents on that desk over there?"

Penny pointed to McAvenny's cache.

"Yep, those. I need them scanned."

"Okay."

"Right now, and really, *really* quickly."

Penny's mouth crumpled. "All of them?"

Ingrid thought for a second. "Start with the blue folder and everything in that pile." She paused. "If you can, keep everything in the piles they're in."

"Okay. What about the stuff from DeWalt's diary?"

"Come back to it when this is done."

Penny bundled up a pile of documents and was just at the threshold when Ingrid thought of something else.

"When you get a moment—"

Penny threw her a look.

"Well, *if* you do, can you ask HR about a guy called Zeke McDaniel? I kind of think he was screwed out of a job here and we ought to make it up to him." Ingrid saw the affront on Penny's face. "God no, I didn't mean it like that! It's just, well, we need as many hands on deck as possible."

"You're lucky I know you like me." Penny smirked. "I'll get on to it."

Ingrid followed Penny out into the bullpen and looked out at a sea of heads bowed over keyboards and phones clamped to ears. "Hi," she said. "Hey." She raised her voice. A few of the admin assistants looked up. "I need a couple of volunteers. This is super urgent and super important. If you can spare me half an hour, I need it."

No one looked enthusiastic.

"Okay, your country needs it. Come on, one of you must have thirty minutes of slack in your day."

One of the assistants on the CI team stuck his hand up. "I'll bite."

"Jackson, you little star. Get over here."

The clerks and analysts watched Jackson Brady as he weaved his way between their desks. Ingrid had never seen him in anything other than chinos and plaid shirts. He wore neither garment well. Either the fit or the size was wrong, with the pants stretching unflatteringly over chubby thighs and a too-large shirt failing to disguise a premature paunch. He was one of those men who would look exactly the same at fifty as he did at thirty.

"Reporting for duty," he said, a boyish smile emerging from his pink face.

Ingrid tore off Burridge's details from her notepad and handed them to him. "I need everything you can get on this guy, and I need it fast. I want to know who he banks with, who he works for, who he lives with, owes money to, drinks with, who his landlord is and when he last left the country."

Brady blinked behind his wire-rimmed spectacles. "So not a lot then."

"I like your style. Seriously, set a timer, run every search you can and give me everything you've got in half an hour."

"Is there anything in particular you're looking for?"

Ingrid pressed her lips between her teeth as she thought. "Russia. I don't suppose you'll find anything, but any possible link to Russia would be..." She searched for the right word. "...interesting. Ditto the Metropolitan Police. Even if it's just being arrested for possession when he was a teenager."

"I'm on it."

Ingrid picked up the phone and dialed Cath Murray.

"Mate, how are you?"

Fine, apart from the fact one of your colleagues tried to shoot me the other night. "Good. Busy. And in desperate need of a favor."

"What does that involve?" There were sirens in the background.

"Are you on a call?"

"Don't worry. I'm not driving. Safely strapped in at the back."

"I need you to arrest a suspect for me."

"What's he done?" Cath sounded remarkably calm for someone in a patrol car traveling at high speed.

Ah. What had he done, exactly? Being in the wrong place at the wrong time? "Stalking," Ingrid said. "I really need him brought in for questioning."

"When?"

"Right now."

"I was afraid you'd say that. I'm kinda busy."

"Later?"

"If this goes the way we plan, we'll have seven suspects to interview and process. Sorry mate. You'll have to do it through official channels."

It wasn't unexpected. "Okay. Worth a try."

"Always."

Cath hung up before Ingrid could wish her good luck with the arrests. She dropped her head into her hands and slowly scratched her scalp, as if it would order her thoughts more clearly.

There was no way Burridge being at West Park *and* Century Mills was a coincidence, especially given the photograph of her on the passenger seat. That meant two things: one, Burridge was her top priority; and two, she couldn't be the one to approach him because he had probably been hired to kill her.

Ingrid wrinkled her nose. She had spotted a contradiction. Why would Skylark, or the Russian state, hire a man like Wayne Burridge to kill her? When they wanted to silence Saskia Cole, they sent in professional assassins. Ingrid pictured the look of panic on Burridge's face when she approached his car at West Park. It wasn't the response of a calm, calculating killer. If he wanted me dead, wouldn't he have killed me already? Something wasn't adding up.

"So, this is where my stuff is."

Ingrid turned with alarm to see the disheveled figure of James McAvenny in the doorway. She smiled at him. "Just the man I've been looking for."

35

INGRID GRABBED one of the glass walled meeting rooms alongside the bullpen. She ushered in McAvenny and made him an offer. He could print whatever he liked, but not until she said so. No copy approval, no oversight. He would get his career-redeeming scoop, but in return he would let the bureau utilize Cole's cache. McAvenny also agreed—rather enthusiastically—to contact Burridge on her behalf. The speed with which Burridge had driven away from Century Mills led Ingrid to believe he'd be on his guard for anyone who looked like secret intelligence or law enforcement. An approach from a crumpled, unshaven Australian, on the other hand, had a much higher likelihood of success. "Hell yeah," were his exact words. "Editors go ga-ga for that first-person shit."

Jackson Brady knocked on the glass door and opened it. Ingrid introduced the two men.

"Hi."

"G'day."

Brady dropped a notebook and a sheaf of printed paper onto the table.

"All right," Ingrid said. "What have you got?"

"Okay." Brady sat down. "Wayne John Burridge. Forty-four years old. No criminal record. Works as a locksmith. Self-employed. Banking records haven't come through yet. Been living at 396c Uxbridge Road for seventeen months. Spoke to the letting agent, told her I was getting a reference for an employer. She told me he pays £1,350 a month in rent and has never been late. No complaints from the landlord. The other name on the tenancy is Sonia Hardcastle." He ran a pen over his notes. "What else have I got for you? Here you go. Born in Hampshire." Brady looked up. "No, I don't know where that is either, in 1973. He's not super active on social media, but Sonia is. Into the environment. Lots of placards and protests. She's got an eight-year-old called Bay. Not sure if that's a boy or a girl."

"Probably non-bloody-binary," McAvenny said. "It's all the rage."

Brady's eyes popped briefly, then continued. "Couldn't find any links to Russia, or the police."

"Russia?" McAvenny said. "This is going to be juicy."

Brady looked apologetic. "That's all, folks."

"You got contact details for Burridge?"

"Oh, yes, yes I do." He tore off a corner of his notepad. "That's the details of his business."

Ingrid glanced down at it. "Thanks. Don't suppose you live in west London, do you?"

Brady's mouth pursed. "Um, no. Camberwell Green."

Ingrid pushed her chair back, opened the meeting room door and, for the second time in an hour, shouted at the bullpen. "Can I have everyone's attention please?"

The chatter lessened. The typing slowed.

"Sorry. If I could have everyone's attention, please."

People stopped their work and looked at her in puzzlement.

"Thank you. Anyone here live in west London?"

"Which bit of west London?" someone asked.

Ingrid wasn't going to be fussy. "Shepherd's Bush ideally, but anywhere west of Hyde Park, and not as far out as…" She struggled to think of somewhere. "Richmond."

"I'm in Hammersmith."

"Who said that?"

One of the admin assistants assigned to the CI team stood up. "Me. Hi."

Ingrid strode purposefully toward her. "Don't suppose I could borrow your apartment for a couple of hours, could I?"

Ingrid sat in the smallest bedroom of Berta Hoffman's very nice Hammersmith apartment with the drapes drawn, while James McAvenny paced outside the front door. The modern building had twelve apartments, four on each level, accessed via external walkways overlooking a parking lot. It looked uninviting from the rear, but the front of the building faced the Thames at a very leafy curve in the river. Ingrid pictured Berta and—she presumed—a husband sitting on their terrace with a French press and pastries, reading the weekend papers as a family of swans sailed past. Ingrid must have run in front of the apartment a hundred times on the riverside path.

McAvenny had called the locksmith saying he'd just

returned from a long flight and discovered he had lost his keys. He certainly looked the part. Burridge hadn't wanted the gig, but the Australian had laid it on thick. He'd tried everyone else. He'd been up for forty-eight hours. He'd pay double. He'd leave a review on Google. It worked. Burridge was due any minute.

Using a civilian was definitely unethical, so Ingrid had taken a couple of precautions. Sam Sherbourne was parked right outside, and she had brought a Taser in case Burridge turned violent. McAvenny's instructions were to leave the moment Burridge got the door open.

The bedroom was next to the front door. Ingrid sat on the floor beneath the closed window—the room was stifling—to eavesdrop on McAvenny's interview technique.

"Mate, am I glad to see you," he said, perhaps a little too loud.

"You James, yeah?" London accent.

"Yep."

"Got here as soon as I could. Right, okay. One Chubb, one Yale. You definitely locked both?"

"You know what, mate. It might only be the top one. I know I should always lock both, but I often forget."

"What, while you've been in Oz? You must have locked both. It might be on the river, but this is still Hammersmith."

"True. But this building has so many cameras, I always feel safe." McAvenny's Irish ancestry had endowed him with the power of Blarney.

Ingrid felt a vibration through the wall as someone pushed against the door.

"You might be right." Burridge's voice. "There's a bit of movement there."

Ingrid had deliberately only used the latch lock, what Burridge was calling the Yale, so as not to cause any unnecessary damage to Berta's doorframe. Or, more accurately, her landlord's doorframe. Ingrid had been on enough raids in her career to know that jimmying a latch lock took all of two seconds and a very simple tool. She wondered if Burridge would say as much, or if he would draw it out and charge more.

"You don't have much stuff," Burridge said. Ingrid heard him rummaging inside his tool bag.

"Bloody Qantas. My bag is apparently still in Singapore. Part of the reason I really need to get inside. I don't even have a change of underpants."

Burridge snorted something indeterminate.

"I suppose I could buy a heap of stuff. But that just seems wrong. Save the planet and all that." McAvenny could definitely keep a conversation going. "I mean, it's bad enough flying half way round the world."

Burridge grunted. "You one of them, then, are you? Bit of a tree hugger?"

"I hug every tree I meet."

"My missus is like that. Waste of time if you ask me."

"So, can you get me in?" McAvenny asked.

"Course I can. Stand back."

Ingrid heard Burridge get to work, both through the window and via the hallway. A scraping sound, a clunk, and then a rush of air as the door opened.

"There you go."

"Wow, and you charge seventy pounds for that?"

"You said you'd pay double."

"I did, didn't I? After you. I've got cash somewhere in the kitchen," McAvenny said.

Ingrid heard footsteps in the hallway and then the sound of the door closing.

"Hey," Burridge said.

"Hey."

He turned and saw Ingrid. His eyes bulged.

"Recognize me?"

Burridge glanced over his shoulder at the closed door.

"Don't try it," Ingrid said. "I've got a team on the other side of that door, and if you want to run the other way, it's forty feet down into the river."

He dropped his tool bag. It landed with a bone-shaking clatter. He stood legs hip-width apart, arms slightly away from his torso. A defiant stance. He was five-eight, lithe, and angry. He had a rockabilly haircut and the turn-ups of his jeans revealed boxer boots with red laces. Tribal tattoos stretched down his toned biceps from under a red tee. A figure moved in the frosted glass behind him. Sherbourne.

"Why were you at Century Mills yesterday?" Ingrid asked.

He looked puzzled.

"It was only yesterday. Surely you remember?"

"I'd have thought an FBI agent would have figured that out already. Supposed to be the world's finest, aren't you?"

"It's a straightforward question," Ingrid said.

"And I don't have to answer it, do I?"

"One of my colleagues was killed and you're my number one suspect. You might find life gets a little tricky if you don't cooperate." The heat inside the apartment—the windows had been closed to create the illusion McAvenny had been away—was intense. Ingrid was desperate for a gasp of fresh air. Her wet palm slipped over the Taser in her right hand.

"Interesting, though. The Met obviously don't think I did it, otherwise they'd be here. Wouldn't they?"

Ingrid took a different tack. "When I saw you in West Park, you had a photo of me in your car."

He stuck out his bottom lip. "And?"

"How did you get hold of it?"

His eyes lit up. "Ooh. Interesting. I see where you're going with this." He bit the inside of his lip and looked at the taser. "A friend gave it to me."

"Why?"

"Why do you think?"

"I think someone wants me dead. Or silenced."

He put a hand in his pocket.

"Keep your hands where I can see them." Ingrid gestured the Taser in his direction.

"All right, love." He returned to his gorilla stance. "Jesus, I'm not a bleeding hitman."

"Then why did someone give you my photo?"

"I guess they must be interested in you." He smirked. "Not romantically, obviously."

"And why would they be interested in me?"

He jutted out a hip and adjusted his feet. "Listen, love, you don't mind if I call you love, do you?"

He knew damn well that she did.

"You've got no powers of arrest here. You use that Taser on me and you've got yourself an assault charge and a diplomatic incident. I don't have to tell you anything any more than I have to tell the woman at the bus stop. But," he balled his fists, "I'll throw you this tasty morsel. West Park, the Serpentine, Century Mills, what do those three places have in common?"

"You tell me."

"You, you dozy mare."

Ingrid was thrown. "Not DeWalt?"

"De what?"

"Jacob DeWalt."

"I don't know who the hell you're talking about."

She believed him. "The man who died yesterday."

"That's got fuck all to do with me."

"Then why drive off? If you were there for me, why leave?"

He almost smiled. "You know who turns up when someone dies? The old bill. If it's all right with you, I'd prefer to stay out of their way." He grimaced. "I think I've said enough. We both know you're not going to use your little toy there, so I'm going to turn around and walk out that door, and you and your brethren are going to let me."

His self-assurance was unnerving.

"You'll be tailed."

"Not for long." He turned slowly and opened the door.

Sherbourne, almost silhouetted against the bright sunshine, looked to Ingrid for instructions. "Follow him," she said.

He nodded and turned. Ingrid closed the door and walked down the corridor toward the living room with its views over the river. She opened the sliding doors and gulped down the fresh air on the balcony. *Cocky bastard.* She stared into the middle distance, largely unaware of the rowing race taking place in front of her, and exhaled hard, forcing all the air from her lungs. Her head swayed from side to side.

She didn't want to believe him, but she did. And if he hadn't known about DeWalt, then he definitely hadn't killed him. And the very fact that she was still alive was evidence he hadn't intended to kill her either. So, why the hell was he following her? And on whose orders?

There was a knock at the door. "*Govno.*" Ingrid kicked the balcony wall petulantly, knowing who it was. She closed the door, padded down the hallway, but stopped half way. Burridge had said something, hadn't he? West Park, the *Serpentine* and Century Mills. Ingrid hadn't seen him at the Serpentine. A shiver ran up her spine as she opened the door.

"You going to tell me what the hell that was about?" McAvenny asked.

Ingrid fished Berta's keys out of her pocket, stepped outside and locked both locks. "No, no I'm not. But you'll get your story." She looked over at the parking lot where Sherbourne's BMW was following Burridge's work van out on to the street. "The deal is, you get to observe, you can print what you like, but you can't print until I tell you."

"Yes boss."

Ingrid's phone vibrated in her pocket. An embassy number. "Skyberg."

"Hi, um, Ingrid. This is Jackson. Jackson Brady. With the counter-intelligence team."

"I know who you are, Jackson." She gestured to McAvenny to take the stairs ahead of her. "What have you got for me?"

"I just, er, I thought you'd like to know. One of my searches on Wayne Burridge just came back with something… interesting."

Ingrid didn't like the sound of interesting. "Go on."

"So, I searched for all the records with the registrar. You remember, he was born in some place called Hampshire in 1973."

"Sure."

"Well, he also died there. I'm looking at the death certificate of Wayne John Burridge. August second, 1982."

Ingrid came to a halt. She turned and got a glimpse of Burridge's van as it disappeared down the road. "Say that again."

"He died. Aged nine."

Then who the hell had she just been talking to?

36

Ingrid handed the keys back to Berta who looked up from her screen. "Nice apartment," she said.

"We're enjoying it while we still can."

"You leaving?"

"Reluctantly. Our landlord has given us notice. He's decided to sell up." She performed a one shoulder shrug. "We'd buy it if we could, but we just can't afford it."

"London property prices are crazy, that's for sure." Ingrid wondered how much the landlord would want for it. "Good news, no damage done, and everything's locked up."

"Thank you," Berta said.

"No, thank you. It was a big help."

Ingrid dodged her way between the bullpen desks and emerged at the other end where her office was. Penny was still at Libby's desk. "Hi."

"Hi," Penny said. "Get what you need?"

"Hmm. Not sure." Ingrid sat down so heavily that her chair rolled backward.

"Have you mislaid your journalist friend?"

"No, he's in the process of moving hotels. Figured the least the FBI could do was to pay for his accommodation." McAvenny had been keen not to spend all the budget Saskia Cole's father had given him. "I don't suppose we'll see him again today. Were you able to scan everything?"

"Yes. It's all on the system."

"Is it searchable?"

"Should be."

Ingrid logged on and saw she had two hundred and eleven unanswered emails. She couldn't ignore them all.

"I've also got messages for you," Penny said.

Ingrid didn't want to know the answer, but she asked anyway. "How many?"

"Sixteen. You get a lot of calls, don't you?"

"More than I did when I worked in Marshall's office."

Penny's face crumpled slightly at the mention of Marshall.

"Either I've been really off my game for the past month, or the work has just been manic. Feels like every field office needs something in the UK right now." Ingrid looked away from her screen to Penny. "How many of them are urgent?"

"Probably all sixteen."

Ingrid stretched her fingers. "Okay then, let's run through them."

Two hours later, Ingrid finally came up for air when Penny placed a bowl of chicken noodles from the commissary in front of her. Ingrid looked up at her and smiled. "You remembered."

"I hadn't seen you eat, so I figured."

The smell of the chicken made Ingrid's stomach grumble. "I, er, let me give you some cash."

"Really, don't worry about it." Penny started packing up her bag as Ingrid scrabbled around for her wallet. "Listen, I'm really sorry, but I have to go. I can come back later but I have a doctor's appointment and I don't want to miss it."

"Everything okay?" Ingrid asked, proffering a fiver.

"Hope so. Just some irregular bleeding." Penny waved away the cash.

"Always important to get that stuff checked out," Ingrid said, her arm still outstretched. "Take it."

"If you're sure."

"You know I am."

Penny took the cash reluctantly. "Thank you."

"There's no need to come back after. You got me all DeWalt's diary stuff? His medical report? Phone records?"

"It's all on the system. Though the medical report didn't come through. They were waiting for his doctor to sign something." She slung her bag over her shoulder. "It should be here by six."

It was five-thirty.

"Listen, take it easy this evening. See some friends. You've had a big shock and you shouldn't be alone."

"Okay, mom."

"Sorry," Ingrid said. "Didn't mean to patronize. And thanks again for the noodles."

When Penny had left, Ingrid picked up the bowl and chopsticks and wandered over to the intern's desk. Her list was still there.

1 People have been calling my number for him
2 The following people have been killed to protect his identity. David Steiner. Saskia Cole. Jacob DeWalt. Mulroony's assistant (coma)

3 Before Mulroony was extracted, Skylark was a code-name for a suspected double agent inside MI5 or the Met
4 Until his death, I thought it could have been DeWalt.

The other piece of paper just said:

Why would DeWalt frame Mulroony if he wasn't Skylark?

Ingrid stared at the list and shoveled in a mouthful of food. She realized her own name had come close to being added to the list at Tilbury. She checked the clock and scooted over to her desk to dial Sam Sherbourne. It had been a couple of hours since they'd last spoken.

"Hey." He sounded weary.

"Any news?"

"No, he's still sitting in the beer garden of the Green Goblin pub not drinking very much, and I'm still sitting at the table opposite keeping an eye on him." He sighed. "He even bought me a drink."

It was very strange behavior for someone being tailed. Just sitting there, brazenly waiting for Sherbourne to, what? Get bored? Get a better offer? Fall asleep? Normally, it took six agents to maintain surveillance, but Burridge was letting the FBI do it with one.

"And is he doing anything?"

"Nope, looking at the paper, looking at his phone."

"It'll run out of juice soon," Ingrid said.

"So will mine."

Fair point. "You want to call it a day?"

"Dunno. I'm kind of intrigued. It's so alpha I think I want to know where this is heading."

"If you're sure."

"I'll let you know if anything changes."

Ingrid scrambled in a few more mouthfuls of food and returned to the spare desk. Her eyes settled on the single line of scrawl on the second piece of paper: *Why would DeWalt frame Mulroony if he wasn't Skylark?*

She thought about what Libby had said about his buddies and his favors and his frat obligations. Was Skylark a friend of DeWalt's? Or someone he owed a massive favor to? It wasn't the most outlandish theory she'd ever come up with.

Sensing she might be onto something, Ingrid pulled up the folder Penny had created and went through DeWalt's diary appointments for the preceding week. Her cell vibrated on the desk. Svetlana. "You'll have to wait, Mom."

DeWalt's workload was familiar. The Monday morning meeting with the Legat and representatives of the Agency and the NSA. The Tuesday afternoon briefing with the State Department team. Speaking engagements at security conferences and appearances at committee meetings. His workload didn't seem any heavier than when she had been covering the desk.

Her cell buzzed again. Svetlana. Again. The best way to get rid of her was to answer it. "Mom, hi."

"How can you say hi at a time like this?"

Ingrid held the phone away from her ear and snarled at it. "Is that no longer the correct way to answer a call?"

"And why do I always have to call twice to get you to answer? Huh?"

"Mom, I'm at work."

"You think I don't know that?"

Actually, yes, the number of times you call me, I think that maybe you don't.

"Work is all you do. Always work, work, work."

Ingrid inhaled deeply through her nose. *In with anger, out with love.* "Mom, I really am very busy."

"Which is why you not even know what is happening."

"With the trial?"

"Yes, with the trial. The defense has rested. The jury is deli-delibery—"

"Deliberating."

"And now you make fun of my accent."

Ingrid eye-rolled. She did not have time for this. "Mom, my other phone is ringing. I'll call you back tonight."

Just as she ended the call to Minnesota, her desk phone did indeed start ringing. "Skyberg."

"Oh, hello Ingrid, I don't know if you'll remember me." The voice—female, English—was alarmingly familiar. "It's Dr. Ives. You used to come to my house."

"Yes. Yes, I remember." Her skin rippled with discomfort. Ingrid had been forced to visit a psychotherapist against her wishes when she was undercover. "This is unexpected."

"I must confess, I didn't expect to be speaking to you today either, but your name was on a request I received."

Ingrid was suddenly back in Dr. Ives's front room. Her body tensed accordingly. "It was?"

"You asked for Jacob DeWalt's medical records?"

"Ah." So he had also been a patient of hers. "You have been told that he's died?" Ingrid said tentatively, unsure of the protocol.

"Yes, that information accompanied the request. And

the reason for my calling is that I do not have a psychological report ready for Jacob, and it would take me several weeks to prepare one." She paused. "So I thought it was best if I relayed my findings over the phone. Perhaps you could make notes?"

"Um, yes." Ingrid looked around her chaotic desk for a pad and pen. "Yes, that would be great." Ingrid scribbled on the pad to make sure the ink was flowing. "Please, go ahead."

"First of all, can I ask how he died?"

"He fell. From a fifth-floor balcony."

"Did he jump?" Ives asked.

"That's what I'm trying to determine."

"I'm rather afraid that he did."

It was as if Dr. Ives had slugged her in the chest. Ingrid let out an involuntary pocket of air and sat with her mouth ajar.

"In our most recent sessions, he had been exceedingly morose. I last saw him two days ago, and he told me he had done a terrible thing."

"I see," Ingrid said, though she didn't.

"He said he didn't think he could live with what he had done. Or that he could withstand his children finding out."

Ingrid couldn't believe what she was hearing. She ran a hand through her hair and closed her eyes. "And what had he done?"

"Well, that he didn't tell me. My job is to help him understand what he is feeling, not to subject him to the Spanish Inquisition."

Ingrid shuddered as she recalled Ives's probing to explore how she *really* felt about things.

"This thing he was referring to? Did it relate to his work, or his family?"

"The situation with his ex-wife had been a source of strain and upheaval for a long time, and it didn't help him to think clearly, or be optimistic, but it was a work thing. Ingrid," Dr. Ives paused. Ingrid had always hated the way Ives said her name. "This was a very profound shame he felt. This wasn't about not getting the bad guy, or overlooking a vital piece of evidence."

"Then what was it?"

Ives sighed. "He exhibited signs of disgust, of very deep loathing, emotions I generally only see in patients who have done something against their own moral code, who have breached their own ethical boundaries."

"But you have no idea what it was?"

"I could speculate, but that would go against my own moral code." Ives cleared her throat. "The reason why he was struggling so much was because he was a deeply moral person. Most law enforcement clients are."

Ingrid was still reeling from the news that affable, likeable Jacob DeWalt had been in such turmoil. She couldn't think what questions to ask.

Ives continued. "He said he knew that good people occasionally did bad things, but that he had done something so wrong that he could no longer claim to be one of the good guys. Ingrid, I have been a therapist for twenty-five years; I have rarely seen a man wrestle with his conscience like this." She inhaled audibly. "I can't tell you what he did, only that he said he never meant to, and that he could not live with having done it."

Ingrid took a moment to absorb what Ives was telling her. "Never meant to?"

"He said it started with a favor, a small thing, and then

he had been asked again, and suddenly he realized that he was compromised, and then finally that he was complicit."

That was sounding familiar.

"I worked with Jacob for four years. He was a man who could tolerate a lot of gray. He accepted, for instance, that it was a lot to expect a man and a woman to remain faithful to each other for decades, and he could understand why criminals who had been rehabilitated deserved their freedom. His morals were actually quite flexible. So…"

"So?"

"So, whatever it was that he couldn't live with was not a small thing."

Not a small thing. What the hell did that mean? All Ingrid's loathing for Dr. Ives's platitudes and equivocation surged to the surface. "Is there anything else?" she said through gritted teeth.

"Only that I am very sorry you have lost a colleague. If you want to talk to me about it, you know that we can always resume our sessions."

Over my dead body. "Thank you, that's very kind."

Ingrid ended the call and walked over to the spare desk and looked at her list. She shook her head as she crossed out DeWalt's name from the list of people Skylark had killed. Within seconds of putting down her pen, Ingrid's cell buzzed on her desk.

"Jesus, can I just get a moment alone?"

She was down to nine percent battery life. She searched in her drawer for a charging cable as she swiped to answer. "Cath, hi. Sorry about earlier. I didn't mean to put you in an awkward position. Did your arrests go well?"

"Actually, they did. But that's not why I'm calling."

Ingrid found a cable and plugged her phone into the

USB port on her computer. She leaned over, as the cord was too short to allow her to sit upright.

"I just had a very strange call from the Chief Super at another station. Highly unusual."

"You been tapped up for another promotion?"

"No, listen." Cath lowered her voice. "He needed to get an official message to you unofficially."

"Okay. Sounds intriguing."

"Apparently you've got a Wayne Burridge under surveillance?"

"Ah, yes. Yes, we do."

"You need to tell your team to step back."

Team? It was just Sherbourne. "Why?"

"He's one of us."

What? "He's a cop?"

"He's undercover."

Why would an undercover cop follow me? "Oh."

"And your operation is in danger of blowing his cover."

Ingrid was stunned into silence. "I thought he was a locksmith."

"Good cover, eh? I gather he's embedded with Extinction Rebellion, and they're always suckers for men with vans."

It explained Burridge's cockiness. And the death certificate: he must have assumed the identity of the child who died.

"You've gone awfully quiet," Cath said.

"Can I ask you something?"

"Of course."

"Do you know any reason why a Metropolitan police officer who's undercover with Extinction Rebellion would have me under surveillance?"

"Hmm. Not a scooby," Cath said. "But I can ask around."

Ingrid left the phone off the hook and turned off the vibrate function on her cell. She needed to think. She needed space. And silence.

There was a knock at the door.

37

Ingrid groaned then turned round. Marsha was leaning against the door frame, arms folded, a concerned look on her face. Ingrid managed something approaching a smile.

"You look beat," Marsha said. "How's it going?"

Ingrid flapped her hands uselessly in the air. "I have no idea. I need a little time to think."

Marsha stepped inside and closed the door. "I think you've got the best air conditioning in the building. Can I move in, please?" She pulled over a chair and sat in front of Ingrid. "To be honest, I just needed five too. You can ignore me. I figured in here I can't hear my phone, and I can't see my emails."

"Tough first day?"

"I feel like I've run an ultra-marathon in heels." She kicked off her sling backs and rubbed her bare feet. "Sorry, is this gross?"

Ingrid slumped back against her chair. "Not at all." Now that she thought about it, her own feet needed some respite from her shoes. She kicked them off, instantly feeling a little less anxious.

"You can ignore me," Marsha said.

"You are the least ignorable person I know." Except, perhaps, Nick Angelis.

"Is that a good thing?"

Ingrid wasn't sure. Was it just that they had a complicated history? Was it Ingrid's own discomfort that meant she couldn't look away when Marsha was in the room? She felt they should have 'the conversation', the one that made it clear nothing was going to happen between them. Maybe if she cleared the air, then she could ignore her.

"Okay, don't answer that. Do your thinking. I'm just hiding. Unless you want a sounding board?"

Ingrid rose slowly to her feet and grabbed the sheet of paper with the single question on it: *Why would DeWalt frame Mulroony if he wasn't Skylark?* "Give that some thought," Ingrid said and returned to the notes and photos on the spare desk. Marsha joined her, standing a fraction too close.

"You haven't actually shown me these before. These are what started it all, huh?"

Ingrid gestured to the ceiling tiles. "Yup."

"You want to talk me through them?"

Ingrid told her about Steiner's book, his suicide, the Hawking Review into the Met's bungled investigation of the dissident Dmitri Andropov's murder. She explained about the Post-its and the file number and the cake and wondered if she was going crazy.

Marsha pointed at the photo of the diary. "What year is that?"

"Twenty-twelve."

"Anything else happen that week?"

Ingrid stared so hard at the dates that her vision

blurred. Something was gnawing its way out of her memory. "Can't think."

"Okay, we'll figure that out. And is this what a skylark looks like?"

Ingrid wasn't listening. "I've remembered."

"Yes?"

"March seven, Twenty-twelve. Saskia Cole was murdered."

Marsha arched one eyebrow, then peered down at the photo. Ingrid followed her gaze. The squiggle she has assumed was Mulroony getting the ink to flow suddenly looked a lot like a lower case S followed by a lower case C. Was her brain making a connection where there wasn't one?

"Oh," Marsha said, suddenly unnerved. "Wait here. I won't be a moment."

She dashed out of the office, leaving Ingrid to wonder what on earth she had said. She looked again at the photos. What had she seen? Less than a minute later, Marsha burst back in holding a Post-it. She handed it to Ingrid.

"Really?" Ingrid looked again.

Please call DCI Rushton, sois, New Scotland Yard.

Ingrid flamed with embarrassment. Sois. She saw it now.

"Libby left it on my desk. I had to ask her what sois was, and she said it was just her handwriting. It was SO15." Marsha almost looked apologetic. "So then I had to ask her what SO15 was. Of course she didn't know, but I imagine anyone who's worked this office for more than a week does."

Ingrid sighed. "Special Operations, Group 15. The Met's counter-terrorism command." She tilted her head back and silently screamed at her stupidity. "I thought it was goddamn French!"

Marsha placed a hand on her shoulder. "The good news is it's further confirmation Skylark is in the Met."

Ingrid fizzed with embarrassment. Fury reddened her cheeks. The shame that Marsha—a woman she admired almost more than any other—had been the one to spot her rookie error made her want to wriggle out of her own skin. "I think I pretty much had that confirmed two days ago when he tried to kill me."

"What?"

"Yeah, I thought I'd forgotten to mention that to anyone."

"You goddamn fool." Marsha reached out to Ingrid's face, forcing her to look at her. "You okay?"

Ingrid nodded. "Yes, thanks to a bee."

"What?"

Ingrid filled Marsha in on Tilbury.

"And the man who followed you, who fired a gun at you, you think that was Skylark?"

Ingrid let out an enormous sigh. "Yes, I suppose I did. Up until about an hour ago."

Marsha narrowed her eyes. "Go on."

"I just spoke to DeWalt's psychologist."

"And?"

"She said something that made me wonder if it was DeWalt after all."

"Okay," Marsha said, encouraging Ingrid to continue.

"She told me it was her assessment that he had broken his own moral code, that he had done something deeply shameful." She stopped and looked at Marsha.

"Doesn't that sound a tiny bit like betraying your country?"

Marsha stared at her with serious eyes. "But if he was Skylark, then why did he tell Libby to spy on you?"

Ingrid sucked on her teeth. That was an excellent question. Why indeed? "Because..."

"Yes?"

"Because someone was leaning on him? Penny said he was getting pressure from somewhere." She paused. "Someone."

Marsha smiled at her.

"What?"

"Just admiring. Watching you crack a case is like watching Monet paint."

Ingrid turned away, embarrassed, and returned to her desk. If her new theory was right, then DeWalt's phone records would show who had been leaning on him. If it was Skylark, then his number would likely be in the call log.

Ingrid examined the list of numbers on her screen, aware of Marsha watching her. Her breathing was rapid and shallow as she scanned the list. She didn't recognize any of the numbers, so she inputted them into the FBI's database. If they already had a record of the numbers, then it'd match them to names and organizations. She drummed her fingers on the desk as she waited for the results to spew out.

And then she saw it.

"What is it?"

"Look at this," Ingrid said.

Marsha crossed the floor in bare feet and stood behind her. "This is the call log of DeWalt's cell—"

"What about his landline?"

"Different file. We'll check that next. But." Ingrid pointed to the screen. "DeWalt jumped at seven fifteen. But look." She jabbed her monitor. "He received a call at seven oh-seven."

"What are you waiting for?"

Ingrid dialed the number, a UK-based mobile. Adrenaline flooded her veins as she waited for the call to connect.

"I'm sorry. The number you have dialed has not been recognized. Please check the number and try again. I'm sorry—" Ingrid exhaled and ended the call to stop the message repeating itself.

"What?" Marsha asked, eagerness lighting up her face.

"Number doesn't exist. I don't suppose you have any really good contacts in the data forensics team?"

"Course I do," she said with a smile.

Marsha called her contact in DC and asked for a full report on the number within an hour. Ingrid checked DeWalt's landline—nothing—then looked to see which numbers from the log were already in the FBI's database. An initial glance suggested he had made the same sorts of calls he always did, his ex-wife, his bank, the office. She wondered if she should call Penny and ask her to come back to the office after all. She needed someone to match up his call records with his diary appointments, and she didn't have time. Ingrid exhaled hard.

"You look like a woman in need of a shoulder rub," Marsha said. "I would offer, but I don't want to cross any boundaries. I mean, technically, I'm your boss."

"Technically, you used to be my instructor."

"I seem to remember you had graduated." Marsha stepped away, putting some distance between them.

"Oh yeah," Ingrid said. "I'd forgotten how ethical you are."

"Ethical? That's your abiding memory of me?"

"You know it's not," Ingrid said quietly. She looked away as a recollection surfaced. Her last night at Quantico. Almost everyone from her intake had made the grade, and they'd gone out to celebrate. On the way back to their barracks, they bumped into Marsha. Ingrid remembered with acute embarrassment the choice she made that night. Marshall or Marsha. Marsha or Marshall. At least neither would notice if she called out the wrong name in the heat of the night.

And although it had indeed been a hot night, at sunrise Ingrid had left Marsha's bed and walked dreamily through the town to the Quantico complex. Finally certain of something, she knocked on the door of Marshall's dormitory. Yes, she told him, she would go out with him.

They had followed each other's careers and had exchanged occasional emails, but Ingrid hadn't seen Marsha again until she'd given her speech in the bullpen that morning. She remained the only woman Ingrid had ever been intimate with. There had been enough men since to convince her she had made the right choice.

Marsha wandered back over to the spare desk and tapped one of the photos. "This is the skylark, right?"

Ingrid stood beside her and checked which image she was pointing to. "Yes."

Marsha tapped the next photo. "So, what's this bird?"

"It's a starling."

Marsha froze. Only her Adam's apple moved. Then her eyes popped. "You're kidding me."

38

INGRID CARRIED on staring at Marsha. "Tell me."

"I… I just need a minute." She walked over to the window where a diffuse pale sky leaked through the slatted blinds.

Ingrid heard her heartbeat in her ears. "Tell me!"

Marsha ran her tongue over her teeth, looked over at Ingrid, and narrowed her eyes. "It might be nothing."

"Geez, Marsha, just spit it out!"

Marsha blew out her cheeks. "Okay. About eighteen, nineteen years ago, a Russian diplomat walked into the New York field office and said one of our men was currently having a meeting with his boss. The codename we gave our traitor was Starling, in part, because it gave us deniability." She pressed her lips together. "Anyone asked about 'Agent Starling' we could tell people they were confusing fact and fiction. If they searched for Agent Starling, they got a photo of Jodie Foster and a review of *The Silence of the Lambs*." She paused. "It was the perfect codename for an agent hiding in plain sight."

"Okay," Ingrid said. "So, who was Starling?"

Marsha eyeballed her. "No one. It was a wild goose chase. We gave the operation a team of agents. They put saint Frank Geest in charge, gave them a separate office, a separate building in fact. It turned out to be an impossible task because Starling didn't exist." She inhaled so deeply her chest heaved upwards. "We're more familiar with Russian disinformation campaigns now, but this was one of the first. Setting us against ourselves, tying up our resources, and demoralizing our guys because their mission was doomed to failure." She shook her head. "Guys killed themselves because they were accused of being traitors."

Ingrid's skin rippled with a shiver. "And what do you think now?"

Marsha scrunched up her face. "Either Starling is still out there, or Skylark is just another goddamn goose chase."

Ingrid folded her arms across her chest as she parsed what Marsha had said. "So we go back to what we know for sure."

"And that is?"

"That Dennis Mulroony is being held in the hell wing of the Black Dolphin prison."

Marsha didn't say anything.

"Nick Angelis—"

"Nick?"

"You know him?"

Was Marsha blushing? "We go way back."

Ingrid's lip curled. Why wasn't that a surprise? "According to Nick Angelis, the Kremlin will extract Skylark tomorrow night. That gives us one day to find him and save the life of an agent who deserves that we do everything we can to bring him home." Ingrid stood in front of Marsha and looked her right in the eye. "If this is some Russian mind game, it only lasts for another day, right? And if it isn't, then we're close on Skylark and we get to rescue Mulroony."

Marsha nodded. "Okay. Twenty-four hours. We give it everything we've got."

"So..." Ingrid stood a little straighter and ran a hand through her hair. "I need to analyze DeWalt's phone records, his diary. I need to scrape and analyze all of these." She gestured to Saskia Cole's notebooks. "Who is there who can help?"

Marsha shrugged. "You know I can't allocate resources to this. We make too much noise, then you risk someone marching in here and shutting this down."

The muscles tightened in Ingrid's neck. "So much for brothers-in-arms. Promise me, if I'm ever where Mulroony is, you won't let me rot."

"Not a chance. Listen, I have to take a meeting, but then I'll come back to help. I think that Brady guy is still at his desk. Where's Penny?"

"Right here."

Ingrid and Marsha both turned to see Penny in the doorway.

"You came back!" Ingrid said, relief infusing her voice.

"Nowhere else I'd rather be."

"You sure? What about the doctor?"

"I'm not actually ill."

"You're sure?"

"Yes."

Ingrid smiled. "Okay then, let's get started."

Marsha departed for a meeting and Penny got to work cross reffing DeWalt's diary, his phone contacts with any possible link to the Metropolitan Police. Ingrid busied herself with the scanned and digitized versions of Saskia Cole's notes. She found another interview with Sidney Baxter, and this one had clearly been conducted after the arms dealer had been sent to prison.

SC: I need to verify what you're saying. Who can prove that these arms sales aren't about profit but about ideology?
SB: It's not ideology, it's blackmail.
SC: Who can verify that?
SB: [long pause] The only name I can give you is the man who blackmailed me. He's hardly going to fess up, is he?
SC: Give me his name, anyway. Let me investigate him independently. If I find enough to put him in jail, you're a hero.
SB: [heavy sigh] No, I won't. It's more than my life's worth, but—
SC: Yes?
SB: I'm going to give you a different name. He's a detective in the Metropolitan Police. I think he's investigating this stuff. He might talk to you.
SC: Great. What's the name?
SB: [heavy sigh] It didn't come from me.
SC: Understood.
SB: No. Changed my mind. Too high a price.
SC: Really? For the name of a detective?
SB: No. I'm not saying anything else. But if you sit at the bar in a place called Mojito Joe's for long enough, the story will more than likely come to you.

Ingrid tapped the desk with her forefinger and stared at the screen. She could almost sense the pieces of the case circling her head, threatening to coalesce into a single, coherent whole. Although her brain was revving, the gears weren't engaged, and she realized she wasn't going anywhere, no matter how hard she glared at her computer.

Ingrid pulled up Libby's list of the people who had attended the gala at Mojito Joe's. Was Skylark's name on the list? She studied the names of the celebrities and business executives she hadn't heard of. Not knowing one of them from the next, her only option was to google. Sure enough, a Russian businessman was on the US sanctions list. It felt like progress.

Stop. Slow down.

It wasn't progress, was it? It was another distraction. She was in danger of following Cole's line of investigation, rather than her own. She wasn't looking for an illegal arms dealer, she was looking for a spy. The clock was ticking. She didn't have time for diversions.

Mulroony certainly didn't.

"Duh." Why hadn't she thought to enter the word 'skylark' into the digitized cache? Annoyed at herself, typed in the letters, but before the results populated, Penny cleared her throat. "Ingrid?"

"Yep."

"You might want to take a look at this."

Ingrid crossed the office to see Penny's screen, her bare feet sticking to the carpet. "What have you got?"

Penny looked up at her. "Can I just preface all this by saying that I normally book meeting rooms and make diary appointments. This isn't exactly my forte."

"I worked with you enough to know you can turn your hand to anything." *Don't you know you're Wonder Woman?* "What have you found out?"

Penny tapped the screen. "These are the calls DeWalt

made on his cell in the five days before he died." She paused. "God, it's weird saying that. I mean, I might as well just say the calls he made last week." Penny bit her lip, then continued. "And these are the calls he made from the office. Same time period."

"Okay. Is there a pattern?"

"There's almost an absence of one. Completely different numbers for each phone." She shrugged. "Not that surprising, I guess. But, there is one number he called from both. The Ravensbourne Golf Club. He was a member there." Penny glanced up at Ingrid. "He loved golf."

Ingrid pictured the set of clubs in his apartment.

"On Friday, he asked me several times if the club had called back. I didn't really pay attention—it's all sportsball, isn't it?—but I think he wanted to get a non-member in for a round, or to let a non-member play on the main course. I dunno. It was tedious boys' stuff, so like I say, I didn't pay attention." She pointed to another open document. "This is his diary. And the weird thing is that there's no golf in it for the weekend."

Ingrid chewed the inside of her cheek. "And was that sort of thing normally in his diary?"

"Yah, you bet." She scrolled through and showed Ingrid not just entries for golf, but for soccer and handball. "So, it's a bit odd that this super important golf match—are they even called matches?—wasn't in his diary." Penny pulled up another document while suppressing a smile. She had found something. "This is an AGM report from the golf club. It has an addendum of all active memberships. And this," she said, opening yet another file, "is our database of Met officers. It's not been updated much recently, but it's a record of all our liaisons with the Met.

Most of the entries for the past few years have been made by you." She filled her lungs. "And this is the crossover. Met officers who are also members of Ravensbourne Golf Club."

Ingrid leaned in to get a closer look. Eleven names. "Penny, this is fantastic information, well done."

"For the record, it is way more fun doing this than working for the SSA."

Ingrid raised an eyebrow. "Well, there may be an opening." She really didn't want Libby back. If she could have Penny *and* Zeke, that would be a dream team.

Penny sat a little taller. "You want me to phone these eleven people?"

Ingrid peered at the names. "No, I know a couple of them. Let me call them first. Can you email me the list? And then can you call the golf club and tell them we need the name of everyone who played a round on Saturday."

"They'll just tell me?"

"They might."

Penny looked dubious. "Okay, I'll give it a go."

Ingrid returned to her desk. The search results for 'skylark' in the Cole cache were on her screen. The word appeared twice in her documents. She clicked on the first entry and found herself looking at a handwritten note in a page of jotted notes, as if Cole were making a record of a phone call.

DSS/Met. No active investigation. London trade is 'Total black hole' for MI5. FBI turns blind eye. US embassy 'willfully' ignores requests for assistance.
Mole/spy/double agent? Really??

'Mole/spy/double agent' was circled in a different

colored ink. An arrow led from the circle to another note that said, simply, 'Skylark?' The note was dated March 1, 2012. Six days before Cole was killed.

Ingrid re-read the note, then scrolled through the neighboring pages. Lots of the entries started with a similar code. AW/Deloitte. HG/Raytheon. FM/Pentagon. It seemed to be the initials of the person Cole was speaking to, and the name of their employer. DSS/Met. Whose initials were they? She checked the list of the eleven golf playing officers. None of the names had the initial DSS. Maybe DS was Detective Sergeant? None of the last names began with S. Ingrid got over the disappointment and clicked on the other entry for Skylark in the digitized cache.

"Ah," she said out loud.

Penny looked over, irritated, every time Ingrid made a noise.

It was a scan of another note from a different notebook. This one had the word Skylark and three phone numbers written next to it. One of them was Ingrid's direct line, which explained the calls she'd been getting. One number had a Florida dialing code, and the third was a UK mobile. She instinctively lifted the phone to call it, then thought twice. Far better to get some analysis on both numbers before cold calling.

"Ooh. Maybe, if I'm really lucky…" She switched back to her emails.

Marsha's contact had been good to his promise and had sent over the analysis of the phone that made the seven-oh-seven call. Ingrid immediately emailed back and asked for further assistance on the Florida number and the UK cell. As she was typing out the numbers, she stopped. She checked. Then she checked again.

"Bingo."

The UK cell in Saskia Cole's notes was the same number that had called DeWalt minutes before he died. Ingrid swallowed hard and blinked at the screen. The number had to belong to Skylark, didn't it?

39

INGRID TOOK her time walking back from the commissary. She hadn't wanted anything to eat, but she had been in desperate need of a break from her screen.

The walk made her realize that McAvenny was a distraction. The Cole cache was useful, but it wasn't going to help her find Skylark before the Spetsnaz team extracted him. She needed to go back to basics. She needed to be sure of her facts. There was too much information swirling round, and not enough knowledge. She saw the irony: flooding the world with information, and never letting on what was real and what was not, was straight out of the Kremlin playbook.

Back at her desk, her mind partially cleared, Ingrid opened up the analysis of Skylark's number. Unsurprisingly, it was an unregistered SIM. It had been in use for six years but was mostly turned off and therefore only traceable when making or receiving a call. In six years, it had only made seventy calls, to twenty-three different numbers, mostly to other UK cell phones. It had called

DeWalt's number precisely five times; three times in the past month. That looked like a pattern of escalation.

The number it called most frequently, a total of twenty-two times in six years, belonged to a man called Patrick Lawson. There was an asterisk next to Lawson's name. Ingrid scanned for the footnote.

Leader of England for the English (EFE), a political party, currently serving a sentence for aggravated assault in Belmarsh Prison.

Ingrid's instinct was to jump on the bike and head straight to Belmarsh, but she couldn't spare the manpower. Instead, she looked at the most recent call it had made. A London number, a few hours beforehand.

"Penny?"

"Yep."

"Can you find out who this number belongs to?"

"Do I just call it?"

"Absolutely not." She gave Penny the number and turned to the next page of the report, and her mouth fell open. It was a map of all the locations the phone had been used. At first, it looked like it had only ever made one call. Then Ingrid zoomed in. "Oh, my." Her eyes bulged. "Oh my, oh my, oh my."

"What is it?" Penny asked.

"The phone that called DeWalt before he died?"

"Yes?"

"I'm looking at a map of all the locations it's ever made calls from."

"And?"

"Every single call has been made from the exact same place."

Penny looked puzzled. "That can't be that unusual, can it? I mean, most of my calls are made from my house."

"These calls aren't being made from inside a building."

"Okay, now I'm a teensy bit intrigued."

"They've all been made from the middle of Parliament Square." Ingrid looked again at her screen. "You know what I want you to do now?"

Penny's expression suggested deep thought. "No. Remember, I'm new to this."

"I want you to request all the CCTV footage for Parliament Square at..." She looked back to the previous page of the report, "at three-oh-five this afternoon. There must be a hundred cameras there—it's right by the Houses of Parliament, Westminster Abbey, New Scotland Yard. Downing Street is just a few yards away—because one of them must, *must*, have caught whoever made this call."

"Okay. How do I do that?"

Ingrid blinked slowly. She needed to be patient. She got up, went to Penny and showed her the list of contact numbers and access codes. As she was talking her through the protocols, she saw the website on Penny's screen.

"What's that?"

"I, um, I googled that number you just gave me. It belongs to this pub."

Ingrid recognized the name of the pub. She had heard it recently. The Green Goblin. Why the heck was that ringing a bell? Ingrid's jaw fell. A sigh sank out of her mouth. It was the pub Wayne Burridge had spent the afternoon in. She gripped her scalp with both hands.

"Okay," she said slowly. "I need to speak to Scotland Yard."

"Why?" Penny asked.

Ingrid clenched her teeth as she recalled Burridge's cockiness. Wiping the smirk from his face had just become her new mission. "Ah."

"What?"

Ingrid was still holding her head. "I also need to speak to Sam Sherbourne, don't I?"

"Do you?" Penny was lost, unable to follow Ingrid's thoughts.

Sam had been in the Green Goblin all afternoon too, hadn't he? Ingrid's mind flashed back to seeing him in West Park. Her mouth contorted with a silent scream. He was their goddamn Russia expert.

Penny rolled her chair to face Ingrid. "What's going on?"

Marsha appeared in the doorway. "I was about to ask the same thing."

Ingrid beckoned her in. She closed the door behind her. Marsha held up a six pack of Michelob, the brown bottles glistening with condensation. "Found them in the fridge in my office. Guess they must be DeWalt's." She set them down on Ingrid's desk, popped a cap on the edge, and offered the bottle to Ingrid.

"No." Ingrid shook her head.

"Penny?"

"I haven't drunk beer since college." Penny didn't take her eyes off Ingrid.

Marsha took a pull on her beer, saw Penny's fixation on Ingrid, and realized she had interrupted something. "What is it, Ingrid? I know that face."

Ingrid filled her in on the lines of inquiry. The call to the Green Goblin. The CCTV in Parliament Square, Burridge, the phone number in Florida, but with every sentence that left her mouth she sounded more and more demoralized. "This is a week's work for a team. Unless we get lucky with the CCTV. And even if we do, we still have to actually find him."

Marsha kicked off her shoes and took a long swig from her bottle. "I think you've forgotten something."

Ingrid gestured for her to elucidate.

"You already know who Skylark is."

"Huh?" Ingrid tugged at the collar of her blouse, loosening the fabric from her shoulders to get some air on her skin.

"An hour ago, you told me that, two nights ago, a Metropolitan police officer tried to kill you."

Penny's ears perked up. "What?"

"I didn't say that was Skylark," Ingrid said. Somewhere in her brain, a cog started turning. "It could be someone close to him."

"I'm not so sure. We know he kills to protect his identity, don't we? That author, Steinway. Either he pulled the trigger or he made the man kill himself. DeWalt, same deal. Either he pushed him or he persuaded him he needed to jump. Those killings don't have the hallmark of the Kremlin, do they? There's no specially manufactured nerve agent, no obscure herb in the smoothie at the gym. No forensics trail to embarrass Number Ten or the White House."

Where was she going with this?

"The journalist in Australia. She was assassinated, right? The Kremlin left enough clues to make sure everyone else was scared off. But it's different with Skylark."

Ingrid rocked back on her heels. She clasped her face in her hands. Marsha was right. "He is killing in such a way that no one sees a conspiracy."

Marsha raised the bottle in salute. Penny looked at them both, her head twisting round like an owl's.

"It's like he wants to make sure there's no investigation." Ingrid swiped the bottle from Marsha and took a glug. "Which kind of makes sense if he's a cop." She paused, letting another cog grind through the motions. "Penny?"

Penny looked surprised to be called on. "Yes?"

"That list of eleven names? The police officers who play golf?"

"Yes?"

"Can you check them against the Operation Pinball personnel?"

"Operation Pinball?"

"Tilbury? DeWalt must have mentioned it."

"Ah, yes." She turned to her computer and hammered her keyboard.

Ingrid leaned against her desk and handed the bottle back to Marsha. "And killing me the other night could have been put down to the failings of the operation. He could have switched the casings, made it impossible to say which gun killed me."

They looked at each other and smiled. Progress felt good. They listened to Penny type, waiting for her to tell them who Skylark was.

"There's something else," Ingrid said, not taking her eyes off Penny.

"Uh-huh."

"It's like he's quietly taking care of business."

Marsha's lips contracted. Her head nodded rhythmically. "You're right. Like the kid that cleans up the party before the parents get home."

Ingrid lifted her eyebrows. "It's like he doesn't want to get into trouble." She turned to Penny. What was taking her so long? It was only eleven names. She reached down and pulled a beer out of the pack. She knocked off the cap on the edge of the desk. "Penny? You found anything?"

Penny looked apologetic. "No, I mean, I don't think so. Diaries and meeting rooms, remember."

Ingrid strode across the office and looked over Penny's shoulder. She peered at the files she had open. There was no correlation between the list of names. Penny hadn't missed anything.

"Nothing?" Marsha asked, reading Ingrid's face.

"Nope."

If Skylark wasn't one of those eleven men, then they were as far away as ever. Marsha saw the disappointment in Ingrid's face.

"Then, we try a different tack."

"Such as?" Ingrid asked

Marsha ran her palm over her face, then looked at Ingrid very deliberately. "How many hours do we have?"

Ingrid looked at the clock. "I really don't know. If Nick is correct—"

"He's very rarely wrong."

"Then we maybe have fifteen hours. Twenty at most."

"Okay, then."

"Okay?"

"If we can't find Skylark in that timeframe, then we have to make sure he finds you."

Ingrid's eyes widened.

"He's already tried to kill you once. We just need to give him another chance."

40

"YOU MEAN USE ME AS BAIT?"

"I mean, obviously, we'd make sure you were fully protected, but yes, that is what I'm suggesting. He wants to silence you, doesn't he? He wants to tidy you up before Papa Putin comes home and gets angry about the mess he's made. So, we just need to tempt him to take another shot. Only at a time and a place we control." Marsha drained her bottle.

Penny wriggled in her chair. "Is this something we really do? I mean, can we do things like this?"

"Not every day," Marsha said. "But when you haven't got time to play by the rules, you gotta write yourself some new ones."

Heat bloomed under Ingrid's shirt. Her heart rate ticked up. Marsha was right. They could set a trap. "I have an idea. Well, half of one." Her skin was tingling.

"Fire away."

"If I was going to kill me, I know where I'd do it." Ingrid stopped herself. "That was a very strange thing to say out loud." She took a sip of beer. "I go for a run almost every day. Since I've been living at the hotel, it's always been through Hyde Park. A lap of the Serpentine and a route through the woods. There's no CCTV, there are ten escape routes. Also," she added. "Burridge told me he'd followed me there and I had no idea."

"You think Burridge, or whatever his real name is, is the scout?" Marsha said.

"I don't know. Maybe. The point is, Hyde Park offers Skylark lots of hiding places."

"It'd make our job harder," Marsha said.

"But it also makes it more likely he'll take his chance. If he knows he's about to be extracted, and if you're right that he would rather tie up his own loose ends rather than have them tied up for him, then he knows he's only got a few hours to accomplish what he tried at Tilbury."

Marsha pursed her lips together and nodded. "Okay. So we let Skylark know your run route. Are you on social media? Can you post something? Strava?"

"I have a Facebook account, but it's just family and friends. My privacy settings are maxed out. Besides, Skylark needs to know I'm going for a run *tomorrow* and take action *tomorrow*."

Marsha exhaled. "Then it's just as well we've got a journalist on the team. Can't McAdoodle-doo place a story somewhere?"

Penny looked from one to the other like a spectator at a tennis match. "Sorry, are you two really contemplating arranging for Ingrid to be shot in Central London? Am I missing something here, because this sounds like something out of a very bad movie."

Ingrid and Marsha exchanged a look to decide which one would answer. Ingrid won. "I'd be very surprised if he tried to shoot me. We know he's a Met officer with access to firearms, but those firearms have to be signed back in at the end of every shift." Ingrid paused. "Besides, guns are too… traceable. If he's a cop, he'd try something… else."

"Like what?" Penny asked.

"Baseball bat," Marsha said, very matter of fact. "Kitchen knife."

"Gee, thanks." Ingrid got up and retrieved a list from the spare desk. "These are the people we already know he's killed." She looked at the names. "David Steiner. Shot himself in woodland but there's reason to think the wound wasn't self-inflicted." Ingrid paused to consider if the next name really was also one of Skylark's victims. "Jacob DeWalt. Either blackmailed into taking his own life or was pushed. And then there's Mulroony's assistant."

"Who's that?" Marsha asked.

Ingrid tried to remember the woman's name. "Julie Something. Jen told me she was attacked with a hammer walking home. She didn't die, but she spent months in a coma and now needs full time care. She never recovered. Julie Bairstow. That's it."

Marsha and Penny both winced.

"If he's done it before… I mean, if that's how he tries to kill women…" Marsha paused. "I don't need to pull out the profiling handbook to know misogyny when I see it. His male victims get swift ends they probably didn't know much about, yet the last thing his female victim sees is his hand wielding a hammer at her face." She stopped, unwilling to go on.

The three of them were silent for several moments before Marsha spoke again. "So, we, correction, *you*, lure him to somewhere he feels powerful, and we have a team in place to intercept him before he can land a blow." Marsha turned her head. "Penny, can you find out everything we know about how Julie Bairstow was attacked?"

"Um, yes. Of course."

Marsha got to her feet. She was taking charge. "Ingrid, what story are we going to give the press? And where the hell is that Australian?"

"Sleeping, I imagine. To be honest, I'm not sure he's that useful, anyway. Skylark isn't going to be reading the Australian papers. It's got to be a London title. And even they're not just going to print my run route, are they? We have to give them a story."

"They'll want photos too." Marsha sighed. "Can you catch a purse snatcher on Oxford Street or something and go viral?"

A sense of calm descended on Ingrid. "Actually, there might be a story. There's even a photograph."

Marsha and Penny listened as Ingrid outlined the scoop.

"And, well, you know, the First Lady thing," Penny said when Ingrid had finished. "I mean, six months ago they wanted to put you on the cover of Vogue."

"She's right," Marsha said. "They will definitely want to run something about the FBI's poster girl in London. It could work."

"I'd want to read that story," Penny said, helpfully.

Marsha's head started to bob up and down. A decision had been made. "Do it."

Ingrid scrolled through her contacts until she reached the Ts. Her finger hovered over Angela Tate's name before she tapped it. Her stomach somersaulted as she waited for Tate to pick up.

"Special Agent Ingrid Skyberg, what a pleasure," Tate

said. "It's almost nine on a Friday night, so I'm thinking this is going to be tasty."

"Not sure how tasty it is, but I've got a story that I need to run tomorrow. I'm figuring you've got the contacts to make it happen."

"Depends on the story. Luckily for you it's a Saturday tomorrow. Papers are always looking to fill space at the weekend."

Ingrid told her about the pictures of the retail magnate drenched in wine at Sabrina's.

"I can see the headline," Angela said, her voice unusually girlish. "'FBI's golden girl saves the day… again'."

"And you understand the story needs to be a profile of me? It must include that I go running every day, same route, same time—"

"Geez. I remember when I had to extract teeth to use your name in a story. Now you want to be a bleeding leading lady."

"I don't want to, Angela, but I've got no choice. And it's got to run tomorrow."

"Understood. First, let me see if any of the agencies still have the photos. If they do, then I reckon I can get it on BuzzFeed this evening. They'll pay a little for it. I'll negotiate a syndication deal. The Mail Online will deffo pick it up and if I hold back a couple of choice quotes and to offer exclusively to the *Sun*. That way they'll probably run you on page nine." Ingrid could almost hear Angela's brain working. "I could even make five hundred quid out of this."

"More importantly, you might also save a life," she said, thinking of Mulroony. "But I can't give you that story unless this one runs tomorrow, okay?"

"Leave it with me."

Ingrid hung up. Marsha was leaning over Penny's shoulder and looking at her monitor. Ingrid joined them and saw they were examining a map of Hyde Park. "If this is your route round the Serpentine, I calculate we'll need a team of six to protect you. I'm in, but we still need five more agents. So, Ingrid, who do you trust?"

Penny almost laughed. "Ingrid famously trusts no one."

Ingrid's eyes widened at her assistant's candor. But Penny was right. Who did Ingrid trust? Who did she trust enough to protect her from a rogue agent desperate to save his own skin?

41

Angela Tate had done her job well. The paparazzi pictures found their way online by midnight, and in the morning, gossip pages on both sides of the Atlantic had picked up the story. Ingrid's circled face appeared in the panel above the main headline of the *Sun* with the teaser 'Look who saved the day… again! See page 9'

The article itself featured a small inset photograph of Sir Richard Black, the owner of several retail chains, his red wine stain enhanced to look like blood, a photo of the chichi Italian restaurant and a larger image of Ingrid walking away. Either the photographer had managed to capture her from an angle that made Sol invisible, or—she suspected—he had been photoshopped out. Along with a fabricated quote from an eyewitness who wouldn't lift a finger to help the loathsome Black, Tate had got a quote from the man himself. "I honestly thought I was going to die," he said. Ingrid was billed as 'an everyday hero' who didn't like attention and mostly kept to herself. *"Most days are exactly the same," the modest Skyberg claims. "My life is really very dull and routine. I eat the same thing for breakfast. I even run the same route through Hyde Park every evening, always the same time between seven and eight, always two laps of the Serpentine."* Tate had made up the bit about breakfast. Ingrid didn't even care *if* she had breakfast, let alone what she ate. It didn't matter: the line had been cast, and now they had to hope their prey would take the bait.

Ingrid pretended not to see Natasha McKittrick standing outside the Queen Mother gates of Hyde Park as if she was waiting for a date. She ran straight past her and into the park, running alongside the flower garden toward the main path that led to the Serpentine. Ingrid had never understood how the L-shaped lake had acquired its name—on a map it looked more like a skinny whale than a snake—but it was the centerpiece of London's biggest green space. The eastern part of the park near her hotel was mostly grass, but toward the middle, the trees thickened into woodland, before giving way to the formal lake. Beyond the water were Kensington Gardens, the Serpentine Gallery and Kensington Palace, still most famous as the place where a shocked nation came to lay flowers after the death of Princess Diana.

Instinctively, Ingrid checked her pace on her watch, forgetting that she had deliberately not enabled the feature. It would be too easy for her to start focusing on her time or cadence. This way, every time she looked at her watch—a square electronic screen connected to her phone—and saw the time, it would remind her that this wasn't a normal run. Somewhere in the park, Nick Angelis was tracking her phone, which was fitted with spyware. It enabled him to record everything her phone camera saw, even when the phone was switched off. Her headphones had an inline mic that allowed her to communicate with Nick and Marsha, who was soaking up the last of the summer rays on a picnic blanket at the point in the route where they thought an ambush was most likely.

Ingrid checked behind her. She couldn't see Zeke, but he would be a few hundred yards behind. Ralph hadn't sufficiently recovered from his injuries to play the part of a fellow jogger, so he was in a boat on the water operating a drone. Ingrid didn't know where Cath was, but she was out in the park somewhere. She was quite pleased that she had been able to come up with a list of six people she trusted. Sol had been willing to get on a plane, but accepted the damage he had done to his lungs over the years didn't make him the best asset to deploy on this particular field of combat. Marsha's plan assumed his first strike would come from close quarters, using a hammer or something similar. If her assumption was wrong, and Skylark did use a gun—they even speculated that he could try a crossbow—they were counting on him missing a moving target with his first shot, allowing Ingrid to take evasive action before a second.

Ingrid had rejected a bullet-proof vest. It was simply too bulky to run in and would only attract attention. Instead she had opted for Kevlar sleeves—they looked like leg warmers for her forearms—to help her fend off a knife attack, and inside her water bottle was a mace canister. Ultimately, her best defense would be her fitness: she could outrun any attacker.

Ingrid had a sense of what Skylark looked like from the warehouse in Tilbury. About her height, so five ten or thereabouts, and muscular. A rugby build rather than a long-distance runner. She was on alert for any man who matched that description.

"How are you feeling?" Marsha's voice piped into her ears.

"All good. What are you seeing?"

"Still a lot of people about. I think you should leave the lake and head into the woods as soon as you can."

"It might also be an idea to slow down." Nick's voice. "I realize it goes against everything you believe in, but if you're a total Billy the Whizz, you'll just be a blur. Ah, that's your phone ringing."

"You can hear that?" Ingrid asked. The ringtone pulsed in her headphones.

"Right now, your phone is my phone. It's your mother, by the way."

Ingrid looked down at her watch. An alert with Svetlana's name flashed up. She always did pick the worst moments to call.

"I take it no one has seen a man who fits the bill?" Ingrid asked.

After a short delay, Nick replied. "Negative."

A pale blue sky stretched behind high, light clouds and the air was still a very warm seventy-two degrees. Consequently, the park was full of runners, cross-country skiers on wheeled skis, promenading couples and groups of friends tossing balls and frisbees. It felt like a festival. Glastonbury without the music. Ingrid dutifully slowed down, in part to allow an unsteady woman on rollerblades to swerve round her.

Ingrid joined the wide path on the north rim of the lake, where customers lined up outside a café for ice creams and soft drinks. Others crammed at the water's edge to feed ducks and innumerable swans. Ingrid scanned as she ran, looking for the man who wanted her dead.

This isn't where he'll strike.

She passed the pontoon where row boats and paddleboats were for hire. She glanced out to the water but didn't see Ralph. Nor could she see or hear his drone. Ingrid had a choice: take Marsha's advice and turn into the wooded area, or continue along the lakeside where the path narrowed and passed under a road bridge. She chose the lake.

Ingrid had run the route often enough to know the next hundred yards were among the most vulnerable. Not only did her opponent have a potential vantage point on the overhead bridge, but the path was shrouded in thick shrubbery just where the lake was at its widest. It was a rare example of a place in Central London where you could feel isolated if another runner didn't come the other way. *If I was going to kill me, this is where I'd do it.*

A man on a bench eyed her as she ran past. He looked like he might shout 'nice tits' or 'speed up, love', a crime that would unfailingly be dealt with by Ingrid's middle finger, but he said nothing. She ducked into the arched tunnel under the bridge. Even after weeks of sun, the ground was still slightly damp and smelled faintly of piss. When she emerged into the light on the other side of the bridge, she clocked the drone over the water, thanks to a dad crouching to point it out to his delighted son.

The next stretch of the shore was usually the quietest, which was reason enough to stay on high alert. Overhung by trees, the path was darker and cooler and less picturesque. A pair of moorhens squabbled in the reeds as a trio of mallards raced overhead in formation.

Ingrid soon reached the top of the lake where a formal Italianate garden hosted fountains and statues under a limestone lake house. She dodged a woman struggling with several dogs on leashes and crossed to the other side. She turned south, back toward the bridge.

"Anyone seeing anything?" she asked.

"Cath is reporting something," Nick said. "Heavier than usual police presence around Kensington Palace. Their royal highnesses must be on the move. Something to be aware of."

Suddenly, the prospect of Skylark being armed was more real. What if he was a royal protection officer? They routinely had MK5s and handguns. He could reasonably say he feared for the life of his principal and opened fire.

"That's your mother again," Nick said, two seconds before her watch vibrated and the ringtone drilled into her ears. "Persistent, isn't she?"

"That's one word for her." Ingrid ran on, a light sweat forming on her brow. She passed the Peter Pan statue where a gaggle of tourists held out food for bright green parakeets that were now a regular sight in London parks.

"How are you feeling?" Marsha asked.

"Good," Ingrid said snappily. She actually felt surprisingly calm for a woman with a target on her back. Though that might change on the second loop of the lake, when Ingrid figured he was more likely to make a move. The first loop was a recce for them both. Ingrid glimpsed the palace between an avenue of trees and thought she spotted Cath's stocky figure. When her vision swerved back to the path, she was immediately alarmed.

"Who has eyes on me? Man, white vest, black shorts running in my direction." She checked his hands for a weapon. He was clutching something black. "Does anyone have eyes on?"

There was only static in her ears.

"Anyone?"

He was fifty yards ahead. Mid-forties, broad chest, skinny legs. Sweating profusely. Not a regular runner. He stared at Ingrid, a blank shark-like gaze. Ingrid checked left and right for backup, but didn't see any of the team. Zeke was too far back. She slowed slightly, trying to work out what he was holding. Something square.

"Anyone?" she said again. This time panic inflected her voice.

"Negative," Nick said. "Drone finding it difficult to lock on to him."

"Shit." The backup team was an illusion. Worse, it was a danger. It had given her the confidence to leave the hotel room, but now—when it really came down to it—she was on her own.

"Pervert," she shouted as he passed, staring at her chest. "In case anyone is interested, he was holding a Walkman. A Walkman!"

"Well, the nineties are making a comeback," Nick quipped.

Ingrid carried on back toward the bridge, then into the foot tunnel under the road. Out in the open again, she had the Princess Diana memorial fountain—a strange granite loop carved into an expanse of lawn—on her right and the Serpentine on her left. Up ahead was the swimming club where a rectangle of white buoys indicated the safe swimming area and another café. A quartet of well-built men wearing slightly too many clothes for the weather stood in line for coffee. "Anyone got visuals on the café?" Ingrid checked over her shoulder to see if Zeke was still with her.

"Mind out!" A cyclist nearly clattered into her while she was looking the other way.

"You shouldn't even be here," Ingrid shouted after him, uselessly. "Pedestrians only!" Her eyes homed in on the four men. "Four males, thirties. If they're not police officers, they're private security. Anyone see them?"

No reply from Nick.

Ingrid was close enough to spot one of them had a transparent coil leading to an earpiece. She felt a sudden need for water, but her bottle was full of something she wouldn't even drink in a desert. Private security in the park wasn't unheard of—the Mandarin Oriental hotel was just a few hundred yards away, and next to that was One Hyde Park, a development of the most expensive apartments in the world.

The men didn't seem the least bit interested in her. She ran on, past the swimming club and headed east, back toward the Hilton. This was the safest part of her run, where the path widened and families strolled, selfies were taken and couples held hands. Ingrid began to think it wasn't going to happen. The park was too busy. Her head dropped. This was a waste of time.

She started the second loop with a sense of despair, passing the first café where McKittrick was now propped up against a wooden table, sipping her coffee. Ingrid made a mental note to mention the Hammersmith apartment to her. She made another mental note to concentrate on the job at hand.

Part of the joy of running had always been that it let her mind wander. Now she needed to rein it in, to focus. She passed a group of rollerbladers setting up cones to slalom through, and a shoal of boys on Santander rental bikes rolled toward her, parting like a stream around a rock as she ran through them.

"It is her," she heard one of them say. At least someone had read the article in the *Sun*. Hopefully Skylark had too.

"I'm going to take the woods this time." Ingrid was getting out of breath, though this still constituted a recreational jog for her. She hung a right to veer away from the water and onto a path between the trees. In the middle of the wooded area were several buildings—gardeners' lodges, hothouses, toilets and an education center—but at this time of day, none of them were in use. As most of the park visitors were trying to get the last of the evening's sun, she suddenly felt very alone. The drone couldn't follow her through the canopy of leaves overhead and a quick glance over her shoulder told her Zeke was a long way behind.

Ingrid gasped. A man appeared from the bushes, adjusting his shorts. He'd had too many beers and way too much sun. He wasn't a threat, but Ingrid didn't like that she hadn't seen him until the last moment. *Concentrate.*

She spotted Marsha on a blanket at a point where the grass gave way to undergrowth. The temperature dropped further as the branches knitted together over her head. It was darker too. Some of the shadows deepened into black.

This was the place.

Ingrid instinctively checked for Zeke, but he was round a bend and out of sight. No drone. No Zeke. Until she emerged on the far side of the woods, she was on her own. Her eyes darted left and right. She gasped as a black and white dog careered out of the undergrowth, causing her to turn sharply. Her heart thundered as its owner shouted for it to come to heel.

Two trees with thick trunks were up ahead. They offered Skylark a defensive hiding place, so Ingrid steered to the other side of the path, putting an extra step between her and the trees.

Govno!

He stepped out from between the trunks, striding out in long dark trousers. He pulled something from a pocket.

Ingrid accelerated toward him. She needed all the momentum she had to push him over.

"What the—" His eyes widened with alarm. He held up his arms to protect himself, a packet of Wet Wipes in his hand.

Ingrid swerved away from him just in time. She breathed hard, the warm air jabbing her lungs. She had never heard of a man relieving himself in the woods and then actually *cleaning his hands*. She was still shaking her head with disbelief when she emerged onto a wider path where a group of skiers forced their way up an incline. Uphill skiing. Hyde Park was full of surprises. Just not the one she had planned.

Ingrid looped her way back to the water, back to the Italianate garden, the Peter Pan statue and eventually the swimming club. Skylark wasn't going to strike now. Too many people. Too much open space. "Well, that was a colossal waste of time," she said when she neared the Queen Mother gates.

"At least you're still alive," Marsha said. "Okay, everyone. Let's give Ingrid a chance to shower. See you all back at the hotel in thirty."

Ingrid was pissed off. The last thing she wanted was a debrief. "What the fuck do you think you're looking at?" she said to a man in the elevator as she rode back up to her floor. Inside her hotel room, Ingrid slumped against the closed door and emptied her lungs. A deep, desperate sigh turned into a wail. It was over. She had failed. Skylark would be extracted by his handlers within hours and Mulroony would rot in hell.

Her watched buzzed. A text from Svetlana.

Kathleen is dead. Maybe now you'll call me back.

42

INGRID SPLASHED cold water on her face and looked at herself in the bathroom mirror. She looked away. She should have called Kathleen. She hadn't even sent her that book. Disgust simmered through her veins, contorting her mouth into a scowl. A heavy ache radiated from her ribs as her heart reached out across the ocean to be with Kathleen.

The apple pies. The tomato sandwiches with the crusts cut off. The racoon in the garbage pail. The lock on their downstairs bathroom with the knack to it. The hugs, the extra cookies in the picnic basket, the made-up bed in the box room just in case Svetlana was having one of her impossible days. Somehow, Kathleen—the kindest woman Ingrid had ever known, the woman who had shown her what being mothered felt like—had survived her daughter by two decades, sustained in no small part by the deep-seated need to find justice for Megan. That she had died without it, possibly just hours before a verdict that might have brought her a tiny speck of solace, was an injustice Ingrid's body could not contain.

She didn't know where to put herself. Her head shook,

seemingly the wrong size for her neck. Her veins bulged with too much blood as rage detonated deep inside. Her face reddened and the tears surged. Howl after howl drained from base of her throat. Her torment wasn't just grief, it was resentment. Resentment that Svetlana would say she hadn't cared enough to answer the phone, resentment at the maternal mind games to come, resentment that the poisoned politics of her relationship with her own mother would shape her grief for Kathleen.

Ingrid staggered out of the bathroom and stood at the window. She stared down at Hyde Park, the scene of her most recent failure, and smacked the glass, fantasizing that her fist smashed the window to drive pain into her flesh. The urge to break something, to inflict injustice on something else, anything else, was restless.

Ingrid knew that every minute she delayed only gave Svetlana more ammunition. She dialed Minnesota.

"Hi."

"So, now you're calling?"

Ingrid worked so hard to suppress her tears that she couldn't get any words out.

"Shame on you, Ingrid Skyberg, shame on you."

Ingrid wiped her wet cheek with the back of her hand.

"You know you did this to Kathleen, don't you? Testifying for the defense? It killed her. You realize that?"

Ingrid's face crumpled. She could barely stand upright. She wanted her dad. She wanted him to bend down and tell her that sometimes your mom gets like this, but she doesn't mean to be cruel. *Deep down, she loves you more than sunshine or blue skies or butterflies, remember that.* It had been okay when he was alive, when he could soothe the wounds his wife inflicted. Here she was, thirty-six years old and wanting her dad to tell her she'd done nothing wrong. But she had. She hadn't called Kathleen, and so she stood there and took Svetlana's acidic medicine.

"Don't even bother coming home for the funeral. You don't even ask me how I am."

And you haven't asked me either.

Ingrid's sobs became uncontrollable. She couldn't hold on to the phone any longer. It dropped to the ground, still emitting a stream of bile from Minnesota. She understood that her mother was angry. She knew that in a few days Svetlana would phone back and call her *Malyshka* and Ingrid would bury her confusion because she craved her mother's approval so deeply. Knowing that was their twisted pattern of behavior made it so much worse. Even at the darkest of hours, they were still playing their power games. She hated her mother. There, she had said it. She despised her. And she despised her all the more because in two days' time she knew she'd love her again.

Ingrid ignored the knock on the door. It was probably Marsha. Her room was on the same floor and she would be asking if Ingrid wanted to walk to the debrief together. The debrief would have to wait. With the verdict so close, Kathleen's death would make the news and they would understand why she didn't show.

Ingrid fell on the bed and stared at the ceiling. It felt like her heart was emptying, deflating, removing itself from her body. Her body was paralyzed with grief, but her brain churned. If she hadn't found the photos. If she hadn't started digging. If she had listened to Sol… then maybe DeWalt would still be alive, Mulroony wouldn't be in hell and she would have had the grace to call Kathleen.

When Ingrid woke up, it was just after ten thirty. She wasn't actually sure if she had slept or had merely been suspended in a catatonic state. There was something dreamlike about her room, as if she wasn't fully present. She checked the date as well as the time, suddenly wondering if she had been asleep for more than twenty-four hours.

Still wearing her running gear, Ingrid sat up and slung her heavy legs over the side of the bed. She remembered about Kathleen, and her head fell into her hands. A surge of loathing for Svetlana curled her lip and pushed her to her feet. She had to get out. She had to burn away her anger. She swiped her swimsuit from the towel rail in the bathroom, threw a hair brush, tee shirt and sweat pants in her gym bag and picked up her phone. No messages from her mom. There wouldn't be for a few days. And then the deluge would arrive.

The smell of chlorine pricked her nostrils as the elevator doors opened onto the basement spa. There were a few men in the cardio room on treadmills, but the reception area was empty. A sign on the desk stated that no lifeguards were on duty and patrons used the facilities at their own risk. She pushed through the swing doors to the ladies' changing room. She didn't have a token for the locker, but she had never seen another woman use the fitness suite this late at night. She made a neat pile of her clothes, hiding her phone inside it, and slipped into her swimsuit.

The pool was the single best thing about living in a hotel. Dim lighting gave the place a spicy, hammam-like feel, with burnt orange walls with ochre accents. The pool, lit from below, was a deep turquoise, and the loungers down one side were dark, tropical wood. It was intoxicating to have it to herself. She stood with her toes over the edge and looked down at the shimmering water.

Ingrid closed her eyes, swung her arms back, bent her

knees and pushed off, diving into the silky water, needing the cold to cover her. She stayed beneath the water for half a length, rising greedily for air, then diving again, trying to make herself disappear. Muscle memory kicked in. Her limbs started to move, her legs pushing out the anger and her arms dragging the cleansing water over her, purifying her rage. Ingrid picked up speed. The more her lungs burned, the more her muscles ached, the more she could purge her acrid mood. By concentrating on her strokes and her breathing, the less space there was to think about Skylark, or Mulroony or Operation Pinball. She was just a body moving through water. No will, no desire, only motion. A form of physical meditation.

Ingrid became an automaton, plowing the lane, up and down, over and over, in a quest for total depletion. She would swim until she couldn't, staying in her secret isolation until her burdens were spent.

On a turn from one length to another, a man came out of the changing rooms. A tiny spike of hatred pricked her brain. This was *her* pool, *her* time. She didn't want to share the space, but nor did she want him to think he had intimidated her into leaving. Her defiance insisted that she carry on. She tried not to look at him as they passed each other in the lanes. She wanted to give the impression that she hadn't even noticed his arrival.

After a few more lengths, the calm she had swum into her limbs had evaporated. Her petty annoyance was coiling into anger. She needed to get out of the water and be alone. Angry, Ingrid hauled herself out of the pool and padded quickly to the changing room. She would go for another run instead.

Ingrid sat on the bench, a towel over her head, and let her tears merge with the chlorinated water dripping from her face onto the sandstone beneath her pruned feet. Her chest burned with exertion and grief.

The blow landed without warning, smashing her head against the lockers behind her. A hand clasped the towel against her face, covering her mouth and nose. His other hand gripped the back of her skull. She raged against his grip, writhing her neck to twist free. Blind and desperate for air, she moved her legs and stamped, but hit stone instead of flesh. She tried to stand up, but couldn't.

Panicked, she struggled to the edge of the bench and jabbed her elbows upwards, trying to make contact. She needed air, she needed oxygen. Heat bloomed across her skull. She began to feel faint. He adjusted his grip, and she seized her chance to slip down, out of the towel and onto the floor. She saw his bare feet briefly before the towel covered her head again. At least she could be sure that a man wearing swim briefs was unarmed. She sucked in air before his hand pressed the towel into her mouth and her head into the stone. His other hand plunged onto her neck, gripping her tightly. His breaths were deep and rasping. The swim had taken something out of him. If she could hold on, he would fade.

Ingrid let him pin her down. *Let him think he's winning.* She could breathe more than he realized. *Think.* He adjusted his position to straddle her, keeping one hand on her neck and the other on her head. His knees were on either side of her head, allowing him to exert more pressure. Pain radiated from her cheek bone as he pressed down. She didn't struggle.

"You nearly ruined everything."

The same voice from Tilbury. His grip strengthened, and he forced his palm harder against her windpipe. Stars appeared in Ingrid's vision. There wasn't enough oxygen in her system. He was winning. Ingrid's body went limp. She stopped resisting. She thought about her hyoid bone. The same fate as Megan, twenty years apart.

He pulled his hand from her face. His grip weakened against her throat. And that's when Ingrid raised her head, crushing her forehead into his balls.

"You fucking bitch, you—"

He slumped forward and she rolled out from under him. Her breaths were jagged as she curled up onto her knees and aimed her right fist into his chest, landing a blow on the bruise she'd given when she'd fired a bullet into his Kevlar vest. He winced and collapsed to one side. She pinned her knee against his neck and looked down at his reddened face.

It was Andy Scott, member of Parliament, Secretary of State for Justice, and a former SO15 detective. One thing was for sure: he was no longer a future Prime Minister.

The door opened and Ingrid's neck twisted to see a familiar figure.

"Looks like I'm a little late," Nick Angelis said.

"What the hell are you doing here?" She dropped her head as her chest heaved.

"Your phone, remember?" He waved his own at her. "I heard about Kathleen. I waited in case you needed a friend." He tipped his head to one side. "Well, here I am."

Ingrid didn't know whether to kiss him or kick him in the shins.

43

THE REASON ANDY SCOTT had chosen the changing room to attack Ingrid was the same reason they were able to smuggle him out without involving the police: for privacy reasons, there were no cameras in the women's changing room. A discrete team from Fortnum Security arrived and escorted them to a secure facility near Biggin Hill airport on the outskirts of London.

Ingrid and Nick sat with him in an armored truck inside a hangar at the edge of the airfield, as ambassadors were summoned, the Prime Minister was called and the Chief Constable was briefed. It wouldn't be long before the phone would ring in the Oval Office and a decision would be taken. They were expecting a plane to arrive from a USAF base in Suffolk that would then take Scott to an airfield in Germany. He would be held there until the exchange for Mulroony could be arranged.

"I think you can be fairly sure the Brits will abandon you," Nick told him. "Our American friends here are offering to cover up all the embarrassments you've caused. A far-right sympathizer, a member of the banned group

England for the English, a quisling cop who allowed himself to be blackmailed by a foreign power." His lip snarled. "Believe me when I tell you the Prime Minister will gladly accept Washington's offer to make that clusterfuck of headaches disappear. A Russian asset sitting at the cabinet table? A meteoric rise based on Kremlin kompromat? A Prime Minister in waiting? It's the political scandal of a generation. The kind of thing that destabilizes governments. Trust me, when the phone rings, it won't be Number Ten."

Nick had made the call not to provide Scott with clothes: humiliation was a surprisingly effective negotiation technique. For every answer Scott gave, he could have an item of clothing. Yet, after three hours, Andy Scott was still in his swimwear, the purple bruise on his right pectoral deepening by the hour. He'd prided himself on his Action Man physique, and he sat with his legs apart, his privates bulging against his briefs in an act of absurd machismo. Nick had turned up the air conditioning and was counting down the minutes until Scott started cooperating.

Ingrid's phone rang. "Marsha, hey."

"Hey."

"Have you slept yet?"

"I had a power nap. Listen, something came up I thought you'd want to hear."

"Go on."

"Penny's just sent you the recording."

"Of what?"

"The seven oh-seven call Scott made to DeWalt. Jacob recorded it. We found it when we searched his phone."

Ingrid's tired eyes widened. Her mouth fell open.

"What?" Nick asked. "What?"

Ingrid slapped him away.

"But before you listen to it, you remember that Florida number?"

"Sure."

"It's a telephone booth on the beach in Sarasota. I called a contact in Tampa. He told me he knew someone who lived at almost exactly the relevant intersection. A retired agent, no less."

"Who?"

"You won't believe it."

"Who?"

"The legend that is Frank Geest."

Ingrid's jaw slung even lower. "Is he…" She couldn't believe she was going to say it about the great Frank Geest. "Is he… Starling?"

Scott's eyebrows raised at the mention of Starling.

"It would certainly explain why the operation Geest ran in the Nineties to find him failed."

"Oh. My. God." Ingrid was stunned.

"Tampa's putting a file together. I imagine they'll be knocking on his door before the sun comes up."

Ingrid's phone dinged: Penny's file had downloaded. "Scott is right here. Should I play the file in front of him?"

"Hell, yeah." Marsha ended the call.

"What?" Nick said again.

"Just wait a minute." Ingrid navigated to the audio file and hit play. Her heart practically stopped while it buffered. She looked at Nick and smiled.

"… do it."

"Just reassign her. Send her to Timbuktu for a few weeks. Get her out of the fucking country."

"So you can arrange a plane crash in the jungle? I told you, I won't do it. I won't do anything anymore."
"Sounds like you've forgotten about the photos, mate."
"You honestly think I'd have done any of this without those goddamn photos? Five years ago, you asked for a favor and that guy Mulroony disappeared off the face of the planet. I kidded myself that it was a coincidence, but it wasn't, was it? I don't know why you wouldn't see her the other day, why I spent six hours in a fucking elevator, or why you wanted her security pass, but that's it. Release the photos. I won't have her death on my conscience too."

Ingrid watched Scott as he listened. She'd seen it happen in court many times, the moment when the guy in the dock realizes he's going down. The stare fixes, the jaw clenches, the color drains. A living rigor mortis.

"Greencoat College, isn't it?"
"You leave my kids out of this."
"Be terrible if something happened to them on the way home from school, wouldn't it? You don't seem to understand, mate. You do what I say, or I make you do what I say. How many fingers do I have to send you in the post before you realize I'm serious?"

Ingrid could hear DeWalt's heavy breathing. She could feel his anguish. She remembered what Dr. Ives had told her about DeWalt's mental health, about his moral code.

"Who do you think is paying for your fucking penthouse, Jakey boy? It isn't me, is it? You don't like dealing with

me? You really couldn't handle the shit I have to shovel every day."

"Wow, you're actually trying to make me feel sorry for you, you sick, sick fucker? What happens if you do get the keys to Number Ten? What will you be like then? No, I'm not going to help you anymore."

"Then start looking over your shoulder. Comply or die. How many times have I told you that? You've seen how they do it. Polonium in your tea, novichok on your door handle, they won't just push you under a train. They'll leave a signature. They'll want the world to realize you were a traitor."

"What?"

"You heard me."

"I, I thought…"

DeWalt fell silent as he realized who his friend really worked for.

"I thought it was some alt-right shit."

"You knew. Don't pretend you didn't."

There was a long pause in the conversation. In the background, Ingrid heard the sounds of Parliament Square, buses and car horns and tourists.

"So, you'll get rid of her?"

Another pause.

"Fucking answer me man or this is not going to end well."

A muscle in Scott's jaw started to twitch.

"Answer me!"

There was another thirty-three seconds of audio. Footsteps and traffic. And then it cut out. Ingrid pictured DeWalt pacing in his apartment. Taking a last swig of beer. Opening his balcony doors. She didn't want to imagine the rest.

The three of them sat in silence for several minutes.

"That sounds like a plane," Nick said. "If you don't want to spend the whole flight in your trunks, now would be an excellent time to start answering my questions."

Scott scratched his balls.

"How eloquent," Nick said. "Those military planes tend to be very cold at twenty-thousand feet."

Scott wasn't going to talk. The only power he had left was his silence, and he was holding on to it.

Ingrid's phone rang. Marsha again. "That's some recording. Who's heard it?"

"Ingrid, that's not why I'm calling." She sounded serious.

"What is it?"

"It's just come up on the news. The jury's filing back in."

Hairs raised on Ingrid's neck. Ice plunged down her throat. She didn't know if she could speak. "Really? Now?"

"Reporter says they've reached a verdict."

Ingrid swallowed to lubricate her mouth. "Oh."

"Have you got a TV there?"

Tears stung the corners of Ingrid's eyes. "I... I can watch on my phone."

"I'm here if you need me, okay?"

Ingrid yanked open the truck door and stepped into the cavernous hangar. Several Fortnum cars surrounded the van, and their drivers stood in a huddle. They looked at her as she strode past them and out into the humid night.

A frozen picture of the courtroom loaded quickly, but there was no sound. Ingrid leaned against the hangar wall and looked up at lilac clouds buffeting a crescent moon. The runway lights stretched out to the north, where one of the stars was moving. The plane was coming.

Ingrid kept her chin up, looking at the sky, unable to glance down at her phone. She had carried the uncertainty of what happened to Megan for twenty years. It was like a major organ and she didn't know if she would be able to function without it.

Her phone emitted a short burst of sound, and then another, and then the audio finally kicked in. "And on count three, the murder of Megan Avery, have you reached a unanimous verdict?"

"No."

"Have you reached a verdict on which ten of you agree?"

"We have."

"And how do you find the accused?"

Ingrid couldn't bear to listen. Her entire body trembled.

"Not guilty."

Her head fell back against the hangar, pain erupting from her bruise. She stared up at the sky, her mouth agape. Tears spilled down her cheek.

"And on count four, the murder of Rebecca Bradlington, have you reached a unanimous verdict?"

"We have."

"And how do you find the accused?"

"Guilty."

Ingrid's chest heaved. She tried to drag oxygen into her lungs as the subsequent guilty verdicts came in. She wiped away her tears and steeled herself to look at her phone. A breaking news banner confirmed the not guilty verdict for the first three victims.

Svetlana would be ashamed of her. She would blame her. Punish her. She would say she was the reason there was no peace for Kathleen. Or justice for Megan.

Ingrid slumped down onto her haunches. She felt she would collapse. If there was a single speck of solace, it was that Kathleen had been spared the agony that now coursed through Ingrid's body.

Ingrid had only ever found one way to deal with her pain. It was a promise. She had originally made it for Megan, but now she looked to the sky and made it for Kathleen too. "One day, I will find him. I swear. One day."

Run Girl - Prequel (A novella)

SECRETARY OF STATE Jayne Whitticker is in the middle of delicate negotiations when her favorite grandchild disappears from Paris.

Special Agent Ingrid Skyberg is hauled out of her FBI training session at Scotland Yard to head the hunt for the eighteen-year-old girl, who the FBI believe is now in London. Will she succeed in her unexpected mission? Or will her failure lead to the collapse of the crucial peace talks?

FREE to download when you join Eva's mailing list at evahudson.com

Fresh Doubt - Book One

A story of lies, secrets and deadly mind games.

Two hours ago, brilliant American psychology student Madison Faber found her roommate lying in a pool of blood. Now she is in police custody and suspected of murder. Madison persuades Special Agent Ingrid Skyberg to find the real killer, but the investigation soon puts Ingrid in danger. Can she unmask the murderer before she becomes a victim herself?

Kill Plan - Book Two

An American trader is poisoned in his office in the City of London. Two days later, a Latvian immigrant is discovered floating face down in the River Thames. These seemingly unrelated crimes are the work of an audacious serial killer working on both sides of the Atlantic.

When Special Agent Ingrid Skyberg starts putting the pieces together, she also puts herself in the firing line.

Deep Hurt - Book Three

In a seedy hotel in central London, the baby daughter of a US Air Force pilot lies lifeless in his wife's arms. Accused of killing the fourteen-month-old in an uncontrolled rage, Kyle Foster flees, taking his eight-year-old son with him.

Will Ingrid find Foster before he hurts anyone else? Or will she succumb to the old demons she's been trying to escape for the last eighteen years?

Shoot First - Book Four

A teenage girl disappears after witnessing a gangland murder in Chicago. Nine months later, and heavily pregnant, she arrives in London only to disappear again.

Special Agent Ingrid Skyberg has just two days to find the girl and get her to testify or else a brutal killer walks free. But Ingrid isn't the only person looking for the girl, and a war that started on the streets of Chicago is about to explode in the peaceful English countryside.

Below Zero - Book Five

Stockholm is under siege. A bomb has gone off, a series of high profile people have been kidnapped, and the city is in lockdown. Unfortunately for Special Agent Ingrid Skyberg, everything is kicking off on the same day she is in town to complete a dangerous assignment that is so secret, and so illegal, that neither the FBI or the US government can ever know about it. Her instructions are simple: no ID, no credit cards, no trace. If she ends up in jail, or floating face down in the harbor, there can be no way of identifying her.

No badge, no gun, no backup: this time Ingrid is on her own.

Final Offer - Book Six

A shadowy UK-based group has been trying to hack the US elections. When Special Agent Ingrid Skyberg is assigned to find out who's funding the hackers, she finds herself up against an invisible enemy who is extremely powerful and utterly ruthless.

To bring them to justice, Ingrid must go undercover and infiltrate the world of super-rich Russian oligarchs. But money buys all kinds of protection and Ingrid soon realizes that by taking on this battle she's putting everything on the line – her career, her future, her life.

In a nail-biting race against time, Ingrid sets out to solve the mystery and unmask the conspirators before they can silence her. Forever.

Flight Risk - Book Seven

Ingrid is ready to walk away from her life. She wants out of London. She even wants out of the FBI. But when she attempts to board a flight at Heathrow and sneak away without telling anyone, she's arrested on suspicion of causing the death of a man she's never heard of.

Now Ingrid must stay in the country, and the Bureau,

to prove her innocence. There's just one problem: she can't remember if she killed him or not

Look Twice - Book Eight

When Ingrid discovers an undeveloped roll of film left behind by her predecessor, she isn't sure what to make of the strange photos he took. A map of Scotland, an out-of-print book, a rare bird, a cluster of Post-It notes, an office party… do these images have something to do with crimes he committed as a Russian double agent known as 'Skylark'?

Ingrid starts digging and becomes convinced that – far from being a traitor – her predecessor was just another victim of the mysterious Skylark who has killed many times to protect his identity. When a case file she has been using is suddenly deleted from the system, Ingrid knows that Skylark is now watching her… and the race is on to find him before she becomes his next victim.

EVA'S OTHER BOOKS

The Loyal Servant

Winner of the Lucy Cavendish Prize for Fiction, *The Loyal Servant* is a whistleblower thriller that topped the Amazon political fiction chart. Investigative reporter Angela Tate investigates scandal and corruption in the corridors of Westminster.

The Senior Moment

Sixty-five-year-old Jean Henderson arrives in New York to find her son and his pregnant wife missing from their apartment. When she reaches out to the cops for help, Jean discovers how invisible older people really are and concocts a plan to get noticed: by robbing a series of banks.

The Deadly Silence (formerly The Third Estate)

Thirty-three years ago two little girls disappeared. Today, the man convicted of murder three decades ago is back on the streets as another girl vanishes. Angela Tate covered the first disappearances and is dragged into discovering the terrible truth behind the latest.

ABOUT THE AUTHOR

Eva was born and raised in London. She worked as a local government worker, web editor, dotcom entrepreneur, portrait artist and singer. In 2011, Eva won the inaugural Lucy Cavendish Prize for Fiction for her first novel, *The Loyal Servant.* The book was also shortlisted for ITV's People's Novelist Award.

Eva's Ingrid Skyberg thrillers have topped sales charts on both sides of the Atlantic. Tragically, Eva died after completing the third book in the series. She left an unfinished manuscript for a fourth book, and extensive notes for future Skyberg adventures. *Look Twice* has been written by Eva's long-time editor and collaborator Jo Monroe. You can find out more about their collaboration at evahudson.com / about-eva.

To find out more about Eva, Jo or Ingrid, please visit evahudson.com. You can get the latest on all things Skyberg at twitter.com / eva_hudson and facebook.com / evahudsoncrimewriter.

Printed in Great Britain
by Amazon

66687996R00251